ALSO BY KENNEDY RYAN

All the King's Men

The Kingmaker

The Rebel King

Queen Move

Hoops

Long Shot

Block Shot

Hook Shot

Hoops Shorts

Soul

My Soul to Keep

Down to My Soul

Refrain

Grip

Flow

Grip

Still

Bennett

When You Are Mine

Loving You Always

Be Mine Forever

Until I'm Yours

Standalones

Reel

Before I Let Go

the Rebel King

KENNEDY RYAN

Bloom books

Published by Bloom Books, an imprint of Sourcebooks
P.O. Box 4410, Naperville, Illinois 60567-4410
(630) 961-3900
sourcebooks.com

Originally self-published in 2019 by Kennedy Ryan.

Cataloging-in-Publication data is on file with the Library of Congress

Printed and bound in the United States of America.
VP 10 9 8 7 6 5 4 3 2 1

Dedicated to the sisters we didn't hear
never looked for
never found

AUTHOR'S NOTE

Lennix, this story's heroine, is a proud member of the Yavapai-Apache Nation, an American Indian tribe. Some tribes mark the transition from girl to young woman through a puberty ceremony known by various names. My story pulls from the Western Apache's version of this rite of passage, generally known as the Sunrise Ceremony or Sunrise Dance. *Na'íí'ees*, which means "preparing her," ingrains in young girls the qualities deemed important for adulthood. The completion of this rite holds consequences for the entire community—blessings, health, and longevity. For the four days of the ceremony, the young girl is believed to be imbued with the power of Changing Woman, the first woman, according to the tribe's origin story.

Banned in the late 1800s by the U.S. government in an attempt to Westernize and assimilate Native people, such ceremonies became illegal, necessitating that they be practiced in secret until 1978 when the American Indian Religious Freedom Act passed. This rite of passage is sacred and pivotal in the life and development of many young Yavapai-Apache women. I approached even writing about this rite with respect, reverence and only under the guidance of several Indigenous women to ensure I would not misrepresent this or other traditions. I also consulted a medicine man who oversees these ceremonies to ensure the integrity of its portrayal. Any mistakes are mine, not theirs. I would also like to amplify Indigenous own voices in romance. Please consider supporting Indigenous authors highligthed here:

https://bookriot.com/romance-novels-by-indigenous-authors/

https://bookshop.org/lists/romances-by-indigenous-authors

In addition, the ladies below opened my eyes to the epidemic of Missing and Murdered Indigenous women, which is addressed in this story. I owe a debt of gratitude to the following for their assistance:

Sherrie—Apache/Yavapai
Makea—Apache/Yavapai
Andrea—Yavapai
Nina—Apsáalooke Nation
Kiona—Hopi Tribe, Liswungwa (Coyote Clan)

PART 1

"Tell me a story.
Make it a story of great distances, and starlight."
                    —Robert Penn Warren, Tell Me a Story

CHAPTER 1
LENNIX

I'M RUNNING.

Desert wind whistles past my ears and whips through my hair. My feet are feathers, light, quick, but my arms and legs are lead, the muscles aching and burning. The shouts, the encouragement of my tribe spur my spirit when I fear my body will fail.

Run.

Nistan.

The Apache word thumps in time with my heart and races through my veins as I run in the four directions.

East.

South.

West.

I turn north but falter, coming to a halt when I see the beautiful woman standing solemnly among the cheering crowd. The wind lifts the dark hair from her shoulders, and her eyes fix on me.

"Mama?" The strangled whisper catches in my throat. I stumble toward her, the ceremony forgotten. The run abandoned. Tears roll over my cheeks, and my hands reach out. Beseeching. Begging for my mother's touch just once.

The unique blend of her soap and shampoo and natural scent floats to me. Longing, desperate and sharp, spears through me with aching familiarity. I'm almost there, can almost touch her, but she points a finger over my shoulder. She points in the direction I have not yet run.

North.

"Finish, Lennix," she says, the words firm and unyielding.

"What?"

Her lips tighten. Her eyes are slits. She is the fierce warrior who lives inside the gentle mother, and she shouts.

"Run!"

I jerk awake in complete darkness, startled, disoriented.

Panic rips my mouth open on a scream, and the sound shatters, falls around my ears. I can't move my arms. Ropes bite into my skin, my wrists bound in front of me.

Oh, my God. Where am I? What's happening?

I want to be strong, but a whimper dissolves on my lips.

"Lenny," a voice says to my right.

I know that voice.

"Wall?" The word grates painfully inside my throat. "Is that you?"

"Yeah. Thank God you're awake."

"I can't see," I tell him, choking back tears.

"They put a bag on your head. On mine, too."

I turn toward the sound of his voice, and coarse fabric brushes my cheek. A stale scent clogs my nostrils. I'm entombed in burlap and uncirculated air.

"Shit, Lenny," Wallace says, relief and torture in his tone. "I thought he was gonna drop you."

Drop me?

The memory rushes back up at me like the ground when you fall, inevitable and jarring. The horror of a masked madman dangling me over the side of a mountain. The feel of his fingers slipping around my throat. The sight of him straining and struggling to keep me aloft. The utter indifference in his eyes about whether I lived or died.

The images set my heart on fire in my chest, the burning, pounding muscle beating so fast my head starts spinning.

"How long have I been out?" I ask.

"I don't know. They shot us up with something that put us out. I just woke a few minutes before you did."

"So you have no idea how long we traveled? Where we could be?"

"No."

"Ahh, you're awake," a disembodied voice says, coming at me suddenly, an unforeseen intrusion into the darkness sheathing my eyes and ears. I hear the crunch of booted footsteps, sense a presence in front of me and tense, my muscles braced for a blow or a bullet. I have no idea which.

The bag is yanked off my head. We're in some kind of cave, and the light flooding in from the opening, though dim, hurts my eyes. It's just Wallace and me and the madman who brought us here. I squint up at him, masked as Abraham Lincoln, the grinning monster with wild blond curls who dangled me over the side of a mountain like an insect trapped between his fingers.

"I thought you could do with a nap while we traveled," he says. "For your own comfort, of course."

"What do you want with us?" Wallace asks, his bag removed, too.

"You've created something extraordinary, Dr. Murrow," Abe says.

Wallace frowns. "Extraordinary? What do you mean?"

"Oh, don't be modest." Abe places the barrel of his rifle on the ground and leans his elbow on the butt. "You've made a thing of beauty in your lab, and there are many people who will pay a lot of money for it."

"Wall, what's he talking about?"

Wallace looks back to me, fear and horror dawning on his face, and shakes his head. "Oh God, Lenny. I'm so sorry I got you into this."

"Into what? What the hell? What's going on?"

"What's *going on*, pretty lady," Abe interjects, "is none of your damn business since it has nothing to do with you."

"If it has nothing to do with me, then you won't mind letting me go."

His low chuckle rumbles, and interest flares in his eyes. "I like a little spirit in a woman." His laugh dies abruptly. "But not that much. Keep it up and you'll die even sooner than I've planned."

"Planned?" Wallace echoes, his eyes wide, his brows bent.

"Oh, yes. Everything is planned," Abe says pleasantly. "There's actually no way for you to come out of this alive, lady, but you'll go when I say you do."

His words are a loaded gun, pointed to my head, waiting for the trigger to be pulled. I feel the pressure as surely as a barrel at my temple.

"But firrrrrrrst," he says, eyes shining with anticipation, "let's have some fun."

He points the gun at us again. "Get up. It's time for the show."

CHAPTER 2
MAXIM

I HATE POLITICS.

Politics and oil are two of my least favorite things. My brother is running for president, and my father is an oil baron, if we're still using words like "baron."

So fuck my life.

"Did you hear me, Maxim?" Kimba asks, seated across from me in my office. "This is important. Don't think because it's *The View* they'll throw softballs. These ladies grill candidates."

I swing my chair around to view DC through my office window, searching out the echoes of Parisienne architecture, ironic because two cities couldn't be more different. "I'm not a candidate," I remind her. "And O hasn't even officially announced yet."

"You'll *be* a surrogate for the Democratic Party's forerunner." She leans forward, propping her elbows on my desk. "And you were just voted one of America's most eligible bachelors. Use this appearance to build some goodwill for your brother. They'll mention him."

Would it be immature to stick a finger down my throat and vomit up my lunch? It wasn't much. Avocado toast or some shit Jin Lei brought in. It would barely stain the carpet.

I've been voted one of America's most eligible bachelors for several years running and have *never* gone on *The View* or even acknowledged this…dubious honor. But for Owen, Kimba's making me do it. Should I decorate myself like a float in the Macy's Thanksgiving Day Parade, too? That's only *slightly* less pomp and circumstance than this appearance on *The View*.

"You need to get used to representing your brother on shows like this." Kimba's still talking. "You have to remember where *he* stands on things like climate change."

Oh, this grabs my attention.

I swing back around to face her. "You mean the fact that I advocate a much more aggressive plan for climate change than Owen does?" I ask, fake-mildly.

"Yeah. It's just scooting a little to the right on this issue."

"I don't scoot."

"Everyone scoots center when they're running."

"I'm also not running, but if I were, I for damn sure wouldn't scoot. Everyone and their mama knows where I stand on climate change. You think I'll lie about it now?"

"I would never ask you to lie," Kimba replies stiffly. "I'm just asking that you articulate your brother's position."

"I'll be happy to do that," I agree with a nod, "and say I think his position should be stronger."

"Maxim, come on."

"People aren't stupid, and their memories aren't that short. They know my brother and I don't share exactly the same views on climate change. It's fine that there's some daylight between us on this issue. Ignoring our differences is not how we fix problems, and neither is focusing on them. People are sick of bickering. They're tired of politicians locking horns and comparing dicks and getting nothing done. They want leaders who'll set their differences aside long enough to actually help somebody."

"Ya know." Kimba frowns a little and tilts her head to stare at me. "That kind of made sense."

"Of course it did." I grin and wink. "Just because I don't like this stuff doesn't mean I'm not good at it."

We both laugh, and Kimba returns her attention to the list of "fun things" she wants me to remember.

"Is that all?" I ask after another twenty minutes of reviewing Owen's position on several issues. "We done?"

"We're done." Kimba packs her iPad and notebook into her bag. "Good talk. I'll email you notes and circle back with more specifics on *The View* appearance."

"I'll try to contain my excitement in the meantime."

"Look, I know your brother appreciates you being all in like this. Having a surrogate as high-profile and popular as you makes the job a lot easier for Lenn and me."

When Kimba mentions Lennix, I automatically check my phone as I have for the past two days. Still nothing.

"Have you heard from her? Lennix, I mean."

"No, but that's not unusual when she goes on these service trips. Reception is usually bad, and Wi-Fi is spotty. She'll call when she can."

"Yeah, of course, you're right."

"And Wallace is there with her."

"Should that make me feel better?" I stand and walk around to lean against the corner of my desk. "That she's in a jungle with her ex?"

Kimba shifts her bag on her shoulder and levels me with a glance that is half amused, half exasperated. "You're kidding, right? You know she and Wallace are—"

"I know they used to date. Not fake date like she let me believe this time, but dated for real."

"That was years ago, and it didn't last long."

"Yeah, you're right." I shake my head. "Maybe I'm just paranoid. Something feels…off."

When you put yourself in perilous situations often enough, your survival instincts become better honed, and you learn to trust them.

"Well, nothing's off," Kimba says. "Believe me. I've been through seven of these trips now with Wallace and Lennix. They're fine. Oh! I have one last thing I forgot to tell you."

Her phone rings, and she glances at the screen. "Just gimme a sec. It's Viv."

She answers. "Hey, Viv. I'm in a meeting. Lemme call you right—"

Her brows bunch, but she chuckles. "Damn, V. Slow down. I can't understand a word you're saying."

Kimba's frown deepens, her expression going from amused to confused to horrified in a matter of seconds. A gulp moves the muscles of her throat, and she draws a shaky breath. "Who? Who has Wallace?"

That niggling intuition that's bothered me for days flares into a full-blown sick feeling. I stride over to stand right beside her. I know I'm too close, crowding her, but I need to hear exactly what's being said.

"Who has him?" I ask. "Is Lennix okay?"

"I-I…" Kimba closes her eyes and presses her hand to her forehead. "V, I don't understand."

"Kimba, what the hell? Is Nix okay?"

"Viv, I'm gonna put you on speaker." Kimba pulls the phone from her ear, taps the screen, and turns it faceup. "Maxim's here with me."

"Maxim, hey." Vivienne's wobbly voice comes over speaker. "I'm sorry I'm all over the place. I just—" Her voice breaks on a sob.

"Vivienne, can you tell me what's happened?" I try to keep my voice level. "Who has Wallace? What's going on?"

"My… My parents got a call about an hour ago from CamTech."

"Who's that?" I demand.

"It's the lab Wallace works for," Kimba says.

"Yeah, they called to say they'd received a video," Vivienne continues, her breath thinning, distressed.

"What kind of video?" I ask.

"A ransom video," Vivienne says. "A group in Costa Rica has taken Wallace hostage."

"And Lennix?" I force the words out. There's a good chance she wasn't with him at the time. She may be safe.

God, please let her be safe.

But something in my gut twists like it already knows the answer.

Vivienne's distress is palpable even over the phone, even before she answers. "They have her, too."

Rage, frustration, fear—a toxic cocktail of emotions stirs inside me. I didn't know you could actually *see red*, but it's like someone poured a bucket of blood over my eyes. Bloodlust, murder, vengeance—those things are smeared red all over me.

"Who the fuck has her?"

Kimba's eyes snap to mine, widening.

"He wears a mask, so we don't know," Vivienne says. "The guy on the video is wearing a mask."

"There's a video? I need it." I stride to my open office door. My assistant is at her desk, poring over reports we were discussing before Kimba arrived.

"Jin Lei, get the CEO of—" I swivel my head back to Kimba. "What was the name of the company again? CamTech?"

"Uh, yeah," Kimba says, blinking rapidly, still holding the phone.

"Get the CEO of CamTech on the phone right now," I tell Jin Lei. "And Grim. Get me Grim. Wherever he is, whatever he's doing, get his ass on a plane. He can call me from the air for an update, but tell him not to wait."

"Got it." Jin Lei nods and picks up her phone.

I cross back to Kimba and Vivienne, still on speaker.

"What else can you tell me?" I ask. "You said they contacted your parents, Viv. Do you know if they've contacted Mr. Hunter?"

"Um, yeah. I think so," Vivienne replies. "He was talking to CamTech."

"Shit." I shake my head. "I need to get to him. I don't want him dealing with those pharma parasites. They won't level with him. My guess is that this is a K&R situation."

"K&R?" Kimba asks faintly. "Like kidnap and ransom insurance?"

"They didn't mention insurance," Vivienne says uncertainly.

"They wouldn't," I tell them. "As soon as you advertise that you have K&R, it's nullified. In most cases, employees don't even know the company has a K&R policy on them. Otherwise, some might set up a hostage situation to collect the payout for themselves. High-value targets like CEOs have to have it. The company pays the ransom, and then the policy reimburses the payout. You can't talk about it, but kidnappers know how it works."

"Mr. Hunter's gotta be freaking out." Kimba gnaws on her bottom lip.

"Call him," I say. "We need to know everything CamTech said and what they've told the kidnappers. And I need that video, Vivienne."

"Uh, I don't have it," she says. "They told my parents not to share it with anyone, and they wanted to follow every instruction to a T. So I literally watched it through FaceTime with them."

"Don't worry," I say. "I'll get it. I need to call Nix's dad now, but keep us posted."

"Okay," Vivienne says, a tremor in her voice. "You really think we'll get them back?"

"Damn right we will. And the son of a bitch who took them will be the one who pays."

"Hang in there, girl." Kimba says. "Love you."

She disconnects the call with Vivienne and holds the phone to her chest for a second.

"God, I'm dreading this call," Kimba says, her brown eyes solemn. "I can't believe it's happening to Mr. Hunter again. This is exactly what he's dreaded since her mom disappeared."

"Nothing is happening again." I refuse to even consider that Mr. Hunter will never see Lennix again. That *I* won't. "Call him. I need as much information as quickly as I can get it."

Kimba nods and dials, keeping it on speaker.

"Kimba?" Concern weights the man's voice on the other end. "I was just about to call. Someone has Lennix."

"Viv told us," Kimba says, blinking at tears. "What do you know?"

"Not much. CamTech called to say they'd been contacted by a group in Costa Rica holding Wallace hostage, and they have Lennix, too."

"Did they give you a name for the group?" I ask.

The line goes silent, and I practically hear the cogs turning in the professor's quick mind.

"Sorry, Mr. Hunter," Kimba says hastily. "I should have told you. I have you on speaker so Maxim can hear, too."

"Maxim?" he asks. "Maxim who?"

"Uh, Maxim Cade, sir," I reply.

"The environmentalist?" he asks, obviously confused.

"Uh...yes?"

"How are you involved with my daughter's case, Mr. Cade?"

He doesn't know me. It stings for a second that I met Lennix when she was seventeen and I've never *come up* in a conversation with her father.

"I'm—"

"He's a friend of ours," Kimba interjects, stretching her eyes at me warningly. *Later,* she mouths.

"Oh, yes," Mr. Hunter says, understanding in his voice. "I do remember her saying she was managing your brother's campaign, but it wouldn't be publicly announced until February."

My brother. Wow.

"Yes, sir. Nix is, ahem, a close friend, and I want to help."

"Nix?" He laughs weakly. "I've never heard anyone call her that before."

Good. That's mine. She's mine.

"The group?" I press. "Did they give a name?"

"No, on the video—"

"Can you send us the video?"

"Well, the CamTech rep said I can't share it with anyone," Mr. Hunter says, his words dragging like he's unsure of what to do.

"Maxim's got lots of connections, as you can imagine," Kimba says. "Of course, we won't share it with the media or anyone else, but we need it if we're going to help her."

"Okay." A rule keeper's reluctance still lingers in his voice. "I'll send it, but I need to warn you. The video... It's bad, and they've hurt her."

My blood freezes in my veins.

"What do you mean they've hurt her?" I ask, my words blunt, curt.

"You'll see on the video," Mr. Hunter says. "Her throat... God, what if they...if she—"

"I'll get her back." I smooth my voice into false confidence. I've never been more afraid in my life.

"You still have my email, Mr. Hunter?" Kimba asks, pulling the iPad from her bag. "Just send it there."

"Yes," he replies. "The video's not long. I'll just stay on the line while you watch and you can tell me what I should do next."

In moments, Kimba receives the email and clicks the link to the video.

A face—or, rather, a mask—appears. A tall man, ripped with muscles and wearing a Kurt Cobain T-shirt and an Abe Lincoln mask, adjusts the camera. They're in some dark space, illuminated dimly with a few lights strung along the back wall.

"Hi," he says, his voice as American as the president he's hiding behind. He waves, and the mask shifts with his grin. "Don't be thrown off by the mask. I know it's kind of"—he touches his chin like he's searching his mind—"comical, but I assure you I'm completely serious."

He tips his head, beckoning someone off camera to come forward. Wallace steps into the frame, his steps reluctant and his eyes darting nervously from the camera to the hulking armed man.

"State your name," Abe says.

When Wallace doesn't respond right away, Abe taps his head with the butt of a semiautomatic weapon. Wallace winces.

"Name," Abe commands again.

Wallace glances at the camera from beneath a heavy frown, his eyes anxious, hollow. "Wallace Murrow."

"As the team at CamTech knows," Abe says, "Dr. Murrow here has been up to some revolutionary things with that vaccine of his."

Kimba and I exchange a quick look. I lift my brows, silently asking if she knows what-the-hell vaccine. She gives a swift negative shake of her head and returns her attention to the video.

"I want to keep this simple," Abe says. "You want your wonder boy back, it'll cost you ten million dollars and the formula for the vaccine he's been developing."

"What can you possibly think you'll be able to do with it?" Wallace asks, his voice pitching high, his eyes stretched open wide.

Abe hits the side of Wallace's head with the butt of his gun. Wallace grunts in pain and stumbles back, and another masked man, this one wearing Richard Nixon, drags him from the frame.

"As you can see…" Abe sighs dramatically. "I'm still training Dr. Murrow how to behave, but I have another hostage. He knows the deal."

He tips his head toward the camera, and Nixon returns, marching a hunched figure with a black bag covering his head into the frame.

"This is Paco," Abe says, ripping the bag from the man's head. "Paco, say hello to the nice people back home."

Time has chiseled deep grooves alongside the man's mouth and into his forehead. His swarthy skin sags around his jaw, and his once-dark hair is more salt than pepper. In his eyes, when he glances up at the camera, there's fear and a solemn resignation.

"I *said*," Abe emphasizes, "say hello to the people back home, Paco."

There is fear and a solemn resignation in Paco's eyes when he glances up at the camera, but he remains silent.

Abe leans down and loud-whispers, "You're making me look bad, buddy."

"Hello," Paco says, the English sounding forced and foreign on his lips.

"Paco here," Abe says, "is what I like to call disposable. Wrong time, wrong place. I don't need him. I only need Dr. Murrow, but fret not! Paco *does* serve a purpose."

Abe pulls a .357 magnum from the waistband of his camouflage pants and presses it to Paco's temple. The older man immediately starts whimpering, eyes closed. He lifts his plastic-cuffed wrists and presses his palms together in prayer. I catch the odd "*dios*" and "*ave maría*" strung into a rosary of fear and pleading.

Abe's voice goes wooden, his eyes like marble. "Paco's going to demonstrate that I mean business."

He pulls the trigger without further warning, the bullet firing into Paco's temple in a spray of blood and violence. Paco drops like a domino, setting a billion things inside me into motion.

"Jesus!" Kimba drops the iPad onto my desk like the blood and gray matter could have splashed on her clothes. It lands facedown, and I steady my hands to turn it back over so we can keep watching.

"See?" Abe's pleasant tone is back, his mask stained with Paco's blood. "Business. I don't do idle threats, Mr. Vale."

"Who's Mr. Vale?" Kimba asks, her voice and hands trembling.

"CEO of CamTech," Jin Lei answers from the door. "He's on the line."

I don't reply but hold up a staying finger to Jin Lei so I can watch the rest of this lunatic's macabre show.

"You're already responsible for the death of one innocent person," Abe says and turns to Nixon. "Bring her in."

Kimba and I stare at one another in a silence so tense, the muscles in my neck and back scream, braced for what will happen next.

The man in the Nixon mask guides a woman forward wearing a

T-shirt, jeans, and a black bag over her head. Abe pulls her to stand directly in front of him.

"Now this second hostage, though as disposable and useless to me as good old Paco…" He pauses and crosses himself with the gun. "Rest in peace, Paco."

He chuckles maniacally.

"Where was I? Oh, yes. My *other* hostage. She's probably worth more to some of you than dear Paco. I hear she's a pretty big deal back home. Allow me to introduce the next person who dies if I don't get my vaccine in forty-eight hours."

He rips the bag from the woman's head, and a river of inky hair tumbles around her shoulders. Abe presses his gun to her temple, and everything slows down. The world comes to a complete stop, and the only thing still in motion is the blood galloping through my veins like wild horses, like mustangs. Even with the riot of my emotions, an icy preternatural calm falls over me. In this moment, I know two things like I know my own name.

The first is that I can no longer call what I feel for Lennix obsession, mere attraction, or anything less than what it is. I'm absolutely, irrevocably in love with her. I know this because it feels as though Abe is holding that gun to *my* head. I know that if her life is over, in every way that counts, so is mine. We are inextricably joined at the heart, even separated by thousands of miles. I wish I'd been clear-eyed enough, brave enough to tell her before she left. I wish standing there in the grip of this lunatic, she already had the assurance of those words—the certainty that I love her this deeply and will not stop fighting, searching until she's safe. Until she's home.

The second thing I know with absolute certainty is that I will kill this masked man myself. *Personally.*

The only sound I hear is my heart beating a lethal rhythm.

Die. Die. Die. Die.

Black and purple bruises ring Lennix's throat like someone has tried to choke her. She glances at the dead man on the floor and gasps, closing her eyes for just a moment.

"Look into the camera, pretty lady," Abe says, his voice pleasant yet as hard and cold and unhinged as an ice floe. "Now tell them your name."

When she doesn't speak, he bunches her hair in his fist and jerks, forcing her to look into the camera. In one glance, those eyes transport me back to Antarctica, a horizon foretelling storms ahead. Lennix's water-sky eyes, her warring eyes, tell me she's not done yet.

He presses the gun's barrel deeper into her temple until she winces. She draws a deep breath and raises her hands, bound at the wrists by plastic cuffs, to push stray stands of hair from her face. The compass bracelet I gave her glints in the light.

It's because we found our way back to each other.

My words from the night I gave her the bracelet haunt me. Did we find each other again only to have our second chance ripped away? I should have told her then that I loved her. I should have smothered her with it—should have kept her with me and ordered her not to go. That would not have gone over well, but my gut sensed danger. Even when Wallace assured me it was safe. Even though she's done several trips and nothing's gone wrong, I should have stopped her.

I failed.

"I said, tell them your name." Abe grounds the harsh words up and spits them into her ear.

Lennix's chin tilts in that defiant way I've seen since the day we met, and I silently beg her to comply, to cooperate until I can get there. Until I can find her and kill this son of a bitch for her.

"My name is Lennix Moon Hunter."

"And she—" Abe starts.

"Lennix Moon Hunter, Yavapai-Apache Nation," she says, her voice fierce, her eyes lit for battle. "The last warriors to surrender. And I am the girl who chases stars."

She turns her head to meet bright-blue eyes through the slits of the mask, every line of her body a declaration of war. My heart constricts with fear for her. She's vulnerable in every way possible. He could shoot her right now. He could rape her. He could cut off her head. He could take her away from me forever, and if she's not frightened, I'm terrified enough for both of us.

A long moment stretches between them, and it's not clear who is conquered and who is the conqueror, but I know who holds the gun.

"You have forty-eight hours," Abe repeats, holding her eyes a second longer before looking directly into the camera for his final words. "And then she dies."

CHAPTER 3
MAXIM

AN EERIE SILENCE PRESIDES OVER MY OFFICE FOR A FEW SECONDS when the screen goes dark. I allow the full weight and peril of the situation to crowd in on me, and then I approach this challenge the way I have every other one. Focused, methodical, and only considering a favorable outcome.

"You still there, Mr. Hunter?" I ask.

"Yes." He clears his throat, but fear is stubborn and lingers in his voice. "I'm here."

"When did they send this video?"

"Um…a little under an hour ago. Fifty-seven minutes. I set the timer on my watch."

I do the same, my heart racing in time with the rapid seconds once I press the button to count down.

"What did CamTech tell you?" I glance up at Jin Lei, standing in the door and mouth, *Vale's next.*

"They said they have a negotiator dealing with the kidnappers," Mr. Hunter says. "And that he has no demands for Lennix separate from the vaccine."

"What does that mean?" Kimba asks.

"It's what he meant by her being disposable," I say grimly. "They'll use her to impose additional pressure on CamTech to get what they want, but there's nothing they're asking for

Lennix's release. Just the ten million and the vaccine in exchange for Wallace."

"So what do we do?" Mr. Hunter asks, panic threading his words.

"Let me work on this, sir." I nod to Jin Lei, indicating that I'm ready for the CamTech CEO. "In the meantime, I'd like to fly you out here to DC. I can have a plane there in a few hours."

"Fly out there?" he asks. "Why?"

"Because I'm taking the lead on this. I need you to trust me. We can't leave Lennix's safety to CamTech. They have no vested interest in saving her. We need to establish our own line of communication with the kidnappers. You understand?"

"I think I do understand, Mr. Cade," Lennix's father says softly. "And I think you're more than just Lennix's friend."

I'm tempted to assert exactly what and who I am to his daughter, but if she hasn't told him, that's not my place.

"My assistant, Jin Lei, will get your information and send you details," I answer instead.

"Will she…" His voice breaks, and tears thicken his voice. "That's my little girl, Mr. Cade. You understand? I can't… I can't lose her."

I can't lose her either!

I want to shout it. Scream that it's taking all my discipline to remain focused and keep forging ahead when my brain just wants to spiral with every awful possibility.

"I swear I'll find a way to get her back." It's a promise I make to him and to myself.

"Thank you." He sniffs and clears his throat. "Sorry. I—I'll be there as soon as I can."

When he hangs up, Kimba and I stare at one another for a handful of tense seconds.

"Maxim," she says, pressing her lips together and blinking rapidly. "I know you'll try your best, but what if—"

"Don't say it." I pick up the phone with the flashing light on my desk. "Don't even think it."

Her tearful gaze holds mine for a moment before she nods, releases a long breath and leans back in her seat. Pressing the handset to my ear, I touch the button and bring the CamTech CEO who's been waiting on the line.

"Mr. Vale, thank you for holding. Sorry it took so long."

"Mr. Cade." A cultured voice comes across the line. I know Ivy League when I hear it. "I'm surprised by your call but pleased, obviously."

Obviously. "I'm calling about your hostage situation in Costa Rica."

His pause on the other line telegraphs surprise and caution. "How…um, what do you know about our situation?"

"I know your employee, Dr. Murrow, is being held hostage along with Lennix Hunter. I know one hostage has already been executed and that the kidnappers are threatening to kill Ms. Hunter in forty-eight hours unless your company meets their demands."

"Only family and significant others are supposed to have that information."

"I *am* significant," I say, struggling to keep the rough demand out of my voice. "Tell me what we're dealing with."

"I'm sure that you, as a CEO like me, understand the confidential nature of a sensitive operation such as this."

"I'm not a CEO like you. I could buy you out several times over, and you know it, which is the only reason you took my call. I asked for the status of these negotiations, and I'd appreciate it if you'd stop bullshitting me."

"Look, Cade," he says, his tone hardening into cement. "This is a confidential company matter and none of your concern."

"Ms. Hunter is my concern. Do you want to tell me what the hell is so special about this vaccine they're demanding? Or would you like for my team to start digging? Because if we start digging, there's no telling what we'll find, and I won't hesitate to turn it over to the FBI and the CDC, which I suspect you should have done by now."

He's quiet on the other line, silently confirming that my instincts are not misleading me.

"Am I right, Vale? This vaccine must be awfully special, and if you haven't brought the CDC in yet, which it appears you haven't, then you're still trying to keep it off their radar. I promise if you don't tell me everything, I will blow the whistle so hard on your shit, the FBI will be at your door in the next hour. Am I clear?"

He *ahems*. "Yes, I hear you."

"Then talk."

"There's an international humanitarian organization that has created certain…incentives for pharmaceutical companies who find ways to increase the effectiveness of vaccines in developing nations," he says. "And, before you ask, I cannot disclose the name of this organization."

"Go on."

"Dr. Murrow leads the CamTech team that has spent the last eighteen months focused on the efficacy of a strain of the TB vaccine."

"And?"

"And he made incredible progress. I urge you that what I'm about to say must stay between us."

"I have a security specialist who may become involved with the negotiation process for Ms. Hunter's extraction. He may need to know, but I can guarantee his silence and trustworthiness."

Vale's frustrated exhale comes across the line. "If this gets out—"

"Every minute you waste is a minute Ms. Hunter is losing. Tell me what I need to know. Now, and no bullshit."

"Dr. Murrow developed a super vaccine of sorts. Of course, you know how vaccines work. They contain enough of the disease to trigger our bodies' defensive process. When we first encounter infection, we have cells that learn how to fight it." He clears his throat, a sound of hesitation and discomfort. "In trying to create a vaccine for TB that would be stronger and more effective in developing nations, Dr. Murrow inadvertently created something so strong it essentially 'tricks' the body's defensive mechanism into *believing* it has learned how to counter the infection but then actually increases the symptoms until you die."

Shit.

"Die?"

"All the animal trials we've conducted so far." Vale continues. "Show the markers of something quite groundbreaking."

"And dangerous. You haven't alerted the CDC about it yet? Surely there are guidelines that would require you to."

"Mr. Cade, our plan was to notify the CDC when it became more clear what we actually have and how it might be used. It was top secret. Someone privy to the details must have leaked the project. We're trying to flush out our rat now."

"And how does this kidnapper want to use it?"

"I'm speculating, of course, but I believe he has…clients who see the potential value of weaponizing the vaccine."

"In biochemical warfare, you mean."

"Yes, I would assume so."

Air hisses through my teeth at the staggering effect this thing could potentially have.

There's no way in hell CamTech will turn that vaccine over. They can't.

I draw a calming breath to keep from hurling the phone through my office window. "So your plan is what?"

"We've opened negotiations with the kidnapper," Vale says. "I'm sure you know how this works. The U.S. government doesn't negotiate with terrorists and rarely engages in private foreign hostage situations. If they find out about the vaccine at this stage, they'll confiscate it and any pertinent records. If my rat finds out we no longer *have* the vaccine and tips them off—"

"You'll have no leverage with the kidnapper."

"Make no mistake, Cade, we will never turn that vaccine over. Our only hope is to convince the kidnapper to settle for the money.

Can you imagine this as a weapon at what would essentially be a black market auction? No way we'd let that be tracked to us. That would be a public relations nightmare."

"Not to mention all the *people* who might die if it falls into the wrong hands," I say. "Or did you forget about that?"

"Of course, that's our primary concern."

"Of course it is," I say, my words heavy with sarcasm. "So again, what is your plan?"

"We have K&R on Dr. Murrow. Our insurance provides a negotiator to intervene and drive the ransom as low as possible."

"Which typically takes weeks, sometimes months." My hand clenches into a knot at my side. "That motherfucker will kill Lennix in forty-eight hours."

"We'll, uh…do our best to include Ms. Hunter's safety in the terms we negotiate."

"This is a madman, Vale. He may want your money to fund whatever his agenda is, but that's not what's *fueling* him. The money won't be enough."

"Well, we cannot turn over the vaccine. You know that. What would you suggest?"

"Like I said, I have my own security specialist, Brock Grimsby. Authorize your negotiator to fully apprise my guy of the situation. I'll determine what we'll do from there."

"*You'll* determine? Don't think you can come in and take this over. This is still my operation to manage. We have a crisis plan."

"He's given Lennix forty-eight hours to live. From what I'm hearing, your crisis plan doesn't include a way to stop him, so I'm damn well taking this over. Get in my way and get crushed, Vale. You and that glorified drugstore you're running."

"Glorified—"

"I don't have time to pander to you. I don't have time to stroke your ego. There is one thing I care about right now, and that's getting her home."

"And Dr. Murrow?"

"Yeah, him, too, but at least the kidnapper might negotiate for him. He considers Lennix disposable." The awful image of Paco's execution replays in my head. "And we've seen how he treats disposable hostages. They end up dead."

CHAPTER 4
MAXIM

"CamTech can't help us, King."

Grim's blunt assessment lands on me with crushing weight. I've tried all day to attack one thing at a time to sort out this shitstorm. I haven't allowed myself to think about what's happening to Lennix right now or to even consider that she won't come home.

Grim's words, though, spoken with such deliberate, honest force, send me to collapse, weak-kneed, in my seat. I rest my elbows on the desk in front of me and steeple my hands, pressing my forehead to the tips of my fingers.

"What'd they say?" My voice sounds calm, but there is a riot in my head, an angry mob throwing stones and setting fires in the streets.

"First of all, they have no idea where they're being held," Grim says, sitting on the other side of the desk, probably watching me for signs of detonation. He's the one who has kept tabs on Lennix for a decade. He knows what she means to me. "They were last seen at the Bribri reserve where they were staying, but Talamanca is mountains and jungle so dense and wild, you could hide for years if you tried hard enough, and no one would find you. It's about as off the grid as you can get."

An image from Nix in the video passes through my mind. Pushing her hair back, the bracelet I gave her glinting in the light.

"The bracelet," I say, some hope flaring in the so-far-bleak news. "Can we use it to find her?"

"You mean even though you didn't activate the geotracker *in* the bracelet?" Grim asks, one brow cocked.

"What was I supposed to say? 'Nix. I know this is our first date in, oh, ten years, but could you wear this tracking device so I can monitor your every move? Thanks.'"

"You could have explained that it's standard practice for people in your position to issue tracking devices to significant others, yeah. This is why."

"It just wasn't that kind of night."

"Well, I hope you had a nice romantic *fuck*, but now it'd come in really handy if you had activated that chip."

"Solutions, Grim," I say through a cage of teeth. "Can you activate it remotely? Is it too late?"

"Not sure. They could be underground. Underwater, for all we know. There's no way to know the conditions where they're being held. With them being in such a remote place with no Wi-Fi, satellite, or electricity—finding that signal could be like pulling a single thread from the rain forest."

"But that's exactly what I need you to do. If anyone can, it's you."

Grim gives a terse nod and rubs a hand over the back of his neck. "I've had an initial conversation with CamTech's negotiator."

"And?"

"Like I said, I don't feel good about it."

"I expected as much. What's their position?"

"They don't have one. The kidnapper wants ten million dollars and the vaccine. We both know they'll never hand over that vaccine. Their only hope is getting them to settle for the money. They're actually willing to pay the ten if they have to because K&R will reimburse that payout. And apparently Dr. Murrow is a pretty big deal. He's the brains behind this vaccine they've developed, and they see its potential."

"Its potential to kill millions of people, you mean?"

"Hey, war is a dirty business, but it's still business. They may be required to report it to the CDC before they issue it as a drug, but they could eventually *sell* it to our government, even if only to keep it from the hands of any other government, and they know it. Bringing him home is a huge priority for them."

"And Lennix? What about bringing her home?"

He shakes his head, his expression grave. "The kidnapper has tied their hands on it. Maybe they can talk this guy down and convince him to cut his losses, grab the ransom, and run without the vaccine, but I'm not sure we'll get there in forty-eight hours."

He pauses, flicks me a careful glance. "The best we can hope for on this abbreviated timeline is that the kidnapper stretches out the threat of killing Lennix."

"Stretches it out? What do you mean?"

"Instead of killing the hostage right away, it's common practice for kidnappers to…assert pressure by sending fingers, toes—"

"Fuck!" The expletive explodes from my mouth. I pull my hair until it hurts and pace my office like a trapped animal.

"I can't take it, Grim." I stand still long enough to tell him. "Getting her back in pieces…" I close my eyes and drag in a breath tainted with fear and rage. "What do you recommend?"

"*If* we can activate that tracking device remotely, we may be able to attempt a rescue, but we should try a conversation with this guy first."

"A *conversation*? With the man who held a gun to her head? I don't want a conversation with him. I want him to know how it feels to have a gun held to *his* head…for about thirty seconds before I blow it off."

"King—"

"I'm serious, Grim. I don't want to negotiate with the guy on that video. He killed an old man to prove a damn point. He'll kill Nix, so I'm killing him first."

Grim scowls his exasperation. "It's not a matter of packing a lunch and taking off for the jungle. A rescue mission in conditions like these would require extensive tactical planning, strategy, assembling the best team possible. Time."

"We don't *have* time. We have to get her out of there."

"In half these K&R rescues, someone dies. Often the hostage."

That alarming truth sinks in alongside the just-as-alarming alternatives.

"Let me at least try to speak with him," he says. "I asked CamTech's negotiator to inquire, to see if this guy will talk to us."

"And?"

"He will."

"When?"

"Today. If you're saying yes, we'll try to talk to him as soon as we can."

"We don't have time to waste, Grim."

"Believe me, I'm aware."

———————

"You have to let me handle this."

I nod and keep my face straight when Grim says it. If he suspects how close I am to completely losing my mind, he'll try to lock me out of the room. And I refuse to miss even one second of this negotiation call. I douse my whole being in *Namaste* and hope Grim doesn't detect the shackled demon under the three-piece suit.

"Maxim, excuse me," Jin Lei says from the office door. "Kimba's here, and she has Mr. Hunter with her."

I thought the first time I met Nix's father would be at Christmas or some special occasion. She'd introduce me. Her dad and I would get to know each other over a beer and maybe a football game. I'd be nervous in that way a man is when he meets the father of the woman he loves. I'd have time to convince him I was worthy of his daughter, even though I know I'll never be good enough for Lennix.

Now, I just don't give a damn. When I get her back, I'm keeping her. I'm nervous about this first time meeting her father, but there's a lot more at stake than his blessing.

"Mr. Hunter," I say, stepping forward with an outstretched hand. "Thank you for coming right away."

"Of course. Thank you for the, uh…plane."

His uncertain smile reminds me I'm not the guy most girls bring home. In some ways, there's less mystery because he feels he already knows me, but most of what he's heard is probably bullshit, so he knows less than he thinks he does. It will take time to sort the truth of who I am from the gossip and speculation. And right now, time is one thing we don't have.

"Glad you made it," I tell Mr. Hunter, splitting a glance between him and Kimba. "Grim's about to speak with Abe."

"Abe?" Kimba's dark brows crinkle.

"What else should I call him? Coward, maybe? Hiding behind that mask."

Grim walks over to shake hands with Mr. Hunter and Kimba.

"We're expecting the call in the next minute or so." Grim gestures to a table in the middle of my office. "You'll hear us on speaker, but I'll use the handset so he's only actually speaking to me. We'll also be recording the conversation to review it later in case he gives anything away about their location or any other pertinent details."

"So there's no lead on where they might be?" Anxiety spikes Mr. Hunter's voice.

Grim and I exchange a look, silently asking each other how much we should divulge. Hell, if Nix was my daughter, I'd want to know it all.

"We're working on a lead," I say. "I, um, gave Nix a bracelet before she left."

"I saw it," Kimba says with a smile. "It was beautiful."

"There's a tracking device in it," I say, refusing to look away when her eyes widen then narrow.

"Does she know?" Kimba's tone turns starchy.

"No, I hadn't activated it. I wanted to discuss it with her before I took that step."

"Considerate of you," she drawls.

"It's standard practice for the significant others, wives, and girlfriends of men like Maxim to wear such devices," Grim says absently, not looking at us but checking the telecommunications setup.

"Girlfriend?" Mr. Hunter asks, brows lifted.

"Oh." Grim glances up and looks between Mr. Hunter and me. He shrugs. "Sorry."

Thanks for that, Grim.

"Here we go." Grim presses a button, which switches on a green light, and he picks up the phone. "Hello."

"Well, hello," the caller says. I recognize the taunting voice. "I heard you want to discuss my little squaw."

I nearly lunge at the phone. *This motherfucker.*

I bite into my frustration, let it burst in my mouth like a bitter pill. My hands curl into fists in my pockets. I think I'm doing a decent job disguising my anger until I look up to find Mr. Hunter watching me, glancing from my tight jaw to the bunched fists I'm hiding. An answering outrage flashes in his eyes, and we just nod to each other in recognition. Losing our tempers won't help Lennix.

"Yes, I'm authorized to negotiate Lennix Hunter's freedom," Grim says, his tone brisk, professional.

"Freedom?" Abe's laugh echoes harshly in my office. "Who said anything about freedom? I entertained this call to let the arrogant prick who thinks he can buy his way into my good graces know that he can't."

"It's in your best interest to—"

THE REBEL KING   31

"Don't presume to know my interests," Abe snaps, any traces of faux pleasantness vacating his voice. "You can let the man hiding behind his *purse* and his mouthpiece know I cannot be bought out of my convictions."

"Convictions?" I spit, fury and indignation torpedoing the word from my mouth.

Grim arrows a glare at me and presses a finger to his lips. "Look, there must be something you need or want that we could—"

"My vaccine." A loaded silence follows his words. "Can you get me that?"

"CamTech is handling that aspect of the negotiations in connection with Dr. Murrow."

"You're confused. CamTech is handling *all* the negotiations because they are the only ones who have what I want, and if they don't give me the vaccine in...oh, ticktock, forty-two hours now, then I will put a bullet in her head."

I speed to the table, jerk the phone from Grim, and strangle it in a tight hold.

"Listen to me," I grit out. "Name a price. There must be something you want."

"Oh ho ho," Abe chuckles. "You must be the man behind the curtain. I guess you're old moneybags, huh? To whom do I have the pleasure of speaking?"

"Tell me your name and I'll tell you mine," I say, swiping at Grim when he tries to take the phone from me.

"That's not how the game works."

"This isn't a game. It's someone's life."

"*It's someone's life*, he says." Abe's flippant tone sours. "Like that matters to the government, to the drug companies, to our fucked-up health-care system. But when your precious is affected, all of a sudden *it's someone's life* and it's not a game."

"Our health-care system *is* fucked up," I agree flatly. "The drug companies *are* leeches. The government *doesn't* do enough when it's needed and butts in when it's not. You're right, but taking her life won't change any of that. How does this help?"

His bark of laughter is a switchblade—short, sharp, cutting. "I'm not interested in helping. That shit's beyond helping, but they'll at least pay."

"Paying doesn't have to mean killing. And does it really get you what you want?"

"I want my mother back. Can you give my dead mother back to me, Mr. Moneybags? Can your wealth and power reverse how this ruined system left her for dead?"

I close my eyes, hearing the bleak fury in his voice. I'm completely ill-equipped to do a damn thing about it.

"I'm sorry for your loss," I say after a moment, "but what will this prove?"

"How does it help? What does it prove?" he mocks. "You're a pathetic negotiator. You're supposed to figure out what's important to me, and neither of those things matter at all. Nothing does anymore. That's the point you're missing. So I'd just as soon shoot your little girlfriend's head off as take a piss out in the jungle. She doesn't matter."

That red rage replaces any sympathy I might have felt for this lunatic.

"Nix matters to me, and I'll give you whatever you want."

"Nix, is it?" His voice is again lilting, taunting. "She must hold a very special place in your heart, Moneybags."

"There's not a price too high. Just name it."

"I've told you what I want. My mother back. Got a wire transfer for that, do you?"

"So you punish innocent people in your mother's name? I'm sure she'd be so proud."

Grim's head drops to his hands, and he releases a frustrated exhale.

"You're a dumb fuck, aren't you?" Abe demands with a caustic laugh. "I've got your piece of pussy right here, and you dare insult me. I have six men who don't mind sharing. There's seven, but one of them doesn't like girls, so you know. To each his own."

Fear sends my heart nose-diving. Rage breathes fire down my neck.

"Don't," I choke out. "Don't hurt her."

"Say you're sorry and maybe you'll win the game."

Die. Die. Die.

"Say it, you idiot," Grim snaps. "If you don't want her dead before he hangs up, say it."

Kimba's gasp, her tears. Mr. Hunter's wide, terrified eyes. Jin Lei's anxious frown. The disdain of Grim's stare.

I messed up, and if this psychopath harms even one hair on Lennix's head because of my stupidity, I'll never forgive myself.

"I'm sorry."

"Very good." His pause screams delight and contempt. "Now beg."

"Please." It comes easily because I'd say anything to save her.

"I'll think about it."

The line goes dead.

"Dammit!" I bang the handset on the table once, twice, three times, four, until it cracks down the middle.

"King, stop," Grim says. "Breaking the phone won't change anything. You messed that up real good, brother."

"I… I'm… Shit." I push shaking fingers through my hair and squeeze the bridge of my nose. "I know. I'm sorry. God, I'm sorry. He just… He has her, Grim. What will he do to her?"

He shakes his head and shoots a furtive glance at Mr. Hunter.

My gut knots at the finality in that look.

"We *have* to find her," I tell him. "We *have* to go get her."

CHAPTER 5
MAXIM

"I FOUND HER," GRIM SAYS A FEW HOURS LATER, STRIDING INTO MY office, triumph and trepidation equal shareholders on his face.

"The signal?" I ask. "The tracker?"

"Yup. Wherever they are is remote for sure, and at first we couldn't pick it up to activate. They may have been in a forest so dense we couldn't grab it. They must have left an area we couldn't detect it for a place where we can."

"When do we leave?"

"We?" Grim cocks one brow.

"You can't possibly think I'm letting you do this without me. While I do what? Stay here like some house pet waiting for you to come back? The fuck. You know me better than that. He has my girl, Grim."

"You're not trained for this."

"I'm an excellent shot."

"Shooting what? Geese? Shooting for sport on your daddy's ranch? A human target is different. Shooting a person is…" He pauses, leveling a warning glance at me. "Killing a person is different."

"I wouldn't hesitate to shoot him or anyone threatening her, if that's what you're worried about."

"Taking the shot is not the same as living with the weight of that death on your conscience."

"This motherfucker held a gun to Nix's head and, by the looks of it, tried to choke her to death. If I get a shot, I'm taking it, and I'll sleep like a baby."

Our stares interlock, and he searches my eyes in that way Grim has that peels back your skin to see what you're made of. He gives a terse nod.

"I'll get things organized, but if you come, we can't have a repeat of that phone call. No taking over. It's my operation, and you follow *my* rules."

I just stare at him because when was the last time I followed any rules except the ones I made up? I don't challenge him now, but surely he knows I will if necessary. I nod to satisfy the demand on his face.

My cell rings, and I grimace when I check the screen. "O, what's up?"

"What's *up*?" Owen asks, irritation prickling his voice. "When were you going to tell me Lennix had been taken hostage?"

Shit.

"I'm sorry." I blow out a weary breath.

"She's my campaign manager, Maxim. She's my *friend*. Kimba told me what's going on. I should have heard it from you as soon as you knew."

"I've just been focused on finding her and figuring out how to get her back."

"And did you find her?"

"Yes. Grim's strategizing now."

"How are you?" he asks, concern breaking past his initial irritation.

Something about my brother asking, about talking to Owen, batters the wall I've been building around my emotions to get through this crisis.

"Not good." I pass a shaking hand over my mouth. "O, what if…?"

I can't say it aloud.

"Max," he says, his voice softening. "We'll get through this. We'll get her back."

Even knowing he can't guarantee it, can't promise it any more than I can, hearing Owen say it, too, eases the band around my chest.

"Thanks, man," I say.

"I called to see if there's anything I can do. Of course, you know officially the American government does not negotiate with terrorists or involve itself in international kidnapping and ransom situations."

I'm about to tell him I'll rescue Lennix without help from anyone else when he surprises me.

"But unofficially," he says, "what do you need?"

CHAPTER 6
LENNIX

"Rabbit ears, Britney Spears, iPhone, *Home Alone*."

I'm not even aware I'm singing the words and familiar tune until Wallace nudges my foot with his shoe.

"What're you singing?" he asks, leaning his shoulder into mine against the wall of the cave they brought us to this morning. At least it feels like morning from what I can see outside. It's like that first gasp of dawn, with sunrays cutting through misty-breath clouds. I have no real sense of time after being drugged and waking up God knows how many hours later. But it feels like a new day.

It feels like the last day of my life.

A misplaced smile cracks my dry lips. "'We Didn't Start the Fire.'"

"Oh, I remember that. Elton John?"

"Billy Joel." I twist my wrist in the plastic cuffs to touch the compass charm dangling from my bracelet. "Maxim and I sang it in Amsterdam. He made up all the words, and we…"The little doomed smile dies, and tears sting my eyes. "We saw the tulips that day and the windmills. We rode bikes along the coast by the water, and it was a perfect day."

I close my eyes, and the memory rises so rich and vivid that the dankness of this cave fades, and fresh air filters into my lungs. Sea spray cools the sweat from my skin and sprinkles salt on my lips.

Raised voices speaking Spanish beyond the mouth of the cave

yank me back, and reality turns the sea spray on my lips to the salt of my own tears. I swipe my body's confession of fear from my cheeks, determined these fools won't have the satisfaction of seeing.

"By my calculations," I say, my voice soft and resigned, "my forty-eight hours are almost up. I'm out of time soon."

"He won't…" Wallace's voice fades, and his eyes glaze over. I wonder if, even as he assures me Abe won't kill me, he sees Paco's body, his blood spilled on the ground. Because I do. The sight will haunt me forever. "We'll figure something out."

"I don't know," I whisper, pressing my back into the cave wall. "It doesn't look good."

Wallace grabs my hand. "Don't lose hope."

How do I tell him I lost hope long ago? Now I live between flashes of faith and glimpses of hope, even as I fight. The one thing that has given me hope, the one thing that has renewed my faith, is another thing I'll lose.

Maxim.

"Wall," I say, squeezing his hand with new urgency. "I need you to promise me something."

"No." He shakes his head, his eyes panicked. "No promises. You'll make it out of this."

"You have some leverage. Maybe not much, but promise me you'll try to do what I ask."

"What…" He swallows and looks down to the dirt of the cave floor. "What is it?"

"My body," I choke, blinking back tears. "Make him send me home."

"Lenny, no." Wallace hangs his head, clenching his eyes closed. "Please no."

"Yes." I lift my cuffed hands under his chin, forcing his gaze to meet mine. "Try to do this for me. My father can't go through that again. Not knowing. Never seeing. Not sure. He needs closure, no matter how bad it is." I stuff a sob back down my throat.

"And Maxim," I say, "he'll need that, too. God, I never got to tell Maxim I love him, and now it's too late."

Tears leak from under Wallace's closed lids, dampening his lashes. He shakes his head. "I hate that you got dragged into this. I'm so sorry. It's not fair."

"It's not your fault." My tears win, coursing over my cheeks.

I cover my mouth, capturing the painful sob before it escapes and reveals my vulnerability to the bastards guarding the cave. Hot tears leak over my fingers and burn a trail down my neck. I close my eyes and draw a deep breath from the well of strength inside me that I pray is deep enough for what's ahead.

"You sound like you've accepted this," Wallace says. "That's not like you. You're a fighter. You don't surrender. Remember?"

"You can still fight with fear in your heart." A watery chuckle escapes me. "Sometimes it's the greatest motivator. The fear of what you'll lose can make you that much more determined to win. My life is at stake, and I'll do whatever it takes to get out of this alive, but if I don't, I have to think about the ones who mean the most to me." I discipline my mouth into a firm line. "I'll be prepared for the worst and fight for the best."

I reach over and grab his hand, our shackled wrists overlapping. "There are two things that *do* give me hope, Wall."

"What?"

"Did I ever tell you that I dream of my mother?"

The question seems to startle him. His brows lift, and he fixes all his attention on me. "No. What do you dream?"

I recall the night I huddled in Maxim's arms after a nightmare and can almost feel the strength, the comfort I found in him.

"It's different, but sometimes the same. Sometimes a recurring nightmare, sometimes a memory."

I find Wallace's eyes in the dim light of the cave. "I dreamt of her. We were back at my Sunrise Dance, this rite of passage for young girls in my tribe. She looked right at me and told me to run."

I shake my head, a slight smile curving my lips. "I'm hoping she's reaching me somehow, letting me know when the time is right, to be ready. That gives me hope."

"And the other thing?" Wallace asks. "What's the other thing that gives you hope?"

"Maxim," I say with soft certainty. "If there's a way out of this, he'll find it. If there isn't…" A hot knot of emotion and tears crowd and burn my throat.

"If there's not," I tell Wallace, "just remember your promise. I have to go home."

The words I don't say chill the silent air between us.

Dead or alive.

CHAPTER 7
MAXIM

"You stay here."

Grim's words cut through the thick jungle humidity like a machete.

"I told you I'm a great shot," I say, my voice gravelly and frustrated.

"It was short notice, but between my contacts and your brother's, I've assembled a great team of *qualified* guys," he says pointedly. "You might be a great shot, but you ain't qualified, brother."

"I can still help."

"I don't want you anywhere near the action. We shouldn't need your help, but if the action comes to you, you got that." He nods to the gun holstered at my hip and then glances at the nine men checking their weapons and preparing for the strike. They're some scary motherfuckers. Like a group of Grims going into battle.

The sight should reassure me, but nothing will put me at ease until I can touch her. Until I can feel Lennix's heart beating against mine again, confirmation that she's gotten out of this alive.

"You remember what you're supposed to do?" Grim slots a knife inside his boot.

"Yeah. Wait here like a neutered cocker spaniel."

"You want her back?" Grim asks, not looking up from the watch he's been checking since we left DC headed for Costa Rica. It shows 3:022:02 and counting down. Just over three hours. All Nix has left, if that shitbag sticks to his timetable. He doesn't strike me as the type to back down.

"Yeah." I look up at the overcast sky, primed for storms and reflecting my own uncertainty, the turbulence whirring inside me. "I want her back."

"Then follow the plan. You wanted the gun, you got it. For once in your damn life, fall back and follow orders. Leave this to the guys actually trained to do it. What are your orders?"

I grit my teeth, unused to following anyone else's lead. "If I see a bad guy," I say stonily, "shoot him."

"And?" He cocks one thick eyebrow at me, looking very The Rock-ish.

"Don't get my ass killed."

CHAPTER 8
LENNIX

"GET UP!"

Abe's barked order makes my heart somersault and my belly flop.

Is it time? I have no concept of how long it's been since he recorded that video and flipped an hourglass on my life. I've felt the sand falling, every grain piling up, taking me closer to a gruesome end. Now that I'm facing my own death, I want to comport myself with honor—to die unflinchingly. For my enemy to see war in my eyes even as the life drains from them. How did my ancestors feel with an army ahead of them and certain death behind? The warriors at the Leap, who jumped from a cliff instead of surrendering? Did panic crawl up from their bellies, the insidious thief of courage? Or were they brave, resolved until their last breath?

In the near-dark of the cave, I hope there is just enough light for this monster to catch defiance in my glare when I stand and look at him.

"You, too, Dr. Murrow." He kicks Wallace's leg and flicks his head toward the opening of the cave, swinging his automatic rifle between us. "Move."

Wallace stands, and we share a quick, confused glance.

"I said"—he pokes Wallace in the hip with the gun—"move."

We take a few cautious steps toward the mouth of the cave. Is there a camera out there? Will he shoot me out in the open? Will he make Wallace watch? I have no idea what's about to happen. Fear claws through my skin, and anxiety leaks from every pore. Wallace stretches his cuffed hands toward mine and gives my fingers a reassuring squeeze.

Outside, I squint against the sudden brightness of the sun. Nixon stands with the six other men who have shadowed our every move, traveling with us since the brothers intercepted our jeep on the narrow mountain trail.

"Where'd you say you saw movement?" Abe asks, his big body deceptively relaxed. I sense tension coiled in his every muscle, tightening every line, even though on the surface, he seems almost indolent, his blue eyes placid behind the mask.

"Down there," one of the dark-haired men replies in heavily accented English, pointing toward the river barely visible through the tall trees and tangled foliage below. "I counted ten men."

I hold back a gasp of relief. Movement? Ten men? Has someone found us? Has *Maxim* found us? I caress my compass charm, a touchstone for the dregs of faith I'm drawing from.

"Ten, you say?" Nixon frowns. "We gotta move then."

"Yup," Abe agrees. "And we need to travel light. You know what that means."

"Plan B?" Nixon asks flatly.

"Plan B."

"You sure?"

"I'm sure." Abe fires in quick succession, shooting each of the three men to his left in the forehead. In a cruel choreography, Nixon executes the three other men with clean shots through their foreheads, too. The men fall like dominos, some still wearing the wide-eyed, gaping-mouthed expressions of sudden death.

"Shit!" Wallace shouts. He closes his eyes, clamping his lips together so tightly, a white ring forms around his mouth.

I swallow a sob, refusing to show Abe and Nixon my horror, my terror. I deaden my eyes, focusing on a point above where the mountain range kisses the sky. I even suppress the hope springing in my heart at the possibility that someone has found us. That someone is coming for us.

Maxim?

I shift my glance to the monster with the cherubic curls, and for one mad moment, I want to urge him to hurry. To put as much distance between us and our potential rescuer as possible. I've seen him kill Paco and the six men on his own team in cold blood and with a heart of stone. He could kill Maxim. My imagination conjures the awful vision of Maxim slumped to the ground, a bullet through his head, that same startled death stare stamped on his face.

"Let's go," Abe says, stepping over one of the dead bodies and shoving the gun's barrel into my side. "Move."

I step quickly in the direction he pushes me, glancing over my shoulder to see Nixon poke Wallace, who walks up and falls into step beside me. Our backs are to them, and Wallace slants a sideways smile my way, one filled with surreptitious excitement and hope. With a set of malevolent eyes burning blue fire in the back of my head, I don't even dare smile back.

"I hope we don't regret going to Plan B so soon," Nixon says just a little behind us.

"We need to travel light." Displeasure colors Abe's voice. "Don't punk out now."

"I'm not punking out. I'm just thinking if there are ten men chasing us, it'll be good to have some backup."

"Our contact didn't make arrangements for a group that size. He's made arrangements for three."

Three.

Not four.

A lump of trepidation forms in my throat, and I blink at tears. If there is a rescue being staged, it may not be in time to save me.

We march through the brush, and the more distance we put between us and the cave, the more conflicted I feel. Obviously Abe's men spotted some kind of rescue team heading in our direction. By the time they arrive at the cave, we'll be long gone. Absorbed into the lining of the hungry forest's belly. Untraceable.

We've walked at a quick pace for about fifteen minutes when we reach the river. The water rushes, the rapids intense and raging. As soon as we wade in, we'll be taken. They may as well shoot us now if they're going to toss us to those turbulent waves.

"Go," Abe tells Nixon with a curt snap of his head toward a cluster of mangled branches. "Get it. Hurry."

Nixon nods and runs toward the trees.

Abe grabs my chin, tilting my face up and peering down at me with masked malice.

"I'm usually a stickler on deadlines," he says, evil gleaming from his eyes. "And technically we have another two hours before I'm supposed to kill you, but I'm flexible. I didn't account for a rescue party. I wonder if it's Mr. Moneybags?"

I struggle to control my breathing. "Who?"

"The man who tried to negotiate for your life. Apparently, no one told him money doesn't buy everything. I think I'll leave your dead body here on the shore to teach him."

It must have been Maxim. I can't even imagine his fury, his frustration with Abe's brand of callous impudence. I've never heard the words from Maxim, and he's never heard them from me, but I know he loves me. And I hope he knows that I love him, too. I thought him having my body would bring some kind of comfort, the way having my mother's would have for me, but now I don't think it will, and my heart aches for him.

A yellow raft emerges from the trees bordering the river. Nixon pushes it out to the edge of the water from behind and then jogs over to join us.

Abe nods toward the boat. "No room where we're going, lady. This is the end of the road for you."

"No!" Wallace steps forward, but Abe puts the gun to his forehead.

"I suggest you cooperate or get your head blown off, too," Abe says, every word like a bullet. "Don't make me forget I need you."

"Come on!" Nixon shouts. "We gotta go."

"Time's up, pretty lady," Abe says with mock-woefulness and turns toward Nixon. "Take Dr. Murrow to the boat."

Wallace grabs my arm even with his hands cuffed. "No. Please."

Abe shifts the pistol down, aiming at Wallace's leg. "I could shoot off your kneecap and still get my vaccine."

"Wallace, go," I say, my voice soft but insistent.

"I won't leave you." Wallace says, his hands tightening. "He'll have to kill me."

"Oh, well," Abe says, shifting the gun to Wallace's head again. "These things happen."

"No!" The word rips from me. I'm horrified and absolutely certain he would do it. "Wallace, just go. Please."

"I love you, Lenny."

"I love you, too," I whisper, heedless of the two men listening or of the tears wetting my cheeks.

"Come on." Nixon pokes Wallace in the back with his automatic weapon. "Get in that boat."

Abe raises his gun and points it to my forehead. Everything in me wants to squeeze my eyes shut, to take refuge in that darkness, but I force my eyes open. I refuse to hide from evil, locking my glance with his through the slits of his mask. The last time he sees me, I won't be cowering, I won't be in fear.

The shot fires.

I wait to fall and wonder if I'll float above my body, look down on myself dying on the ground...but I'm whole and unharmed. Abe's gun falls. He howls, grabbing the hand that was holding his gun moments ago, which now gushes blood. Nixon looks in the direction of the shot, but before he can fire, he's hit. Still holding the gun, he wears that startled look of the men they shot not even an hour ago. Blood gurgles from a hole in his throat. He drops the gun, both his hands going to his neck to stop the gushing.

"Jack!" Abe shouts.

My feet are planted in the sand. I'm paralyzed for long seconds while Abe takes in the scene, the emotion on his face reshaping, skewing the mask.

Wallace looks at me, his eyes wide and his mouth gaping. We stare at one another for a moment, both shocked and strangely immobile.

"Run!"

At first it's my mother's voice, my dream, and I think my imagination is still playing tricks on me.

"Nix!" a voice yells a second time from the edge of the woods. "Run!"

As soon as I hear my name just that way, called in that deep voice, my heart pounds against my ribs.

"Maxim?" I look around, frantically searching the tangle of wild bushes and trees. And then I see him. Running toward us, a gun extended, aimed.

"Run!" he shouts again, not looking at me, eyes locked on Abe. "Murrow, get her out of here."

Wallace, as if snapping from a trance, grabs my arm awkwardly with one cuffed hand and takes off, dragging me along with him. I glance back. Fury tautens every line of Abe's body. He looks from the dead man on the ground to Maxim and picks up Nixon's automatic weapon.

"No!" I scream, breaking away from Wallace and running back. Before Abe gets off even one shot, the report of a bullet splinters the air. Abe stumbles back, a scarlet bloodstain blossoming on his shoulder through his T-shirt. He covers the wound with his hand and takes off toward the boat. Another shot rings out, but Maxim hasn't raised his gun again. A huge man dressed in camouflage pursues Abe, who pauses long enough to lift his gun despite a grimace of pain. The man in fatigues shoots him again, this time hitting the other shoulder. Abe stumbles toward the river where the boat waits, lunging, his body half on, half off the vessel. Another shot fires, this one hitting him in the back. He falls overboard into the rushing water, which drags him downstream. The man in fatigues keeps running, wading along the river's edge in the direction the water carries Abe.

"Don't let him get away!" the man in fatigues shouts.

It's only then I notice the group of men following him, all dressed in camouflage, black greasepaint smeared on their faces. Several of them jump in the yellow raft and follow Abe's body, bobbing along and farther away. With narrowed eyes, Maxim watches the violent waves, blood streaming behind Abe in a scarlet wake.

"Doc!" I run and hurl myself at him, not even sure he's ready to catch me. But he does. His arms encircle me so tightly it almost hurts and it's still not tight enough. Maxim's muscles flex with leashed power, but with my arms and cuffed hands trapped between us, he trembles against me. It feels like I'm rescuing him, too.

"Nix," he says, his voice rough. "I thought…"

"I'm okay." I press into him, sobs shaking my whole body—relief, joy, shock. Too many emotions to contain, and they leak from me in a torrent, wetting his neck, his shirt with my tears.

"You're okay?" He pulls back to search my face, to look into my eyes. "Did he hurt you?"

Those are two separate questions with different responses. Yes, he hurt me, but I'm okay. I have no idea how what Wallace and I experienced will affect me tomorrow or the next day, but in this moment, in Maxim's arms, I know how I feel right now. "I'm okay."

His sharp look narrows on my face. "Nix—"

"I'm fine. Doc, I'm fine. I promise."

He nods, pushing my tangle of unwashed messy hair back. I'm sure I look bad, my cheek swollen from the blow of Abe's gun, my face smeared with God knows what. I haven't been able to brush my teeth in days. I should feel self-conscious with him watching me so closely. His stare consumes every part of me, and I feel eaten alive in the best way. I don't care about my appearance when he looks at me like that, like he sees me.

"I love you, Nix." He says it so softly, Wallace and the few members of the rescue team standing nearby couldn't have heard him, but to me, it sounds like he's shouted it to the stars. I'm overcome with every possibility for happiness I never thought I'd find or even care about, right here in front of me. He's gloriously masculine and perfectly mine.

I say the only thing I can with so much emotion burning and clogging my throat.

"Same, Doc," I whisper, tears leaking from the corners of my eyes that have nothing to do with what I just went through and everything to do with what's ahead of me. Of us. "Same."

CHAPTER 9
LENNIX

"MORE TEA, LENN?"

My stepmother Bethany's solicitousness is so sweet, but I'm tired of being fussed over. It's surreal to be safely ensconced in the downy luxury of my bed, the lights and sounds of DC just beyond my window. After a few days in a cave, half of the time spent with a bag over my head, even the dim light of my bedroom lamp seems like too much. It feels like the walls are squeezing me, like that inordinately affectionate distant relative who gives you socks each Christmas and hugs so long and too tight. It should feel so good, but…it's too much.

Kimba, my father, Wallace, Bethany, and the doctor Maxim brought in stand around my bed, all eyes on me. I touch my throat self-consciously. I caught a glimpse of myself earlier in my bathroom mirror and saw for the first time how bad the bruises look. How bad *I* look. What a difference a few days in captivity make.

"Does your throat hurt?" Wallace asks, his frown anxious.

"Just a little." I force a weak smile to reassure him, to reassure them all. "I'm fine, but what about you? You were there, too, Wall."

"He didn't hang me over the side of a mountain by my throat," Wallace says.

"No, he didn't," Maxim says from his chair in the corner. He's barely spoken since we got back. He's been watching me the whole time, and my father keeps flicking curious glances his way.

"You need rest more than anything," the doctor says. "That sedative should be kicking in soon."

Maybe sleep will make them go away, leave me alone for a while. I droop my eyes deliberately and yawn on cue.

"We should let her get some rest," Kimba says. "We're all up in your space."

"It's okay." I smile at her, concerned by her concern. She never looks worried, and I've never seen her like this. "*I'm* okay, Kimba."

She doesn't look convinced but nods. "Viv's coming from New York. Says she needs to see you both for herself."

Wallace and I smile at each other, yet another bond formed through the ordeal we just survived.

"We have a hotel," Bethany says, "but maybe we should stay here. We can't leave you alone."

"She won't be," Maxim says from the corner.

Everyone turns to look at him. Bethany clears her throat, shooting a questioning look at my dad, like he may be able to offer some insight into the big man periodically growling from the corner.

"You need rest, young lady," the doctor says. "We'll clear out." He glances at Maxim. "Since it sounds like you'll be here, Mr. Cade—"

"I will be." Maxim stands and approaches the bed, giving the doctor his full attention.

"Good. You have my number. Call if she needs anything." The doctor walks out, and Maxim follows him, stopping at the door as if waiting for everyone else to come.

"Oh," Bethany says, gathering the lozenges and lotion and other items I'm not sure how she planned to use. There's even a ball of yarn and knitting needles. I'd laugh if I wasn't so tired and ready to be left alone.

Not alone.

With Maxim.

Maxim follows everyone out of the room, probably ensuring

they actually leave. My father lingers, picking up my hand on the bed once they're gone.

"You sure you're okay, kiddo?"

He hasn't called me that in a long time, and the endearment, the love behind it, makes my eyes water. "Yeah, Dad. I'm okay."

He met us on the tarmac, squeezing me so tight and weeping. This traumatized him in a way I think only he and I can fully comprehend. What we went through with Mama…I'm just so grateful he doesn't have to go through that again.

"Maxim is"—he widens his eyes and smiles—"intense."

"He is." My chuckle sounds like it's in a blender. "But I like it."

"I can see that. Why didn't you tell me you were dating Maxim Cade? He's a pretty big deal."

"He's a very big deal to me."

"He's not who I would have expected you to choose," Dad says carefully.

"Yeah," I agree wryly. "We met when I went to Amsterdam."

"You've known him that long?"

"We hadn't seen each other in years. We reconnected when I started working on his brother's campaign. You'll love Owen, by the way."

"Everyone seems to. I haven't seen this much excitement about a candidate in a very long time."

"He's the real deal. Kimba and I feel very lucky to work on his team."

"*He's* lucky to have you." He pauses, darting a quick glance over his shoulder and then turning back to me, lowering his voice. "How serious is it between you and Maxim?"

"We're keeping it private. I don't want the drama of us dating to cast any doubt on why Kimba and I got this job, and it would only distract from Owen's campaign at this point, but I love him."

"And he obviously has very strong feelings for you."

"He loves me."

Dad pushes my hair back. "Who wouldn't?"

"Spoken like a daddy." A real yawn, not like the one I faked to get rid of everyone, catches me by surprise. "Guess I *am* tired."

"Love you, kiddo. Get some sleep."

I nod, determined to see Maxim before I close my eyes, but I don't last.

CHAPTER 10
MAXIM

"I want to see his dead body, Grim."

The words vibrate in my chest, rattling across my rib cage. I grip the cell phone tightly and run a hand through my hair, keeping my voice low in the front room of Lennix's apartment.

"I know." Grim sounds as weary as I feel. "My team's doing everything short of draining that river to find him. You and I both know his odds of surviving in that current with four bullets in him are almost zero. The rapids alone would probably drown him, and if they didn't, he'd bleed out in the middle of nowhere with no medical assistance available."

"I don't want odds. I want proof. I don't care if he's facedown, blue and bloated in that river. Until I see for myself that he can't get to her again, this isn't over."

"King, it *is* over."

"You don't believe that. You just want me to stop harassing you about it while *you* keep searching because you need the same closure I do."

His silence admits that I'm right.

"What about his partner?" I ask. "Get anything from him yet?"

"The body's back in the States. We're cross-referencing fingerprints and DNA with state records, FBI, Scotland Yard, every database available. We're hoping there's some biological or documented connection between the two of them that will also give us clues to Abe's identity."

Hearing the fake name for the masked man makes me grit my teeth. Coward hiding behind a mask and threatening my girl. Putting a gun to her head. Fury contracts the muscles in my belly.

"He called Nixon 'Jack,'" I say, recalling the volatile scene by the river. "He was beyond distressed. I bet they're related."

"Yeah, I heard. We'll get everything we can from the body and go from there." Grim pauses and then sighs heavily. "Look, I know you said you'd be okay if you had to kill, but taking a life is some heavy shit. If you need—"

"Like a baby. That's how I told you I'd sleep if I had to kill one of those motherfuckers to get Lennix back, and that is exactly how I plan to sleep tonight." I glance at the closed door to Lennix's bedroom where I hope she's sleeping peacefully. "Like a baby."

"All right." A dark chuckle comes from Grim's end of the line. "I knew you were a ruthless son of a bitch, but even I underestimated you. You handled yourself well, and you aimed straight. Right in the throat on the first shot. Not bad. You sure you shouldn't have enlisted?"

The panic of those moments rushes back. Adrenaline coursed through every vein and deployed to every vital organ in my body when I saw that man pressing a gun to Lennix's head. I knew something had to have gone wrong if Grim's team wasn't on their tail but didn't have time to process that.

Grim had a location, and the team struck out for the cave where Lennix's geotracker had led them. They must have been detected somehow because the team found six locals dead and the cave empty. Grim had half-joked about the action coming to me, but it did. I was in the trees, waiting for instructions, an update—something—when Abe and Nixon came into view, guns trained on Wallace and Lennix and headed for that boat. I didn't even pause to think.

Aim. Fire.

It was as instinctive as when my father taught me to hunt. I felt more for the first deer I put down during hunting season than I did for that cretin who held Lennix hostage.

"King?" Grim asks again, all humor stripped from his voice and replaced by concern. "Maxim, you there? You sure you're okay?"

"Yeah." I release an extended breath. "I'm sure. Just a long few days. And to answer your question, my father would have lost his shit if I'd enlisted. Owen, yeah. He could have, since the military looks good on your record when you're running for president. But me? Nah. He wanted to keep me close so I could run his empire."

Ironic, since wanting me close ended up pushing me so far away.

"Speaking of your brother," Grim says, "thank him for the reinforcements. With those time constraints, pulling a team like that together would have been much tougher without him calling in some special ops favors for us."

"Yeah. Between his guys and yours, we got it done. I know I was being a tyrannical asshole, but—"

"They had your girl. I would have been the same if I were in your shoes. And you know I'll always have your back. How many scrapes have we gotten each other out of?"

"A helluva lot," I answer with a chuckle, "but this one meant more than all the others combined." *Nix* means more. Grim knows that better than anyone.

"How's she doing?" he asks.

"Sleeping."

"The doctor said she's okay?"

The images of Lennix's swollen, discolored cheek and the black and blue bruises ringing her neck, where that bastard choked her, haunt me, torture me. I want to fly back to Costa Rica and drain that damn river myself until I find him.

"Uh, yeah," I reply, swallowing a fresh wave of rage. "The doctor said it's just bruising and getting the drugs Abe gave her and Wallace out of her system."

"They saw some intense shit. There could be some PTSD, some trauma, nightmares. The mental and emotional toll might be greater than anything we see on the outside."

"Yeah, she has a therapist she sees regularly. They'll discuss it in her sessions."

"And all this is still under the radar, right?"

"Miraculously, yeah. Or maybe not so miraculously. It was in CamTech's best interest to keep it on the low. They never went public with the kidnappers' demands, so it didn't get beyond friends, family, and a select few high-ranking CamTech execs. Since they were scheduled to be away for a few more days, Nix's staff here was none the wiser."

"And the service team?"

"Paco's family was told about the failed kidnap attempt, and we're taking care of them. The rest of the team believe they got stranded in the jungle. Not too unusual for Talamanca."

"Almost like it never happened."

"Except it did," I remind him tersely, "and it's still happening until we find that body."

"Working on it." Even though we aren't face-to-face, I can picture Grim's scowl, and the irritation is clear in his voice. "Why don't you get back to your actual job, taking over companies and saving planets and shit?"

I allow myself my first real grin in days. "Believe me. I am. Jin Lei's head might explode if I don't get some work done. I'll dive into one disaster at a time until Nix wakes up."

"I'll keep you posted on what we find."

My grin fades at the reminder that Abe may still be out there, even though the odds are slim.

"Thanks, Grim. For everything."

He hangs up without acknowledging my gratitude. The closeness between Grim and me is different, obviously, from the closeness I share with my brother, but he feels like family. We've bonded around peril and adventure and all the things young men chase when they have no real sense of their own mortality, their limits. We spent our wanderlust together in dozens of cities in a hundred different ways. Spent it on more women than I can count, but none of them were ever Nix.

I sit on the couch and open my iPad on Lennix's coffee table. Despite the exhaustion weighting my arms and legs, I force myself to return emails and address the issues Jin Lei held while I focused on getting Lennix back. I need some serious libations to get through this pile of work that's been waiting for me. I search the kitchen and cabinets, the small bar in one corner of the room, but all I find is wine.

"Damn, babe," I mutter, reading the bottle of Bordeaux. "I was hoping for something stronger."

I poke the fire and remove my socks and shoes, settling at the coffee table again. I'm not sure how long I work, but the fire goes out, and the bottle of wine is almost empty when Lennix's bedroom door opens.

The sight of her arrests me. It's her beauty, yes, as she leans into the doorframe like it's the only thing holding her up. But more than how impossibly beautiful she is, it's her *life* I appreciate most. The simple lift and fall of her chest with each precious breath. I want to feel her heart pressed to mine, beating reassurance into every part of me until I'm sure that she's actually safe.

Dark hair tumbles around her shoulders, and there's a sleep print etched into the smooth, unbruised skin of one high cheekbone. In her white-silk pajamas, she's soft and sleep-mussed.

The thing I've been trying to ignore since I held her in that jungle rears in me. It's primitive and too rough and too soon after what she's been through. Every cell in my body screams with the need to reclaim her physically. To stamp myself into her skin and feel the imprint of her burned into mine.

But I can't because it wouldn't be gentle or soft or considerate. It would be a hard and pounding and unrelenting fuck. I need to feel her under me and know she's safe in my bed, in my arms. To have her to myself so completely, the fear that somebody will one day take her from me subsides. I need to fuck that fear away, but I won't do that to her. It's selfish and base, and she's the best thing in my life. I won't corrupt her with that.

"Hey," I greet her.

"Hey." Her voice is husky with fatigue. "What time is it? Why are you out here?"

Because I don't trust myself with you right now.

"Work," I answer instead, pointing to the iPad and the papers sprawled over the coffee table. "Jin Lei's already cracking the whip."

Lennix nods and walks farther into the room, coming closer. I swallow hard. The sight of her looking so pure in the snowy pajamas, her pretty bare feet peeking from beneath the wide silk bottoms, is more than I can take right now.

"It doesn't take long to get behind," she says, sitting beside me on the couch.

"No time at all." I force my eyes back to the iPad, even though the letters of the document run together onscreen. "Been taking the last few hours to start catching up."

"I'm sorry you missed work."

I abandon the pretense of working to reach over and cup the uninjured side of her face. "Baby, there was no question where I needed to be. I couldn't have thought about another thing until I had you back."

She leans her cheek into the palm of my hand. "He said someone tried to negotiate for me. Someone he called Moneybags. I guess that was you?"

"Yeah." A harsh chuckle rumbles in my throat. "I almost screwed everything to hell when I lost my temper. Grim was handling things, and I jerked the phone from him and took over. I fucked it all up royally. I thought that bastard was going to…" I can't even bring myself to articulate what I know he would have done to her had we not found her in time.

"He was going to kill me."

I look up again, and the vestiges of fear in those water-sky eyes are my undoing. I reach for her, barely trusting myself but needing her to know I'll keep her safe. I pull her onto my lap and brush the long hair back over her shoulders and away from her face.

"I wouldn't ever let that happen." I press our foreheads together. "I would have moved heaven and Earth, *bought* heaven and Earth, to get you back."

"But it was never just the money for him." She grips my neck and huddles closer. "I knew I was going to die, Doc, and all I could think was that I'd never told you I loved you."

"Yeah." I make a conscious effort to loosen my fingers from her waist and thigh. "That's all I could think, too."

"And I'd never heard you say it." She looks up, her gray eyes darkening, shining with tears. "But I knew you loved me, too."

"So much." I dip my nose to her neck, absorbing the smell of the soap from her bath and the alluring scent that is hers alone. "It was killing me that you might not ever know."

"I knew," she whispers, drifting kisses over my face until she reaches my mouth. "Maxim, I knew."

Pulling her chin between my thumb and forefinger, I pry her mouth open and command the kiss. I try to exercise restraint but instantly take her tongue, licking into her with possessive strokes, so hungry, so desperate. Swallowing the little sounds she makes, I pull her closer, wanting so badly to be tender, to take my time, but desire and need suffocate my good intentions.

I press her back into the sofa cushions, squeezing her breast through the silk pajama top. My hips are notched between her thighs, and I thrust, the movements aggressive and compulsive. She whimpers, and I go still.

Dammit. Am I hurting her?

She's not ready for this. She's been through an ordeal. I need to put this fucking wolf on a leash.

I pull back, sit up, rest my elbows on my knees, and tunnel my fingers through my hair.

"Nix, I'm sorry." I lick my lips, my dick going harder at the taste of her lingering there. "Baby, go back to bed. You need your rest. It's been…uh, a crazy few days."

She caresses my back, and I jump like she's touched an exposed nerve. I'm that attuned to her hands on me.

"Are you…" She sits up, too, leaning forward. I feel her eyes searing my profile. "Do you not want to—"

"You know I do." I whip my head around to meet the confusion in her eyes.

"Then why?" She leans in to kiss me, her lips soft and gentle, two things I already know I'll forget to be as soon as I touch her. "I'm *alive*, and I missed you."

I jerk away from the sweet contact of the kiss.

"I want it too much," I grit out, shamed by my lack of control but helpless to do anything about it with this wildness prowling inside me. "You've been through a lot."

"You think I don't want it?" she asks softly. I search her eyes, surprised that the heat, the desperation there matches mine. "Is that why you stayed out here when you should have been in bed with me? Talk to me. Tell me, Doc."

I close my eyes, which is a mistake because her scent, her warmth—everything about her rises to the surface of my senses, increasing my gut-level urge to reunite our bodies, reconnect our souls.

"It's like I came so close to losing you," I say stiltedly. "And something in me wants to lay claim to you. I don't think it'll be gentle. It's some caveman shit. I know that."

"Then I must be on some cavewoman shit," she says, her smile widening, even though her eyes remain solemn. "Because I feel the same way."

"You do?" I barely allow the words out in case she says no.

"I do. I was lying in bed, and the sedative worked at first, but I woke up, and you weren't there. Just staring at the ceiling felt wrong. I almost died, and I want to *feel* alive. Nothing makes me feel more alive than making love to you."

I couldn't put words to it, but she did. She summarized exactly what has me clawing out of my skin to be inside her. But even after hearing it from her lips, I need her to make the first move. I need to know she's fine—that if I lose control, she won't break.

She stands and walks back toward her bedroom. Leaning against the doorjamb again, eyes intense and stormy and locked with mine, she tugs the first button of her pajama top loose. The second, third, and last buttons follow. The white silk slides down her arms, baring her breasts, full, high, tipped with berry-brown nipples.

I gulp, my chest heaving with the control it takes to remain on this couch. Not to charge and fuck her where she stands. It's animalistic, and I want to be, if not gentle, at least civilized. But there's nothing civilized about how I feel when the pajama bottoms glide like water over the curve of her hips and down her legs. Lustrous hair bathes her shoulders in black silk and slips over her breasts, her distended nipples taunting me through the long strands. She turns her back to me and slowly bends over to pick up the discarded pajamas, giving me a clear view of the plump lips and slit of her pussy.

My mouth goes dry. I can't *not* do this.

I'm on my feet and in the bedroom before she's even reached the bed. I grab her arm, being careful with her, and turn her to face me. Only her bedside lamp is on, washing us and her bedroom in golden light. The regal bone structure of her face is marred by one swelling cheekbone. Black and blue bruises shackle the slim line of her neck. Rage and helplessness flood me again, as if she's still hundreds of miles away. I sift strands of her hair through my fingers, brush my thumb over the discolored rise of her cheek, bend to dust kisses in the shallow well at the base of her bruised throat.

"He hurt you," I say, my voice strangled.

"I'm okay." She cups my neck and slides her fingers into my hair.

"I'm furious." I span her waist, tightening my hands on her, feeling the delicate bones through her warm flesh. "He's probably dead, but I want to hunt him down. I want to kill him for hurting you. I don't know what to do with all these feelings."

"I do," she says, tugging at the hem of my T-shirt and pulling it over my head.

"Are you sure?" My hands tremble with the need to touch every inch of her naked golden-brown skin.

"I'm messed up right now." She undoes my belt, glances up from the task to meet my eyes straight on. "I won't pretend that what happened hasn't scarred me—hasn't changed me. It has. I don't even think I know how it's affected me yet. What I do know is that I love you, and the thing I regretted most when I thought I would die was that I never told you. So let me tell you." She steps back and sits on the edge of the bed, which is covered in a cream-and-gold-silk comforter. She spreads her legs in blatant invitation. "Let me show you."

The seduction of her movements, of her eyes, pained and yet passionate in her drawn face, pulls me to her and over the line of restraint. I take my place on my knees between her legs, pressing her open wider. I bend and press my face against the soft heat of her, at first just lightly running my lips over her pussy, then spreading her and taking her clit into my mouth. I groan at the taste, the texture.

"Doc," she moans, her fingers tangling in my hair. "Yes. Please."

I eat, reminding myself to go slowly, but I get lost in this delicious universe between her legs, and I'm ravenous. My fingers are inside her. My tongue is firm and darting into her, lapping at her wetness. I rain kisses over the insides of her thighs and bite the firm flesh. She gasps, and I check her face for pain. A startled kind of pleasure warms her expression.

"Do that again," she demands, her fingers tugging my hair. "Bite me again."

I bite a trail up her thighs and between her legs until she comes, flopping onto her back, bucking and thrusting and writhing on the bed, her cries filling the room. Her response is as wild as my passion for her.

When her body stills, I undress and crawl onto the bed to lie beside her, watching her pretty face twitch with the aftershocks of her orgasm. I take one nipple into my mouth, sucking hard, biting. He had no right to mark her with violence. I mark her with my love, with my tenderness and care. I follow the circle of her areola with love bites, ringing her breasts with tiny hickeys, all the while fucking her with my fingers and circling, pinching her clit until she comes again.

She's gasping, panting, her eyes languid and lustful and wet from tears.

I haven't been rough. I want her fiercely, but I would never hurt her. I'm not capable of it. It would be like hurting my own body. I thought I couldn't trust myself with her, but I had nothing to fear.

That's not to say I won't fuck her hard.

The sheets feel the same way *she* will feel under me, like satin decadence. I position myself between her thighs and slide in. We gasp together at this perfection. She's tight and slick and hot, and my cock has a mind of its own, ignoring my attempts at control. As soon as I'm inside, all pretense of civilization disappears. I want to get past every barrier, anything that would keep me from the inner-most part of her, the part she used to guard and protect.

I want *that* part.

With grunts and curses, I piston into her. Any feelings we've held back spill out with the lock and slide of our bodies together. The room is silent except for the pounding rhythm of each thrust. I zone out, not hearing any sound, not seeing anything except the darkness behind my closed lids, but then I hear it.

She's crying.

Wrenching sobs that quake through my chest where she's pressed into me.

I stop, tilting her head up so I can look into her eyes.

"Nix?" I ask, fearing I've hurt her—that by not waiting I've ruined something that should always be pure between us.

"Don't stop," she says through her sobs. "Please. This is what I needed. Oh, God. Please don't stop, Doc."

She grabs my ass, pushes me back in deep again.

"Shit," I hiss.

"I'm not hurt," she says, but tears still clot her words. "I just love you so much. Nothing's ever felt like this."

God, hearing it this way strips any final defense I may have had. Yesterday she said "same" when I told her I loved her. To hear her say it outright with such an offering of emotion is more than I can take. My pace picks up, and I plunge in relentlessly.

"I love you." She reaches until she finds my hand to link our fingers. "Don't stop."

Her love is a potion that makes me crazed—that makes me come harder than I ever have in my life. The world literally goes black for a moment as I empty myself into her body in the most elemental way a man can.

When I've spent everything, we fall onto the bed, and I pull her back into me, stroking her damp hair and kissing the curve of her shoulders, caressing the swell of her hip, tangling our legs together.

"I love you," I whisper into her hair. I feel so reverent when I say it. We exchanged those words like sacred prayers. With our bodies, through our confession, we made our own religion. She is the temple, and I am the priest, worshipping.

"I love you, too," she says, her voice still shaken with emotion, with tears.

"Are you okay?" I'm afraid of her answer but prepared to do whatever she needs if she says no.

"I will be okay," she says, turning over to look at me after a few moments. "It may take some time, but you love me, and I will be okay."

CHAPTER 11
LENNIX

"So how are you really?"

Mena's question pokes the pat answers I've given everyone except Maxim since we returned from Costa Rica two days ago. I can't hide anything from him. I don't want to. Kimba, Vivienne, my dad—they've all asked how I am, but I don't know if they're ready to hear how this has affected me. Or maybe I'm just not ready to admit it to anyone. But ever since the Sunrise Dance, Mena and I have shared a unique bond no one else understands. She probes when others take me at my word.

"I'm getting there," I settle on saying. "I talked to my therapist on the phone yesterday and told her some of what happened. She's prepared to tailor some sessions to make sure I'm processing things the right way. We're meeting next week."

"I'm glad," Mena says.

She takes a bite of the blue-corn pancakes she's prepared for us. "These turned out pretty good."

"They're delicious. I need the recipe. I love that you've been cooking with so many original ingredients." I wash down a mouthful of the pancakes with a sip of my tea. "I need to get back to that. I'm always so busy, I end up doing too much takeout."

"We've been focusing on ancestral eating, just understanding values-based food choices before colonialism and industrialization."

She takes a small bite of her corn pancakes. "Revolutionary. Jim's cholesterol was a little high at his last annual. The doctor wanted to put him on some meds, which we'll do if we have to, but I wanted to try following a more ancestral eating lifestyle first. His numbers are already better."

"That's awesome." I pull up one leg and rest my chin on my knee as we sit at the dining-room table. "I know my therapist will help me process everything, but I also think there are some basics I need to get back to that will help me heal."

"Like what?" Mena asks, sipping her freshly squeezed juice.

"Running." I drag my fork through the maple syrup on my plate. "I dreamt of Mama when I was there, Auntie."

"You dream of her often, though, right?"

"Yes, but in this dream she told me to run. Remember when I was a water protector in high school? The marathons I organized and all the running I did to preserve our culture and fight for what I believed in."

"You're still fighting. Just in a different way. Politics is a complex path to get our people what they need. Not everyone can do what you and Jim do—can navigate this cutthroat world so well. You're doing good work."

"Thanks, Auntie, but I do think running may help me. Not just physically, but in other ways, too. It made me feel connected to the land, to our struggle in a way that nothing else does."

"All the training you did for your Sunrise Dance? Running was probably one of the hardest parts of the ceremony."

"For sure." A sad smile settles on my lips. "That night, when it was over, I was so relieved, and Mama was so happy."

"She was proud of you. Even if you hadn't gone through the rite, she would have been proud, but that meant so much to her. I'm glad she got to see you become a woman before she crossed to the next world."

"God, I thought she'd never stop taking pictures," I say, laughing even though tears well in my eyes. My emotions are so close to the surface, it feels like anything could make me cry, but I don't fight the tears right now. Giving in to this memory of Mama, even though it stings my heart, makes me feel closer to her.

My bedroom door opens, and Maxim enters the living room. He's on the phone, speaking what sounds like Chinese or Japanese. He strides into every room like he owns it—like there's no one in it he can't persuade, convince, or recruit. The force of his charisma is a tangible thing, a hook that lures you before you even feel it in your mouth.

Dark hair is brushed back from his handsome face, but one lock falls over his forehead like he got ready in a hurry because he usually does. He wears a navy-blue three-piece suit with a silvery-gray shirt that's open and tieless.

Lord above, he looks delicious.

The vest molds to his broad chest and flat stomach, and the impeccably tailored trousers pull and flow with each step, emphasizing the powerful muscles of his thighs. I take a sip of my tea, watching over the rim of my glass, eating him up with my stare. He flashes us a smile, still talking on the phone in a language I don't understand, before disappearing into the kitchen.

After that first time last night, I woke him before sunrise and fucked him again. Putting my knee down, I squirm in my seat, pulsing between my legs at the sight of him, at the memory of our bodies locking, grinding.

Is this trauma horniness? I can't get enough.

He was worried about being too rough so soon after I returned from such a harrowing ordeal, but I wanted that physical reunion as much as he did. Maybe more. It feels like I've been pardoned from an execution. I felt the chilly breath of death, saw my gory end through the barrel of a gun, but was spared at the last second. And I want to take life by the balls, by the horns, by anything I can grab and make the most of it.

Maxim is definitely *the most.*

"Get a room if you're going to look at your boyfriend like that," Mena says, a twist of humor to her lips.

I look at her, my eyes wide and my cheeks burning. Am I that obvious? "Excuse me?" I ask, trying to play it off.

"Oh, honey, don't even." Mena chuckles and pushes her empty plate away. "You're lit up like the Vegas Strip. I know that look. I give it to my own husband every day."

At that, we both let out throaty laughs and sit back in our seats. I enjoy her company the way I do few others'. She and Senator Nighthorse have a place here in DC, but she splits her time between being here in town and Oklahoma, the state Jim represents.

Maxim comes through the swinging door separating my kitchen and dining room, holding a glass of the orange juice Mena squeezed. "What's so funny, ladies?"

"Just some girl talk," Mena says with a smile. "Morning, Mr. Cade."

"Morning, Mrs. Nighthorse," he returns with a grin.

Mena knows my history with Maxim, and even though very few people know he and I are together now, she was one of the first and few I brought up to speed before I left for Costa Rica.

"Good morning," he says to me, his green eyes darkening as he leans down to kiss me. He pulls away after a brief contact, but I reach up and bring him back for a kiss that lingers, exploring him for a few seconds even with Mena watching. I can't help it. Seeing him dressed to leave makes me want to tie him to my bed so he can't get away. I don't know if it's clinginess or neediness, but I want him as close as possible as much as possible.

"You have to go?" I murmur against his lips.

"Yes." He looks down at me, eyes blazing with love and affection and desire. "Unless you want me to stay? I have a meeting at Café du Parc, but I can cancel if you need me to."

"No, of course not. Power breakfast, huh?" I ask, lifting my brows at his meeting spot near the White House.

"Something like that," he says wryly. "Peggy Newcombe was on that Antarctica expedition with me, and we've stayed in touch over the years."

"Senator Newcombe?" I ask, surprised.

"Congresswoman then. She's an ally for climate change and is sponsoring a bill I want to see pushed through. I've canceled on her three times already, and she's leaving on a month-long trip, so I'd like to catch her." He searches my face, a frown pinching between his thick brows. "But if you need me to stay—"

"No, I'll be fine. I think I'll go out a little later myself."

His frown deepens. "You've only been home two days, Nix. You'll get back to your routine soon enough. Get some rest. Schedule a session with your therapist. Take it slow."

"I don't have time for slow, Doc. Your brother's announcing his campaign very soon."

"I don't give a damn if O is announcing he's going to the moon. Kimba and your team have everything under control. Don't rush it."

"Are you presuming to tell me when I should go back to work?" My tone is light, but he needs to know. I love him, but he won't run my life.

He sighs and rolls his eyes up to the light fixture suspended over my dining-room table. "I would never presume, but can I be concerned?"

He leans down to cup my cheek and locks our gazes together. "I just don't want you feeling pressure."

The stiffness gathering in my neck eases at the love in his eyes. "Thank you, but you have to trust me to know what I need, and I need to work. I won't break."

He nods slowly, searching my face before straightening. "Well, I have to go meet Peggy, but I'll be back. I can work from here."

"Work from your office. It's fine. I think I'm going for a run and might swing by my office just to pick up a few things and check in."

He stiffens. "What time? When?"

"Maxim, really?" I laugh and take a sip of my juice. "I'll be fine."

"One of the guys will go with you," he says, an expression I can't quite place crossing his face.

"One of what guys?" I ask.

"Oh, you mean the battalion stationed outside the door? In the hall?" Mena asks, her tone dry. "Or the one in the lobby?"

"Battalion?" I look from my auntie to my boyfriend. "What's she talking about, Doc? And what guys?"

"Just a precautionary measure," he says. "I've assigned you a security detail."

"A what?" My back goes straight and rigid. "The kidnapping was specific to that country, to those circumstances, and was about Wallace and the vaccine. It had nothing to do with me. Don't generalize the danger. I've never needed security, and I still don't."

His full lips tighten, but he doesn't speak for a moment. "This is a broader conversation we should have tonight when I get home."

My heart contracts when he refers to my apartment as home. I melt at the thought of us sharing a home together, but I set my mouth and my will, too.

"I may go for a run a little later," I say through stiff lips, "and I do not want to be followed. Am I clear on that, Maxim?"

He glances at that insanely expensive Richard Mille watch on his wrist. "I need to go. We'll discuss it later."

His tight expression loosens, and he offers Mena a natural smile, charm oozing from every pore. "Goodbye, Mrs. Nighthorse."

"Please call me Mena. I think we'll be seeing quite a bit of each other."

"I'm sure," he replies, flicking his glance back to me.

"I'll walk you out." I stand and follow him around the corner to the small foyer of my apartment. He leans against the front door and pulls me into him, dipping his head to delve into my mouth without speaking. The tension that had crept up between us drains away, and I return every thrust of his tongue, groaning into the kiss. He slides his hands down my back and over my ass, smoothing the silk of the pajamas over my skin.

"I love these on you," he says. "Almost as much as I love them off. Wear them again for me tonight?"

I nod, settling my feet back down to the floor. "You have plans for tonight?"

"You. You're my only plans." A frown usurps his smile. "When are you talking to your therapist?"

"Doc, please don't fuss over me."

"I almost *lost* you, dammit," he says, tightening his hands at my hips. "Don't tell me not to worry about your safety, about your well-being, about *you* because that shit's not gonna fly. I don't want to infringe on your independence, but I'm also not letting a damn thing happen to you. Am I making myself clear on this?"

"Let me make *myself* clear," I fire back, stepping out of his arms and putting my hands where his were on my hips. "I'm responsible for my safety and well-being. Thank you for rescuing me from a lunatic who had a mind to kill me, but we're home now. And I don't need someone to caretake my life or to monitor my comings and goings."

He blows out an exasperated breath, disrupting his hair when he runs a hand through it. "I have to go, and Mena's waiting for you. I want you to have time with her. We'll discuss this tonight, okay?"

"Yeah, okay." Now that he's leaving, I want to wrap my arms and legs around him and lock the door to keep him with me a little longer. "I love you."

His expression softens, and he looks at me in a way I've never seen him look at anyone else. And I know it's because I'm the only one he loves in just this way. He leans down to give me a quick, searing kiss and whispers his reply over my lips, "Same, baby. Same."

I stand there for a moment after he leaves, absorbing the scent of him lingering in the foyer before rejoining Mena at the dining-room table.

"Sorry about that." I grimace. "About all of it. We clash from time to time."

"You both have incredibly strong personalities. It's to be expected, but there's obviously a lot of passion there." Mena grins and tilts her head, considering. "And love, if I'm not mistaken."

"You're not mistaken." I toy with my fork and smile. "I love him, yeah."

"I'm so happy for you, Lennix. You know I've wanted someone to get past that guard around your heart for a long time."

"He got past it all right. I just hope we don't screw it up. He likes to piss circles around me, and as you can imagine, that doesn't always go over well."

"He's a very dominant man. Many politicians are. I know. I married one."

"Well, he is dominant, but he's not a politician. Thank God."

"Maybe not by trade." Mena levels a speculative look over her coffee mug, sipping. "But he obviously has aspirations."

"No, he has convictions. Principles. Goals for the world, no less, and he understands there has to be some intersection with politics to accomplish them, but he's not *into* politics. I think that's partly why we work."

"The two of you also work because he wouldn't settle for you *not* working. When you resisted, he kept coming. That's a man always looking for the next mountain to climb."

"I have my own mountains," I say, pushing around what's left of my pancakes. "He knows that."

We share a look, and there's some knowledge in Mena's eyes that I don't want to ask about. After breakfast, we clear the dining-room table and head into the kitchen. Mena leans against the counter and watches me load the dishwasher.

"What?" I ask, glancing up from a row of plates in the rack. "You have that *I've got something on my chest* look."

Mena smiles and nods. "I was thinking of what you said earlier about incorporating some of the old practices into your recovery."

"Yeah?" I close the dishwasher door and lean beside her against the counter. "And?"

"I do think incorporating some of the ancient practices in your healing process is wise. If running makes you feel connected, do that. Smudging can be incredibly powerful, too."

I can't remember the last time I engaged in the practice of smudging. Growing up, Mama's house always smelled of sage, and the sacred smoke drifted through every room.

"I'll bring some things over for you to use," Mena says, wrapping her arm around my shoulder. "I'll give you the tools, but you have to do the work."

At every juncture, she's there, stepping into so many gaps. I believe Mama sees us and is grateful for how Mena has guided me time and time again. "Thank you for always being there for me, Auntie," I say with watery eyes.

"Oh, honey, I always will."

CHAPTER 12
MAXIM

Laughter reaches me even before I step off the elevator to Lennix's apartment.

So much for another night alone with my girl. I hadn't planned to be away all day, but we're at a critical stage in several deals. Jin Lei reminded me, not too gently, about several things that needed my immediate attention. Lennix texted to say her friends were coming over. I don't begrudge them time with her. They almost lost her, too, and no doubt need to feel assured she's okay the same way I do, but damn if I didn't want time alone.

When she mentioned Owen announcing soon, it reminded me that the pace of our lives doesn't leave much time for each other. In addition to my business interests, I'll be on the campaign trail for O. With Nix *running* the campaign, I don't foresee us slowing down to enjoy each other anytime soon.

I blow out a long breath and step into the hall.

"Everything good?" I ask the plain-suit security guy positioned near the door.

"Yes, sir."

"Did she go out today?" I ask, frowning.

"No, sir. Mrs. Nighthorse ended up visiting most of the day." He nods toward the apartment. "Ms. Hunter didn't leave her apartment."

"Good. The entire team knows if she leaves—"

"To trail her, yes, sir."

Lennix's response to just the thought of a security detail let me know she won't be thrilled about the geotracker in her bracelet. She knows Grim found her and probably assumes he used his resources to track them down. We haven't gotten into details, but I thought we'd discuss that tonight. Laughter and the sound of glasses clinking tell me there may not be much time to bring it up. I have to admit putting that argument off is no hardship.

When I use the key Lennix gave me to enter the apartment, everyone turns to look at me. Bottles of wine seem to be on every flat surface along with plates loaded with something that smells delicious. Kimba and Vivienne stretch out on the couch. Wallace and Lennix sit on the floor with their backs against the love seat.

My blood boils a little at the sight of Wallace Murrow. It's not jealousy. I'm secure in Lennix's feelings for me. No, that idiot promised he'd keep Lennix safe on that service trip, and she ended up almost dead. Though it technically wasn't his fault, on some level, right or wrong, I blame him for entangling Lennix in the drama with his experimental vaccine.

"Maxim!" Kimba says and crosses the room to hug me. "The man of the hour."

"I am?" I return her squeeze and grin. She has quickly become one of my favorite people. "How so?"

"You went and got our girl," she says, her smile wobbling a little, tears coming to her eyes. "And, of course, our guy."

"Not getting her wasn't an option," I reply, looking at Murrow long enough to let him feel my displeasure, even if he doesn't fully understand it yet. His eyes drop after a few seconds, and it takes everything in me not to demand how he could be so careless.

"It's been years, Maxim," Vivienne says, getting up from her spot on the couch and coming for a hug, too. "I always knew you'd weasel your way back into Lenn's life, and thank goodness you did."

I haven't seen her since Amsterdam more than a decade ago. With fresh eyes, I note the resemblance to her brother.

"Good to see you again, too, Vivienne. How's Manhattan treating you?"

"Great. I don't get off that island much, but I had to come make sure Wall and Lenn were okay." She squeezes my hand and looks directly into my eyes. "Truly, thank you for going to get them."

I don't respond but am moved by her sincere gratitude. I just nod and squeeze her hand in return.

Lennix stands and walks over to me wearing a wide smile, leggings, and a sweatshirt with DEFEAT THE PATRIARCHY emblazoned across the front.

"Hey," she greets me warmly, stretching up for a kiss. I don't really give a damn that her friends are watching. I take her by the chin and kiss her thoroughly, groaning when she kisses me back with the same enthusiasm and disregard for anyone else. It's only a few seconds and nowhere near satisfying, but it soothes my agitation at having to be away from her all day. I haven't wanted her out of my sight since we got back from Costa Rica. It's an overreaction, and she's safe, but I can't ignore the niggling worry that something will happen again, especially with no confirmation on Abe's body.

"I missed you," I whisper in her ear when we break the kiss. "I'm trying really hard to be nice to your friends, but I want you to myself."

She pulls back, and I expect that she'll at least teasingly scold me, but the desperate heat I saw in her eyes last night is still there. "Missed you, too," she whispers.

That only makes me want to kick everyone out even more, but instead I turn to her friends and pull her into my side. "What are we eating? I'm starving."

"Mena left some bison and kale," Kimba says, nodding toward a loaded serving dish on the table.

"Is that okay?" Lennix asks with a slight frown. "The bison, I mean?"

"You're a vegetarian?" Wallace asks, a forkful of the meat halfway to his mouth.

"No," I serve some of the meat onto my plate. "But I limit my cattle intake because of how deforestation contributes to global warming."

Wallace nods, but his sister looks baffled.

"Can I admit I don't understand how those things actually relate?" she asks with a wry smile.

"They clear forests for pastures, grazing and raising crops to feed livestock," Lennix answers before I can. I love that she cares about these things, that she feels deeply connected to nature and the land even more fundamentally than I do. My concern is largely pragmatic. For her and her tribe, it's just as much spiritual.

"When those trees are cut down and burned," Lennix continues, "carbon dioxide is released, which I believe is the main source of global warming. Is that right, Maxim?"

"Right," I say. "In addition to being what we call ecologically inefficient, basically meaning it costs us more than the benefits it yields."

"What's an example?" Vivienne presses. "'Cause I don't get it."

"Well, beef, for example, uses about 60 percent of all agricultural land globally but only yields about 5 percent of its protein."

"So we just stop eating beef?" Kimba asks. "Don't take my Jack in the Box, Maxim."

Everyone laughs, including me, because Kimba's straightforwardness is so authentic and irresistible.

"I don't tell people they should stop eating meat," I say. "But eating more chicken than beef is a great start, and buying deforestation-free meats is a huge help, too."

"Also, methane is produced by cow manure and the stomachs of cattle," Wallace adds. "That's a heat-trapping gas, right, Doc?"

"Don't call me Doc."

The sharp comment pinpricks the good humor in the room, leaving behind an awkward silence. We were all getting along so well until the good doctor had to put in his two cents. I don't know if I'll ever like him the way Lennix wants me to.

"Uh, sorry," Wallace says, lowering his head and digging back into his meal. "I just heard Lenny calling you that and—"

"Precisely. She's the only one who calls me that."

Lennix stretches her eyes at me in a WTF warning. I shrug, brush off her silent rebuke, and pile my plate with more kale than bison.

Soon Lennix's coffee table is littered with full wine glasses and empty plates. Her friends continue talking, laughing with the familiarity of years together. I'm not the kind of person who feels left out, so it doesn't bother me that I don't have much to say or find many natural places to contribute to the conversation. I'm content to observe this looser version of Lennix that her close friends draw out. I'm also having trouble concentrating on their discussion, which ranges from politics, obviously, to fashion and, for some reason, *Mary Tyler Moore* reruns. I must have missed something, though, because *why?*

My watch garners most of my attention, sending stock alerts every few minutes. Our deal in Hong Kong will go south if the market keeps fluctuating the way it has been all day.

"That's some watch, Maxim," Vivienne says teasingly. "Is that... no way. I've never seen one in real life. Is that a Richard Mille?"

I glance from the watch to her excited face and nod.

"Wow." She gives Lennix a knowing smile. "Wait till I tell the girls back home that your boyfriend's a baller, Lenn."

"You know you can't, right?" Lennix's expression borders on horrified. "We're not telling people."

"What?" My head snaps around, and I meet her eyes head-on. "The hell. What do you mean we're not telling people?"

"Maxim," Lennix says almost patiently, like I missed a memo. "We didn't have much time together before I left, but I've been careful that we haven't been seen in public or around people we can't trust not to out us."

"Not to *out* us? We have nothing to hide. I'm not pretending we're not together."

"It's just not a good look if the press finds out while Owen's running," she says, her own frown growing heavier. "I guess we haven't really talked about it, but I thought you knew... Well, I have certain rules for my team, and I have to follow them, too."

"What rules?" I demand.

"We have a strict *don't fuck the candidate* policy," Kimba says and sips on her third glass of wine.

"I'm *not* a candidate. My brother is. Problem solved."

"You're candidate-adjacent, though," Lennix says, "which means you're close enough that a relationship with someone from the team would distract the press from covering the real issues and, consequently, the public from voting on them."

"I'm not hiding my relationship."

"You're not the only one *in* this relationship," she fires back.

"Apparently neither of us is, if appearances are to be believed," I say with increasing irritation.

"It's taken us a decade to get our consulting firm off the ground in what is, as you know, a man's game. If they get past the fact that I'm a woman, then I'm also a person of color. In some circles, that's two strikes against me before I even open my mouth. I can't afford some gossip rag undermining my credibility by insinuating I slept my way into this."

"Seriously? You think a consensual relationship between two adults will ruin your career?"

"Of course you wouldn't get it," she says, exasperation clear in her voice, on her face. "You don't have to worry about things like that. Nothing could penetrate all those layers of privilege to even touch you."

In the awkward silence that follows, I set my wine glass down on the coffee table and stand, heading to the kitchen.

"Doc—"

"Is there no hard liquor in this whole damn place?" I cut in, ignoring all of them and going straight for the stainless-steel refrigerator as soon as I enter the kitchen.

The swinging door behind me opens, but I don't turn.

"I'm sorry," Lennix says.

I don't answer but keep moving things around in the fridge in the quest for something to drink. I'd settle for a beer.

"Did you hear me, Doc?"

I close the refrigerator and turn to face her. Even though she's just across the room, it feels like we're farther apart. "I like bourbon."

She blinks and frowns. "Okay. I'll get some."

"Ask Jin Lei."

"Ask her…what?"

"The bourbon. She knows the one."

"All right."

"Fine." I lean against the counter and wait for her to go on.

She licks her lips and heaves a sigh. "I said I'm sorry."

"We won't work if I'm some idea to you, Nix. If I'm a concept. I'm your man, not 'one of them.'"

"I don't think you're one of them." She leans against the wall and crosses her arms over her chest. "But I do think there are things about my experience, what it means to negotiate my life in this world, that you don't, *can't* understand."

"I know that. I was born with platinum spoons in my mouth. A whole set, if I'm honest, and you're right. I have layers and layers of privilege I couldn't shed if I tried. I don't want to shed them. If I didn't have those advantages, I couldn't leverage them for people who don't."

She draws a deep breath and nods. "Thank you for seeing that. It's what allies should do, and you've always done an excellent job of it. I didn't mean to imply you don't. I'm sorry for that, but maybe you can understand my hesitation about people finding out we're together until the campaign is over."

"I'm sorry. I don't understand or agree. I don't give a fuck what people think."

"Even not giving a fuck is a privilege I don't have," she says, her frown back. "It's not about that. It's about understanding how people's minds work, about their assumptions. They'll think Owen chose me because I'm sleeping with you, not because I was the best person for the job. Can you even grasp what it means for a Native American girl raised on the rez and a black woman to be running the campaign for the probable next president of the United States?"

The weight of it, the pride tucked into the crevices of her words, dismantles all my reasons for pushing back on this. I breathe through a sinking feeling at what I need to do, to tell her.

"I suggested that Owen hire you and arranged for you to be on *Beltway* with him."

Her eyes saucer, and her mouth drops open. "You *what?*"

"Baby, I—"

"Do *not* call me baby right now."

"He would have hired you anyway."

"But you just helped him along by recommending that pretty little thing you fucked years ago?"

"Don't be reductive."

"*I'm* being reductive?" She slams her hand against the wall, fury spitting from her eyes. "So if I had been a man, I wouldn't have this job now because a man doesn't have a pussy for you to play with."

"Dammit, Nix."

"How dare you manipulate something this important for your own ends, your own desires? This is the fate of a nation, and you wanted me back in your bed so you *arranged* for your brother to hire me?"

"It's not that simple. You were the best for the job. He recognized that, or he wouldn't have brought you on."

"Oh, I know Owen wouldn't have hired me if he didn't believe I could do it. I'm talking about *you*. Did you even *care* that I could do it? Or did you just want me back?"

"Both," I say with unflinching honesty. "I believed you could do the job, and I would have done anything to get you back. You can call that privilege or arrogance. I don't know what it is, and I don't actually care. I care about you. About us."

I cross the kitchen in a few strides, coming to stand right in front of her, placing my arms on either side of her head, caging her against the wall with my body. She holds herself stiffly, looking down at the floor, a ring of tension around the lush curves of her mouth.

"I'm sorry," I say, dipping to kiss the tight line of her jaw.

"Doc, don't." She turns her head. "This is a big deal, and we can't gloss it over."

"Do you think you're capable of leading O's campaign?"

She swivels an indignant look up to me. "Of course I'm capable. I have a track record. Kimba and I have worked our asses off proving we're capable."

"And Owen knows that." I push a swath of dark hair away from her face, over her shoulder. "I know you're capable, or I wouldn't have suggested you. I would have found another way to get you if you'd been bad at your job. Lucky for me, you're the best in the business. You're the Kingmaker."

She shakes her head. "It's hard for me to believe you now."

I lift her chin, hold her eyes so she can see the truth. "I watched you work. I knew you'd be able to do it when you won that city council race in New Mexico."

She frowns. "That was a tiny race. How did you—"

"And the county commissioner in Montana. The secretary of state in Virginia."

"Doc," she says, the chill thawing from her eyes. "You saw those?"

"The mayor in Nashville," I continue, bending to breathe it over her lips. "The congresswoman in Tallahassee."

She closes her eyes and listens as I recite every race I watched from a distance, document every moment I saw her rise in her field.

"I was proud of you then." I dip to kiss her, just a quick brush of our lips. "And I'm proud of you now. Of course I know you can do this."

She leans forward and takes my bottom lip between hers, the sweet, hot suction of it so perfect I groan and slide my arms under her thighs, lifting her up, her back pressed to the wall.

Shit, I'm hard.

Any anger still lingering in the air blurs with our building passion, and I want to fuck more than I want to fight. I kiss her neck, licking lovingly at the fading bruises. I push her higher until her chest is level with my face, and I suck her tits hard through the thick material of her sweatshirt. She moans and drops her head back to the wall. With one arm on my shoulder, she uses the other to lift the sweatshirt. She's not wearing a bra, and I latch on to one naked nipple greedily, not even caring that I'm sucking so hard the noises I make are loud. The sweatshirt drops over my head, and I'm in a cave of cotton, lost in the clean scent in the valley between her breasts, feasting on the plump tips until they turn tight and hard in my mouth.

"Jesus, Doc," Lennix pants, circling her hips on my cock. "I'm gonna come."

I don't let up, savoring her nipples and thrusting between her legs, helping her get off. Through the sweatshirt, I hear her breaths coming faster, harder. She grunts with each thrust until finally, her groan releases long and hard, tiny cries of suppressed pleasure reaching me in the scented dark of her clothes. I continue laving her breasts, relishing the right. She is exactly what I want in every way, down to how her nipples fatten in my mouth and the sounds she makes when she comes. I don't want any man to ever hear her unravel that way again.

I tighten my arms under her, pulling her close. She's mine completely. And I, unequivocally, belong to Lennix Moon Hunter.

I pull my head from under her sweatshirt, let her legs drop to the floor. Her expression is dazed wonder and satiation, her eyes hazy. Teeth marks dent her lips where she trapped her pleasure inside.

"Think your friends know what we're doing in here?" I ask.

She swipes shaking hands over her face and grins, pointing to my crotch. "They'll know we didn't finish with that huge pipe between your legs."

"Nothing to be done about that right now." I adjust myself as well as I can. "But you're deep throating my cock tonight, by the way,"

"Gladly," she says, swinging the door open.

Kimba's impish grin teases me over the rim of her wine glass. Vivienne avoids eye contact, but there is a carnation-pink flush washing her cheeks. She's either embarrassed or turned on. Maybe both. Wallace, sitting in the window seat tucked into the corner with Lennix's bookshelf, holds some tome open on his lap.

Vivienne stands and brushes a hand over her skirt. "Um, I have an early fuck... Ahem, I mean an early *flight*. I have an early *flight* to catch."

Kimba's hearty laugh booms. "Real smooth, Viv. Let's go back to my place so I can get alone and work out all these *feelings* Lenn and Maxim have inspired in me."

"Ugh." Lennix drops her head into her hands. "Could you just not rub this in?"

"Girl, I'm rubbing it *out* soon as I get home." Kimba winks.

"You didn't hear anything," Lennix says, biting her nail like she hopes they didn't.

"I didn't hear a thing," Kimba says. "Except *ahh, ahh, that's it, Doc. I'm gonna co—*"

"Okay," I cut in, fighting back a huge grin. "It's been great catching up. Kimba, I'm sure we'll connect about the campaign now that things have settled down."

"Yes," she says, still smirking. "I think we'll save *The View* until after Owen announces."

"Fine with me. Just coordinate with Jin Lei to make sure I'm in the country."

"Good seeing you again," Vivienne says, reaching up to hug me. "You guys are still adorable together."

She turns to Lennix, and tears gather in her eyes. "Oh, Lenn, I'm so glad you're home. It would have been like losing my sister *and* my brother."

Lennix nods, blinking at the tears rimming her lower lashes. "Love you, Viv. I'll be in New York with Owen soon, and I want to see my niece."

"She would love to see Aunt Lin Lin." Vivienne turns toward her brother. "You coming, Wall?"

"Uh, yeah." He stands and slides the book back into its home on the shelf. "In a little bit. I need to chat with Lenny first."

I tense at Lennix's side and fold my arms across my chest. If he thinks I'm leaving the room, he's deeply confused.

"Good," he says once Kimba and Vivienne leave. "You're staying, Maxim."

I look at him, unblinking, waiting for what he has to say.

"What's up, Wall?" Lennix asks, her brows knitting in that tender way she seems to reserve for this particular friend. I know it's not a romantic way, but it's closeness. And I want to be closer to her than anyone else, so it bugs me.

"Maxim," he says, looking at me and swallowing convulsively like I scare him. "I think we got off on the wrong foot."

"Oh, you do?" I ask, cocking one brow. "How so?"

"I sense a certain…hostility, and I can only assume it's because you know Lenny and I used to date, and you were under the mistaken impression when you first came back that she and I were—"

"That's not why I'm hostile." I slide my hands into my pockets, deliberately relaxing my posture. "Maybe when I thought you were still dating I didn't like you, but you're right. I'm angry with you now."

His expression clouds. "What? Why? If we—"

"At Owen's house, at dinner, I asked you outright if this trip was safe, and you told me it was. You said you would never do anything to put Lennix in danger."

"Doc, come on," Lennix says. "You can't—"

"I can." I don't look away from Wallace. "I'll never trust you with her again."

"Obviously I feel awful about what happened," he says. "But how could I have known about the kidnappers?"

"I'm not saying it was your fault. But I'm very exacting about her safety in a way that you don't know how to be."

"You can't be serious." Lennix laughs, but there's more outrage than humor in it. "You're *exacting* about my safety? What does that even mean?"

"I told you there's a broader conversation we need to have," I tell her, keeping my voice even. "And it does not concern Wallace, except for him to know he will never be in charge of your safety again."

"He was not *in charge* of my safety in Costa Rica. I'm in charge of myself."

"How'd that work out for you?" I ask.

"I'm not a child you tell to look both ways before I cross the street, Maxim. I'm a grown woman."

"*My* woman, and that shit show from last week won't happen again."

"Look," Wallace says, "this is between the two of you, but we'll be extra careful on our next service trip if you'd just—"

My laughter cuts in on his stupid words. "Next service trip? What part of 'never again' do you not understand, Dr. Murrow?"

"Talk to *me*," Lennix says. "I'm the one who decides if I go on another service trip."

"I'm not saying you won't," I tell her with a shrug. "I'm saying I'll be involved because I don't trust anyone else to keep you safe."

"I'm gonna leave now." Wallace walks toward the door.

"Excellent idea," I say.

Lennix angles a chastising look over her shoulder at me while she walks Wallace out.

"When do you go back to work?" she asks him.

"Tomorrow." He squeezes the bridge of his nose. "It's weird because they didn't have to pay anything to get me back and didn't lose the vaccine. It's like nothing happened. Nothing's changed."

"Have they informed the FDA yet?" I ask.

"Not yet." His eyes meet and then skid away from mine.

"Well, let's hope your company's rat doesn't blow any whistles or link up with another psycho and try to steal the vaccine. I don't have to tell you how powerful and dangerous something like that would be in the wrong hands."

"Agreed," Wallace says. "I'm pushing for them to hand it over, but these things take time."

"Don't take too much time," I say, warning with a look. "I know about this now. I have no deniability if it comes out. Get your boss to do the right thing, or I will."

Wallace stares at me for an extra moment before nodding. He bends down to kiss Lennix on the cheek and then goes.

She turns to face me, her back to the door, arms folded behind her. There's a somber cast to her face. I'm braced for more disagreements, especially when I tell her about the geotracker, but I don't want them. Not tonight.

"Let's not fight," she says, like she's reading my mind.

"I don't want to."

"It feels like we disagreed so much tonight." She pushes off the door and crosses the room, stopping right in front of me. She steps so close that her clean, fresh scent surrounds me and I could drown in those water-sky eyes.

"After seeing us fight tonight, your friends may wonder if we'll last." I loop my arms and link my hands at the base of her spine, bringing her closer.

"My friends remember how I was when we were together

ten years ago." She stares at the floor and pushes long, dark hair behind her ear.

"How were you?" I kiss her temple and work my thumbs into the tense muscles in her back.

"Oh, that feels really good." She moans and closes her eyes, resting her head on my chest.

"How were you when we were together ten years ago?"

She shrugs one shoulder. "Sure. I knew the first night in Amsterdam I would sleep with you. This from a twenty-one-year-old virgin." She glances up, speculation in the look she gives me. "How were you?"

I cast my mind back to the darkened streets of Amsterdam and the first blush of what we had. "I was shocked that we'd found each other again, and I was determined to make the most of it."

"You mean by having sex?" she asks, her grin wry.

"No. I mean, yeah. Of course that was part of it. But mostly, I knew we would be going our separate ways after a week, and I wanted as much of you as I could possibly get before then." I hesitate before going on. "And I was conflicted because you didn't know about my family—my last name, who I really was."

"You're wrong. I was wrong. I knew exactly who you were. I know it caused problems, but now I'm glad I met you before I knew you were a Cade. You're not your last name. You're not your father. You're someone wholly unique. I don't know that I would have been able to see that if I'd known you were a Cade right off the bat."

I resolve to tell her about the geotracker.

"Now I know you're a Cade," she says, tipping up to kiss my lips, "and I still want you."

"Is that a fact?" I ask, smiling lazily.

She walks to the bedroom, the swing of her hips mesmerizing.

"I believe you said something about me deep throating your cock?" She raises her eyebrows, all innocent.

I'm on her in seconds, scooping her up. The geotracker can wait until tomorrow. This erection has waited long enough.

CHAPTER 13
LENNIX

Run.

The word pounds through my head like footsteps as soon as I wake. My arms and legs practically tingle with the need to move. A glance at my bedside clock tells me it's only five in the morning. There's a gym in my building where I often work out before dressing and then eating breakfast at Royal, where Maxim ambushed me and declared his intentions, as they were.

In my bed, he holds me from behind, his grip as tight and possessive in sleep as when he's awake. We've only been back three days, but having him here has me imagining how our lives could be, our dreams intertwining, our goals intersecting.

Our bodies interlocking.

Good Lord, this man can fuck.

As promised, his cock was as far as it could possibly go down my throat after my friends left, but he repaid the favor. The girl who chases stars finds them every time we make love. I didn't know any better when he lied in that alleyway and told me you sometimes find the connection we have with others.

You don't.

I never have, and I have no desire to keep searching.

"Nix," he sleepily mumbles into the curve of my neck, his arms tightening around me. One hand wanders to my breast, and even half-asleep, he squeezes. My body responds instantly, my nipples pebbling, and I'm wet in seconds. If he wakes up, that's it. No run. No early start to a day I'm determined will be more normal than the last three have been.

The doctor warned me I might have bad dreams after the traumatic events. Bad dreams are nothing new for me. I haven't had any about the ordeal in Costa Rica, but something *is* off. Flashes of fear, unease? Something I can't articulate but makes a liar of me when I say I'm fine. Something has retreated inside me, threatened by death and mayhem, but it's time to advance. Kimba and I have the opportunity of a lifetime managing Owen's campaign. I won't allow "Abe" to derail that. And Owen deserves my full attention. He's been amazing, making sure I was okay and telling me to take my time coming back, but I have to resume my regularly scheduled life.

I ease from the comfort of Maxim's powerful arms, careful not to wake him. After we made love, he jumped on a call to Hong Kong and must have been up long after I fell into a love-drowsed sleep. I woke briefly when he slipped into bed and pulled me into his arms, but only long enough to kiss him and fall back asleep. He needs to rest. I thought *I* worked hard. This man never stops but also never seems to tire. He's a phenomenon. *My* phenomenon. I've never been with a man like Maxim. There *are* no men like Maxim. Not for me.

Run.

I stand, pad into my closet, and slip on my running gear. In minutes, my hair is pulled into a ponytail, my sneakers are on, and I'm ready to go. I pause as I'm leaving the room to glance at my bed. The predawn light teases the strong lines of his face from the shadows. He's beautiful, there's no denying that, but beyond his physical beauty, he's principled and brilliant and funny.

And so damn intense.

If I leave now, there might still be time for a morning quickie when I return. I step into the hall and jump when a large man with a jagged scar bisecting his forehead stands right outside my door, his eyes as alert as if it's noon instead of just past five a.m.

Mena referenced Maxim's "battalion," but this is my first time encountering it. First order of business when I return from my run is to get rid of all this security. It's unnecessary and impractical now that there's no real threat. Are they going on the campaign trail with me? Hopping planes to crisscross the country as I follow Owen to all the states we need to hit? I don't think so.

"Um, good morning." I offer a tentative smile to the grim-faced giant guarding my hallway.

"Good morning, Ms. Hunter." His words roll out hard and rough like bits of gravel.

I walk to the elevator and am peeved when he gets in with me.

"You don't have to come," I say, smiling even as my brows pinch together in a frown. "I'll be fine, but thank you."

"We have our orders, ma'am." He pushes the button for the lobby.

I press the button to hold the doors open. "Your orders don't come from me."

"You *are* my orders, Ms. Hunter." Now he starts frowning and presses the lobby button again.

I stab the doors open button and hold my finger there. "Get off. I don't want company on my run."

The elevator buzzes, signaling that the doors have been held open too long.

Apparently unbothered by the annoying noise, he folds his arms and leans against the elevator wall like he has all day.

"I'm serious," I snap, losing patience. "If you follow me, I'll call the cops and tell them you're harassing me."

"My job is to protect you."

"Then you need a new job. I'll tell Mr. Cade so when I return from my run, which I plan to take alone." I nod to the hall beyond the open elevator doors. "Off."

With a shake of his head and an exasperated huff of breath, he steps out of the elevator.

"And tell your buddies downstairs to back off, too," I say, remembering Mena mentioning more guards in the lobby. I've lived my whole life without security. I had a close call in Costa Rica, but it was an isolated incident, extenuating circumstances. I don't need to spend the rest of my life under guard.

When I exit the elevator, a man speaks into an earpiece and tracks my progress past the lobby desk and out the door. Hopefully, the bridge troll upstairs informed him I'm free to leave my own building unaccompanied.

The bite of the cold January air invigorates me instantly, stinging my cheeks and snapping at the little bits of skin my thermal running clothes leave exposed. Swift steps carry me to the park not far from my building, and I nod and smile to the other runners out this morning. DC has been voted the fittest city in America for several years, partly because we have so many great running trails and options. I was in a runners' group that met a few mornings a week, but my schedule ate that ritual up and spat it out when we managed a few tough campaigns back-to-back. I'd forgotten how good the community and camaraderie of it feel. Still, nothing compares to the deep kinship I had with my fellow students when we ran across the country raising awareness about water crises in Native communities and on protected lands.

In the park not far from home, I stretch for a few minutes, my breath forming little puffs in the chilly air while I start gentle exertions to ease my body into the demands of the run ahead. I begin at a moderate pace, waking my muscles and stirring my blood. The trees decorated with cherry blossoms in the spring are stripped bare, their spindly branches reaching out like bony fingers when I jog past.

My favorite section of this path lies ahead, a picturesque cobblestone bridge that provides just a moment of shelter from the sun overhead in the summer. In the fall, leaves wallpaper the stones, and in winter, they are sometimes kissed with snowflakes.

Today there are no autumn leaves, no blanket of snow. Just an archway to break the monotony of the path. I cross under it and yelp when a tall figure stands from a nearby bench. I automatically reach for the mace I left behind, but he steps out onto the path so I can see his face.

"Maxim?" I press a hand to my heart and bend over to palm my knees. "You scared me to death."

"Sorry."

It steals my breath, how beautiful he is this morning. Dark, amber-dusted hair slumps forward in silky chunks over his forehead, like he rolled out of bed and came straight here. A smile barely moves his lips, and there's a somberness to his expression that gives me pause.

"What are you doing here?" I ask. "How'd you even find me?"

He watches me for a few moments and then nods to the bench where he sat waiting. "Let's talk."

"Let's talk?" I glance at my Fitbit. "Baby, you're literally breaking my stride. Can't we talk when I get back to the apartment?"

"Well, that's what we need to talk about." He sits and gestures to the empty space on the bench beside him. "Please."

I let out a choppy breath, my heart still racing from the run and the fright, but take the seat.

"Is this about your goon? Because he was mistaken if he thought I needed him to run behind me through the park. And you're mistaken if you think I'll have a cohort of security guards trailing me around the country during the campaign. It's unnecessary and impractical."

"Okay. We can discuss…modifications, but you do need security."

"I've never needed it before."

"You weren't my girlfriend before. Once people know they can get to me through you, you can't expect me to let you wander around unprotected."

"*Let* me wander around? You mean like an unaccompanied child in an amusement park?"

He answers only with an impatient frown and a tightening of his lips.

"No one knows about our relationship yet, Doc."

"And just how long do you think I'll accept that?" he asks, his voice quiet, unyielding. "Accept people not knowing we're together?"

"Maybe for the next eighteen months while I'm running your brother's campaign?"

Even as I say it, I know he won't agree. It sounds exhausting even to me, hiding how we feel for that long, but I want to protect what Kimba and I have built, and I don't want to detract from Owen's platform with sidebar romance fodder for the tabloids.

"We can compromise and ease into discussing our relationship," he says, resting his elbows on his knees and turning to look at me, "but I'm not going through this entire campaign pretending not to be in love with you."

My heartbeat stutters even hearing him say the words. The intensity of his stare warms my skin in the frigid morning air. I scoot closer to him on the bench.

"We can work something out," I say, dropping my head to his shoulder. "But not this early in the campaign. Owen hasn't even announced, and Kimba and I need to establish ourselves and prove that we can do this on merit first."

I turn my face into his shoulder, drawing in the scent of him. "Later. We'll let people know later. So you see, no need for security quite yet."

He doesn't respond right away but reaches up to cup my head and lift my chin, catching and holding my eyes for a moment. "Let's talk about how we found you in Costa Rica."

His statement catches me off guard. "Well, I know your friend Grim owns a security firm, called in some favors, and arranged the rescue. So I assumed through his contacts."

"No, not his contacts."

"What do you mean?" I try to laugh, but he looks so dour. "You're being cryptic."

"We used your bracelet to find you."

"My bracelet?" I touch the compass dangling from the links he clipped around my wrist. "I don't get it. What do you mean?"

"There's a geotracker in your bracelet."

The air seems to go even chillier around me. "A geo—"

Anger stunts the words in my throat. I swallow a string of curses and accusations. This relationship, this man is precious to me, and I know the first things to spew from my mouth will be words I could never take back—words that might damage us irreparably. I stew in outraged silence for a few more seconds before trusting I won't have a nuclear reaction.

"You've been tracking me?"

"Not at first, no." He sits back on the bench and stretches his long legs out in front of him.

I strip my glove off with my teeth, and my cold, stiff fingers fumble with the bracelet's clasp.

I can't get the damn thing off.

"Stop." He puts a staying hand over mine. "Don't take it off."

"I thought it was a gift, not a monitoring system."

"It *is* a gift. I meant it as a gift."

"It just does double duty as a tracking system for your pet girlfriend. Isn't that how people make sure if their dogs get lost, they can find them? I guess this is much more efficient than putting posters of me up in the neighborhood if you *misplace* me."

"Will you listen to me and stop talking just to vent your anger?"

"I *get* to vent my anger." I stand up and pace in front of the bench. "Me talking only when you want to hear me and shutting up when you don't like what I have to say is not communication."

"I know that, but if you work yourself up—"

"You mean like a tantrum?" My harsh laugh is an explosion of white, puffy air that disappears as quickly as it comes. "Make up your mind, Maxim. Am I a pet or a spoiled child?"

He drops his head to the back of the bench and sighs. "When I gave you the bracelet, it was our first date in ten years, and I didn't think that was the best time to bring up…tracking you."

"Is there ever a good time really? Right after sex? Over morning coffee? Before a dangerous service trip?"

"I intended," he continues, sitting up and looking at me without acknowledging my sardonicism, "to tell you when you came back from Costa Rica, and I didn't activate the chip. I wouldn't have done that without your permission."

"Well, you don't have my permission." I fumble with the clasp again. "Take your damn tracker back."

He's in front of me in seconds, towering over me and pulling my hands to his chest. "Stop. Please listen to me, and after we talk, if you want to deactivate the chip, we can, but I would like for you to keep the bracelet because I wasn't lying about why I gave it to you."

He dips until our foreheads kiss. My cold skin against his impossibly warm. "I found you when you were seventeen." He lifts my hand to kiss my wrist. "I found you again in Amsterdam." He brushes his lips over my knuckles, setting a thousand feathers free in my belly. "And I found you after a decade of waiting for just the right moment."

"Is it really finding when you arrange the meeting, coerce a television host, and recruit your brother?" I ask dryly.

"Details," he says, his husky laugh dusting my fingers and chasing the cold away for the space of a breath. "My point is, this bracelet is significant. It's symbolic of the fact that I've been all over the world, but you are my one place."

I close my eyes, scrambling to reinforce my defenses but failing with him so close. "This is not okay, Doc."

"I know. Let me explain."

I nod, fixing my eyes on the compass charm dangling between us like it will guide this conversation and tell me what to do, how to feel and respond.

"Like I said, my plan was to have this conversation when you returned from Costa Rica and ask your permission to activate the chip after I'd explained to you why I think it's necessary, but you were taken." He closes his eyes and swallows deeply. "And I hated myself for not talking with you before you left and activating it. At first, Grim couldn't pick up the signal. You guys were in the jungle or forest or somewhere so remote, he had trouble."

"We were in caves part of the time." My pulse picks up and sweat breaks out on my lip and forehead in the freezing cold remembering the helplessness with that bag over my head and the dank smell of the cave filling my nostrils. "Why do you think it's necessary?"

"There have been eleven attempts to kidnap me."

My eyes zip up to meet his, and fear crawls over me, making my hands clammy. "Eleven?"

"Yeah, but none were ever successful because I have great security."

I look around meaningfully. "They seem to be lax on the job."

"You won't always see them, but they're never too far away. The K&R insurance CamTech was going to use to get Wallace back—I have a K&R policy, but it's worth a lot more."

"I can imagine."

"Can you? If I die or something happens to make me even slightly vulnerable, that could drastically affect our stocks, investments, and every person employed by every one of my companies all over the world. Their spouses, their kids. Their futures."

He laughs and shakes his head. "I sound like my dad. He used to talk about satisfying investors, keeping shareholders happy, and taking care of employees and their families. I didn't get that then, but I do now."

"Can we go back to the part where you've almost been kidnapped eleven times?"

He takes my hand and walks us over to the bench. "All failed attempts, but it's not unusual. CEOs are big money in the kidnapping game, so it can be really expensive to insure us for K&R. One of the conditions of my policy is that I use some type of GPS tracking. It increases the likelihood of recovery if an attempt ever proves successful."

He taps the face of the watch Vivienne admired so much last night. "Mine is in here. I'm sure soon we'll advance to implants, but we aren't there yet."

"So I get why you need one, but why do I?"

"Many significant others wear tracking devices because family members are sometimes easier to get to than the executives themselves and the people they care about end up being taken."

I glance down at the gift on my wrist, which meant so much to me.

"I know I probably wouldn't be sitting here with you now were it not for this bracelet, Doc. I don't want to seem ungrateful, but my independence is important to me. I don't need looking after."

He caresses the inside of my wrist where the bracelet brushes up against my skin.

"But *I* need to look after you. I need to know that you're safe and that I can find you. I can get to you. When Grim couldn't pick up the signal and the clock was ticking, I felt absolutely helpless. That lunatic could have shot you in the head, or…" The muscle along his jaw tightens. "I couldn't get to you. Your father couldn't get to you. Can you imagine how he felt knowing you could die at any moment and there was nothing he could do about it?"

"Oh, that's low." I link my hands behind my neck. He knows how sensitive I am to my father's anxiety.

"I don't mind playing dirty when I care this much about something." He leans over to take my top lip between his and then my bottom. "About someone. What do you say?"

"It's one or the other," I tell him, balling my fist in my lap to keep my hands off him long enough to negotiate with a clear head. "Either this pet tracker or the security. Not both."

I know which I prefer, so I barrel forward when he frowns, like

I haven't given him any choice at all. "The security is less important until everyone knows we're together anyway. And it's impractical. I'll be on the road constantly once the campaign is fully underway. I'll be with Owen most of the time, who has security of his own. I'll be safe with him."

"Are you sure now that we're together," he says, leaning over to kiss behind my ear, inciting goose bumps that have nothing to do with the morning chill, "you don't want to swap with Kimba? Come on the road with me instead?"

Visions of us fucking in the back of a campaign bus fill my head. I pull away, glancing around the empty park to make sure no one is around. "Um, I don't think going on the trail with you is a great idea. Now, I won't do this bracelet *and* security, so which will it be?"

He pulls back, and our eyes meet for long seconds. Those green eyes could persuade me to do just about anything he asked.

"Wear the bracelet."

CHAPTER 14
MAXIM

"I HAVE NEWS."

Grim's words make me pause, my stylus poised over my iPad.

"What's up?" I stand and walk to the window of the hotel suite. The Champs-Élysées spreads itself like a sultry woman beneath me, flashing alluring glimpses of the Eiffel Tower in the distance. The most beautiful avenue in the world and I feel nothing but indifference for the glittering lights and elegant lines of the buildings. Not just because I've seen this view a hundred times or more, but because what Grim has to say is the most important thing in the world to me right now.

"Jackson Keene is the one who died," Grim says.

My remorse for killing the man doesn't deepen knowing his name.

"It took us a while," Grim goes on, "because he'd managed to scrub himself from the records we'd typically check. These guys have been off the radar for a while. They may have been running a pretty rudimentary operation, but that seems to have been intentional. They've kept their digital footprint almost non-existent the last few years."

"Jackson," I murmur, tugging my bottom lip and frowning. "Abe called him Jack."

"Abe is actually Gregory. Jack's brother, Gregory Keene. Stanford grad, computer science. Master's degree from Harvard. Lots of scholarships, but there was also a lot of loan debt. Not one payment's been made since his mother died."

"What the hell?" I turn my back on the shimmering city and scowl. "That cretin's better educated than I am."

"That's relative, *Doctor* Cade," Grim says dryly. "He's a genius, though, yeah. In the literal sense, not colloquially. The little I've been able to dig up on him all predates his mother's long bout with cancer. After she died, the trail dries up for the brothers, too."

"And any luck finding his hopefully decomposing body yet?"

"No, but at least now we know who he is. We have a face and a name, which we probably won't need because he's probably dead and the body has been eaten by some wild animal or devoured by a shark."

"Sharks in a river? Not likely."

"You know what I mean. We've had no activity since. Not even a ping."

"Considering he managed to *not* ping for years, that doesn't ease my mind. If he survived…"

The tortured voice screaming his brother's name haunts me for a moment. I've thought more about that than I have about the man I shot. It was the sound of genuine human pain. I hope I'll never be so callous that it doesn't affect me, even coming from the man I hate.

"We'll keep our feelers out there," Grim says. "I'm not giving up, just telling you there's nothing yet and we're probably in the clear."

"'Probably' is not damn good enough with Lennix traipsing all over the fucking country in crowds and at rallies and vulnerable."

"She wouldn't be vulnerable if you'd let me put my guys back on her, King."

"She doesn't want that." I clench a hand in my pocket. Each day I'm away from her, it takes everything in me not to order a stealth security detail she'd never even detect.

"Fuck what she wants. Since when did you hand your balls over to a girl?"

"You've obviously never had your balls well handled." My

roguish laugh echoes in the empty, palatial suite. "Lennix takes very good care of them for me."

"Spare me the details." Rare humor enters his gruff voice. "How the mighty have fallen. You go almost forty years without tying yourself down, and this little woman wraps you around her finger in a matter of months."

"Months? I met her when I was twenty-four years old, Grim. You know she started winding me around more than her finger years ago."

"God, yes. You were so whipped even in Antarctica. Staring at her photo on your phone all the time."

I don't bother telling him I've reinstated that photo of us in the tulip field as my phone's screensaver. Lennix would have a conniption if she knew, afraid someone would see us together. I've yielded on enough. The hell if I won't at least have a photo when she's a whole continent away.

"I don't mind being whipped as long as she's the one holding the belt."

"Be right back. I need to go mourn your manhood."

"Ironically, she makes me a better man. She's the most important thing in my life, and I got a lot of important shit in my life, brother."

"I know. We'll keep her safe, even though she's being a brat about it."

"Watch it. No one calls Nix a brat but me."

"When was the last time you told me what the hell to do?"

He's right. I'm invested in his security firm, but I've never been Grim's boss. Everything he does for me is out of friendship, years of it.

"Also, why couldn't you fall for some nice girl who would be quiet when you gave her jewels, suck your dick before breakfast, and follow you all over the world instead of trying to elect the next president?"

"One out of three ain't bad."

It takes him a second to catch it, and his guffaw draws an answering chuckle from me.

"Lucky son of a bitch," Grim mumbles.

"Exactly, and as soon as I get back to the States I plan to take full advantage of my good fortune. Being away from her is hard as a motherfucker."

"Well, we know precisely where she is at all times. At least you didn't punk out on the tracker."

"I love her," I tell Grim softly, seriously. "I don't own her. You don't hold back someone like Lennix because the beauty is in how she flies. I want to see her soar. I just want to make sure she always lands safely. You know?"

Grim is silent on the other end for a moment. "I'll keep working on Keene. Dude's dead as a doorknob, but if by some miracle he shows his pretty face, we'll see it."

Pretty face? The image of wild blond curls rioting behind the Abe mask comes back to me.

"You prepared a file on him, right?" I ask, biting the inside of my jaw.

"Yeah, of course."

"Send me everything."

CHAPTER 15
LENNIX

IT FEELS GOOD TO BE OUT ON THE TRAIL AGAIN. WHEN OWEN announced his candidacy, the response was exactly what I expected. Pandemonium. He's the best candidate I've ever managed and the most exciting one the American public has seen in a long time.

Hope generates a unique energy, and that's what I sense in these crowds, in these people as we travel the country and lay the groundwork for what will be a massive campaign. Hope that Owen *is* as good as he looks. That he might effect change to actually make life better for them. That he'll make this *country* better. No matter how many campaigns I manage or scandals I have to spin or counterfeit candidates I meet, on the inside, I'm still like every eager face crowding the front of Owen's stage.

I still hope for the real thing.

"There's a long road ahead," Owen tells the people huddled into their coats and scarves in the February cold. He leans into the mic, his blond hair disheveled by the bitter wind. "But that just gives you more time to get to know me."

With that boyish grin, he'll be collecting hearts and votes for the next year and a half, all the way to the booth next November.

"And I hope when it's time to pull that lever," he continues, "you'll remember Owen Cade. For the people."

The applause is thunderous when he steps away from the podium, waves, and walks offstage. Never far away, his two security plain suits flank him as soon as he hits the ground and starts signing autographs, air-kissing babies, and posing for selfies. We often make rock stars of our politicians. Large crowds, theme music, slogans. Owen, with his three-hundred-dollar haircut and five-thousand-dollar suit, somehow makes people struggling to pay rent feel he understands their pain. Never having gone a day in his life suffering any lack, he *does* seem to understand the plight of working people. I marvel again that Warren Cade raised Maxim and Owen. From such a privileged background and with such a jerk for a father, they both managed to become good men, empathetic and caring about others who have a lot less.

"Must be the mom," I mutter, pulling out my phone to double-check the itinerary for what comes next. A text grabs my attention right away.

Maxim: This shit isn't funny. It's been two weeks. I want to see you.

My heart does that little hiccup he always inspires, accompanied by the ache of missing him. It *has* been two weeks since we saw each other. I've been on the trail. He went to Paris and then Prague for business. We're just beginning, but the pace is already hectic, and at the end of every day, alone in whatever unfamiliar bed the hotel provides, I think of Maxim. We talk every day, even if only for a few minutes with time differences and schedule demands, but he's right. It's been too long.

Me: I know. I miss you, too. We're in DC next week because Owen has to come home for a vote. Then?
Maxim: Then. I was scheduled for Germany, but I'll have Jin Lei rearrange.
Me: You sure? I don't want to disrupt your business. I know how crazy your schedule is.

Maxim: I need to fuck you. I haven't jerked off this much since I was fourteen.

I giggle and start my reply when Owen walks up. I shove the phone into my pocket and tune back in.

"Ready?" I ask him. "The car's waiting."

"Yeah." He gives me that auto-smile he's probably defaulted to after a full day of photos and questions and rally stops, but then I see the shift. He dips his head to look directly into my eyes, his smile softening and turning genuine. "You look tired."

"Says the pot to the kettle." I fall in step beside him, the two guards not far behind us. "It's been a grueling day."

"Yeah, but it's Pennsylvania. How many times will we come through this state over the next year and a half?"

"Oh, you'll lose count. Pennsylvania, Ohio, Michigan, Florida. We have to hit these swing states hard and often, starting now. They went red last election, and we need to turn them blue again if we have any hope of winning in the general."

"Don't get ahead of yourself." He glances down at me from the same great height his brother has. "We have to win the nomination first."

"I'm not worried about the nomination. You're so far ahead in the polls for a reason, Owen. There's not a candidate from the party who can touch you, but you're right. The Iowa caucus is our first proving ground. We've got a year to ensure it's a knockout punch. I want as many of those delegates as possible. I want to debilitate the competition—steal their hearts right out of the gate. Make them feel it's a lost cause before they even start fighting in the primaries."

"Ruthless little thing, aren't you?" Owen asks with a smile as we approach his black SUV at the curb.

"If politics doesn't make you at least a bit ruthless and, in my case, at least a *little* bit of a bitch, you aren't doing it right."

He laughs and turns to his two guards when we reach the car.

"Guys, I need to chat with Lennix. One of you take the front seat with the driver, and the other trail in the car behind?"

They nod and split up accordingly. I'm not sure why we need privacy. The guys, whom I know now by first name—Bob and Kevin—kind of melt into the background, and we discuss strategy, schedule, and everything in between in front of them. Owen and I climb in, and he rolls up the privacy partition.

"That went really well." I settle into the seat facing him and pull out the pad from my bag I use to jot down notes when he's speaking. "There was one thing you said about health care that we need to clarify, though, before the Wisconsin rally tomorrow."

"That's what I get for going off-script," he says, grabbing a bottle of water from the small cooler built into a raised table between us. "Should have stuck to the speech. Before we go there, though, I wanted to make sure you're doing okay."

I glance up from my pad with a frown. "Doing okay? What do you mean?"

"Lennix, you were held hostage just a few weeks ago." Even with the partition up, he still pitches his voice low. "You were back after a few days. We announced my candidacy not long after and hit the ground at jet pace. Of course I want to make sure you're okay."

"Owen, I'm fine. I've been talking with my therapist some by video chat. She's helping me process everything, but I *need* to work."

I don't mention that niggling disquiet of my soul, the restlessness of my mind. I've tossed those into the basement and locked the door so I can function. They aren't banging to get out yet, so for now that's good enough for me.

"Please take care of yourself," Owen says. "My brother's driving me crazy making sure I'm not wearing you out or leaving you alone for even one second."

I stiffen. Owen and I haven't discussed Maxim at all. In our last conversation about his brother, I said I wanted nothing to do with him, and now we're in a relationship and Maxim is being all over the top, like I knew he would.

"I'll speak to him," I say, keeping my voice even. "I don't want him distracting you."

"Are you kidding?" Owen's grin slides into a tilt. "It's awesome. He hasn't called me this much since he went away to camp in sixth grade."

My startled glance collides with his teasing one.

"Maxim has never been the typical little brother," Owen says wryly. "He never got that he was supposed to look up to me or depend on me to defend him against bullies. No one dared bully that kid. Even then, he was tough as nails. Our father made sure of that."

I just nod, not wanting to discuss Warren Cade ever.

"I know you don't like my father," Owen says, "but he's not so bad. He's typical of his generation."

"I'm sure the people who spat on children desegregating schools consider themselves typical of their generation, too."

His smile dissolves. "My dad's not a racist, Lennix."

"Maybe he's what I call not *not* a racist. All I know is he feels entitled to steal land that doesn't belong to him, and it's often from people who look like me."

"He's a capitalist. So is my brother." He sits back in his seat and folds his arms. "They're a lot alike. You know that, right?"

"Don't ever say that to me again," I say with a fierceness that even surprises me. "All Maxim's life he's heard that, and I'm dreading the day he actually starts believing it."

"You just don't want to believe you could care for someone who is so much, at his core, like the man you hate. Let me give you a word of advice."

"I didn't ask for advice on my personal life, Senator."

"It concerns my brother, so forgive me if I overstep, *Ms. Hunter*." He leans forward, elbows on his knees, and looks at me directly. "They may be estranged, but my father and brother love each other very much."

"I know."

"At some point, they'll reconcile. They'll need each other. Don't make Maxim choose between you and my father. He would choose you, but he'll need Dad, too."

I drop my eyes to the notepad in my lap.

"Dad's so hard on Maxim because he's always seen his potential and was afraid he wouldn't reach it."

"And you?"

"He thought president of the United States was the best I could do, but he knew Max could run the world. Maxim's his favorite."

I'd concluded the same thing, and Warren's florid face as he warned me off his younger son on New Year's Eve only confirmed it.

"Don't feel sorry for me, though," Owen says with a wide grin. "I'm Mom's favorite."

We laugh together for a moment and then fall into an easy silence.

"Do you love my brother?"

The question startles a cough from me. I reach for one of the water bottles, unscrew the top, and sip. I wanted to keep my relationship with Maxim as separate from this campaign as possible. Discussing my feelings for him *with* the candidate doesn't exactly align with that goal.

When I look at Owen, though, he's patiently waiting for my answer, none of his boyish humor in evidence. He's serious. He's the big brother making sure his little brother isn't being played and that he won't get hurt.

"I love Maxim very much, Senator, and you're a better big brother than you think."

He chuckles, but I suspect he's pleased by the compliment. "Well, he's obviously crazy about you. Just look at all he's done to have you back in his life."

"About that." I look up to hold his blue stare. "I'm going to impress you more and more every day managing this campaign because I'm smart and I'll work my fingers to the bone for you, but I need to know. Did you hire me because you believed that or because your brother wanted me back in his bed?"

He barks out a laugh. "Well, tell me how you really feel, Lennix."

He unknots his tie, flinging it onto the seat beside him. "I've seen you and Kimba shake up the political world over the last few years, and I knew I needed the kind of innovative, principled team you put together. And, frankly, having a Native American and an African American woman on either side of me helps significantly with the minority and female vote. I can win the white guys on my own. In addition to being highly capable, the optics of you and Kimba will help me with the rest."

Cold, hard facts and calculated moves.

My fave.

"Just making sure." I open the pad and find the notes I took during his speech. "Now let's talk health care."

CHAPTER 16
LENNIX

I BARELY HAVE ENERGY TO ROLL THE SUITCASE INTO MY APARTment. I don't even bother turning on the lights, relying on the glow from the streetlights to stumble back to my bedroom. I flick on my bedside lamp, tempted to fall into my bed wearing the silk blouse and tailored pants that were crisp in New Hampshire, rumpled by Vermont, and probably slightly funky by the time Owen's plane landed at Reagan National.

"Ugh." I moan and drag my listless body to the shower, leaving a trail of carelessly discarded expensive clothing in my wake. The rainfall showerhead pours warm, life-giving droplets over my hair and shoulders, massaging the cramped muscles of my neck. I stand there a few minutes, just letting the water cascade along my nakedness, not even reaching for the body wash on the shower ledge. My knees are weak, and my heart sits like a barbell in my chest.

The sting of tears surprises my eyes, and before I realize what's happening, a sob shocks my body. I slide down the wall of the shower and land on my butt, pulling my knees to my chest. Rationally, I know what this is. Exhaustion has chipped at my armor, leaving me vulnerable to things I could typically easily withstand. The things I locked away in the basement want out. Even knowing it, I can't make it stop. I have no defense when memories from Costa Rica unexpectedly splash across the canvas of my mind.

Abe forcing me at gunpoint to step across Paco's lifeless body on the floor. The six men so close to me when they were shot, I saw the blood and gore of their brains spray the air. So close I stared into the dead eyes in their shattered skulls. The lethal threat of the gun's cold barrel digging so hard into my temple it broke the skin.

Suddenly, I'm not in the shower. I'm dangling over the side of a cliff, a tangle of trees and the winding river hundreds of feet below. Iron fingers clamp my neck, feeling like they'll crush my windpipe, cutting off my breath. My heart slams desperate fists behind my chest, *pounding, pounding, pounding* painfully until I can't take it anymore. I try to gasp, but there's no air. I try to scream, but I have no voice.

Black spots dot my vision. The last thing I see are those malicious eyes, maniacal blue, laughing at me through the slits of a mask, and then the world goes dark.

I'm probably only unconscious a few seconds, but I jerk awake still slumped in the corner, the shower a domesticated waterfall, nothing like the untamed waters of the jungle in Costa Rica. The river there has a gaping mouth, thirsty to drown anything that falls into it. I brace my hand against the wall, using it to carefully stand and turn off the shower. I dry off, toweling the water from my hair half-heartedly, the taste of fear still souring in my mouth.

In my closet, I rummage through my gowns and thermals until I find the white silk pajamas Maxim loves. It's foolish for something of mine to make me feel closer to him, but I don't care. I relish the feel of the cool silk against my overheated skin like it's his arms around me. He'll be home tomorrow. He canceled his trip to Germany to be with me.

The thought soothes my raw emotions. We'll only have a few days before Owen and I hit the trail again, but I'll savor every moment with Maxim.

With the horrific tableau of events so close to the surface of my imagination, I assume I won't be able to sleep for hours, but my body can't resist the pull of much-needed rest, and in minutes, I drift off into the dark again.

CHAPTER 17
MAXIM

I'M EAGER AND HORNY AS HELL.

I unlock Nix's door but turn to the guard in the hall with me before actually opening it.

"No one even rings the bell," I tell him. "If someone wants to come in, call me and I'll decide."

"Yes, sir," he says, his face cast into lines of impassive professionalism.

"You on for the rest of the night?"

"Second shift comes at six tomorrow morning." He hesitates and then, with a grimace, goes on. "What if she tries to go run by herself?"

"Let her go," I force myself to reply.

"You sure?" he asks, brows lifted.

I clench my teeth, seeing Greg Keene's "pretty" face staring back at me from the file Grim sent. "If I'm asleep and she leaves without me knowing, alert me that she's left."

"Yes, sir."

I ease the door open and roll my huge suitcase in behind me. I have more clothes than I need because I plan to leave some things here. She doesn't want people to know we're together yet. Fine. Doesn't mean we won't *be* together.

Her bedroom door stands open, and the light from the lamp

reveals her small outline under the comforter. Even seeing just the curve of her ass and one slim arm makes me want to wake her up and slake all this lust immediately, but her schedule has been as taxing as mine. Sex can wait, but I need to hold her and have wanted to wake up beside her every morning since I left. Jin Lei's not speaking to me for canceling the Germany trip, but no way was I missing the few days Lennix would be in DC before she and Owen hit the trail again.

I've unbuttoned my shirt and tossed it onto the bench at the foot of her bed when she makes a sound that freezes my hands on my belt. I've heard that sound before—the night she cried during her nightmares in Amsterdam.

"No," she says sharply, turning so the comforter falls back. "Please, don't."

Her eyes remain closed. Her brows scrunch, distress twisting the fine lines of her face. Tears streak her cheek, and it feels like someone is squeezing my heart until it bleeds. I walk to her side of the bed and touch her shoulder.

"Don't touch me!" she shouts, swatting at my hand. "Leave Wallace alone."

My hand drops. *Wallace.*

This isn't like the other dreams of her mother. This is about Costa Rica.

"Nix." I gently shake her shoulder.

She claws at me, raking her nails over my hand hard enough to tear the skin away.

I ignore the sting and the faint drops of blood, gathering her wrists in one hand. "Lennix, it's me. Maxim."

"Doc," she sobs, her slim shoulders suddenly going limp and then shaking. "I love you. Don't leave me."

Emotion singes the inside of my throat. My muscles tauten with rage. Rage that I can't seem to help her now, that I couldn't help her then. Not in time to spare her these dark memories.

I sit on the bed and carefully gather her to me. She's unresistant, her tears splashing against the bare skin of my chest.

"Nix, baby." I push the tumbled hair back from her face and thumb the tears on her smooth cheeks. "Wake up for me."

Her body goes stiff in my arms, and she slowly pulls back, blinking wet, spiky lashes.

"Doc?" Her voice is hoarse, and I wonder how long she's been crying and crying out in her sleep. "You're here."

"I'm here."

She drops her head to my chest and the tears come faster, the sobs shaking her slim body. My teeth grind together at the tortured sound, and I realize I'm holding her too tightly. I loosen my grip, but she shakes her head, burrowing into my throat.

"Hold me tighter," she whispers through tears. "Love me as hard as you possibly can."

"I do, Nix." I kiss the top of her head. "God knows I do."

Her breaths are jagged, punctuated by sniffles. I stroke her hair and caress her back until the muscles loosen and she breathes evenly, finally finding enough peace to sleep.

CHAPTER 18
LENNIX

I KNOW I'M NOT HUNGOVER, SO WHO LET THE GUY WITH THE hammer inside my head? I sit up tentatively, pushing tangled hair back and squinting at even the little bit of morning sun sneaking through a gap between the drawn curtains.

"Morning."

The voice beside me makes me do a double-take. I massage my temples at the discomfort caused by the sudden movement. Maxim sits, back pressed into my tufted headboard, chest bare and sculpted, with his iPad on his lap and papers fanning on the bed around him.

"Doc." I smile despite my aching head. "I thought I dreamt you were here."

"Nope. Flesh and blood." He pushes the iPad off his lap and slides down, facing me and propping his head on his fist.

"You're home early." I lean forward and press my forehead to his, absorbing the *him* scent that both soothes and excites me. I kiss the base of his throat, the tan skin firm and warm beneath my lips.

"I wanted to wake up with you." He pulls back a little and palms one side of my face, his eyes concerned and searching. "How are you this morning?"

I'm not sure how to respond. Worse than the pain in my head is the turmoil of the flashback still swirling inside me. My therapist did warn that the traumatic effects of the kidnapping might sneak up on me when I least expected. Exhaustion exacerbated my response, but I still can't believe it was this bad and this sudden.

I realize I've been quiet too long when Maxim's brows fall into a deep bend.

"I'm fine," I say hastily and reach up to brush back the thick hair that likes to fall over his forehead in the morning.

"You sure you're okay?"

"Why would you think I'm not?" I sit up and swing my legs over the side of the bed. The room spins a little.

"Because you were crying in your sleep last night," Maxim says behind me, still in the bed. "A lot. It was hard to wake you up, and you seemed really distressed. You don't remember opening your eyes and talking with me?"

I suppress a groan.

Damn it all to hell.

I'm glad Maxim's here, but I wish he hadn't walked in on that hot mess. Knowing his protective nature, he won't let this go. I glance over my shoulder, calling up a casual smile. "You know I have bad dreams sometimes."

"About your mom, yes, but I didn't realize you were having nightmares about Costa Rica."

I sigh, letting my casual smile fall. "I haven't been. Last night was…different. I'd never had one before."

He gets out of bed to face me, still wearing his slacks, but the top button is undone, parting to display the taut muscles of his stomach and the black briefs he wears beneath. That's sexy as hell, and my neglected libido reminds me this specimen is mine to do with as I will.

"Come here," I order, my voice rolling out like a command swaddled in a purr.

"No." He crosses his arms over his chest. "I see that look in your eyes. I want sex, too, but we need to talk about these nightmares. What does your therapist say?"

"*This* nightmare." I walk to him, since he won't come to me. "Not these. I told you last night was the first, so she and I haven't discussed it yet."

"What do you think triggered this one?" His dark brows gather into a storm on his face. He's so intense about everything. I absolutely love it most of the time, but I don't want to talk about my nightmares when the man of my dreams is standing in my bedroom looking so highly fuckable.

"Exhaustion." I stop in front of him, dwarfed by his height but not daunted by his resistance.

I've got something for that.

I slip off my pajamas, drop to my knees, and peel the waistband of his pants back.

"Nix, no." He glances down at me from beneath the unjustly long curl of his lashes, trying so hard to look stern even with his erection practically poking my cheek through his pants. "We need to talk."

"Okay." I yank his zipper down. "Let's talk."

With admirable efficiency, I have his cock out and in my mouth in a matter of seconds.

"Holy shit," he gasps. "Lennix, do *not* distract me."

I say, "I'm not distracting you," but he probably doesn't understand since his dick in my mouth distorts my speech. I watch as the vibrations of my words around his cock force his eyes closed in pleasure. I slide my mouth up and down his length, alternating my strokes between fast and slow. I press my tongue into the opening at his tip, making love to it with reverent licks before easing him in and down inch by inch until the well-loved tip invades my throat.

"Fuuuuuuuck." He fists my hair, bringing my head down even farther until I choke. I know that sound turns him on, so I choke again, my lips swollen around his cock.

"You want to distract me, huh?" He growls, cupping my head with both hands. "You don't want to talk?"

I shake my head and hum "mmmm-mmmm." He jerks from the

vibration and starts fucking my mouth like a madman, his movements jerky and out of control, his fingers in my hair desperate and tugging. He pushes in farther, and I cannot breathe. I cherish the sensation of being completely full of him, literally wanting him more than my next breath. I draw in air through my nostrils and tighten my jaws around the rod of steel pistoning in my mouth and down my throat. I slide my hands into the waistband of his pants, which hang loosely around his hips, and urge the pants and briefs down his legs. I run my hands over his powerful thighs and cup his ass, squeezing a rhythm in time with his aggressive thrusts into my mouth.

"Nix." His head drops back, the cords of his strong throat strained, his broad shoulders heaving with panting breath. "Suck my balls."

I immediately release his cock and angle my head to take one large ball into my mouth. I take his cock in hand, continuing to pump his length even as I give each ball my wet, eager attention. His growls and moans spur me on, and I tighten my fingers around his swollen dick. I release the ball long enough to shove my finger into my mouth, wetting it liberally. He glances down at me, watching the in and out motion of my finger. Never letting his gaze go, with my free hand, I reach around and insinuate my soaked finger between the tightly held muscles of his ass.

"Hell, yes." He loosens his clenched muscles and widens his stance, opening for me. "Do it."

I ease into the tight hidden hole, and his cries become hoarser, louder. He grabs my chin and pushes his dick back into my mouth. I'm soaked between my legs, and I widen my knees. The cool air kisses the tight, wet bud nestled between my pussy lips. In time with my finger fucking his ass, I begin stroking myself. He reaches down and pinches my nipple.

It's overwhelming, the choreography of our lust, of our love, fingers and lips and tongues and cock in concert, working toward mutual bliss. My mouth drops open on a scream, and his cock comes out. His cum streams over my neck and shoulders and breasts. For seconds, I'm tremoring, barely lucid, dazed with pleasure.

He picks me up and lays me gently on the bed, leaving my legs to hang over the edge. Standing over me, he slowly, deliberately, rubs his cum into my skin, his eyes narrowed and connected with mine. He massages it all around my nipples and over my belly and then slips his hand between my legs.

"My pussy," he mutters and goes down to his knees, spreading my legs. He licks at the wetness smattered inside my thighs, groaning and reaching under me to cup my ass, dragging me deeper into his mouth. With each loving stroke of his tongue, a knot loosens inside me until it completely unravels, and I'm sobbing, my hands clawing his scalp, tugging his silky hair.

"That's it, baby," he whispers between sucks and licks. "Break for me. Show me."

And I do, drawing my knees up until my heels hit the backs of my thighs, spreading myself wide for him. Exposing everything. I can't hide from this man. He proves that every time I try. He licks the fresh wetness leaking from my body, an offering for him, and sucks my clit into his mouth hard. "No one else ever puts their mouth on you again. Do you hear me, Lennix?"

Wave after wave of pleasure washes through me, and the muscles in my lower back and legs tighten, quaking with another orgasm.

"Lennix, did you hear me? No one—"

"No one," I mumble, my head turned into the pillow.

"My pussy."

"Your pussy." I lift up just enough to catch his eyes. "And that cock is mine."

His lips are wet and shiny, full and swollen. His eyes are happy, bright with love. "Oh, I think you established that."

CHAPTER 19
MAXIM

THIS SHOULD BE FUN.

I'm being facetious. Persuading Lennix to leave DC with me won't be fun at all. We'll fight, but in the end, I *will* get her out of this town and out of the campaign grind for a breather. She may have distracted me with the most mind-numbing blow job of my whole life… Okay, she *did* do that. That definitely happened, *but* I haven't forgotten about her distress last night.

"I have a few meetings at the office," she says, standing nude in the bathroom and testing the shower with her fingertips. "But I can be home early afternoon if you want to try to do something."

"I did have something in mind actually." I stride into the bathroom, as naked as she is, and climb into the shower behind her. I grab the shampoo and massage it into her hair.

"Oh, that feels amazing," she moans, leaning back so her shoulder blades press into my chest. "What'd you have in mind?"

"I was thinking you won't go to work at all today."

"Oh, no." She turns to face me, the spray from the shower bouncing off her back. "I have to at least be there for the update—make sure we're all on the same page."

"You've been on the campaign trail every day. Kimba can do the update." I dip to capture one wet, shiny nipple in my mouth.

"Doc," she groans. "Don't you dare—"

"Distract you?" I knead her other breast and trail kisses up her shoulder and neck, sucking at the skin hard enough to leave a mark. "Now you know how it feels."

"Maxim!" She jerks back, thick strands of wet hair clinging to her arms and throat. "I can't show up at my office with a hickey like some oversexed teenager."

"Exactly. No work for you today." I turn her gently but firmly by the shoulder to face the shower wall, angling her hips and ass for me, bending her until her palms press into the shower bench.

"I can't just skip out on…"

Whatever she planned to say doesn't get said once I push in.

"I missed that last part." I rock into her, reaching to the front and sliding my fingers between her lips to pinch her clit. "What were you saying?"

"Shut up." She presses back on me. "Is that all you got? That's how you fuck your woman? I barely feel it."

My cock swells, pressing even tighter against her slick inner walls at the taunting words.

"Don't provoke me," I growl, cupping her neck and pressing my hand into the small of her back.

"I need it hard, Doc," she pants. "I want the wolf."

Her words are like the pull of the moon, and that tenuous hold I keep on civilized behavior snaps.

"You want the wolf?" I slap her ass. "Do you have any idea how hard I could fuck you?"

I let myself off the leash, ramming into her on repeat, her cries of pleasure echoing a desperate refrain in the bathroom. I grip handfuls of her wet, sudsy hair and pound into her relentlessly. She uses the bench for balance while I screw into her as deeply as possible. I want to twist so far in I feel her pulse throbbing on my cock—to break past every barrier. I want us so close our bodies whisper secrets and our heartbeats are indistinguishable.

"There's no one like you, Nix."

God, it's true.

"Jesus, Doc. There's nothing like this." Her words break on a sob, and the elegant line of her shoulders trembles. "No one like you."

I palm her breasts, squeezing the tight nipples between my fingers. Her indrawn breath tells me she likes it.

"Anything you want," she pants, circling her ass on me. "Take it."

"I want today with you," I say, changing the angle of my thrust slightly but hitting a new spot that makes her moan.

"I can't."

I force myself to stop abruptly and start easing out.

"No!" She reaches back and grabs my ass. "Don't you dare."

I stop pulling out but don't move. She squirms, tries to grind on my cock, but I grip her hips, holding her still.

"Son of a bitch," she growls. "Finish me, Doc."

"No."

"Do you think I don't feel how hard that cock is? You want this, too."

"Obviously," I force my voice to casual, like it doesn't matter to me one way or the other. "But I want a day with you more. I told you Kimba's got it. What's it going to be?"

I push in and give her a quick, shallow thrust.

"Oh, yes." She starts circling her hips, and I stop again. "Bastard!"

"I've told you my terms."

My cock hates me, silently cursing me in four different languages for not finishing this right now.

"One day," she concedes breathlessly. "I can give you one day."

I take off the reins and fuck her until we're both shaking. We almost fall when our orgasms hit. I ease out, sit on the shower bench, and set her on my lap. Greedy, thirsty, we kiss until my lips are numb, her fingers burrowing into my wet hair, my fingers tunneled into hers. I break the kiss, taking her face between my slick hands and searching her eyes.

"One day," I remind her, panting.

She nods, sucking my bottom lip and smiling. "One day."

CHAPTER 20
LENNIX

"CALIFORNIA?"

I glance over to Maxim in the driver's seat, dragging my eyes from the panorama of vivid blue water and mosaic sky, streaks of pink, purple and orange painted through the clouds.

"I wanted to get far from DC," he says, "but knew we didn't have time to leave the country."

"So we flew across it."

"I know you. If I didn't get far enough away, you'd cheat."

"Do you honestly think I'm the workaholic in this relationship?"

"Oh, I'm indisputably a workaholic, but there are a few things I'll drop everything for. You're one of them."

He did cancel his trip to Germany to be here this week, and he's proven more than once that I'm his priority. The least I can do is show him I feel the same way, but I'm having a tough time turning my brain off. There's so much to do for the campaign, and some disturbing news that broke right before we left DC keeps distracting me.

"Are you thinking about Middleton?" Maxim asks.

I turn surprised eyes his way at the uncanny guess. "Yeah, a little."

The Arizona senator who brokered the backroom, last-minute deal with Warren Cade to sell my tribe's land announced his candidacy, becoming the Republican front-runner.

"You don't actually think that idiot can beat Owen, do you?" Maxim quirks a skeptical brow.

"This country is a lot more conservative than you think if you only watch CNN and MSNBC all day."

"I don't have a problem with people being conservative. I just don't like it when people are assholes, and from my experience, there are assholes on both sides of the aisle."

A damn independent. Me, true blue, fell for a purple.

"Believe me, I'm well aware that you don't consider yourself a Democrat," I reply. "Regarding Middleton's chances against Owen, I meant he may be a jerk, but a lot of people won't care about that. They'll just vote the party line."

"Say my party nominates an antique like Middleton who couldn't lead me in a chorus of 'Twinkle, Twinkle, Little Star,' much less lead this country," Maxim says. "You think I'd vote for him simply because we're registered to the same party? Bullshit."

"Your views on the two-party system are well documented and duly noted."

"I don't understand a nation that grew so powerful using capitalism, which is essentially about choice and options and hard work, being so lazy as to give us only two options, usually bad ones, in something as crucial as leading the free world."

"God, you're such a capitalist."

"Never denied it, but back to my original point. I'm telling you, Middleton's nothing to worry about. Owen's the kind of guy voters cross party lines for." His voice rings with conviction and, if I'm not mistaken, a note of pride.

"I love seeing that you and Owen have grown close. In Amsterdam, you seemed so disconnected from your family."

"I was. My fight with my father was fresh. I never imagined it would last this long."

"Do you think he'll be conflicted if the Republicans put

Middleton up?" I ask, frowning. It would look pretty bad if the candidate's own father supported his opponent.

"Oh, hell no. He's wanted a Cade in the White House since Owen took his first steps. Middleton was expeditious for that pipeline deal. My father has no ongoing relationship with him."

I toy with the compass charm dangling from my bracelet. "You so rarely talk about your dad."

"He's not exactly your favorite person."

"No, he's not, but I don't want you feeling like you can't talk to me about him. I know you miss him. I'm sorry the animosity between him and me makes things even more awkward between the two of you."

He doesn't speak, but his fingers court mine in the space between us in the car, linking, caressing. "It's not awkward for me that you and my dad don't get along because I love you both, but I'll always choose you."

He'll choose you, but he'll need Dad, too.

I shift, angling my back against the car window so I can see Maxim better.

"I'm not that college kid who couldn't handle being with you because you were a Cade."

"I know." He flicks a quick, searching glance from the road to my face.

"You won't lose me because you love your father."

"The problems with my dad predate you and are too complex for an easy fix." He releases a long sigh. "Or we wouldn't still be on the outs fifteen years later."

"Tell me about him," I say, keeping my face clear of disgust or disdain. "About the parts of him you love."

He nods after a few moments, eyes fixed ahead on the road. "I was his shadow growing up. I know it sounds ridiculous because I was a kid, but I believed we were best friends. We did everything together."

"What kinds of things?"

"Fly-fishing, horse riding. He'd take me to the office with him. He taught me to shoot."

"So I guess, in a roundabout way, I have him to thank for my rescue," I say wryly. "I was pretty shocked to even *see* you with a gun, much less able to shoot someone from that distance."

"Yeah, my dad used to joke that I could shoot the wings off a flea. I'm not anti-guns. I know that probably breaks your little liberal heart."

"I don't need you to be anti-guns. I need you to be pro–smart gun laws, and I know you are that."

"Definitely that. I don't esteem my right to bear arms over another person's right to live and not get shot by some idiot with weapons that belong on a battlefield, not in the hands of a civilian."

"See? We agree, and my liberal heart is safe."

"Your liberal heart is *mine*," he says, tightening his hand around mine. "Does it bother you that I'm possessive and intrusive and protective?"

"Let's just say I like your growl best in bed."

He drops his head back into the supple leather of the seat and chuckles. In the silence that follows, I wonder if I should ask him something that's bothered me since Costa Rica. "Doc, the man you shot…"

"Jackson Keene," he inserts, his voice hardening, his jaw tightening.

"You know his real name?"

"I planned to discuss what Grim has found today while we had some time together, but yeah. And 'Abe' is his brother, Gregory Keene."

An icy finger traces my spine when I hear the name of the man who almost killed me more than once. "But he's dead, too, right?" I demand, my voice going a little higher. "They're both dead."

"Grim thinks so, yeah."

"You don't believe it?"

"I want to see it. I want to see Gregory's body in a morgue the way I've seen his brother's."

"Had you ever shot anyone, killed anyone before?"

"Never. Not until then."

"And have you been… Well, are you okay? How have you been processing it? I should have asked when we first got back, but my head was all over the place. In some ways, I feel like it's just starting to clear."

"I'm not sad or conflicted about shooting Jackson Keene. Gregory held a gun to your head. He almost dropped you off a cliff. If, by chance, he *did* survive four bullets and didn't drown in that river, God help him if we ever meet again because I *will* kill him, too."

A balloon of fear swells around my heart, popping, leaking into my belly.

"Pull over," I say, sudden anxiety making the words breathy.

"What?" He lobs a confused look over at me.

"Pull the fuck over, Maxim."

With a frown, he eases the car onto the shoulder of the road. His legs are so long, his seat is already back to its limit. I undo my seat belt and maneuver over to the driver's seat, straddling him. I settle my knees on either side of his thighs, slotting myself between his big body and the steering wheel. Taking his face between my hands, I trace the rise of his cheekbones with my thumbs, catch his stare, and don't let go.

"I don't want you to see him. I don't want him anywhere near you." My breath gets choppy at the thought of Maxim facing that maniac again. "I just want him to leave us alone. I just want you…" I bury my face in his neck, wrap my arms around him. "Leave him alone, Maxim. If he's alive and not bothering us, just leave him alone."

He pulls back and frames my face between big, gentle hands. "*If* he's alive, and that's an unlikely if, there's always the chance that he *will* bother us," Maxim says, his voice like granite. "And I'll be damned if anyone will bother you again. I'll kill him myself if he's still breathing."

"Please stop talking like this. I don't want you killing anyone for me. Most of all, I don't want you dead."

"I would kill a thousand times for you." His voice throbs with truth. "I'd die a thousand times for you if I could. You asked me what I love about my father. I love *that*. He protects those he cares about at any cost, and I'm sorry to break it to you, Nix, but I am just like him in that respect."

A transfer truck passes so close on the highway, our car trembles. We're so vulnerable on this remote stretch of road. Panic wraps tight fingers around my throat. I've rejected the idea of security, but Maxim's words about killing and revenge take me back to that jungle, to that river; back to the bullets slicing through the air, through flesh. I was literally in mortal danger, but Gregory Keene could have killed Maxim that day. I push away and glare at him.

"Where's your security? Why are we out here in the middle of nowhere alone?"

"Babe, we landed in San Francisco. I hardly think this is the middle of nowhere, and we're fine."

"We're fine? What the hell does *we're fine* mean? Those guys should be trailing this car right now. Does Grim know where you are at all times? I mean, what if your tracker fails? Do you sleep in that watch?" I try to remember if he wore it in the shower. "Is the watch waterproof?"

"Okay, you're kind of spiraling."

"So when I'm concerned for your safety, it's spiraling, but when you're concerned for mine, it's—"

"Perfectly justifiable. Correct." He keeps a straight face, but humor brightens the green eyes that have captivated me since day one.

"This isn't funny," I whisper. "We have a deal."

"A deal? What deal do you think we have?"

"I'll be in love with you if you don't make foolhardy, life-endangering choices."

He sifts his fingers into my hair and tugs, tilting my head back to level me with the penetrative graveness of his stare. "There's no deal, no going back. I'll probably always be a lot more cautious with your life than I am with my own, but I don't have a death wish. Living for as long as I can with you is the dream, but please don't ever think you get to stop loving me or I get to stop loving you. That shit won't happen."

I grip his shirt and pull him so close our breath mingles and I feel his heart beating into my chest.

"I don't *want* that shit to happen," I say, my eyes watering. "But I've lost the most important person in my life once before. Don't ask me to do that again."

CHAPTER 21
MAXIM

"THIS PLACE IS BREATHTAKING."

It's one of the few things Lennix has said since our conversation about Gregory Keene.

"Yeah," I reply, slamming the car door. "Point Reyes is one of my favorite spots in the world."

I walk around to the passenger side where she leans against the car, her eyes fixed on the vivid landscape of verdant coast and azure water.

She drags her gaze away to meet mine. "It is?"

"It is." I hold out the puffy down jacket I had stowed in the back seat for her to slip her arms in. "And it's also considered the windiest place on the Pacific Coast. It gets pretty chilly up here, especially when the sun goes down."

We watch the sun begin its descent toward the sheet of water, taking more light and warmth with it by the minute.

"I assume you have special plans," she says, smiling for the first time since she climbed on my lap in the car.

"I do."

An older gentleman wearing a toboggan, a down jacket, and jeans ambles toward us.

"Mr. Cade?" he asks.

"Yes." I offer my hand. "But please call me Maxim, and you must be Callum?"

"Sure am." He beams at Lennix. "And is this Mrs. Cade?"

I freeze. Hearing Lennix called "Mrs. Cade" has turned something in me, a revolution of the Earth around the sun. It sparks a deep hunger, a longing for something I didn't even know I wanted this badly until I heard it. I've imagined "a future" with her, but I'd never felt the thrill of hearing my name *attached* to her in an indissoluble way.

"Uh, no." Lennix laughs, extending her hand. "Miss Hunter. Lennix Hunter."

"Yes, well," Callum says, flushing maybe from embarrassment, maybe from the wind. "We should probably get started. The sun's going down."

"What are we doing, Doc?" Lennix asks.

"Boating." I grin when her brow furrows.

"Boating," she repeats. "A four-hour flight and almost two-hour drive for boating. Must be some special boats."

Callum opens his mouth, obviously ready to defend his little corner of the world, but I catch his eye and give a quick shake of my head.

"We'll let you see for yourself," I tell her. "Callum, show us the way."

We leave the car in the parking lot and follow him down a long pier to the boat launch where a few kayaks bob along the water's smooth surface. He suits us up with life jackets.

"Now this area is Point Reyes," Callum says, "and this is Tomales Bay where you'll be tonight."

"It's lovely," Lennix comments, her tone polite.

I know her. She's still thinking about Gregory Keene. Or about Middleton. Or maybe she was as affected as I was by hearing Callum call her Mrs. Cade. The hell if I know what she's thinking, but I do know only half of her attention is on what Callum is saying.

"Part of the bay is formed along the San Andreas fault."

"Comforting," Lennix says dryly.

"And these waters are historically protected," he goes on to say.

"Historically protected?" That piques her interest. "What's their historical significance?"

"This whole area was original Coast Miwok territory. That's a Northern Californian indigenous tribe."

"I've heard about them," she says, her smile growing warmer.

"Well, Sir Francis Drake landed in this region," Callum says with a distinct touch of pride. "Drake's Bay."

"Drake?" She rolls her eyes. "Well, of course we'd want to protect his 'discovery.' Figures."

"The interesting thing," Callum goes on, oblivious to how this story might set my girlfriend off, "is that they had all these missions that came in later and forced the Miwok people to assimilate. Settlers killed off the language, the customs, and, in some cases, the people. California has a pretty brutal history with Native Americans in a lot of cases."

Wow. This guy's batting a thousand.

"Yes, well, California is not alone in that," Lennix murmurs.

"But archeologists found evidence of them still being here and using elements of their culture years after the missions were gone. Some of them, at least, managed to survive and continue their practices while modernizing."

"Ahem," I interrupt and give him a meaningful glance. "I think we're all set and I can take it from here."

"Thank you, Callum," Lennix says, offering a genuine smile, which he returns before making his way back up the pier.

"Were you afraid I would lecture poor Callum on Drake's imperialism and probable exploitation of the Miwok tribe?"

"Pretty much, yeah."

Her rich, throaty laugh that always seduces me rings out over the quiet bay. "You're probably right. Now what's up with the boating? Isn't it getting too dark for that?"

She's right. The sun has almost completely set, and darkness blankets the horizon. A few other people come down the pier in groups with a guide instructing them and outfitting them with life jackets.

"We don't need a guide?" she asks, eyeing the people climbing into kayaks and paddling out onto the water.

"I'm our guide."

"Are you sure we'll be safe?" she asks, half-teasingly.

"I'll always protect you." Our gazes hold in the little light provided by the footlights along the pier, and the conversation from the car hangs between us.

"I know," she replies softly, the tightness around her mouth loosening. I kiss her hair and take her hand.

"Let's go." I nod toward not a kayak but a small motorboat.

"Why not a kayak?"

"They're in groups and can look out for each other if someone falls in," I tell her. "We're going to venture off on our own some. The motorboat is a little safer."

"Ahh. Your master plan to get me alone is revealed."

"I'm never subtle about getting you alone," I say, exchanging a quick grin with her. "Get in."

We get settled and strike out on the water. After a few minutes, I cut the motor and allow the boat to drift and the nocturnal beauty of our surroundings to speak. The quiet takes up the small wedge of space between us, broken only by the low murmur of the guides assisting groups a few feet away.

"Tell me about this place," she says after a few moments. "I know you know more than you've shared."

"And how do you know that?"

"You're an explorer." She tilts a small smile at me. "An expeditioner. You don't go to places completely unprepared."

"What do you want to know?"

"Tell me why you brought me here. What did you want to show me?"

"A few times a month, there are moonless nights. It's the darkest on those nights."

"The sky *is* so dark," she says, reclining in the hull of the boat and tipping her head back to stare at the hypnotic swirl of stars overhead. It's a cathedral sky at night, lit with starry sconces and cosmic candelabra. "It makes the stars brighter."

My girl who chases stars.

"It's because there's less light pollution here than in most places," I tell her. "And they protect this bay from mixing with other water sources, which keeps the water free of pollution in a way most aren't. The combination of the really dark sky and the really clear water creates perfect conditions for a unique phenomenon."

She looks around as if wondering what's so phenomenal about a bunch of people kayaking in the dark. I grin, secretly relishing the chance to show her, and take a paddle from the boat floor to run it through the water. Immediately, trails of light flare under the surface. Her startled gasp is followed by an uncharacteristic giggle.

I hand her a paddle. "You try."

She dips the paddle in, stroking slowly through the water, watching it shimmer, lighting it up.

"Oh my gosh." She covers her mouth, laughter leaking between her fingers. "That's freaking amazing."

All around us, the tour groups drag their paddles through the water, and soon, there's so much light shining beneath the surface, we're floating on sunbeams, rainbows, underwater solar flares.

"It's beautiful." She swings her head from side to side and peers over her shoulder, taking it in. "What is it?"

"Do you want to appreciate the beauty or know the boring part that makes it beautiful?"

"Is it boring to you?"

"No, it fascinates me."

"Then you'll make it fascinating for me."

"It's called bioluminescence, which is basically when an organism produces light based on various factors, depending on the species."

"That's a very sexy brain you've got there, Mr. Cade."

I wink at her. "Be a good girl and I'll let you touch it."

"Ew." She scrunches up her face. "You had to go and make it weird."

"It's what I do. So dinoflagellates are here in Tomales Bay, and they produce light when disturbed. A paddle or fingers running through the water or other fish swimming past or brushing against them or even just the boat cutting through the water could set off the light."

The other groups keep moving, so now we're alone on a sheet of glowing water. It casts a blue-green glow on her face, and I can't look anywhere else. Even the glorious underwater show can't compare to the sculpted brows and the sweet sweep of her lashes. The curve of her cheekbones and the obstinate jut of her chin.

"What's the most beautiful place you've ever been?" she asks after a few moments of silence.

"You."

She blinks a few times, shaking her head, giving me a look redolent with affection. "*Place* you've ever *been*."

My answer's the same, but I know what she means. "I don't know. It's hard to compare all these places that offer something uniquely beautiful."

I glance up at the dark sky and mentally impose a curtain of azure, emerald, and scarlet, swirling in an atmospheric lightshow. "I'd love to take you to Antarctica one day to see the southern lights."

"Antarctica, huh?" she teases with a laughing glance. "Sounds like a real vacay."

"Trust me. You'd love it. People always talk about the northern lights, but the southern lights are just as fantastic. Aurora Australis. Antarctica is spectacular."

"Not a word I would have ever thought to apply to a frozen tundra."

"You have to see it, I guess. Don't get me wrong. It's one of the toughest places I've ever been. Nearly uninhabitable, especially in the long, sunless winter, but Grim used to say it was like another planet. You see and hear things there you can't see or hear most other places on Earth."

"Like what? Tell me."

"There are illusions," I say, hearing the eagerness enter my own voice from the memory of the wonders I experienced when we wintered over. "These microscopic ice crystals are suspended in the air, and it changes how light and sound travel."

I wonder if she's bored yet, but in the glow of stars from above and the bioluminescence from below, her eyes are locked on me, rapt, so I go on.

"The cold literally bends the sound waves differently there than at lower altitudes, bending them down toward the surface instead of up. Soft snow absorbs sound energy better and mutes it, but hard-crusted snow like you find in Antarctica doesn't absorb as well. Sound literally bounces off the harder, smooth ice surface." I laugh, knowing she won't believe what I'm about to tell her. "Under the right conditions, you might hear conversations up to almost two miles away."

Her pretty mouth drops open, and her eyes go round, and it's such a look of almost childish disbelief, I want to freeze this moment of wonder and innocence.

"You said you see different things, too," she says after a moment. "Like what?"

"Well, the hot and cold air bend light rays, and that makes the light bounce off clouds, water, and ice to create optical illusions."

After all these years, I finally get to share what makes Antarctica special to me and how it made me think of *her* even when we were apart.

"There's this one optical illusion called water sky. Sailors have used it forever to navigate because the light projects open lanes of water onto the clouds and shows them how to avoid dangerous ice floes. I thought of your eyes every time I saw one."

"You did?" Her smile softens, grows tender.

"Yeah, you have water-sky eyes."

"I'm not sure how, but you've actually made me want to visit Antarctica."

"You just have to be prepared to take the beauty with the bad." I scoot forward and grasp her hands between mine. "You go months with no sun, but then you go months where the sun never sets."

"That's a great way to describe forever." She traces my palm, the thinner skin of my wrist, exciting a response through my body from every point she touches.

I don't answer because I know I'll screw this up—say the wrong thing. The "not yet" thing. The "too soon" thing—that I want an endless day with her where the sun never sets on us. So I don't say any of that but let her guide the conversation, like the paddle in the water, lighting our way with each stroke.

"That was a crazy time in our lives," she finally says.

"Which time?"

"When you went to Antarctica and I graduated college and started working in politics." She glances up at me. "I wonder how different things would have been if I'd listened to you—given you a chance when you came to see me at Jim's campaign headquarters."

"Very different. I'd probably have a lot less money."

"What? Why?"

"You see how I canceled Germany because you had a week free in DC?"

"Yeah."

"It would have been like that all the time. I would have dropped everything all the time, followed you anywhere, I think."

She stares at me, confusion or disbelief gathering in her eyes.

"You were it for me before I even knew what *it* was, Nix," I say with quiet honesty. "What I've done in the last ten years, most people don't do in a lifetime. I don't say that to brag but to say it required *everything*, all my focus, all my life to build what I have now. It's in my DNA to do that. My father, his before him, his before him—they were pioneers, businessmen, entrepreneurs who, when others saw flat plains, saw oil fields. When others saw disaster, they saw opportunity. That's who we are, but I wouldn't have been that with you. I'm already changing."

"You are?"

"It's impossible to be *that* single-minded when your mind is always somewhere else, and I think my mind would have always been on you."

Is always on you now.

"When Wallace and I were held hostage," she says, her voice subdued and her eyes lowered, "I kept thinking we wasted so much time not being together, but maybe we needed that time. We were really young." Her words, the look on her face is wistful. "We wanted to change the world."

"We still do. We still can."

She nods, her mouth lifting slightly at the corners, and crawls carefully over to my side of the boat, turning so her back rests against my chest. I cross my arms at her waist and pull her warm, pliant body into me. I'll never let this woman go, and I hope with everything I have that she'll always hold on to me.

"When you're young, you have ideals," she says, her voice a wisp in the chilly air. "You take that simplicity, that purity, for granted. You don't know how much harder it will be later."

"What's harder?"

"Everything. I used to run to change the world and protest to make my voice heard. Now I'm running campaigns and giving interviews on television and analyzing electoral maps."

"Right. And I'm testifying before Congress." I laugh into the clean scent of her neck. "By the way, I'd rather spoon my eyes out than ever do that again, but you're right. I knew what I wanted to do, but I don't think I knew how complicated it would make my life."

"It's all the compromises you have to make, the ideals you have to set aside, the plans you have to revise. It changes you."

The sweet rasp of her voice and her slim fingers twining with mine make me want to drift on this water indefinitely. To make her laugh all night while she holds my hand.

"But under all the things we've done and become," I say after a few contemplative seconds, "I think we're basically the same."

She tilts her head back to catch my eyes, smiling. "You do?"

And in just this moment, it's like déjà vu, and we've been here before, said these things before. I'm the guy and she's the girl, her innocence reincarnated, my ideals resurrected, and it doesn't matter if we're in a field of tulips or under a canopy of stars. We believe again.

"We had to learn how to play the game," I say, "and the rules may have changed, but our goals haven't. Our endgame is still the same. Make this crappy world a better place."

"I guess you're right."

She pulls my hand to her lips and kisses my fingers one by one, and with that simple act of affection, a rare, fathomless contentment saturates the air. A meridian of seconds where I'm completely satisfied, and at least for this handful of moments, there's nowhere to be, nothing to gain, and this is enough. This, *she* is the first time I've tasted enough, and I savor it on my tongue, hoard it. Fold it into my hands to memorize the feel of complete satisfaction. An entire kingdom fits in this boat. My whole world rests against my heart.

Lennix leans up and takes my mouth in a kiss so gentle, so loving, I believe she's completely content, too. For tonight at least, there's nothing to do, nothing to conquer or pursue. All the power in the universe convenes here, throbbing and humming between our bodies.

And it is more than enough.

CHAPTER 22
LENNIX

Not only did Maxim and I cruise on the glowing bay, watching the dinoflagellates perform their fantastic underwater circus, but we camped for the night.

In a tent. With a sleeping bag.

Considering Maxim's wealth, I expected at least glamping, some tricked-out mansion-tent big enough to drive a Mack truck through, but no. It was just a tent and the most rudimentary camping equipment. We zipped our sleeping bags together and shared each other's warmth, reminisced about the past, and passed our dreams of the future back and forth between each other.

I left Maxim there this morning, still zipped up, his hair slumping forward boyishly into his face, and struck out for a run along the coast. In the months when I prepared for my Sunrise Dance, I trained rigorously to endure the physical demands of the ceremony. Personifying Changing Woman, the first woman, was supposed to help me gain command over my weaknesses and even activate my ability to heal.

I need all those things now more than I did even then, but this woman has a lot more baggage than a thirteen-year-old girl. I find that peace more elusive. They say Changing Woman runs east so she can run into her younger self. What would I say to that younger girl?

With my run complete, I quietly pull my bag from the tent

where Maxim still sleeps and rummage until I find the items Mena gave me. I head for a jutting rock overlooking Tomales Bay. Legs folded beneath me, I spread out the simple elements for smudging: a bowl, sage, wooden matches, and a feather. I light the sage and watch the smoke rise from the bowl before picking up the feather and using it to coax the smoke over my face, my head, my eyes, ears, and heart.

Traditions are the memories of those before us, breathed to life when we carry them on. My hands reach back, straining through time for the peace my ancestors found even in the midst of unimaginable loss and injustice.

I haven't smudged in so long that at first, I feel like a phony. Like I'm going through the motions of something that could be wasting my time, but when I close my eyes, I see Mama in the mornings. She liked to smudge outside. She said when you call on the four directions, you start with the east, and she could never remember where that was. Seeing the sun showed her where to start. We laughed, but really she just loved to be outside, to breathe fresh air.

The idea is that the smoke attaches to the negative things in our lives, in our bodies, in ourselves, and draws them out. They float away with the smoke. There were days Mama was only outside for a minute or so. But there were other days when, through a cloud of smoke, I would see tears washing her cheeks. It's only now that I carry my own pain, that I have my own healing to do, that I wonder what she was healing from. I don't think the smoke is magic. For me, it's one of those practices that connects me to the elders and reminds me of their strength in the face of upheaval and violence and disenfranchisement.

Mena said to start with intention or an affirmation. What do I even say? Do I say it out loud?

"I will live this day in gratitude," I whisper, the words mingling with the smoke I scoop over my face. "Grateful to be alive and breathing and able to give and receive love. I will face every obstacle with the boldness of those who follow me and with the courage of those who came before."

Behind closed lids, I'm suddenly transported again to that dank cave, blind inside the black bag. It's so disorienting my head swims. Just as I feel those iron fingers gripping my throat and the ground falling away beneath me, I breathe in the sage. Fear, panic, and anger slowly recede, and I wonder if it's as easy as breathing in and breathing out; as surviving one breath to the next, one day at a time, healing in my own way.

I've regained my ground and breathe deeply, honoring the four directions, starting with the east, the dawning of a new day—new beginnings. Putting the old behind me and embracing what is ahead.

After a few more minutes, I stand and overlook the bay that used to belong to the Miwok tribe. They'd been here thousands of years when the first settlers came ashore.

Save the man, kill the Indian.

That was what those missions were for—to eradicate everything that made us *us* in hopes we'd become what they wanted us to be. The acculturation of a people who were doing just fine before the boats came. After the missions were long gone, some of the Miwok were still here.

That's me. I have no idea what's ahead, and I'm still healing from the past, but I have to believe that, like the Miwok, I'll remain, planted, rooted, and still standing.

CHAPTER 23
LENNIX

"Owen, Lennix," Millicent Cade calls from up the hall, excitement lighting her voice. "It's on!"

Owen glances up from the red-lined papers spread out on his desk. For the past hour in his Georgetown home office, we've been revising tomorrow's fundraiser speech with Glenn Hill, the campaign speechwriter, and we're all ready for a break.

Owen runs a weary hand over his face and stands. He looks younger, disheveled, the sleeves of his Harvard sweatshirt pushed up to the elbows, the expensive Italian boots he favors replaced by white athletic socks. Nothing like the shiny, pressed, pulled-together candidate I've been crisscrossing the country with.

"You guys coming to watch Maxim on that late-night thing?" he calls over his shoulder as he leaves his study.

Hearing Maxim's name sets off tiny, needy bombs in my pants. I miss him. Tomales Bay was two weeks ago, a brief reprieve before we had to resume the unrelenting pace of our schedules.

"Good grief," Glenn says, highlighting a point in the speech we agreed needed clarifying. "How many more of these do we have to sit through?"

I chuckle, shuffling my copy into a neat pile of papers. "What do you have against the senator's brother?"

"It just feels like ever since he was on *The View*," Glenn says,

"America's all fixated on Maxim instead of on the issues Owen wants people thinking about."

"I know what you mean, but it's according to plan."

"Really?" He quirks a brow, doubt all up in the word.

"Owen just announced last month. This campaign is a marathon, not a sprint. If he's too wonky and blah, blah, blah policy now, when most Americans aren't even paying attention, we're not taking advantage of what they will pay attention to."

"Which is what?" Glenn asks. "One of America's 'most eligible bachelors'? I thought the women in the audience on last night's show were going to start throwing panties. If drool translates to votes, Owen's got this in the bag, thanks to his brother."

The muscles in my neck and back tighten at Glenn's reference to panties. I know Maxim is faithful. I don't even think twice about it, but still, knowing your very handsome boyfriend is out in the world inspiring lust and getting offers from every Tom, Jane, and Harriet doesn't feel great. Especially when you only see him a few times a month.

I should be happy about that because it's easier to keep our relationship on the low, but I'm not happy about it. Talking to him every day isn't enough. Phone and FaceTime sex isn't enough. Nothing is enough until he's back home and in my bed again.

"We better get out there," I say, nodding toward the hall. "Or we'll miss the panties."

Glenn chuckles and follows. This is our fourth campaign together, and he's one of the best speechwriters in the game. We've become friends, but when he touches the small of my back, I still pull away because…I don't know. It feels intimate, and if Maxim were in the room, I'd be squirming and he'd be glaring.

God, what I wouldn't do for one of his glares right now. Or a good fight, where we disagree vehemently about everything and then fuck until I sob because it's so perfect. I've never physically ached for a man, but I do for Maxim.

"I wondered where you two were," Owen says when we enter the living room where he's seated on the couch beside his wife. He drops a kiss on Millie's blond hair, and she tilts her head to capture his lips in a quick kiss.

So many DC power marriages are strategic alliances, negotiated with benefits for both parties involved. Millie is definitely invested in Owen's success, but she's most invested in *him*. She loves *him*. There's an unexpected warmth to her, and I see why Owen is besotted. Working so closely with Owen, I see why she's besotted with him. I've come to admire them both over the past few months, not just for how fabulous they are in front of a crowd but for who they are when there's not one.

She married Owen, and that was it. Millie has a law degree from Cornell, but her own career aspirations seem to have been absorbed like a spill soaked up by a sponge. Since the beginning, Maxim has esteemed my dreams just as important as his. Each couple is different, but I'm glad he doesn't expect me to set aside my ambition. I don't judge Millie's path. True empowerment is about choice—figuring out what we want and going after it. She wants *this*. I just want something entirely different.

It's barely March, and winter's not going without a fight. The fireplace in the Cades' living room, coupled with the hot chocolate Millie made, suffuses the tastefully decorated room with warmth.

I sip my hot chocolate and chew on one of the marshmallows bobbing on its surface while the late-night show's logo appears onscreen when the show returns from a commercial break.

"And we're back," the host says. "We have a treat tonight. This guy was recently voted one of America's most eligible bachelors, and his brother just might be your next president. Please welcome Maxim Cade!"

Maxim strides out from backstage, wearing expertly tailored gray pants and a black sweater molded to his arms and broad chest. Even in understated clothes, he looks like money and orgasms.

The high-pitched squeals of the women in the audience grate on my nerves.

Hussies.

"Well, hello," the host says, motioning for Maxim to take the seat beside his desk. "Thank you for coming on, Mr. Cade."

"Thanks for having me, Connor," Maxim replies, his smile polite and his eyes guarded. I'm not used to this closed-off version of him, but I know this is who he has to be in the world.

"You've been voted one of America's most eligible bachelors for a few years," Connor dives in, "but this is the first time you've agreed to any interviews or talk shows. Is it a coincidence that your brother's running for president?"

Maxim's wide grin comes more naturally. He likes things straight-forward, cards on the table, so that approach would appeal to him.

Point for you, Connor.

"Definitely not a coincidence," Maxim says. "I don't mind answering a few questions about my personal life if it means I can talk about what an amazing president my brother will make."

"That's right," Millie says with a fist pump.

Owen rolls his eyes, but his mouth curls at the corners, and I easily read the pride and affection he has for his brother.

"Yet you and he don't always see eye to eye on issues, do you?" Connor asks.

Maxim shrugs. "Growing up, O thought Batman was the coolest DC comic character, and I called Superman because...obviously. You mean stuff like that?"

The audience laughs, and Connor offers a good-natured grin but isn't giving up.

"I mean on things like climate change and gun control," Connor says. "He has a much more progressive stance on guns, and you have what some would call a radical position on climate change."

"Wow, aren't you supposed to softball it, asking about that special someone in my life or if I have any tattoos?"

"Do you have any tattoos?" Connor laughs.

"I do. One."

"I bet the ladies out there want to know where it is."

"Don't leave the guys out."

"What's the tattoo? If you don't mind me asking."

"No, that's actually better than your first question."

Amusement ripples through the audience again, and Maxim looks out at them, winking like they're in on the joke or sharing a secret.

"One tattoo," he says. "The word *endurance*, after my favorite expeditioner's ship."

"You have a favorite expeditioner?"

"Not as cool as you thought, huh?"

Connor waits for the audience laughter to die down, glances at the little card in his hand, and dives back in. "Don't think I'm letting you off the hook with my first question, but *is* there a special woman in your life?"

I tense in my seat, gripping my little mug within an inch of its porcelain life.

Maxim pulls his bottom lip between his teeth for a second and then grins. "When there is, you'll be the first to know, Connor."

My breath whooshes out, louder than I thought apparently because Glenn looks away from the screen to my face. "You okay?"

"Me?" I frown, like *why are you even asking me this*. "Of course. This hot chocolate's just…hot."

Thus the name hot chocolate.

"Well, now that we've addressed that," Connor goes on, "back to my original question."

"Persistent, aren't you?" Maxim slides down in his chair an inch or so and folds well-defined arms across his chest, spreading his legs the slightest bit. It's a move of subtle masculine power, flaunting his ease and comfort. He's unthreatened.

"How do you reconcile the differences of opinion you have with your brother?"

"I think the better question is why do you want me to?" Maxim fires back, still smiling. "I'm like any other American voter. I look at the choices I'm given and decide whom I trust to make the world better. There will inevitably be some issues I wish my candidate wanted to do more about and some policies where we don't exactly agree, but I believe he's the best man for the job. If I didn't believe that, I wouldn't vote for him, and that's the truth. It would make family dinners awkward, but hey…"

"Speaking of family," Connor goes on. "Your father did an interview recently, too."

I sense tension in Maxim—the slightest narrowing around the corners of his eyes and tightening of his mouth. The casual observer wouldn't notice, but I'm anything but casual when it comes to this man. Never have been. Owen probably recognizes it too, his smile fading as he waits for what's next.

"He was asked who he saw as the most influential business mind of the last decade," Connor says. "Do you know who he said?"

"Uh, I could guess," Maxim says, "or you could just tell me."

"You."

Maxim lifts both brows and nods. "Wow. That's quite a compliment."

He sounds completely unaffected, but there's a flare of response, an alertness to his green eyes belied by his indolent posture.

"You and your father have been at odds for a while," Connor goes on. "How would you characterize the relationship?"

"Like any other family," Maxim says. "We don't always agree, and we let differences get in the way sometimes, but at the end of the day we're still family. Like yours or anyone else's, but our disagreements sometimes play out for everyone to see."

"Will he be on the campaign trail with you and Owen?"

"He's a very busy man, but he knows O has the strength of character to lead this country. He'll know how to best support him."

"Good answer," Owen murmurs, looking over at me. "He

didn't commit Dad to the trail but didn't make it seem like there's a problem."

"Great answer," I agree.

"Now there's also an interesting dynamic with your dad and your brother's campaign manager," Connor says, grinning.

I hold my breath, and Owen narrows his gaze on the TV screen, not looking at me.

"What dynamic is that?" Maxim asks easily.

"They hate each other."

"God, Connor, you make us sound like a bad soap opera."

"No, a good one. Like *Dallas* or *Dynasty*."

The audience laughs, and Maxim does, too, albeit with that guarded watchful look on his face.

"Okay, okay, enough tough stuff," Connor says. "Let me ask the things everyone wants to know."

With his hardest-hitting questions out of the way, Connor shifts to lighter topics, and by the end, Maxim has the audience thinking and laughing and pretty much swooning.

"He's such a natural," Owen says when the segment ends. "Maybe one day, I can convince him to run for office."

I almost choke on my marshmallow. "That's the worst idea I've ever heard."

"Agreed," Glenn speaks up. "Candidates have to be incredibly disciplined."

"You're mistaken if you think Max wasn't intentional about everything he revealed tonight," Owen says, smiling. "Lennix, I'm surprised you don't think he should get into politics."

"I think he's positioned himself as just enough of an outsider that everyday people trust him but as someone so undoubtedly influential that politicians want to use him. The best of both worlds. I think they trust him *because* he's not a politician."

"Gee, thanks," Owen murmurs wryly.

"You know what I mean." I laugh. "He's better off staying out."

I don't add, of course, that Maxim in politics sounds like a nightmare for our personal life.

After the show, Millie goes to bed, but Glenn, Owen, and I put in another hour hammering out the speech. By the time we go our separate ways, I'm exhausted and can barely see straight on the ride home. I'm letting myself into the apartment when Maxim calls.

"Hey," he says, his voice low and liquid.

"Hey yourself, Mr. Late Night."

"I made Kimba promise this is the last one. I have better things to do with my time than answer inane questions for lame latenight hosts."

"It's not a waste of time. The rapport you're building with America will come in handy later when Owen needs you to speak on his behalf."

"If you say so. I miss you."

His abrupt shift from the campaign to personal throws me off for a second. "Uh, yeah. Same."

"It was cute at first," Maxim says dryly, "but I don't think *same* properly conveys how much you should be missing me right now."

"How should I properly convey it?" I ask teasingly, dropping my bag on the floor and stretching out on the couch.

"A picture of your naked tits would be a good start."

"Did we learn nothing from Anthony Weiner? A dick pic is forever, so imagine the half-life on a tit pic."

"Good point," he says soberly. "Soooo…video?"

"Doc." I laugh, kicking my shoes off and wiggling my sore toes. "They're just breasts. Nothing special."

"Shh! They'll hear you."

"God, don't make me laugh. Owen's cook made pot roast tonight, and I ate my weight in beef. And before you ask, no, I didn't check to see if it was non-foresty."

"Well, that's disappointing. Why were you eating at O's place?"

"We were working on the speech for that fundraiser tomorrow

in Baltimore. I watched your segment at the house with him, Millie, and Glenn."

"Ahh. Good ol' Glenn. I don't think he's a fan of me."

"No, he totally is," I say. I'm not sure either, but we can't have tension between two key figures in my campaign.

"Did you hear what Connor said about my dad?"

"Something about you being the greatest business mind?" I ask, keeping my voice neutral.

"I don't know why he said it."

"He believes it, of course. He's right. You are."

Maxim just grunts at my praise. "Dad knew it would get back to me, so he's signaling me something, but I'm not sure what yet."

"Maybe he's ready to repair things between the two of you." I try to keep my voice even, but the thought of seeing Warren Cade on the regular if he and Maxim reconcile may bring that pot roast back up.

"After all these years?" Maxim asks. "Maybe. Sometimes it's hard to remember what drove us apart."

Him being an asshole?

"More than anything," I say, suppressing my internal scream. "I'd love to stay on the phone talking about your father, but alas...I have a life."

I sit up, grabbing my sling-backs by the straps and heading to the bedroom.

"Very funny." He does chuckle but then sobers and says seriously, "I can't wait to see you next week."

Next week.

I want him home now. I want to kick and scream on the floor, but I can't. He canceled Germany for me, and in Tomales Bay, he implied that he was willing to follow me all the time. I can't have that. He has too much to do.

So, with a grin, I say something that will keep him where he needs to be. "Same."

CHAPTER 24
LENNIX

"Maybe we should've left out that part about jobs," I say and try to soundlessly slurp the French onion soup from my spoon. "Employment numbers came out today, and jobs are up. Score one for the other side."

"They haven't been up," Millicent whispers back. "Everybody knows employment has been trending down. Today's report was an outlier, so I think it's okay." She frowns at her own soup. "French onion? Really? The menu at this fundraiser is just sad." She touches her dinner roll with one contemptuous finger. "Hard as a rock."

"Yeah," I reply distractedly.

"And this lettuce is wilted. I mean, iceberg? Kale, at least."

"Millie, uh, trying to listen to Owen here."

"Sorry." Her grin is almost girlish. "I've heard this speech a dozen times, so I know it by heart. He's been rehearsing it since he woke up."

"If it goes over well, he knows we'll reuse it about a hundred times in some form or fashion between now and November."

"I know it's tempting to dwell on the past," Owen says from the stage, looking handsome in his tuxedo, that one rebellious lock of blond hair breaking from the rest, just like his brother's.

"But we still have the future," Millie whispers along with him to finish the line, winking at me. "And we still have each other."

I grin at her and discreetly pull my phone from my evening clutch to make a note of things I need to address with Owen later on the ride home. A message notification grabs my attention before I can start the note.

King: You look beautiful tonight.

I changed his contact name to King just to be safe. I shift the phone under the tablecloth to keep my reply discreet.

Me: You have no idea how I look.
King: That so?

He sends over a picture of me standing with Owen at the bar talking to a Baltimore businessman who consistently supports the campaign. My hair is in a chignon, and my red evening dress looks like it was poured onto me. The red matte lipstick stretches with my smile.

Me: How'd you get this? Spies? We agreed no security. Bad enough you gave me jewelry to transmit my every move.
KING: Not security. My sister-in-law.

I turn to scold Millie, but now she's tuned in to the speech and watches her husband, the look in her eyes titrated with respect and adoration. I'll tease her about the pic later.

King: I'm done here in Palo Alto earlier than expected. I'm already on the flight and on my way home to you.

My heart starts triple-timing to a raunchy little tune. We'll be home in an hour, and I can actually sleep in Maxim's arms tonight.

Me: Oh! Make sure to use the rear entrance.

I've cracked down on the discretion. Us being seen in the same general area could be easily explained, but some snoop snapping photos of him coming and going regularly from my apartment building would be a problem, especially after this goodwill media tour raised his profile even that much more. He wasn't happy about the new "rear entry" policy, but at least it's led to some good anal jokes.

> King: As long as I get that "back door" access we discussed at some point.
> Me: Um...it's up for negotiation. So what changed? I thought you were there till next week.
> King: I asked Jin Lei to expedite meetings so I could take advantage of you being in DC for a few days.
> Me: Lawd! She probably thinks I'm going to ruin your business.
> King: She probably thinks your pussy is lined with gold.
> Me: OMG! I cannot believe you just said that.
> King: She's not wrong...

I'm still not sure if I want to slap him or hump him after that last comment, but there's no time to reply because everyone stands and applauds as Owen leaves the stage.

"Let's get out of here as soon as possible," Millie says from the corner of her mouth. "O's got his car, so we don't have to wait."

Owen is notoriously accessible, always taking "one last" selfie or answering one more question. Millicent and I rode here together since Owen came straight from a committee meeting and met us here.

"I was supposed to go over a few things with him on the ride home," I say, "but he looks as tired as I am. Maybe it can wait till the morning."

"The nanny's been with Darcy and Elijah all day." Millicent glances at her watch. "I'd like to send her home."

"I'm all for a quick exit." I glance down at my phone, at Maxim's last text, before tucking it back into my evening bag. "The faster the better."

Owen's listening intently to an older woman asking about the future of Social Security when Millie approaches.

"Sorry to interrupt," she says, smiling kindly at the woman. "But I'm going to start back home, O, for the kids."

"Of course," Owen says. "You still need to chat, Lennix?"

"I don't think so," I say. "My car's at your place, so I'll catch a ride with Millie and head on home. We can touch base tomorrow."

"Good. Get some rest," he says, looking back to Millie. "You take Kevin and I'll keep Bob. I'm right behind you."

She reaches up to kiss his cheek and gives the woman a parting smile, and we head toward her car.

"Now we can talk about your secret relationship with my brother-in-law," she says.

I glance around to see who's within earshot. "Um, yeah, and maybe we can discuss the ins and outs of what it means to be *secret* while we're at it."

She grins, loops her arm through mine, and starts toward the private back entrance of the country club hosting the fundraiser. A group of red-jacketed valets scramble to get the cars pulled up. Bob takes the keys from the tallest of the young men and holds open the door of Millie's SUV.

"Thanks, Bob," Millie says and climbs in.

I settle into the back seat, facing her. "And since when are you Maxim's spy?"

"You mean the pic I sent him?" She grins and reaches into the little cooler between us, pulling out a Peroni and offering one to me. "That wine tonight may as well have been dishwater. Who organized that menu? Lucky for us, Owen stocks these for me."

I never would have pegged Millie as a beer girl, but that's where we usually mess up, thinking we have people pegged. I shake my head to refuse as the car pulls away from the curb.

"It was just a little fun," she says mischievously. "You two have heated up a lot, huh?"

"Look, I know you guys are close, but I need to keep this discreet and separate from the campaign. I don't want people thinking I got this job because I'm sleeping with the candidate's little brother."

"I think the only time anyone thinks of Maxim as the 'little brother' is when Owen reminds them." She laughs and takes a swig of her beer.

"Maxim's not anyone's little anything."

"Hung, is he?" Millie asks wickedly.

"Not going there with you, *Mrs. Cade*." I pull an imaginary zip over twitching lips.

"I'll just say," Millie persists, giving me a wink, "it runs in the family."

Our bawdy laughter is so loud I check to make sure the privacy partition is up all the way.

"Would you lookie there," Millie says, glancing through the SUV's back window. "Senator Cade managed to extract himself from a conversation in record time. I should've waited a little longer. I really wanted to ride home together."

I look, too, and see that Owen's SUV is already behind us.

"At the next light," I say, feeling lighthearted and happy for how genuinely they love each other, "you could hop out and go ride with him. I'll be fine here by myself."

"You sure?"

"Of course."

I'm already thinking about calling Maxim as soon as Millie hits the pavement. We both peer again through the back window. They got caught at a light and are a little farther back but still within easy sprinting distance if Millie wants to make it happen.

She gives me a conspiratorial glance when we stop at the next light. "I think I'm gonna go for it."

"We should probably let Bob know first."

I roll the privacy partition down to tell him Millie's plan, of which he'll probably disapprove. "Hey, Bob. Millie's gonna—"

But the words, the sound of my voice, and every thought are absorbed by a bone-rattling boom that shakes the car. A sonic nightmare of sound rings a gong in my head and fills my ears, blocks all other noise until Millie's tortured scream pierces the wall holding sound at bay. I lift my head dazedly and through the rear window see bright, angry flames devouring the car behind us.

"O!" Millie scrambles across the seat, lunging for the door. "No! Oh, my God, Owen!"

"Millie!" I reach for her arm, but she evades my grasp and jerks the door open. She trips out of the car and takes off running toward the burning vehicle. I run after her, only catching her when her stiletto turns over and she stumbles. I grab her from behind, wrapping my arms around her waist.

"Millie, you can't," I say, tears burning wet tracks down my face.

She wiggles free again and limps toward the burning vehicle, but Bob streaks past me and grabs her again. Her arms windmill, fighting with an invisible foe. Even with his strong arms around her waist, she still strains toward the destruction, toward her husband, her hands outstretched and trembling.

"O," she moans, her voice jagged and falling apart. "No. Oh, God, no. Owen."

The vibrant, beautiful woman who laughed with me only minutes ago is already gone. This is a sobbing, broken shell, and my heart aches knowing that other woman is being consumed in those flames. Owen is gone, and so is she. We're standing in one of life's awful moments where your breath is a comma, marking the space before and after tragedy, punctuating that nothing will ever be the same.

CHAPTER 25
MAXIM

My father and I haven't spoken since Christmas when I warned him to leave Lennix the hell alone, so I'm surprised when his name pops up on my phone. Right away, I think of the compliment he "planted" in the media and wonder what this is about. I'm reclining, resting on the flight home, but sit up to take his call.

"Dad." I'm not asking a question or offering much of a greeting. Just literally letting him know I've answered.

"Maxim." For a moment, it's only my name, but spoken in a voice I've never heard from my father. Torn. Ragged. *Lost.*

"What's wrong? Is it Mom?"

"No, your mother… She's here with me."

"Where's here? What's going on?"

"We're flying to Baltimore. There's been an accident at the fundraiser."

"Nix?" Her name is out before anything or anyone else occurs to me.

"She's fine, from what I've gathered. It's… It's Owen."

I bite my tongue, not wanting to ask the question burning the tip of it—the question my father's sober tone begs. And, from my father's silence, he doesn't want to answer.

"What about O?"

"He's gone."

There's a wail in the background, a wounded animal with my mother's voice. The moment retards, slows, stretched by her pain, like a drawn-out note in the octave of anguish. It doesn't fall on me all at once, the impact of what my father said. Not like a brick or a boulder, something heavy and flattening in one blow. It's a deluge of pebbles, embedding themselves in my flesh one by one, second by agonizing second, until I'm covered. I can't move. I can't speak. Hurt is my only faculty.

"Maxim?" my father asks, with a hint of his typical command. "Did you hear me?"

"Gone," I say dazedly. "Y-you said Owen's gone… Jesus."

In my seat, I bend at the waist and hold the phone away from my ear, letting it fall to the floor. I can't find my bearings in a world where my brother doesn't exist. I've never been here before. The pain is tornadic, picking up speed, tossing out everything I knew about how something could hurt. There is no point of reference for this. The reality of Owen being gone travels through me, miles per second, and nothing is left untouched.

"Maxim," I hear my father again, a distant echo. "Son, talk to me."

Without opening my eyes, I feel around on the floor until I find the phone and lift it to my ear. "I'm here." That's not my voice, grated up with sobs, but it's coming from my body. "I'm… I'm trying to… Shit."

Words abandon me, and I sit in silence for a moment with my father, and when he speaks, his voice is hoarse and emotion cracks it, and he says the words that I've often wanted to hear, but not like this. Never like this.

"Son, just come home."

CHAPTER 26
LENNIX

THERE IS NO COLDER PLACE THAN A WAITING ROOM WHEN THE waiting is over.

When hope turns off the lights. The held breath is released in tears. The end of faith. It all convenes in a waiting room when death has come and gone.

Millie sits on the hospital's drab, impersonal couch, dry-eyed and lost in her own apocalypse. This is the end of the world as she knows it. I'm inches away in the blast wave of her pain, feeling the shock of it and still seeing the burning vehicle that took her husband. My friend. Maxim's brother.

Oh, God, Maxim.

The police pulled Bob and me in for questioning right away, to reconstruct the timeline as best we could. In all the commotion, I left my evening bag and phone in the SUV. I haven't been able to call Maxim, and I need to hear his voice. I want to be there for him, but also...*I need him.* Nothing settles me like being in his arms, and I'm short-circuiting at how close I came to death...again.

I was supposed to be in that car with Owen.

If I hadn't caught a ride with Millie, I *would* have been.

Is death hounding me?

I haven't had time to process the implications of what could have happened to me because I'm too unraveled by what did happen to Owen; his family, suffering this unfathomable loss. Then I think about the country and the hope and enthusiasm Owen had inspired. Young people wanting to vote for the first time, older voters who had lost faith in the process, eager and wondering if maybe this time…

It's so hard to compartmentalize right now, but I have to remember I'm a friend but also running the country's most closely followed political campaign. Kimba and our team are flying blind right now. I need to call her, but first I *have* to call Maxim.

I glance at the woman seated across from me, one slim arm wrapped around Millie's shoulder. Salina Pérez, her best friend, lives in the Virginia suburbs outside DC and was Millie's first call. She arrived a half hour ago in a whisper of cashmere and Dior perfume, ushering in some degree of calm and comfort in the waiting room.

"Um, could I borrow your phone?" I ask softly, nodding toward the phone on her lap. "I think I left mine in…" It feels wrong to even refer to that scene, to that moment Millie and I witnessed.

"Of course." Her dark, kind eyes are slightly puffy and red-rimmed, but it doesn't detract from her dusky beauty. She hands me the phone. "I'm sure you have many things to take care of. I've got Mill until the family arrives."

I take the phone, stand, but then hesitate. "I'll be right back, Millie."

Millie's vacant stare shifts to me, and an odd little smile quirks her bite-marked lips. "I keep playing that damn speech over and over in my head," she says, as if I hadn't spoken. "We still have the future, and we still have each other."

She nods, and a solitary tear slides over her cheek, meandering into the corner of her mouth. "It's a good line. Good speech."

I stand there helplessly. Shock and grief and this tight dress make it hard to breathe and move. I don't know what to say, how to function in this alternate universe. Last night, Millie was cuddling with Owen on their couch, sneaking kisses and sharing a mug of hot chocolate topped with marshmallows. Now parts of him have been blown away, incinerated. A death so gory I can't even contemplate it and keep moving forward.

After a few seconds of silence and a few more tears, Salina squeezes her arm, and I nod. "I'll be right back."

I duck around the corner and lean against the wall, allowing myself a moment to feel the loss of Owen for myself. To feel my friend gone. To feel my own hope lost for what he could have meant to this country—the possibilities he represented to me and to so many. I choke back a guttural sound, and with the phone like a slab of marble in my hand, I swipe at my tears, clear my throat, and dial Maxim.

I want to slam the phone into the wall when it just rings. There's no message, only a beep. I hang up, completely unprepared to speak into the void of an empty line. I need his *voice*. I need *him*.

Resolving to try him again later, I call Kimba next.

"Hello?" There's an uncharacteristic edge of panic in Kimba's voice. This woman would remain calm facing an army of zombies with a toothbrush, but she sounds like she's falling apart. I recognize that sound.

"Kimba."

"Thank God," she says, her voice breaking. "Answer your damn phone, Lenn. I thought… We didn't know… Where the hell are you? I was worried about you, and the press is up my ass."

"I'm sorry."

"What's going on? There've been reports of some explosion after the fundraiser, but the scene is closed. No press allowed, but there have been rumors that… Are you okay? Owen? Millicent?"

"Yes. No." I close my eyes, blow out a painful sigh. "Millie and I are okay. It's Owen."

"Oh, God."

"A car bomb. There was an explosion. Millie and I were riding together in her car, and Owen…"

"What about Owen?" The question tilts up at the end, hanging, waiting.

"Kimba, he didn't make it."

Her silence on the other end is an epoch, marking our new reality and mourning what we've lost.

"No, oh my God, Lennix."

I slide down the wall, sitting on the floor and pulling my knees up while we cry together, a commiseration of sniffles and hiccups and tears.

"Shit." She blows her nose, and I already hear the necessary shift in her voice, sense it in her famously iron will. "Okay. What do we say to the press? What's the plan?"

"I don't think we *can* plan without consulting the family. Maxim and his parents are en route."

"Maxim. How is he?"

"I haven't even gotten to talk to…"

A shadow falls over me in the narrow hall, and I look up to find Maxim standing there, the green of his eyes swallowed in a pain so dark it makes them look almost black.

"Hey, I'll call you back," I say, never letting my eyes leave his, even though it hurts to see him drowning in agony this way. "Maxim's here."

CHAPTER 27
MAXIM

I DIDN'T KNOW HOW BADLY I NEEDED TO SEE LENNIX UNTIL I rounded the corner and found her there, wearing the whole night like a heavy cloak slumping her shoulders and etching lines of tension around her mouth. Her eyes snare mine, and I breathe, not realizing how anaerobic I've been since my father called. She's my air, and I don't even wait for her to stand but reach down, scooping her up in my arms. I fold my elbows under her bottom, savoring her warmth, the wing-touch of her breath at the base of my neck.

Leaned against the wall with her clutched to me like that, I don't care who walks by or what anyone thinks. Without this, without *her*, I won't make it another step. Every moment I hold her is resuscitating.

At first I don't realize where that sound is coming from. That wrenching, bleating, sobbing noise. It's the comfort of Lennix's fingers ghosting over my neck and sliding into my hair. It's the sibilant, soothing "*shh*" she leaves in my ear that lets me know *I'm* making those sounds. It's me shaking in her arms even though right now, hoisted up against me, her feet don't even touch the floor.

"I'm so sorry," she whispers, her own grief and pain dampening the collar of my shirt where she huddles into me. "I love you so much."

I absorb her words into my lungs like a deep breath and slide down the wall to the same spot on the floor where I found her. She settles across my lap and pushes my hair back. Peering into my face, her water-sky eyes are brilliant and stormy and raining tears.

I pull her to my chest again, compulsively needing to feel her heart thumping into mine. Even though Dad told me she was okay. Even though I've already seen Millie, safe and devastated and desolate, in the waiting room, I had to see Lennix with my own eyes. And now I can't let her go. She's slim and small and willowy against the width of my chest, but she's my tree in this storm.

She pulls back.

"Don't," I mutter with a swift shake of my aching head, tightening my arms around her. "Don't let go."

She nods, the cool, tumbled strands of her hair brushing against my neck.

"When Dad said there had been an accident at the fundraiser, you were the first person I thought about. I could have lost you both tonight."

"You didn't."

"But Owen..." My voice breaks. Something *inside* me breaks, and my emotions are ungoverned, an anarchy of relief for Lennix, grief for Owen, rage at whomever set this tragedy in motion. If I'd lost them both, I'd be living in darkness. Lennix feels like my one tiny point of light, and still I can't see.

"Maxim."

My father stands over us, startling me. His bleak gaze moves between Lennix and me with a kind of dull acceptance.

"Dad," I say, my voice as strong as can be expected through a throat grated by the lifetime of sorrow I've crammed into the past two hours.

"The medical examiner is ready to talk to the family." He looks at Lennix and then away, his mouth a grim line.

"Go," she says softly, lifting wet, spiky lashes to catch my eyes. "I need to call Kimba back. Could you let me know what we should... um, say to the press? The scene has been locked down, but there are already rumors circulating. I don't want us to say anything your family doesn't want us to."

The reality of moving forward with the logistics crushes me. The press will make theater of my family's real pain. Owen will be "the senator," "the candidate" on the morning news and in all the papers, but to my mother, in so much pain she's had to be sedated, he's "the son." To Millicent, dull-eyed, devastated, he was "the husband"—the love of her life. And to the twins, he was "Dad."

To me, he's the big brother I never said "*I love you*" to enough. I didn't voice how much I admired him, not for the laws he passed or any of the things the reporters will commemorate. I admired him for the way he loved his wife and kids. For managing to be a good man who genuinely cared about others when he could have been, by all rights, an entitled asshole who cared only about himself.

I finally nod and dip my head to kiss Lennix's temple. "I'll let you know."

"Thank you." She scoots off my lap, and in the fitted evening dress, it will be hard to get up with dignity. I know she's cognizant of my father's presence here, so I stand and pull her up. She shoots me a grateful look and then shifts her glance to my father.

"I'm so sorry, Mr. Cade," she says softly, a little stiffly. "Owen was one of the finest men I've ever met." Her eyes soften, and her shoulders lose some of their tension. "I mean that truly."

"Thank you," he replies, his tone abrupt but not rude or cruel. He tips his head toward the waiting room. "The medical examiner is waiting, son."

She holds the phone to her chest, and I know her quick mind already has to shift to her team and the press and the shit I don't care about at all right now but know must be done. Leaving her to that, I follow my father into the gruesome new reality that none of us can ignore.

CHAPTER 28
LENNIX

I'VE ALWAYS AVOIDED FUNERALS. I IMAGINED I'D SIT IN THE audience the whole time thinking the family at least "lucky" to have a formal goodbye. To know what the end held and have closure, unlike my family.

This is not luck.

Millie sitting between her twins in the front row before a casket that can't even be opened because her husband is so disfigured and badly burned inside—that's not luck.

Salina sits beside Darcy, brushing her hair with one hand and pressing the little girl's head to her shoulder. "Auntie Sal," they call her. I'm sure, had the campaign gotten further along, we would have had more contact. She seems deeply embedded in the family's lives. Apparently, she was legal counsel for one of Warren's companies before opening her own law firm specializing in immigration law. Seated between Darcy and Maxim, she fits right in, and I can't help but think she's exactly the kind of woman Warren would choose for his son.

"You sure you don't want to sit with Maxim?" Kimba whispers as we take our seats a few pews back.

"I didn't want it to be awkward. His father should be able to grieve with his family without the added tension of our…history."

"And since no one knows about you and Maxim, the press might latch on to that and make more drama."

"Exactly. Drama they don't need. Neither do we."

The press has constantly fed the public's voracious appetite for every available detail of Owen's assassination, as it's been termed. Every time I hear the word, I want to vomit. I've barely had time to process what's happened because we've been responding to inquiries and figuring out what to do for our team. It's been a week, and the shock of Owen's death has reverberated all over the country—the world, really. You can't turn on the television or radio or walk past a newsstand without seeing it. The promise of Owen's campaign had garnered a lot of international attention and coverage, even at this early stage. It's not every day the son of one of the most powerful men in the world runs for the most powerful job in the world.

Owen's gone.

There's nothing I can do to make this better. No lever I can pull. No one I can persuade or situation I can spin to fix things.

I don't understand it. I couldn't have forecast it. I've never lost a candidate. Not just any candidate, but a friend. It wasn't even that long ago when he came asking for our help, and I assumed he was just another privileged white man expecting the best of everything to be handed to him on a silver platter.

But he wasn't. He was so much more, so different, and my heart opened to him in ways I'd never anticipated. He would have changed the world, that elusive concept held together by the last shreds of idealism and hope. He would have achieved it. And I have no idea why now he'll never get the chance. With all the technology at our disposal, with all the security cameras, bodyguards, precautions and protocols, we have no leads on who assassinated Owen. How is that even possible?

With Owen gone, our team is all out of jobs. Technically, Kimba and I aren't, but most of them contract with campaigns. They have families and mortgages and lives to support. We usually have a few elections running at once, especially midterms, like Susan's was in Denver, but we had never run a presidential campaign. It required all of our dedicated resources. We can float most of them for a little while, but people have already started accepting other offers since we're so early in the campaign cycle, still nearly a year from the Iowa caucus. Plenty of time to land somewhere else.

My mind has been split for days, tuned into the stark reality of Owen's death but also managing the very real implications of it. Maxim and I have had nearly no time together. He's been a rock for Millie and the twins and for his mother.

I'm Mom's favorite.

Owen said it, but both parents appear devastated.

Mrs. Cade sits on the front row, bracketed by the intimidating breadth of her son on one side and her husband on the other. I've known Warren Cade as long as I've known Maxim, since I was seventeen years old. For the first time, my heart softens toward the elder Cade.

I'm seated on the opposite side of the church so I can see his profile. Pain has carved new lines alongside his mouth and bold nose, so like Maxim's. I usually try to ignore their similarities, above and beneath the surface, but today it's impossible. The same sorrow hovers over them. They both bend solicitously toward the small woman seated between them whose grief slumps her slight shoulders.

The priest closes his prayer book, having shared a few verses of comfort, and scans the crowd. The Dallas church is filled beyond capacity. Mourners line the streets outside. Millie has allowed the service to be broadcast, so large screens have been set up in nearby parks and all across the country. People are crowding around their TVs at home or huddling around their laptops. Some are watching on their phones. The response across the nation has only highlighted how beloved Owen was from his ten years of service in the Senate and the impression he'd made in the few short months he'd been on the campaign trail.

"This is a difficult day for so many," the priest says. "Most difficult for Owen's family. His brother, Maxim, will now share a few words."

Anxiety scatters briars in my belly. I didn't know he would have to do this.

Maxim takes the stage, so handsome and proud, looking as impeccable as ever, but I know better. I sense the cracks, the lapses in his defenses. The only time I've ever seen him this emotionally vulnerable was by that river in Costa Rica, and not because he'd killed a man, but because he'd almost lost me. I want to cover him—to shield him from prying eyes. They haven't earned the intimacy of Maxim's pain, but it's there for anyone looking closely enough to see.

"I made a really bad little brother," Maxim says, managing to shape the grim line of his mouth into something approaching a smile. "Big brothers protect their little brothers when they get picked on, but I was kind of a big kid and not very nice, if I'm honest."

A small murmur of subdued amusement ripples through the crowd.

"So nobody really messed with me," he continues. "And you're supposed to look up to your big brother, but when I was a kid, I didn't look up to anyone except my father."

I glance at Warren Cade, but the inscrutable planes of his face register no response or emotion.

"As we grew older, in a lot of ways, we grew apart." Maxim glances down and clears his throat. "I wasn't close to my family for a long time, but Owen never stopped reaching out to me."

He aims a brief grin toward Millicent, seated in the front row. "He called me the night he met you at that mixer, Millie, and said he'd found the one. I laughed at him because how do you know after one night, right?"

He scans the crowd for a second until he finds me, his eyes connecting with mine almost imperceptibly, but it sends a jolt of recognition down the center of my body and arrows through my heart.

"I hadn't seen him for months, but he wanted me as best man

at his wedding. I was there when the twins were born." He stares at the closed coffin, his eyes unfocused like he's seeing a kaleidoscope of memories. "He never gave up on me, not just as his brother, but on us being friends."

A deep breath swells his chest, and he goes on. "Owen modeled what it looked like to be a faithful husband, to save your love for one woman and then show her every day that she was worth waiting for. He showed me how it looked to believe in your children and want the best for them without pressuring them or making them feel they had to live up to someone else's standards. He showed me how to really serve this country, not with charisma or charm or with lip service, but with his heart. With hard work on behalf of people who needed help more than he and I ever did."

A deep swallow moves the muscles in his throat. "You were a great big brother, Owen. You were a fine man, and I didn't tell you enough, but I love you, and I *do* look up to you."

When he shifts his gaze to the audience, there's a shift in his demeanor, too. Steel enters his eyes. His broad shoulders seem to stretch. "Someone killed my brother, and they think they ended Owen's life, but they haven't. Not really. His legacy of service goes on in every person who benefits from the laws he voted into existence. He lives on in his beautiful wife, Millie, and my niece and nephew, Darcy and Elijah, who knew his love and his devotion and will carry them with them forever.

"Someone, the person who killed my brother, thinks we should be afraid." His mouth tightens, and his eyes narrow. "I'm not afraid. Don't you be afraid either. You know what scares me? Cynicism. Apathy. Anything that convinces people to settle, to quit. The thought that people will give up on changing this world because of one person's cruel cowardice makes my blood run cold. I would have given up on the system, the way things work, long ago had it not been for Owen. He renewed my faith in the process by which we change things in this country."

He grips the podium so tightly, his knuckles whiten. "Robert Kennedy said, 'There are people in every time and every land who want to stop history in its tracks. They fear the future, mistrust the present, and invoke the security of a comfortable past which, in fact, never existed.' I say comfort, even peace, is an illusion. There is always a cause, but too few believe enough to fight.

"Owen was a believer, and if you were around him long enough, he made a believer out of you. He had a stealthy will of iron. Beneath that easy charm and boyish grin was a tough-as-nails crusader. A brawler for the things and people he cared about, and he cared about a lot of people. They were his mission. *You* were his mission. He was determined not to fail you. If Owen inspired you even once, don't you fail him."

His glance drops to the coffin, and for a moment, he looks shaken. That helpless sorrow passes across his face almost too quickly to detect before he firms his mouth and looks back to the crowd.

"The past is behind us. The future is ours. Figure out how you can change the world right *now*, and don't fear it. Do it."

CHAPTER 29
MAXIM

My polite responses to condolences stopped hours ago. The comfort of strangers feels like an itchy sweater—agitating. I want to strip it *off*. Whoever decided the best way to spend the afternoon following a funeral was with food and well-meaning, awkward mourners should be punched in the face. This reception is absolutely the last thing I want to do.

I haven't been in my parents' house in years, and this was not how I saw myself returning. When I *have* come to visit my mother over the past decade, I've stayed in a hotel. I own homes all over the world, but not here. Even Texas isn't big enough for my father and me.

I flew into Dallas yesterday to help prepare for the service and to support Millie and Mom. This has taken the hardest toll on them.

"How you doing?" David asks, the concern clear in the eyes of my long-time friend.

"Irritable," I reply. "And ready to kick everyone out."

"I can imagine. Actually, I've never lost anyone this close, so I *can't* imagine. Sorry doesn't even begin to cut it, brother, but I *am* sorry."

I nod, grateful for the sincerity of his helplessness. We've been friends long enough not to say stupid, useless shit when we're hurting, though nothing has ever hurt like this.

"Thanks, man," I say.

"You talked to Grim?" David glances around the room. "I thought he might break his no funeral rule this time."

"He's where I need him to be, working with the authorities to figure out who did this. He knows that means a lot more to me than him showing up in a suit and tie."

"I hear ya."

Mom, standing across the room, nurses a glass of her favorite pinot. The congresswoman talking to her doesn't seem to notice the glaze over Mom's eyes or her plastic smile cracking around the edges, but I do. Why is the family expected to entertain? We're not in the mood for finger sandwiches and banal standing-room conversations. Middle finger to the guy who thought *I know what we'll do now that our loved one has died. We'll throw a party.*

"I'll be back," I tell David. "I need to go check on my mom."

I'm headed toward her when a new group enters the dining room. I recognize several of them from Owen's campaign and redirect my steps, walking toward the sharply dressed knot of people.

"Maxim."

I turn my head toward the familiar voice.

"Kimba," I say. "Thank you for coming."

She steps forward and wraps her arms around me, and I squeeze her back.

"I'm so sorry," she says, her voice teary. "We all loved him."

And they all did. From that first night when we all met at Owen's, a bond started forming between Owen and the team Kimba and Lennix led. Millie had asked for their birthdays and anniversaries so her social secretary could get them a little something. She would have made a fine first lady. I don't know what the future holds for her, but I'll make sure it's whatever she wants.

I pull away and scan the group with Kimba. "Where's Lennix?"

"She's coming. There was some press outside the church, and they pounced as soon as they saw her."

I clamp down on my frustration. I want her with me. I haven't pressed on it much. I understand her hesitation. Our relationship hasn't been public and my brother's funeral isn't exactly the best place to debut as a couple. Mostly, Lennix has wanted my father to be able to grieve with the family without her presence, considering the enmity between them. I appreciate her sensitivity, but I need her in ways I can't even articulate. My body and my heart tell me every second of every day that she should be with me.

"Doc."

It's like my need for Lennix drew her to me. Her hair is sleek and long, a shiny dark curtain spilling over the red coat she wears, covering a severely cut black dress. Her mouth is red and full. My arms flex with the effort it takes not to grab her.

"Nix." I keep my voice calm but take her hand and start walking off. "Kimba, excuse us."

I know I was abrupt, but I need to be alone with Lennix. A few minutes where it's just us and no one expects me to be "doing well," "holding up" or "hanging in there." In measured but swift strides, I pull her out of the dining room and down the hall to the nearest closed door, my father's office. As soon as the door shuts behind us, I fold her into my arms. She's winter sunshine, bright and warm on the coldest day of my life. I huddle into her heat and softness. Frustrated by the layer of wool keeping her shape from me, I push the coat over her shoulders and down her arms, letting it pool on the floor around her high-heeled feet, and turn her so she's against the wall. I press into her, bury my face in the silky curve of her neck. She slides her arms around me under my suit jacket, and her fingers seek and find the tension in my back, kneading the muscles through my shirt.

"I missed you." I kiss her forehead and push the stream of hair over her shoulder, exposing the line and curve of her jaw and neck.

"I missed you, too." She cups one side of my face and searches my eyes. "How are you?"

"Breathing. That's about it."

"It's enough." She tips up to kiss my cheek, and I turn my head, brushing our lips together, briefly, but enough to catch fire. We both pause, our gazes cling, and our mouths part, hovering in a shared breath. The flare of passion catches us unaware in the midst of grief, but it's undeniably the same burning want that's never far away when we touch. I grip her by the hips and pull her so close my body is a hard question. Hers is a soft response. A "yes" wrapped in velvet, lined with satin.

The door opens, and Lennix sucks in a startled breath. I brace myself to face my father, but it's not him.

"Mom."

She stares at us, Lennix pressed between the hard wall and my hard body. "Introduce us, Maxim."

Mom's voice is calm, no sign of the wrenching sobs I heard through the walls last night. I step back, and Lennix picks her coat up from the floor. I grab her hand, walking her over to my mother.

"Mom, this is Lennix Hunter. Nix, my mother, Tessa Cade."

"Nice to meet you, Mrs. Cade," Lennix says. "I'm sorry. We all loved him so much."

Mom doesn't reply for a second, tilting her head quizzically, studying Lennix's face. "I thought you'd have horns and scales," she finally says, a small smile making its careful way onto her colorless lips.

"Excuse me?" Lennix looks from my mother to me.

"The way Warren talks about you," Mom continues, "I thought you might be a dragon, but Owen assured me you weren't."

She looks at me with the shadow of her usual sunny nature. "And Maxim's always liked pretty girls and been an excellent judge of character, so I figured my husband was biased."

I haven't told my mother about our relationship, so I assume Owen did. He and Mom always talked about everything.

She steps forward and extends her hand to Lennix, who accepts, a cautious welcome on her face. "It's nice to finally meet you," Mom says. "I saw you at New Year's from a distance, but you were very busy, and we didn't get to speak."

It was only three months ago that Owen first floated his presidential run at the New Year's Eve party in his home. The night Lennix came back to me. We made love in the garden, a dark night under a wild moon, the air heavy with hope and new beginnings. That night feels like a century ago.

My mother slides her glance from my face to Nix's and then drops it to our held hands between us. Her brows lift, and one side of her mouth tilts up. "Owen told me, but I didn't quite believe him."

"Believe what?" I ask, frowning.

"That you were in love," she says.

"He was right about most things most of the time," I reply quietly.

"Or at least he made you think he was," Mom says, her smile wobbling and then dissolving altogether. "I think I'll go upstairs and lie down now. The guests—"

"They'll be fine." I release Lennix's hand and slip an arm around Mom's shoulders, guiding her toward the door.

"Walk her up, Maxim," Lennix says, trailing us out. "Or she'll get stopped a dozen times on her way. I'm gonna go anyway."

"What?" I stop and turn. "Why?"

"I wanted to pay my respects," she says, barely loud enough for me to hear and slips her coat on. "We can talk later."

"When do you go back to DC?"

"Most of the team leaves tomorrow." She licks her lips and glances down at her shoes. "But I'm...um, flexible. I can stay for a while if—"

"Stay." I can't spend another night alone in my bed upstairs, thinking about Owen sleeping across the hall when we were kids. "I'll call."

She nods, and we leave the library, nearly colliding with my father in the hall. For a few frozen seconds, the four of us stand in silence stretched over barbed wire.

"I should, well...get going," Lennix says, looking to my mother. "It was very nice meeting you, Mrs. Cade."

"Nice meeting you, too, Lennix," Mom replies, taking her hand and patting it. "Next time under better circumstances, I hope."

"Yes." Lennix looks up at my father. "Mr. Cade."

"Ms. Hunter," Dad replies neutrally.

"I'll walk you out," I say, laying my hand at the base of her spine.

"No, it's fine." She turns to face me and tips her head toward the dining room. "You still have guests."

"I'll call you." I bend to press a hard, quick kiss on her lips, not caring what my parents make of it, and reluctantly let her go.

CHAPTER 30
LENNIX

MAXIM CALLED AN HOUR AGO TO SAY HE WAS COMING, AND MY heart has been in hummingbird wings mode ever since. It's not eagerness. I mean, I am looking forward to seeing him, but "eager" is too bright for this dense darkness we're living through. There's a sobriety to every second, no escape from the startling new reality that Owen is gone. It's not eagerness as much as need, a hand clenched around my heart.

I'm in the bedroom when I hear three quick raps at the hotel suite door. My sweatshirt and yoga pants don't exactly scream *come hither*, but I was exhausted after dealing with the press, and the initial stages of dismantling the campaign have drained me. My appearance is the last thing Maxim will care about.

I speed walk to the door but stop with my hand on the knob, giving myself a beat to calm down. Anticipation sings along my nerve endings. The rapid *thump thump* of my heartbeat fills my ears, and my palms are actually sweating.

When I open the door, my heart collapses at the sight of him. Maxim's handsome face is almost haggard. His eyes, tortured. I marveled at his composure during the funeral service, delivering Owen's eulogy without breaking down. And at the reception, he stood with his usual strength, though obviously emotional and grieving, but the man in front of me is held together with ropes close to snapping.

"Maxim, hey." I open the door wider for him to come in. The security guy who wanted to follow me on my jog stands in the hall. "Oh, hi."

"Ms. Hunter." He nods, his expression giving away nothing.

Maxim strides in past me.

"Is he, um…" I keep my voice low and tip my head toward the hall. "…staying out there?"

"Yeah. That's okay?"

"Of course." I walk over and grab a chair from the hotel's tiny dining nook and drag it to the door.

"So you won't have to stand," I say, pushing the chair toward him.

Surprise flicks over his face before he carefully stows it away behind the straight line of brows and an unsmiling mouth. "Thank you."

"What's your name?"

"Rick, ma'am." He slides the chair out into the hall and closes the door.

I turn my attention to Maxim. Outwardly, he's as put together as usual, the navy-blue sweater clinging lovingly to the sculpted muscles in his arms and back and chest. The slacks are well tailored and crisp. There's no slump to his broad shoulders. He stands as straight and powerful as usual, but I've never seen Maxim unsure. He always knows what he wants, what comes next, and where he's headed. This is the first time I've seen his compass spinning.

I cross the room and wrap my arms around him, laying my head on his shoulder. "How ya doing, Doc?"

His chest rises and falls against me with a deeply drawn breath. "Not good."

"I know." I tighten my arms around him and blink at the tears stinging my eyes. "I'm so sorry."

He kisses my hair and rubs my back. The pressure of his hands on me feels so good, I huddle closer, needing him, too. He dips to scatter kisses over my cheek and jaw. Cupping the back of my neck, he drags his lips to my ear.

"Nix, I…" he rasps. "I need to fuck you."

My breath catches, and I start trembling, the anticipation I felt before he came building and running in rivulets down my arms and legs.

"Okay." I nod. "Yes."

"I can't explain it," he says hoarsely. "I just need to feel you, to know that—"

I press my finger to his lips and lay his hand between my breasts. "Maxim, you don't have to explain. I'm yours."

"Thank you." He presses his forehead to mine, grips my neck, and kisses me so thoroughly, his tongue so deep and seeking, that my head spins. I grip his shirt to stay on my feet.

"Too much?" he asks, his breath coming fast. "You okay?"

"I'm fine." I lick my lips, gasping for air. "But could we go to the bed?"

He nods, and I lead him by the hand to the back of the suite where the bedroom lies.

"Sit." I give his shoulder a gentle nudge, and he sits on the edge of the bed. "Can I undress you?"

He glances up, eyes flaring, and nods his agreement. I stand between his spread thighs, only a little taller even when he's seated. I tug his sweater by the hem over his head. With his last business trip, it's been two weeks since we made love, and at the sight of his pecs with the bronzed nipples and the taut, tanned skin straining over a ladder of muscles in his stomach, my mouth waters. I get on my knees and trace the word *endurance* inked into his skin. He *will* endure. This is his greatest test yet, and though it's unimaginably hard, he'll get through this.

We will together.

Wordlessly, I ghost kisses over his shoulders and throat, drifting down to his chest and laving the tattoo for long seconds before taking his nipple into my mouth, whirling my tongue around the hardening tip.

"Lennix," he breathes. "I need you so much."

I take the other nipple, setting an aggressive, suctioning rhythm until he groans and curses. I roll my hand over his dick, hard in his pants. With shaking fingers, I undo his belt, free the button of his slacks, and pull down the zipper, reaching into his briefs and taking him in my hand.

He gasps, lifts to free himself of the briefs and slacks. "You know what I want," he says.

I nod, lowering my head and taking his length into my mouth and down my throat.

"Shit." He pushes my head more until I gag a little, and he goes even harder in my mouth. All the while I'm sucking him, I rub my hands over the granite muscles of his thighs. I release his dick from my mouth and kiss his legs, his knees, bend to trace his calves, caress his feet.

"Lennix, hell. You don't have to—"

"Let me make love to you," I whisper.

He watches me intently but nods. I explore the rough brush of the hair on his legs against my cheek, the small birthmark on his hip, the scar on his forearm—the dog bite from the first day we met—all the beautiful, neglected parts of him.

Standing, I lift my sweatshirt over my head. He cups my back and brings me forward to take my nipple in his mouth, so warm and wet through my bra. I drag the lace cups down, intolerant of anything between my aching flesh and his lips. He sucks and bites so hard, I know I'll wear his marks tomorrow, intimate badges of honor. He shoves at the waistband of my yoga pants, sliding them and my panties down until we're both naked.

"Lay back," I give him the gentle command. He drags himself onto the bed until his head rests on the pillow. I crawl up, spreading my thighs across his, opening myself over him.

"Show me what you do when we're apart," he says.

Our eyes cling as my fingers wander to my clit, finding the hot, tight bud nestled between my lips. I rub in gentle circles at first but pick up the pace, increasing the pressure as sensation spreads over my body. My head drops back, and my breath comes in heavy pants. He tweaks my nipple, and I cry out, pausing for a moment to savor his touch.

"Keep on," he demands. "Show me."

My fingers resume the flicking and pinching and stroking between my legs. I bite my lip, choking back moans.

"Let me hear you. I need this, Nix."

I nod, a brush fire licking all over my skin as I let the moan go.

"It's not enough," I gasp.

"What's not enough?"

"I need you."

"Where?" he asks, his voice gentling. "Where do you need me?"

"Inside." Tears gather in my eyes and run over my cheeks, and I don't know if it's grief or lust, but I know only he can make this ache go away. The ache of my body and of my soul. "Please, Doc."

He nods, and I reach between us, easing down, watching his big dick disappear inside me, my body swallowing his entire length. Our breath catches on the same sigh, and I rock over him, squeeze him between my thighs, and ride.

"God, you're beautiful," he says hoarsely. "Take your hair down for me."

I reach up and undo the topknot, letting the hair fall around my shoulders and down my back. He tunnels one hand into the tresses at my neck and grips my hip with the other, controlling the rhythm of our bodies together.

Our gazes lock, and what I see behind his beautiful green eyes breaks my heart. The bleakness. The grief. The need. All distinct and stemming from the same place.

"Oh, Maxim. I'm so sorry."

He sits up, repositioning me so I'm spread over his hips, my thighs resting on my calves. I go still, feeling him swollen and hard inside me, to cup his face between my hands.

"I love you." I kiss his eyelids, wet with tears I've never seen on his hard cheeks. "I love you." I rub our noses together. "I love you." I touch his lips with mine, licking into the hot silk of his mouth, tasting his desperation. He thrusts up hard and goes deeper, stealing my breath and burying his head in the curve of my neck and shoulder.

"Don't leave me, Nix." His words break, *he* breaks, and his tears fall on my naked skin. "If I lost you—"

"You won't." I slide my fingers into his hair, kissing him until he moans and we lose ourselves to the tempest of grief and grind, passion and weeping, our bodies moving with blazing urgency. Groaning, he comes, shouting my name. He reaches between us, stroking my clit until I come, too.

We remain locked together, sweaty and satisfied, the cinders of our desire cooling between us in silence broken only by the harshness of our breaths.

Moments later, he falls back onto the mattress, taking me with him, pulling the covers over us. Turning me to my side, he presses his chest to my back, snakes his arm possessively around my waist, and falls into exhausted sleep.

CHAPTER 31
MAXIM

My phone vibrating on the bedside table jerks me awake with a start. I sit up and look around the strange room. The only thing familiar is the woman beside me. Inky strands of Lennix's hair spill stark against the hotel's white sheets. Her face carries a peace in sleep none of us have felt for the past week.

I grab my phone and walk into the bathroom, closing the door behind me.

"Grim, what's up?"

"I'm in the hall," he says, his tone like a butcher's freezer. "You didn't answer your damn phone, King, so I had to come over."

"Sorry. I had it on silent."

"I bet you did," he says, the harshness easing some. "We need to talk. Now."

"All right." I run a hand over my face. "I'll be out."

I hang up, splash my face with cold water, and walk as quietly as I can back into the bedroom. I put on my briefs and slacks, not bothering with the sweater.

When I glance at the bed, Lennix has shifted, one berry-tipped breast visible over the sheet. My dick goes hard again. I've heard of grief sex, but damn. This is ridiculous. I could make love to her again and probably again before the sun rises. The need to be inside her is so elemental, I can't distinguish it from the need to breathe or blink.

She's come so close to death twice, I need to know she's alive. That's the only way I can articulate it.

I close the bedroom door and walk into the sitting area. When I open the door, Grim stands in the hall, chatting with Rick. They both glance from my bare chest to my hair rumpled in all directions by Nix's fingers, and it doesn't take much to guess what I've been doing the past few hours. Hell, Rick probably heard us fucking. I can't really care. I need her and I need him standing guard, both now more than ever.

I tip my head toward the suite. "Come on in."

He looks past me, a brow cocked. "You sure? I don't want to interrupt."

I give him a wry look and turn away to walk inside. The door closes behind him, and I fall onto the couch, linking my hands behind my head. "What we got?" I ask him.

"He's alive," Grim says, jaw clenched. "Gregory's alive."

I'm not surprised. Even when all signs indicated he was dead, some instinct of self-preservation warned me he wasn't. My greatest suspicion has also been my greatest fear—that he was behind Owen's assassination.

For a moment, guilt tourniquets my throat, and I can't breathe. If Gregory did this, I may as well have planted that bomb—may as well have murdered Owen myself. He'd be alive if not for this vendetta against me.

"How do you know?" I ask.

"He left a message for you."

My eyes cut across the small space separating us, the width of the coffee table. "A message? What the hell do you mean?"

Grim shakes his head and barks out a brief, humorless laugh. "He left a message at your office to call him."

"To call...the fuck?"

"He called CadeCo's U.S. headquarters in New York and left an urgent message that your friend Abe was trying to reach you. They passed his number on to Jin Lei, probably thinking it was some prankster but wanting her to have it just in case. She recognized the name…well, the fake name, and called me."

I hate him. I detest his flippancy and his complete disregard for human life.

"Jin Lei was at the funeral," I say, realizing she and I barely got to speak. "She didn't mention it."

"She wouldn't have said anything there, but she passed it on to me because she knew we'd have to address it. This is the last thing you should be dealing with on the day you had to bury your brother, but I'm afraid we can't afford to wait."

"He did this, Grim," I say through caged teeth and tight lips. "He killed Owen. I know it."

"If he did, that means he's a lot more active and a lot closer than we'd expected."

"And definitely not dead. I knew he wasn't."

"All signs pointed to—"

"I don't care about signs, Grim." I stand and pace, dragging my fingers through my hair. "I knew it in my gut."

"Well, there was nothing we could do about it. Our antennae have been up, and we've been hunting, but there was no sign of him until now."

"Now, after he's killed my brother and left a fucking *message* at my office to brag about it." I slam my fist into the nearest wall, denting it and sending pain shooting through my hand. "Son of a bitch."

The bedroom door opens, and footsteps hurry up the short hall. Lennix appears, a silk robe barely covering her. The curve of her breast tantalizes me, and her robe gapes a little, revealing the sexy sliver of her collarbone. Her lips are kiss-swollen. Tiny red marks dot her slim throat, rising from the neckline. Her hair is silky and tumbled. She looks thoroughly fucked. I never want anyone else, not even Grim, whom I trust with my life, with hers, to see Lennix like this.

"What's wrong?" Her eyes widen, and she rushes over, grabs

my hand, and frowns up at me. "You've hurt yourself. Let me get some ice to—"

"Go get dressed," I say in a low voice, my hand at her back turning her back toward the bedroom.

"What? I…" She glances at Grim and gathers the collar of her robe in one hand. "Grim, hi."

"Lennix." Grim nods but wisely keeps his eyes trained on her face.

"I'll…be back." She nods to my hand. "We need to get ice on that, though. It's already swelling."

"Okay." I walk her toward the hall. "When you come out."

I stride back to the sitting room, standing closer to Grim and pitching my voice lower, glancing over my shoulder. "Let's get this over with."

"You won't be able to keep this from her. You know that, right?"

"If he did this to Owen, he'll…" Horror and rage and fear stunt my words. "She was supposed to be in that car, Grim. If anything happens to Nix—"

"We'll protect her."

"Like I protected my brother?" I choke on self-condemnation, barely getting the words out.

"Owen had round-the-clock security, and if Keene got to him, there wasn't more we—*you*—could have done given the information we had."

"Of course it was him. Who else?"

"We gotta talk to him. If he's being this bold and foolish, he'll slip up and leave clues for us to follow."

"You know that number's a burner phone."

"Still, having the number in advance this way, we can trace the general location and know where he is now. It's something."

"It's not enough."

"It's a start."

I breathe through my nose and force the air through my mouth, trying to calm down. This motherfucker loves getting a rise out of me. He proved that in our first conversation. Whatever he says will devastate me, will enrage me, and I won't be able to do anything about it. I already know that.

"Maxim, make the damn call before he changes his mind."

"Before who changes his mind?" Lennix asks. She's back in her yoga pants and sweatshirt, her hair neatly pulled into a knot on top of her head. I don't even want her in the room when I call this lunatic.

"Baby, could you give us a few more minutes?"

"No." She sits beside me on the small couch. "Tell me what's going on."

I squeeze the bridge of my nose and close my eyes. If she were just biddable from time to time, my life would be so much simpler.

"King, she'll have to know eventually."

My head snaps up, and I glare at Grim. Whose side is this motherfucker on?

My side. I know that, and he's right.

"Keene called."

Lennix stiffens beside me, her eyes stretching to their limits. "What? He's dead. Are you sure it was him? He called you here? Your cell? What... How did he—"

"He left a message for me at CadeCo headquarters in New York."

"That makes no sense." She frowns and rubs her forehead. "Why would he expose himself this way?"

"I believe he's too narcissistic and twisted not to claim his kill," Grim says.

The truth piles up between us—carnage and danger and vengeance.

"His kill?" Lennix divides the question between Grim and me.

"Owen," I say. "We think Keene was behind the assassination."

The full weight and horrific implications of my statement sink in, play out across her expressive face.

"No. Oh, God." She covers her mouth. "This is...my fault. If you hadn't come for me—"

"Nix, no." I pull her to sit sideways on my lap, rubbing her back. "Don't even think that. I provoked him. I shot his brother. It's *my* fault."

"You're both wrong," Grim says. "It's *his* fault. He's a psychopath. He killed innocent people and would have killed literally millions more had we not stopped him selling that vaccine on the black market."

Nix looks as unconvinced as I feel, wearing guilt like a badly tailored jacket. It doesn't belong on her.

"Look, I've been doing this shit all my life," Grim says. "In the process of bringing bad guys to justice, bad guys get killed sometimes. Gregory's brother was a bad guy who got what was coming to him, just like this motherfucker will. You don't blame yourself for evil. You fight it, but evil fights back. That's the nature of this thing since the beginning of time."

Lennix finally nods at Grim's philosophical flash, offering him a small, grateful smile, but I can't accept his rationale so quickly. My brother is dead. My sister-in-law is a widow. Her kids are fatherless, and my mother is barely holding on because she lost her son.

"Give me a few minutes to get set up for the trace," Grim says, "and then you need to call him."

"Won't he suspect you're tracing the call?" Lennix asks.

"Oh, yeah. I'm sure it's a burner," Grim says, unpacking items from his bag and setting up a few pieces of electronic equipment. "And he'll toss it as soon as he's done, but we'll know where he is at that moment. It's a start, a crumb we'll pick up until we find another, and we'll keep following till we find this head case. He knows we'll get this information, so he's planning for it already. But he'll slip up and give us something he doesn't mean to. When that happens, we'll grab him."

"I don't like this," Nix says softly, leaning back to look into my eyes. "I don't want you talking to him. Can't we just ignore him?"

"And what?" I ask. "Wait for him to strike again with no idea what he wants, what his plans are, or where he was last? No, we can't do that."

"It's dangerous."

"All of this is dangerous, and it's given that you'll have security now," I tell her, my tone brooking no argument. "That's nonnegotiable."

"Not dangerous for *me*." She pokes her finger in my chest. "I'm worried about you."

"I have security, too, and I'm not afraid of him."

"Oh, and your security is so much better than Owen's was?"

"Frankly, yes," Grim says, frowning and pulling at a small wire. "Because I manage it."

I would laugh at Grim's arrogance if there was anything remotely funny about this situation, which is life and death.

"I wouldn't trust the government with my goldfish," Grim says.

"You have a goldfish?" Lennix asks.

"Theoretically," Grim says, glancing up at her.

"That's a shame," Lennix says. "I was trying to envision you going home to lovingly feed a few betta fish."

"Aren't those the ones that eat each other?" he asks.

"Exactly," Lennix returns.

He rolls his eyes, but one corner of that hard mouth tips up. He's stingy with whole smiles. Half is usually about as much as you'll get.

"I think he likes you," I whisper in her ear.

"How can you tell?" she whispers back.

"He hasn't shot you yet."

I chuckle at her wry look, the sound rusty and unused in my throat. To feel anything other than immense grief seemed impossible when I woke up this morning, rehearsing my brother's eulogy. And I'm nowhere near fine, but having Nix with me makes everything feel a little better. I knew it would.

I sit on the couch alone when I call, Lennix and Grim seated across from me. Grim has a set of headphones on and some sophisticated-looking equipment in front of him to trace the call as best we can.

"What do the police say about all this?" Lennix asks, right before I start dialing.

"We're not exactly telling them yet," Grim says. "But we will after this, under certain conditions. Mainly that they not go telegraphing our every move and generally screwing everything up."

"But we want all the resources involved, right?" Lennix asks.

"We want the resources *we* want involved," I say. "And the ones we don't need to stay the hell out of our way."

Lennix still doesn't look convinced, but we'll have to have this discussion later.

I dial the number. On the fourth ring, he picks up.

"Maxim?" A familiar voice is broadcast in the room. "Is that you, man? I assume so, since no one else has this number."

"It's me." I try to keep my tone clear of the hatred and resentment corroding my insides.

"Sorry. I was in the shower. Wouldn't want to be less then presentable when the cops arrived after you trace this call."

"What do you want?" I ask, ignoring his bait.

"You don't sound surprised to hear from me, which surprises *me*, since you and your Robocop shot me four times and left me to drown."

"Oh, we came after you. We thought you were dead."

"So did I, Cade," he says, with affected wonder. "So did I, but these nice natives helped me when I washed up on shore. Ya know, I find indigenous people to be so kind. It's really a shame how we've treated them. Speaking of, how's my squaw?"

I don't trust myself to answer. Nor do I even look at Lennix, though I feel her gaze riveted to my face. I hazard a glance at Grim, who mouths, *Stay calm. Keep him talking.*

"What do you want, Gregory?"

"Ahh. Look at you, doing your homework. I guess you used my dead brother's DNA to figure out my name, huh?"

"Yeah. That's how we did it."

"It wasn't enough that my mother died because of the shitty systems America calls democracy and capitalism. You had to go and take the one thing I had left worth caring about in this world. My little brother."

"He held a gun to her head. I had no choice."

"And you're so fiercely protective of the ones you love, aren't you, Cade? It must have torn you up inside when someone got to your do-gooder brother."

I swallow a growl, close my eyes, and beg for patience.

"Funeral was today, right? I saw your speech on television. Nothing to fear. Who are you? Fucking Franklin D. Roosevelt? Of course there's shit we should fear. Things *you* should fear. You should fear me."

"I'm not afraid of you, you demented piece of shit."

"Oh, but you should be. Look what happened to poor Owen. I had this entire speech planned," he says, regret in his voice. "You ever seen *Princess Bride*? What am I saying? Everyone's seen that movie, am I right?"

I don't reply but let my rage simmer.

"So I was gonna do the dramatic Inigo Montoya thing," he says, affecting a bad Spanish accent. "You killed my brother. Prepare to die."

He laughs, but it only lasts a few moments before he slides into demonic silence. The tension is a wire at my throat. "I killed your brother, Cade, and I'll kill you, too."

Lennix draws in a sharp breath, but I don't look at her. Even though I suspected it, hearing Gregory's careless confession tears through my gut. Owen's killer is on the other line, and if I could strangle him through this phone right now, I would.

I clamp down my guilt and rage to remain focused on every word he says.

"Did you know our girl was supposed to be in the car with your brother that night?" he asks, his voice soft and malevolent like poisoned butter. "God, I was this close to completely decimating you. I know how you feel about that piece of ass. It was all over your face when you *shot my brother*."

He draws a shallow breath before going on. "When I'm done with you, you'll know how this feels. Mama's gone. Jackson's gone. What do I have left to lose? You thought this wasn't a game, but it totally is. And I'll win. By the way, I get bonus points for the girl."

And he disconnects.

Controlling my movements, I lay the phone down on the table and lean my elbows on my knees. For Nix's sake, I'm trying to keep my shit together when all I want to do is flip furniture and burn the hotel to the ground.

"You did good," Grim says, narrowing his eyes on a small screen. "We got him, but he knew we would. He's at JFK. Probably already tossed that phone and boarding a plane. At least we can start piecing some possibilities together."

"Uh-huh." I steeple my fingers and clench my teeth.

"What are you gonna do about the fact that he wants to kill Maxim?" Lennix asks. I look at her for the first time, and all the rage and emotion I'm holding back burn in her stare. "That son of a bitch. Did you hear him? He wants to kill Maxim, and you're what?" She gestures toward the table where the equipment is laid out. "Fiddling with your little toys? He's at JFK. Go get his ass. Take him out. We have to kill him first."

Grim and I stare at her in silence. I'm unsure how to respond. Grim's hard mouth lifts on that one side. "I like this one. For your information, Rambo, I have operatives in several high-risk locations, one of which is New York. They were listening in and have already dispatched to JFK, though we know it will most likely be too late. A guy like this doesn't play into your hands. He's already three steps ahead. You just have to take what he gives you and keep looking on your own until he trips up and you get him. Maxim's safe."

He glances at me while he puts away the rest of his equipment. "I'm guessing he's more concerned about you."

"You can put security on me," she says, looking at me across the table. "I'll wear the tracker. I'll be fine."

Owen should have been fine. Every aspect of his event was heavily vetted and the details planned weeks in advance. All of the facility staff had been cleared. We're still sorting out how Gregory penetrated the security to plant that bomb. There was one guy, a valet, who had called in sick at the last minute. We're digging into that and hopefully should have an answer soon.

The police and the FBI are working on Owen's case, and we'll have to share some of this with them. I trust very few people right now, so I don't want to widen the circle beyond those we know can be trusted.

"I have an idea," Grim says, "but I'm not sure either of you will go for it."

Lennix crosses over and sits beside me, taking my hand.

"What's the idea?" I ask.

"Wyoming," Grim says simply. "Think about it."

I have a place in Wyoming. Completely isolated, well guarded. Lennix would be safe, but I'm not completely sold.

"I'm not afraid of that bastard," I say harshly. "I'm not running away from him."

"It's not just the safety," Grim argues. "You both have been through a lot these last few months. Costa Rica and all you witnessed there, Lennix. Now, Owen and the emotional toll it's taking. King, you can work from anywhere, and it won't hurt you to slow down for a few weeks. It'll also give us some time to track this son of a bitch."

"I'm in between campaigns," Lennix says, biting her bottom lip and wiping a tear at the corner of her eye. "Now that Owen..." She draws a shaky breath. "I guess I'm saying I wouldn't mind a few weeks away."

That's not playing fair because she knows I'll do anything for her to feel better, to feel safe. Grim knows it, too, judging by the smug look on his stupid face.

I think through the things I'll need to function out of Wyoming for a few weeks. If I have Jin Lei, Wi-Fi, and good bourbon, I think I can make it work.

And Lennix. She's my survival kit. The girl who chases stars has war in her eyes, and she'll need it. The toughest fight of our lives is ahead. The fight to *heal*.

"Okay," I say, squeezing her hand. "Looks like we're going off the grid."

PART 2

"When you know who you are;
when your mission is clear and you burn with the inner fire of
unbreakable will;
no cold can touch your heart;
no deluge can dampen your purpose.
You know that you are alive."
—*Chief Seattle, Suquamish and Duwamish leader*

CHAPTER 32
LENNIX

"Pusillanimous." I glare at the crossword puzzle and clamp an ink pen between my teeth. "It means lacking courage. A sly dig at *pussy*, like we're the ones lacking courage in this world. You know some *man* made that word up."

"Wow," Maxim says, walking a tray over and setting it on the bedside table. "Glad there are no men around because they'd need to cover their private parts."

"Are you saying I don't think of you as a man?" I drop the crossword puzzle and pen to grin up at him from my nest of pillows and luxurious bed linen. "What do you call last night if not sublime copulation between a man and a woman?"

"Keep using these five-dollar words, and I'm taking your crossword puzzles, and yes. Last night was sublime copulation."

He digs one knee into the mattress, leaning over to kiss me. "Good morning, you."

"Good morning, you. What do we have here?"

"For madam." He slides the tray over my legs. "Breakfast in bed."

"Again?" I smile and pick up my tea, blowing off some of the steam before taking a sip. "And you got my tea exactly right. You're spoiling me, Mr. Cade."

"Took some practice, but I'm nothing if not determined, and it's much too early to start with the patriarchy. I thought we agreed no talk of blowing up the patriarchy before noon."

"We said we'd *negotiate*. I didn't agree to that because sometimes the patriarchy needs to be called out."

He settles beside me and plucks a square of mango from a dish. "Well, if pussy… What was the word?"

"Pusillanimous." I say it slower and with more resentment. "I know you have words you don't like."

"Yes, but my hate words are things like *impossible* and *no* and *never*." He opens his mouth for a forkful of my omelet. "Remember the last time you told me never?"

The memory of us banging in the conference room makes its way from my brain to my nether parts. "Not words like *moist* or *panties*?"

He cocks one brow and talks around a bite. "When have I ever objected to moist panties?"

I almost spit out my tea, and we laugh like middle schoolers, sharing our breakfast from the tray. He drinks his unleaded coffee, and I sip my tea. It's one of the rituals we've developed in our three weeks here on his Wyoming ranch.

I'd never been to Wyoming before this trip. It's not exactly a hotly contested swing state or a cornucopia of electoral votes, so in all my travels, it's never been a campaign stop. I'm glad. I've experienced it as it should be—an infinite plain, disturbed only by the rise of mesas, ascendant mountaintops, and sagebrush sprouting from the terrain. Stretches of wilderness, untouched and inhabited only by lazy bison and ambling antelope. Each mile unveils a view more stunning than the next with navy-blue skies and angel-breath clouds tangling around mountain peaks.

When we first arrived, Rick and a full security team trailed us down a long, unpaved road walled in by towering pine trees. It didn't take long to go from private to remote. I worried we'd have no time alone, but when we reached the gate emblazoned with a heavy brass *C*, Maxim and I peeled off.

It was just the two of us driving down the winding road to his place, a sprawling homestead with a front porch embracing the entire house. Wide windows invite the sunlight in. The dark floors gleam, dotted with vibrant knotted rugs.

The sunroom overlooking a creek has become my favorite part of this property I love so much. I run the paths most mornings freely since there's no access other than through the gate and so few people even know this home exists. Some mornings Maxim joins me on my run, but he usually leaves me to it.

I've also started smudging each morning on the sun porch. Mena was right. My ancestors intuitively understood the sacred connection with the land—that it could heal us—and during this time away out here in the middle of nowhere, with the sun and sky for company and the mountains for shelter, I'm recovering. That, along with regular video calls to my therapist, has helped with the flashbacks and residual trauma from Costa Rica.

I am getting better.

And I've smudged every corner of this huge house. Maxim leaned against the wall, arms folded, curiosity and love in his gaze that tracked me walking from room to room waving out the negative energy with my smoky sage.

"What are you thinking about?" he asks, lifting his brows and piercing the last piece of turkey sausage before offering it up to me. I shake my head that I don't want it, and he bites into it.

"This place. How much I love it here." I hesitate and then confess. "Wondering how much longer we can hide out."

"Hide?" He settles back against the pillows and threads our fingers together on the breakfast tray. "Is that what you think we're doing?"

"You're hiding me." I squeeze his fingers until he meets my eyes. "And as much as I've loved it, needed it, I wonder how much longer it can last."

"Don't let Jin Lei hear you say that. She loves it here."

Jin Lei stays in a guest house about a mile away. We see her when she comes once or twice a week to meet with Maxim, giving him papers to sign, updating him on the things he can do from here. I've never known him to stay put this long.

"I love it here, too, but Kimba called yesterday." I run my fingers through his hair, the longest I've seen it in a long time. "She's fielded several calls from candidates asking us to run their campaigns."

"Isn't it a bit late to still be assembling a team?"

"It's only April. Still ten months before Iowa. Plenty of time if you have a foundation."

He stiffens and flicks a narrow glance up at me. "You're considering it."

It sounds like an accusation, and I sigh, bracing for our first argument in three weeks. "How can I not? It's my job, Doc. It's not just me. Kimba's my business partner. I can't ask her to sit idle while I do whatever we're doing."

"Whatever we're doing." He huffs a truncated laugh, tosses the down comforter back, and climbs out of bed. "I'm sorry you're getting bored with 'whatever we're doing.'"

"You know I'm not bored, but some of the candidates Kimba mentioned might have a shot if we help them, and Senator Middleton's position grows stronger every day. He's the front-runner for the Republicans. If there's anything I can do to keep that mongrel thief out of the Oval, I have to try."

Maxim nods but turns his back to me. The sleeping pants cling to the muscled curves of his ass and long legs. He links his fingers behind his head, burying them in the dark strands of his hair. The wide plateau of his back tightens with the movement but also with new tension.

He strides out to the balcony off the bedroom. Diaphanous curtains billow back and forth, in and out with the breeze. I slip a heavy silk robe over my nightgown and grab his Berkeley hoodie from the bench at the foot of our bed.

Our bed. *Our* place. *Our* life here.

It's the first time we've ever been in the same place this long, and it does feel like we actually share a life. I don't want it to end, but we can't hunker down here forever just in case Gregory Keene decides he wants to try something.

"Hey." I walk up beside him on the balcony and proffer the sweatshirt. "It's cool out here."

He grunts but accepts the hoodie and slides it over his head. It rumples his hair even more, and wearing the Berkeley sweatshirt, he looks so unlike the businessman the world knows. He looks more like he did the day we met when he was still a master's student.

"You're mad?" I ask after a few moments of silence.

Exasperation edges his sigh. "What did Kimba say?" His eyes narrow on my twitching lips. "Oh, God. Do I even want to know?"

My best friend has a way of making even the darkest times a tad brighter. "She said she knows we're in mourning and having lots of grief sex."

"Wow. That's appropriate."

"But she asked when I'll be emerging from what she calls the 'cry hump' stage of grief."

"Cry hump?" He chokes a little on his chuckle. "Like—"

"Like dry hump, yeah, but with tears, according to her definition." I pause. "When did you last speak to Millie?"

He sighs heavily, his shoulders drooping a little like they're carrying Millie's grief. I know in some ways they are and he does.

"A few days ago, briefly. I could tell she didn't want to talk. She and the twins are staying with her parents in Connecticut. I told her I'd come see them soon."

He leans his elbows on the rail and scans the horizon, rolled out like a vibrant mural splattered with teal, chartreuse, forest green, and turquoise—a painter's dream. We've learned each other differently, deeper here, and I understand his reluctance to leave it. Beyond this ranch, there are danger and cynicism and the demands of a crumbling world. Here, he's my only focus, and I'm his.

It's just us.

The world belongs to us, and we have the sky to ourselves, but I know we can't stay here forever.

"I'm sorry for my initial response," he says. "Of course I know we have to go back at some point. I've actually been doing a lot of soul searching these last three weeks about what I want to do when we return."

"Meaning?"

"I'll still run my business, of course," he says. "But I've been wondering about Owen's legacy, trying to figure out how I keep it alive, extend it."

"What are you considering? Like a scholarship fund? Something that supports one of his causes?"

"You know…" He chuckles, shakes his head. "For the first time in a long time, I don't know what to do next, but you said something when we were in Amsterdam."

"Talk about a throwback. Which of the many brilliant things I said do you mean?"

He rolls his eyes but caresses the skin at my wrist. "You said you felt like a missile ready to fire with no launch codes."

Hearing my own words in my ears again, I remember how that felt. That girl was so earnest and naive and young and principled in a way I'm not sure I can ever be again. Not like that. Those words sprung from untried convictions. The purity of idealism untouched by compromise. I still know what I believe, but I've learned what it takes to not only fight my battles but win as many of them as possible.

And I've learned every battle isn't worth fighting.

Maxim's phone buzzes in the pocket of his sleep pants, and he answers. After listening for a few seconds and issuing monosyllabic responses, he disconnects the call. Blowing out a long breath, he slides the phone back into his pocket, a frown plastering his handsome features.

"What is it?" I ask, my shoulders and back exercising muscle memory, tightening with concern like they haven't the past three weeks.

"Not what. Who."

"Then who?"

He stares back at me like he's resigned to this world slipping away from us. "It's my father."

CHAPTER 33
MAXIM

I SHOULDN'T BE SURPRISED BY NOW, BUT I AM. OWEN ALWAYS USED to say our father knew where we were at all times.

You called it, O.

I seem to talk to Owen more now than I did when he was alive, entire conversations I probably would never have initiated. Now, after Lennix, he's the first person I want to share things with.

"I'll be back," I tell Lennix, leaving the balcony and heading into our bedroom.

"Is that your way of telling me not to come down?" she asks softly, following me.

"No, that's my way of trying to spare us all a battle royale. If you want to see my father that badly, you can, of course."

"It's not that."

I stride back to her, tilt her chin up. "I'm always fine with anyone knowing you're with me. You're what I'm proudest of, Nix."

I mean it. She probably doesn't believe me, but earning the love of this woman is the greatest thing I've ever done, and I want to keep doing it for the rest of my life.

I drop a quick kiss in her hair. "I better get down there to see what my dad wants."

I bound down the stairs, automatically pulling my armor in place. My father and I haven't actually been at odds since we argued about Lennix at Christmas, but we haven't been around each other. The week of the funeral, by tacit agreement we called a cease-fire, both wanting to support Mom and Millie and honestly needing the support of each other. Owen's only been gone a month, and though I've spoken to my mother regularly, checking on her at least a few times a week, this will be my first contact with my father.

And it's a sneak attack from him.

When I reach the bottom of the stairs, he stands in the middle of the living room, scowling at Rick.

"I didn't ask for or need an escort," he says, his deep voice like a mallet crushing the words over Rick's head. "He's my son."

Even when we've been estranged for a decade and a half, there's always a certain possessiveness to my father's voice, always has been when he spoke of Owen and me.

"Rick's simply doing his job, Dad." I walk closer and smile at Rick.

"I won't need an escort back either," Dad says.

"It's a big property," I say, trying not to be annoyed. "Rick's just helping."

"Well, you can go," he tells Rick.

Except Rick works for me. He looks to me, brows lifted, silently asking to be released. I nod and wait for him to leave. I sit, gesturing to the collection of couches and recliners in the middle of the room.

"Have a seat. Everything okay? Mom all right?"

"She's doing as well as can be expected." He sits, seeming to hesitate before going on. "Thank you for calling so often. It's been helping her."

"I wish I could say I've spoken to Millie as much, but she rarely answers her phone."

"She's lost the man she loves," my father says, his voice uncharacteristically pensive. "If I lost your mother, I wouldn't want to talk much to anyone for a long time either."

I know he loves Mom, but he hasn't said it often. I stare at him, searching out any other discernable differences between this more subdued man and the ruthless tyrant I've known all my life.

"Any more leads on Keene?" Dad asks, his tone soft but dangerous.

I had to share what we knew with my parents and Millie so they could be on high alert in case Gregory tried to get to me through any of my other family members. Millie was quiet when I told her. She didn't scream or weep. No accusations, which I would have welcomed like a scourge on my back. Just that silence, goodbye, and the *click* when she hung up. She must hate me. There are so many mornings I wake up and the first thing I think about is my brother being dead because of me, and I hate myself, too.

"No," I answer my father's question. "He's lying low, but he'll pop up when we least expect it."

"I want that bastard to get the death penalty."

"Oh, he'll get what's coming to him." I don't mention that I don't intend to hand over the privilege of punishing him to anyone else. They'll find him criminally insane, which is probably true, and he'll live a nice, comfortable life in some asylum, or they'll bungle it some other way. I don't have time or tolerance for all the ways our system screws up justice.

Dad searches my face, his eyes narrowed and his mouth tight before nodding.

"What's going on?" I ask, shifting from Gregory, my new least-favorite word and subject. "I didn't even think you knew about this place. What made you fly all the way out here?"

His stare is a laser. "Several well-placed people have approached me over the last month about you running."

"Running where?"

"Not where, son. For what. Running for president."

I laugh outright and lean forward. "And you flew all the way out here to, what? Have a good laugh?"

"You don't think you could do the job?"

My humor dries up. I hate that he knows how I respond to challenges and knows just which buttons to push. When someone intimates I can't do something, I immediately want to prove them wrong. That was how I broke my arm in third grade. Owen said I couldn't fly.

Right again, O.

But that two-second hang time before I crashed was glorious.

"Not interested," I say instead of what my father wanted to hear.

"You're telling me the job for the most powerful office in the world is open and you don't even want to apply?"

"I'm not convinced it's the most powerful office in the world anymore."

"Look, you want to do good, want to change the world or whatever, this is how you do it. Can't you see that?"

"Owen was a rare politician, Dad. Most of them are so hamstrung by party rules and keeping the ones who scratch their backs happy, they can't do the things people actually elected them to do."

"Then be different. Change things. The men who want you to run are powerful enough to deliver the nomination."

"If I did run, I wouldn't need anyone to *deliver* anything to me. I'd deliver on my own."

Something sparks in my father's eyes. I've seen it when he talked about Owen, but it's been a long time since I've seen it in his eyes for me. *Pride.*

"And I assume you're talking about guys like Chuck Garrett," I say.

"Garrett was one of the first who approached me, yes."

"Why would the head of the DNC want me to run when I've told anyone who'd listen I'm independent, not a Democrat?"

"Maybe he's hoping to change your mind."

"About the two-party system? In one conversation? Wow, check out the balls on Chuck."

"If you decide to run, aligning with the Dems might be your best bet, and Chuck is the road to the party. There's a real chance here,

Maxim. I would never want to trade on Owen's death, but you're in a unique situation."

"I think I'll vomit if you say another word, Dad," I tell him, my jaw so tight it hurts.

"Listen to me, and not with that soft heart you got from your mama. Listen to me with all the parts you got from *me*. There is a window, and if we don't strike now, it will close. Iowa is in ten months. That's no time in the election cycle. Candidates are preparing for debate season, introducing themselves to the American people, but you don't need an introduction. People already know you, and that speech you gave at Owen's funeral has gone viral."

"Dancing cats go viral. Excuse me for not trusting a million hits on YouTube to dictate my future."

"*Millions,*" Dad amends. "While you've been licking your wounds and hiding in these hills—"

"I'm not hiding."

"Whatever. You're not out there. People believed in Owen. They don't see any other candidate who makes them feel that way, who makes them *believe* that way. They've started petitions to get your name on the ballot."

"What?"

"There's a group of independents who have organized something called the Cade Ballot Access Committee."

"What?" I can't seem to find another word to say.

"It's a complicated process, getting onto the ballot, especially when you're not affiliated with a party. You have to go state by state to get on, and every state has its own rules. Some of them require a helluva lot of signatures. This group has teams in every state collecting signatures so they'll be ready when you decide to run."

"And this is separate from Chuck?"

"Yes. Chuck wants you to run for the Democrats. Is that such a stretch? You were a surrogate for Owen."

"That's the point. The *person* I believed in happened to be a

Democrat. Parties prescribe too much, try to strip you of what you believe for the sake of making others believe in you. That's not me."

"The call for you to run, the speculation that you might, is out there. You could still mobilize and have enough of an organization to be ready for Iowa."

This is an echo of the conversation I had with Lennix before my father arrived, but we were discussing *her* diving back in to manage someone else's campaign.

Would she manage mine?

Is this even a possibility? Do I want it to be?

Something stirs in me. I don't know if it's my own ruthless ambition or if it's the optimism Owen brought back to my life—the restlessness I've been unable to place or articulate. I meant what I said in the eulogy. Owen *did* make me believe again. He made me want to be a part of some solution to a world that is broken and fractured in ways that hurt the weakest, the poorest, most.

You really think you can convince a nation to change its ways? And the answer is always yes.

My own voice from another lifetime, from that first night with Lennix, haunts me.

Is the answer still yes?

Even as I ask myself the question, the pain of that phone call when I found out about Owen slams into my chest with fresh impact. I *have* been hiding, but not hiding myself. Hiding Lennix. I wouldn't live through losing her, and risking her on the campaign trail while that psychopath is still on the loose? I couldn't. I can't.

There's my answer.

"I came so you can at least consider it," Dad says, standing. "Let me know your answer."

"Answer to what?" Lennix asks from the top of the stairs. "What's the question?"

CHAPTER 34
LENNIX

"Ahh." Warren Cade looks up at me, his eyes cooling, hardening into volcanic glass. "Ms. Hunter. Never too far away, are you?"

He makes me sound like some grasping whore following his son around from place to place.

"Mr. Cade." That's the only greeting I can offer that's neutral and authentic as I take the stairs down to join them. *Nice to see you* would be a lie. I think even *hello* would smack of phoniness "I repeat, what's the question you came here to ask Maxim?"

"I'm not sure it's any of your business."

I'll let Maxim address that.

He meets me at the stairs and leads me by the hand to where his father stands. "It's very much her business, Dad," he says, frowning. "I wouldn't make a decision this important without consulting the woman I love."

"Damn your mama's heart," Warren mutters. "Power has nothing to do with love, Maxim."

"You're wrong, Dad. You think I'd consider this because of the power it would give me, but the power I *have* could help the country I love. I'm not running, though, so it's a moot point."

"Running?" I ask. "What run? What are you talking about?"

"There's a great deal of interest in Maxim running for president," Warren says.

His words don't sink in right away. It takes my mind a few seconds to process them.

"I've already told him no," Maxim says.

"Don't be hasty." Warren runs a scathing glance over my perfectly presentable wrap dress and ballet flats. You'd think I was dressed like a stripper the way he looks at me so disdainfully. "And don't listen to her."

"I think you should consider it," I tell Maxim.

Two dark heads swivel, and both men stare at me.

"Listen to her, son," Warren says, a smile stretching across his distinguished features. "The girl knows what she's talking about."

I twist my lips scornfully. "This isn't about furthering your agenda, Mr. Cade."

"Then what is it about exactly?" Maxim asks, a frown sketched between his brows.

"For one thing," I say, "the Dems probably have no one who can actually beat Senator Middleton." I slide a contemptuous look toward his father. "And we both know *his* history of partnering with corporations to steal protected lands in addition to many other of his policies that hurt marginalized people."

"Well, I'm glad that after all these years," Warren says, ignoring my not-so-subtle dig, "we finally agree on something. I appreciate your assistance persuading my son to see sense."

"I'm not doing this for you," I say, glaring at him. "It's for Owen. For the people."

I grab Maxim's hand and look into his eyes, blocking out his father's manipulative presence. "For you, Doc. What if this is your launch code?"

A muscle in Maxim's jaw clenches, and he shakes his head. "Then there is no launch because I won't risk you."

"Launch?" Warren asks. "What are you talking about?"

"I'm not staying here while some thief takes the Oval," I say, ignoring Warren's question. "Do you want Middleton to win by default while we hide?"

"And you think you can fix it?" Maxim demands.

"I have to try."

"No." His tone is implacable, but the fear in his eyes is evident. I know it's for me, not for himself. "Crowds? Rallies? Public speeches? A dozen chances, a hundred ways every day for that lunatic to kill you? No. We can't do it."

"You can't stop me."

"Lennix," he says, his voice a warning I have no intention of heeding. "Gregory Keene killed my brother, and you were supposed to be in that car. I've almost lost you twice to this bastard. You think I'll risk losing you again by running for the most high-profile job on Earth in a never-ending public interview process? No."

"Look, I told you I'll accept the security *and* wear the tracker."

"Not until he's caught," Maxim says, frowning.

"So indefinitely? We'll stay here even if he doesn't surface for the next year, two years, three? Another four years while some douchebag is president?"

"Grim has leads."

"Fuck Grim's leads. I will not stay in hiding while my country falls apart."

"Falls apart is a little dramatic," Warren inserts. "Middleton's not that bad, but Maxim is what this country needs."

"Don't you mean what *you* need?" I turn a questioning brow on him. "What's your agenda in all this?"

"I simply believe Maxim's the best man for the job," Warren says, shifting his glance to his son, "and the job is *now*. There's an appetite for your vision and leadership."

"Don't think if he *does* decide to run you'll be pulling his strings. If you want a Cade for your schemes, find yourself another one." I position myself between the two men, pressing my back into Maxim's hard chest and glaring up at his father. "This one you can't have."

CHAPTER 35
MAXIM

My father's head may explode. His will and possessiveness collide with Lennix's, and neither one backs down. He glares at her, red crawling up his neck.

"Dad, if you keep looking at her like that," I say, my voice soft but absolutely serious, "we're going to have a problem."

He flips his heated gaze up to me, and it cools by slow degrees. He's not used to being defied, and he and Lennix have a long history of disliking each other.

"Maybe you should leave so Lennix and I can discuss this?"

"You'd let *her* affect the most important decision of your life?" he spits.

I cup the curve of her neck, caressing the raging, pounding pulse there, reassuring her. "Nix is the most important decision of my life, and you're not helping your case by antagonizing her."

I pause, for the first time noting the toll Owen's death has taken on him. His face is now mine in thirty years, not twenty. He's thinner, more drawn. He's lost a lot, and something in me wants to reassure him, too. "I'll always choose her, but I want to choose you, too."

Lennix looks up over her shoulder at me, her eyes questioning, slightly uncertain. I squeeze her shoulder.

"I want to be able to choose you both. Dad, we lost Owen. We've lost the last fifteen years. I'd prefer we not lose anymore, but you can't hurt Nix. You can't threaten or insult her. You accept her, or there won't be a place in my life for you at all."

My father and I stare, mirroring each other's will and determination. I've always believed I was so much like him, been afraid of it, but he's not evil. Gregory Keene is evil. My father is privileged and arrogant and sometimes misguided, but he's the only father I have, and I want a relationship with him. Sometimes loving your family is awkward and hard, especially when you don't believe the same things, don't choose the same paths, but losing Owen has blown a gaping hole in my life where my family should be. He wanted Dad and me to reconcile, and so do I.

"Do we understand each other?" I ask him, kissing the top of Lennix's head.

He shifts his stare from me to her, and he draws a deep breath. "Yes." He turns and strides toward the door. "I'd like your answer by the end of the week."

And then he's gone.

CHAPTER 36
LENNIX

"Lennix, no."

Maxim throws the words down, a gauntlet. A challenge, not a choice.

He sits on the arm of the couch and draws me to stand between his legs.

I rest my hands on his shoulders. "I'm not afraid of Gregory Keene."

"I am," he says, his eyes pained. "How can I not be? Not for myself, but for you. Baby, this man killed my brother. He almost killed you. A campaign run right now tempts the devil."

"Let him come. Look, I get it. I'm scared for you, too. God, I am, but we can't hide forever. Grim will make sure you're impossible to get to. And you can wrap me in cotton. Give me a dozen security guards. Load me down with diamond-crusted geotrackers. I don't care, but don't let this opportunity pass you by." I frame his face between my hands and look into his eyes. "I'm going to ask you one question, and I want you to answer absolutely honestly."

He hesitates then nods.

"Is there any part of you that gets excited at the prospect of leading this country?"

He doesn't nod, but that telltale flare of passion and ambition I noticed our first night together brightens his eyes.

"Do you believe you could do it?" I ask. "If safety weren't an issue, would you want to?"

"That's three questions."

"You haven't responded to any of them." I lean down to whisper in his ear. "Because you know the answer is yes."

He drops his gaze to our feet, a dark fan of lashes casting shadows under his eyes. I slip my hand in the pocket of his sleep pants and pull out his phone.

"I want you to watch something with me." I turn, slotting my hips between his legs as he sits on the arm of the couch, pressing my shoulders into the chiseled warmth of his chest. I search on his phone's browser until I find the video, slide the progress bar, and press play.

"Someone, the person who killed my brother, thinks we should be afraid." Maxim says on the video, pain and passion etched onto his striking features. "I'm not afraid. Don't you be afraid either. You know what scares me? Cynicism. Apathy. Anything that convinces people to settle, to quit. The thought that people will give up on changing this world because of one person's cruel cowardice makes my blood run cold. I would have given up on the system, the way things work, long ago had it not been for Owen. He renewed my faith in the process by which we change things in this country."

"Jesus, Nix." Maxim grabs the phone and presses the arrow to stop the video. He holds me from behind, his chin tucked into the curve of my neck. "I can't watch that."

I fold my hands over his, holding the phone against my stomach, and wait for him to elaborate.

"That was the hardest day of my life," he continues quietly. "I believe those words. When I hear that, I want to do everything that guy on the video tells me I should."

I turn my head, angling so I can look up at him over my shoulder. "But?"

"But then I imagine having to say those words for you." His

breaths come short and ragged in my hair. "Do you think I'll care if this country goes to hell if you're gone?"

"Oh, Doc." I turn and look up at him, moved by the intensity of his eyes on my face. They're starved. They consume. Has a man ever looked at a woman the way Maxim looks at me? "I've got my own throwback for you."

The uncompromising line of his mouth gentles. "Yeah? What?"

"You once told me it's the dreamers who change the world the most—that something about the present wasn't good enough, so they made the future."

He grimaces and drops his head back, studying the ceiling.

"Hell, Nix," he groans, snapping his gaze back to mine. "You'd accept the security?"

"I told you I would. Every bit of it. Mall cops, K-9 units, special ops, whatever."

"So this was all it took to get you compliant, huh?" he asks, a slow smile softening the hard planes of his face.

"We'll see who's compliant when we get out on the campaign trail." I laugh, reaching around to lightly slap his butt. "And I'm running that ass. You might be the candidate, but I'm the boss."

"*If* I decide to do this, that's one thing I could look forward to." He slides his hands down to cup my bottom. "Screwing my campaign manager."

"Yeah, about that." I bite my lip and squeeze my eyes shut because this point alone could undo all the progress we just made. "I don't fuck my candidates."

He throws his head back, his laughter rich all around me. "Okay, if I run, we'll see how long that lasts."

"I'm serious." I let it sink in and watch the humor drain from his expression.

"You're saying if I run, we can't be together?"

"I'm saying the same issue I had when Owen was running would be even *more* of an issue if you *are* the actual candidate."

He runs his hands down my arms and links our fingers, bending to whisper in my ear, brushing the words over my earlobe. "If I'm your candidate, you think you'd be able to *not* fuck me?"

I lick my lips and pull a few inches back to look him in the eyes. "I *never* fuck my candidates."

His eyes go hot when I deliberately use one of his least-favorite words. He stands from the arm of the chair, flips our positions, and hoists me to sit there. He pushes the panels of my wrap-around dress apart. Carefully, not breaking eye contact with me, he nudges my legs open.

"I think you might make an exception for me," he says, his hand disappearing under the fabric, two fingers sinking into the hot, intimate wetness between my legs. My breath whooshes out, and I want to sit still, unmoved, but his thumb caresses my clit while his middle and index finger fuck me. It only takes seconds for my hips to start churning. He twines my hair around his hand, his fingers working in and out of me, and holds me still for a ravaging kiss, his mouth devouring mine, eating my whimpers and moans.

He pulls back, the forest green of his eyes swallowed by midnight at the centers. "Ask me to fuck you, Nix."

I steel myself against the overwhelming appeal of his body and his desire for me. His cock is hard and ready against my thigh. "No."

The right side of his full mouth tips up into a "so it's like that" grin, and he sinks to his knees, presses my legs wider, pushes the dress up, and pulls my panties down and off. He grabs my ass with both hands and presses his face into my pussy, sucking my clit hard.

"Oh, God." My fingers claw into his hair, and I try to press his mouth harder into me. He resists, flicking a long-lashed stare up at me, his dark hair disrupted by my fingers.

"Ask me to fuck you."

"No." I spread my legs wider, turning the temptation back on him. He closes his eyes and draws in a deep breath.

"Dammit, the smell of you is everything, Nix."

He's so beautiful, kneeling between my knees, and he loves me. He told his father that he chooses me over him, over everything. Beneath my confidence, my bravado, I'm scared to death for him, for us. A campaign is never easy, and if Maxim decides to run, he will face more challenges than most. My greatest fears and the most incredible possibilities tangle. I don't get to choose one without getting the other. Right now, all I can choose is this. All I can choose is him.

"Fuck me, Maxim."

He's up and has me turned around and bent over the arm of the couch in seconds. Cool air kisses my ass when he guides the dress up. His first hard thrust pushes me up onto my tiptoes. His hand at the base of my spine presses me deeper into the couch, holds me in place for the aggressive thrust of his body into mine.

"Nix," he grunts behind me. "Your pussy is…"

He bends me over farther, pushes the gown higher until the hem spills around my ears, sinking in deeper.

"That's it," he groans. "God, yes. Can you touch yourself?"

I nod frantically, so close to orgasm I know it won't take much. I widen my legs and touch myself. My clit is swollen, and the insides of my thighs are wet.

"No matter what happens," he says, tracing up my rib cage to cup my breast, "it's just us, Lennix. Don't forget this. Don't forget us."

And then I'm coming and I'm sobbing, one hand between my legs and one hand gripping the couch. I don't know if my tears are because this pleasure, this feeling is so far beyond anything I've ever known or could imagine with anyone else or because in the days to come, for what's ahead, I'm not sure it will be enough.

CHAPTER 37
MAXIM

CHUCK GARRETT, CHAIR OF THE DEMOCRATIC NATIONAL
Committee, is one of those guys who will always be the manager,
never the rock star. He must instinctively know, and rightfully so,
that he doesn't have what it takes to win a national election, but he
takes pride in holding sway over who *does* win. Right now, he's in my
office thinking he holds some kind of sway over me.

He's mistaken.

I'm only meeting with him because when the competition leans
forward at the card table, you look at his hand. I still have reserva-
tions about Lennix's safety, but Grim assures me he's on it. I haven't
officially declared my run, but I'm close, and if I do, Chuck's guy will
be on the ballot.

"We could have met at Bourbon Steak," he says, settling into the
chair on the other side of my desk. "They do a superb filet mignon.
Responsibly sourced. I know that's your thing."

"My thing?" I chuckle. "I guess it is. Well, I thought meeting
at the Four Seasons on Pennsylvania Avenue, no less, with the
DNC chair would send a very loud, public message that could be
premature."

"Premature? You have some strong early support. Being seen
with me could send an early sign of power for you."

"You think I need to borrow power from you?" I ask.

He stiffens, a frown pushing the wrinkles of his forehead into irritated folds. "Not exactly borrow, but we both know you have no experience, so maybe it would ease some worry about your leadership."

I don't mean to laugh; it just happens. "*You* would do that for *me?*" The man's party is in shambles, and they barely listen to him, so surely he doesn't expect me to.

"You don't even have to ask." He waves a hand, misunderstanding me. "I'd be more than willing to, for the sake of the party."

"That is practically magnanimous, Chuck. It really is."

Jin Lei knocks briefly then pokes her head in. "They're here."

"Oh, good. Show them in."

Chuck twists his head around to look at the door. "They?"

"Hunter, Allen and Associates did such a great job for Owen, I thought it would be smart to bring them in as I'm deciding if I want to run."

"If you don't mind me saying so"—Chuck leans forward and lowers his voice—"those ladies are troublemakers sometimes."

"I actually do mind you saying so, and it's what I like about them most." I give him a hard look as Kimba and Lennix enter. "Ladies, hi. Thanks for coming."

Lennix and Kimba take a seat on either side of Chuck, both crossing their legs and folding their arms over their chests.

"I was thinking that we, uh, would get some time alone," Chuck says, glancing from one woman to the other. "To discuss next steps."

"Yes, well, as you mentioned, I'm so inexperienced and lack any real leadership, so having these experts involved is very helpful to a novice like me."

Kimba snorts. Her eyes twinkle at me across the desk. Lennix, however, has barely looked at me since she entered. I know she doesn't want anyone to think we're romantically involved, but hell.

"What are we here to discuss exactly, Chuck?" Kimba asks.

"There's a lot of buzz about Maxim running for president."

"We're aware," Lennix says.

"And I want to talk to him about being the Democratic nominee."

"If I'm not mistaken," Kimba says, "we have a nomination process for that. Starts with Iowa and goes through all the states. Maybe you've heard of it?"

"Yes, that is the formal process, of course," Chuck says, "but we all know that if I back Maxim—"

"Then you control me?" I ask. "Good luck with that."

"Not control, per se," he says. "Guide. A young man such as yourself with so little experience will need some more seasoned players to ease the public's concerns." He shrugs, studies his fingernails. "I could even join the ticket as VP. Our combination of youth and wisdom may be exactly what this country needs."

"Backroom deals won't decide the next president," Lennix says. "The people will. Do you have anything else for us to hear besides your backhanded compliments and posturing?"

His mouth drops open and snaps closed like a turtle's. "You need me. If you think you'll make it far without the party's backing, you're wrong. And if you want Middleton to win, then run. You'll only peel off support from the Democratic nominee and you'll *both* lose to Middleton."

"Last I checked," Kimba says, "about 29 percent of Americans identify as Democrats."

"And about 27 percent as Republicans," Lennix adds.

"And how many say they're independent, Lenn?" Kimba asks.

"Wow. It's like 42 percent."

"Wow. That's a lot."

"But they vote blue or red, even if they're independent," Chuck reminds them smugly.

"That's because they haven't had a viable independent option," Lennix says. "And I think Maxim Cade is more than viable. Did you see the poll today in *The Times*?"

Chuck turns red and smooths his tie.

"He may have missed it," Kimba says. "Let's help him. The poll put Maxim up against Republican and Democratic candidates."

"He won a majority in each scenario," Lennix says coolly. "Even against Middleton. Now, it was a very narrow margin, of course, but that is with mere speculation since Maxim hasn't officially announced his candidacy. We haven't even started working."

"Right now, believe it or not," Kimba says, "we have the advantage."

"I disagree." Chuck laughs. "The idea of an independent winning a presidential election isn't something most Americans can even wrap their heads around, so they'll do what they've always done. Vote red or blue."

"I beg to differ." I speak up for the first time in minutes, since Kimba and Lennix were doing such a great job. "I'm sure you know what the Overton window is, right? We talk a lot about it in business. I know you don't think that's acceptable experience, but having someone who runs a profit-bearing international enterprise might come in handy for an entity, America in this case, carrying over twenty trillion dollars in debt."

"The concept," Kimba says patiently, "is that you outline the range of possible opinions on any given issue."

"In this case," Lennix says, "could an independent candidate win a presidential election?"

"There will be a range of opinions from impossible to acceptable," I add. "Or something that's popular becoming policy, eventually a majority believing it should be the norm."

"If Maxim decides to run as an independent," Kimba says, "that's what we'll do. Our job will be to move the idea of a viable independent candidate from unthinkable to acceptable to the norm."

"Dare we say, even popular." Lennix winks. "The country is primed for something new and so desperate for change and answers that Americans are open to new things. Maxim could be that new thing. Again, if, and that's a big *if*, he decides to run. We believe he's uniquely positioned to shift the window of what is the norm in American politics."

"He could barely stay on message in the few weeks he was surrogate for his own brother," Chuck says, "and couldn't be bothered to move center to align with Owen's position."

"You mean with the party's position, right?" I ask. "And be careful speaking about my brother, Chuck, in case you say the wrong thing and make an enemy of me and I have to destroy you. I hate it when that happens."

There's pin-drop silence for a few seconds before Chuck dives in. "Uh, no, I wasn't saying…of course, respectfully. Um, rest in peace. I was just saying—"

"I know what you were saying," Lennix interjects. "But apparently, Americans liked that Maxim didn't abandon his opinions to align with a party platform. That he wasn't afraid to say when he and his brother didn't agree on something. They appreciated his honesty and authenticity."

"Now could you tell me again," Kimba says, lifting one brow, "why we need you, Chuck?"

"I actually emailed some of my initial thoughts about strategy to you, Maxim," Chuck says.

"We read those." Kimba sighs. "And you wonder why the Dems lost the last election."

"*Excuse* me?" Chuck asks, obviously affronted.

"Where'd you find those strategies, Chuck?" Lennix asks. "The Smithsonian? In addition to your assessment of how to present a candidate like Maxim being all wrong, it's archaic. There's not one modern thing about it."

"Let me guess. You know exactly what he should do." Chuck sneers.

"Maxim is a breath of fresh fucking air," Lennix says, her jaw set and her nostrils flaring. "A bellwether leader who sees the future like it's today and calculates how to get from A to Z before men like you can even start the math. You run him as a rebel—not as the experienced one, but the *smart* one. The one who won't rely on what he's already learned because he understands that in such a quickly changing trajectory, in a month that might not work anymore. You want someone who learns at the speed of light. You tell Americans that in these perilous times, they don't need the safe choice. They need someone who's not afraid.

"I understand you not knowing what to do with Maxim because you've never encountered anyone like him before," she says, looking at me for the first time, that one glance declaring that she loves me and believes every word. "Neither have I."

CHAPTER 38
LENNIX

"Well, that was fun," Kimba says, standing once Chuck has hightailed it out of Maxim's office.

"Watching the two of you is a master class." Maxim chuckles, leaning back in his seat. "If he's not scared of facing me, he's certainly scared of facing the two of you."

"And will he be?" Kimba asks, leaning against the desk. "Facing you? When will you make your final decision? If we're going to do this, we need to start organizing, and fast."

"We'd inherit the basic structure from Owen's campaign," I say. "And some of the team will come back on board if they haven't already found new jobs with other campaigns."

"And it's a huge help that those independents did the grass-roots organization on ballot access for you," Kimba says. "I reached out to the representative and asked how close they are to being done. They're already about 70 percent there. Signatures were easy, especially after that speech you gave."

"It feels grimy that the things I said at my brother's eulogy spurred all of this," Maxim says.

"Not really," I tell him. "You challenged people not to be afraid. To not let what happened stop them from doing what Owen would have wanted."

We both know if it were up to Maxim, we would totally be

allowing fear to stop us. I'm scared, too, for that matter, but there comes a point where your need to act outweighs the fear of what happens when you do. We're at risk. If he does this, my job will be to make sure Maxim has the best chance of winning. Grim's job will be to keep us safe.

And my privilege is to love Maxim no matter what.

"Well, I'm going to zip back to the office," Kimba says, pausing. "There is one thing we need to discuss if you do this and Hunter, Allen and Associates takes you on."

"What's that?" Maxim asks.

"We don't fuck our candidates," she says. "That has been our policy from the beginning, and it's one of the things we're known for and have built our reputation on. Now, when it was Owen running, I think Lennix could have gotten away with your relationship being public. Not ideal, but we could weather that. If you are the actual candidate, she's right. Women have it hard enough without people assuming every time we get near a candidate we want to screw our way to the top of the ballot, if you know what I mean."

Maxim's expression is hard and flat, the face of a cliff. "I don't think—"

"Here are your options," Kimba cuts in. "Option number one: Lennix does not work with your campaign."

"No way," I pipe in. "If he's running, I'm on the ship."

"Right." Kimba nods. "Option number two: You put your relationship on hold for the duration of the campaign."

"The hell we're doing that," Maxim snaps. "No one can expect a man to love his country *that* much."

I cover my burning face, but Kimba laughs, shooting me a lascivious grin. "That's what I thought. So it's option number three."

She sobers and opens the door. "Discretion. I'm serious. You haven't been out together much, so I can see how you've kept it from the press these few months. We're talking a year. Can you keep it from the public and from our team for a year? Because if one of us starts breaking the rules, that's the beginning of chaos. This is my company, too. My reputation, too." She waves her finger between the two of us. "Y'all ain't about to ruin my reputation because Maxim can't keep his dick in his pants."

"Me?" Maxim points to me. "What about her? She wants it all the time. I'm telling you. I can barely keep her satisfied."

Dead. I'm mortified, and anything I say next will be communicated from the afterlife. This whole conversation just became a séance.

My absolute embarrassment must be slathered all over my face because the two of them lose it laughing when they look at me. Kimba fist-bumps Maxim.

"Now that was pretty good. I gotta give it to you." She stops laughing abruptly and swivels a warning stare between the two of us. "But for real, though. Discretion. None of us can afford the scandal."

Once the door closes behind her, Maxim walks over to stand in front of me and pulls me to my feet. I push at his chest, putting space between us.

"She's serious, Doc, and so am I. You can't stay at my apartment anymore, even using the rear entrance. No more sex every day."

He angles a wry look at me because, really. We rarely only have sex once a day.

"Okay, no more sex two times a day. I know it's unrealistic to think we'll never…slip up. That's why Kimba gave us that option, but we can't abuse it."

"So when do you see us making love?"

"Not often and only under very special circumstances."

"You mean like Tuesdays?"

"Be serious. I don't want to be that cliché—the campaign affair." I close my eyes and shake my head. "The candidate and his piece of ass on the trail."

"Piece of ass?" His hands skim the curves of my butt before sliding back up to my waist. "People can be in love and be in politics. *We're* in love. I'm yours. It's not tawdry."

I reach up to bracket his handsome face with its hard angles and rugged symmetry. "And I'm yours. We know that, but it's about perception at this point. Kimba and I can't afford the damage it would do to our reputation, and once you're a candidate, neither could you."

After a second, he nods. "Well, this is all immaterial if I don't run."

"But you want to, don't you?" I ask, searching his eyes and catching that spark of excitement that's getting harder for him to hide. "I can see it starting to make sense to you."

"It's complicated." He shrugs. "As a preliminary measure, I've had my lawyers start seeing how it would affect my business interests."

"You'd have to form a trust and appoint other people to run CadeCo—be completely hands off if you won."

"It's a lot to give up." He bends a little until we're eye to eye. "But what if those crazy kids who dreamed in a tulip field all those years ago about changing the world, about making it a better place, actually get to do it together?"

I draw a deep breath, not even allowing myself to think about the good we could do if this improbable thing actually happened. "Mr. Cade, that would be what we call," I say, tipping up on my toes to kiss him lightly, too, "a dream come true."

CHAPTER 39
LENNIX

MAXIM ANNOUNCES HIS CANDIDACY FROM COLORADO, THE state he technically lists as his home and where he's voted the past few years. I think I'm more nervous than he is. In the living room of his home, someone is putting powder on him to reduce shine, and he's laughing while the cameras and lighting kit are being set up.

"Did we change that last line?" I ask Glenn, who has rejoined the campaign as a speechwriter.

"Yup," Glenn says. "But he probably changed a lot more than that line after we left."

"Why do you say that?" I ask, already in mild panic mode.

"He strikes me as a guy who goes off map a lot. It won't be the first or the last time, I'm sure. He's not his brother."

"Um, cardinal rule, Glenn."

Our team established a cardinal rule not to draw comparisons between Owen and Maxim and to discourage the press from doing so, too. There will be those who say this is an opportunistic move by Maxim when it's really a huge sacrifice in so many ways. Financially *and* personally.

The producer counts us in, and when the camera's red light pops on, it zeroes in on Maxim.

"I'm here to formally announce my candidacy for president of the United States of America," Maxim says. "No one is more shocked to hear me say this than, well, me."

"Was this in the speech?" I ask Glenn, flipping through my printed copy of Maxim's talking points. "I don't remember this beginning."

"Told you so," he says dryly. "I don't know if he's even looking at the teleprompter."

"Many of you first met me when my brother Owen was running for president."

We said we wouldn't go straight to Owen. *Sigh.*

Maxim chuckles. "You think your big brother's a pain in the butt? Try growing up with the guy who knows from the time he's like five years old that he'll be the president one day. Whole other level of bossy."

Kimba walks up beside me. "I know you're losing your shit over here, but he's doing great. Let him be."

"Why is he not using the speech we spent hours on?"

"Great leaders have a great gut. Trust his, okay?"

I release a long breath and nod reluctantly.

"I never aspired to be president," Maxim says, his smile fading. "I wanted to change the world, and most of the politicians I saw weren't doing that. They were taking care of themselves. As most of you know, I'm a wealthy man. I was born into it. I didn't ask for it, but I have it. That's privilege. I've leveraged it in my personal life to help those who don't have it. Now I want to do that on behalf of those in this country struggling. I'm an unapologetic capitalist. I believe in choices and hard work. That's why I'm running not as a Democrat or as a Republican but as an independent."

He angles a wry look into the camera, a lock of dark hair falling forward and probably winning him some votes. "This is the part where you write me off, right? Because no independent has ever won a presidential election. This is also the part where you'd be wrong. I don't plan to be a footnote or a novelty in this campaign. I plan to be a force in it, always redirecting to the issues when we get distracted by tabloids, shaping dialogue around the needs of every-day Americans even if you have trouble seeing me as one."

He leans forward, elbows on his knees, as I've seen him do a thousand times when he wants to drive home a point. "Maybe you're concerned because I've never governed. I understand the intricacies of government, and I've run a billion-dollar company. I know how to make money, which is something a country like ours, in trillions—yes, with a T—trillions of dollars in debt, could use, but I also don't believe people should be sacrificed for the dollar."

I'm holding my breath, no idea how the public will receive this.

"We face bigger problems than we ever have in this country. We need bold solutions. So many things about the future scare many of you, and I get it. According to experts, automation, robots will be taking a huge slice of the jobs humans do. Whole cities could soon be underwater because of climate change. Tensions all over the world have many of our global neighbors on the brink of war. I won't pretend it's not scary, but I assure you that I'm not afraid. Genius and innovation live in the DNA of this nation. If we face new problems every day, there are those among us who have the answers, who will *find* the answers. And where those answers don't exist, we'll create them. I'm a guy who knows how to make something from nothing. I've done it for myself. Let me do it for you."

The passion in his expression tempers, and a sad smile curves his lips. "I started this talking about my brother, Owen. As you know, he was assassinated not long ago. I'm announcing later than the other candidates because I had no intention of ever doing this. I wanted to support my brother. He would have made an amazing president, and Millie would have been an extraordinary first lady."

He pauses, swallows, and blinks rapidly, a sheen of tears over his green eyes. "I would give anything to have him back—to have him sitting here instead, telling you about health care and Social Security and equal pay and all the things he believed were the *least* we could do as a people."

He looks down at his hands, clasped between his knees, and then back into the camera. "That choice was taken away from me, but this one hasn't been. I choose to do what I always wanted to do—to change the world—and Owen made this cynical, jaded guy a believer again. I'm hoping that I can do the same for many of you. This is not a campaign of small moves but of huge ideas. I've built my life on impossible dreams."

His wicked grin scares me because I know it promises mischief. "Once, I was trying to impress a beautiful girl, and I told her all my big dreams—that I wanted to make the world a better place, that I wanted to change a nation, *this* nation. I asked if that was arrogant or presumptuous. You know what she said?"

He chuckles and presses his hands together. "She said revolution requires a certain degree of hubris. I have hubris to spare. Whether you know it or not, we need a revolution. We need to shake things up. The status quo is insufficient for what lies ahead. Let's not fear the future. Let's make it."

CHAPTER 40
MAXIM

"You have hundreds of messages," Jin Lei tells me in clipped tones.

"Well, I did just announce I'm running for president," I say, not looking up from my laptop. "That tends to get the people going."

"I can't believe you're really doing this," she says, leaning one shoulder against the doorjamb. "Like, president."

"Neither can I, but hey, if I become president, maybe I could give you some job that's much easier than what you do for me now."

"Like what?"

"Secretary of Defense?"

"I wouldn't take the pay cut," she says, turning to leave. "I'm gonna go if you don't need anything else."

"I'm good. I think Kimba's coming by in a little bit with some notes. I had to leave the announcement and almost immediately go into rescue mode on this Hong Kong deal. Apparently, our shareholders don't care that I'm running for president. They want their money no matter what."

I work for a few minutes in blessed quiet, getting more done than I have since I woke this morning. I talked to Millie briefly, and she assured me I had her blessing but then hastily got off the phone. My mom and dad called. Mom cried basically through the entire conversation. There was a lot about how Owen would be proud of me for continuing where he left off. That got me pretty choked up, and then my father got on the line and told me I "did good." As praise from my father goes, that was gushing.

"Knock, knock."

I look up, and Lennix, not Kimba, stands in the door. She's wearing jeans and a shirt that says *Indigenous or Bust*, the words across her...bust. Cute.

"Knock, knock yourself." I push back from my desk. "A pleasant surprise. I was expecting Kimba."

"She had to go to Alabama. There's an election down there that's heating up, and they needed some help."

"So I'm stuck dealing with you, huh?" I shake my head and sigh heavily. "If I must."

She walks farther in the room and sits on the edge of my desk. I want to snatch her onto my lap, but I refrain. We've said we'll try to be good, so I'll let her take the lead. She pulls a small notepad from her back pocket.

"Oh, is this the famous notebook? The one where you write down all the things I got wrong and tell me how to do better next time?"

She glances up with a crooked grin. "Yes."

"Well, go on."

"You ignored the teleprompter."

"Uh, yeah, because it had that speech on it, and I decided not to use that speech, so...no need for the teleprompter."

"Right. You went completely off-script."

"I felt I knew what was right for me in that moment. You don't tell a guy whose instincts have saved him all his life to turn off his instincts."

"Yeah, well, I'd appreciate it if we could at least discuss these instincts of yours before you give in to them in front of millions of people."

"Not too much to ask."

"You started with Owen when we said we wouldn't."

"I had to." I run a hand over the tight muscles in the back of my neck. "He's the whole reason I'm even giving this a shot. I had to acknowledge him right up front. What else you got?"

She stands and walks around the desk and leans down until our faces line up. "I'm very, very proud of you," she whispers, closing the space between our mouths and kissing me. She tastes as pure as she did the first time I kissed her on a dark night on a cobblestone street. I stand and kiss her back with all the hope and love she inspires in me.

I glance over her shoulder at my open office door, finding the hall empty. I cup her ass and press my erection into her.

"So, is it a Tuesday?" I ask.

She laughs and drops her head to my shoulder. "No, Doc. Tuesdays will have to be very rare and special occasions for a long time."

CHAPTER 41
LENNIX

"WE NEED TO GET SOME TOWN HALLS SCHEDULED," KIMBA SAYS, glaring at her laptop. "Damn spinning wheel. You'd think Steve Jobs could have figured this out before he passed away, rest in power."

"He revolutionized the personal computer and changed nearly every aspect of your life with a *cell phone*," Maxim says dryly. "Maybe you cut him some slack."

"Please don't tell me you're a Jobs zealot," Glenn groans.

"Zealot? Nooooo," Maxim denies with a shake of his head. "Should he have a state named after him? Most likely, yeah."

The rest of the senior staff gathered around Maxim's campaign office in New York laugh. Setting up our headquarters here was a power move. Yes, CadeCo's headquarters are here. It's the coolest city in the country, at least by perception, and the center of music, theater, and the arts, but it's also easy to get coverage here. To go viral here, *and* it's within relatively easy striking distance of swing states like Pennsylvania, Ohio, Michigan, and New Hampshire. It also doesn't hurt that Maxim owns an apartment building in SoHo, which is where most of us live while we're in town.

"Hey, speaking of scheduling town halls," Glenn says, "didn't Lacy Reardon used to work with you guys? She developed this SkedAdv app, and it's a scheduler's dream."

Kimba and I exchange a quick "lawd have mercy" look at the

mention of Lacy, the girl we had to dismiss after her affair with Susan Bowden was discovered.

By Susan's wife.

Situations like that make me even more determined to keep my relationship with Maxim under wraps for a while. Though there's no infidelity or misconduct, sex and politics have a torrid past. Anytime they rub up against each other, the public perceives it as scandal. And scandal destroys campaigns.

"Yeah, Lacy worked with us," Kimba replies. "On Susan Bowden's campaign for a while, but she ended up leaving. She's incredibly talented. I heard she recently signed on with one of the Democrats."

"Dentley's campaign, right?" I ask, keeping my tone casual. "Governor from New Jersey."

"Yeah, we did a project together a few months ago," Glenn says. "Maybe we could persuade her to come work for Maxim instead."

"I think we're set," I say. "But you're right. She's amazing. Now, back to these town halls."

"Blech." Maxim shudders.

"Blech?" I ask, laughing. "Are you a fourteen-year-old girl?"

He tosses a plastic-wrapped fortune cookie at me, and it bounces off my boob. He shrugs, looking all innocent. "Oops."

I roll my eyes and can't help but grin. "Town halls—we need some in swing states."

"Hmmm, quick question," Maxim says around the fortune cookie he popped in his mouth. "Will Thomas Jefferson be there? Wasn't he the last person who cared about a town hall?"

"Maxim, we need a way for you to connect with people and answer their questions," Kimba says. "Especially since you've never worked in government and you're so young."

"With so many people talking about my age, when they ask how old I am, I now say I'll be forty my next birthday."

"You're on fire tonight, huh?" I ask.

His glance caresses each part of my face. I stretch my eyes to let him know he's doing that thing again where he looks like he's in love with me. He drops his gaze, grinning and picking up his phone.

My phone beeps a notification a few minutes later when we're still listing reasons Maxim should do these town halls. Even with his changed contact name, I still nearly break a nail diving for the phone before anyone sees it.

> King: I reaaaally need it to be Tuesday soon.
> Me: We're doing so well. Just hang in there.
> King: You don't tell a guy with blue balls to "hang in there."

I snicker and glance up to find Glenn looking at me quizzically. "What's so funny, Nix?" he asks with a grin.

The smile on Maxim's face freezes and shatters like ice.

Oh, shit.

"I, nothing. I'm fine." I pull the elastic band from my hair and then scoop my hair right back up into a ponytail. I don't know what to do with my hands, and I don't know why Glenn called me Nix. It wouldn't be that big of a deal if anyone other than Maxim called me Nix, but *no one ever does.* "Um, so, town halls?"

Maxim's still staring at Glenn, who is oblivious, chatting with Polly, our deputy scheduler, about possible locations. Maxim still semi-glares at Glenn for another few seconds.

"I'm not saying we don't connect with voters and give them a chance to ask questions," Maxim says. "I'm saying I think we need to freshen the concept and make it more consistent with my brand, which is young, progressive, innovative. The words 'town hall' are about as innovative as running water."

"What did you have in mind?" Glenn asks. Maxim still has the heat of a thousand suns in his eyes when he turns them on Glenn, but no one else seems to notice.

"What about pop-ups?" I ask. "Like policy pop-ups."

"I love that." Maxim proffers his fist for a bump across the table, very *buddy buddy* when only weeks ago we slept together every night and ate breakfast in bed each morning. "And if we're strategic about it, we could do a bus from stop to stop. I offset every time I fly and make sure I'm carbon neutral, but that's fine print. The average voter will just see me jetting all over the country in a private plane and wonder how it squares with my stance on climate change. I mean, I have to fly a lot, but whenever we can minimize, I think we should."

"I love the bus idea," Kimba says. "That feels kinda old school but also greener than the plane. Though I promise you I'm not riding a bus all the way to Cali, so you can forget that right now, Mr. Candidate."

Maxim chuckles along with the rest of the team. We hash out a few more things and have some preliminary discussions about the first Democratic debate in June. Maxim's at a disadvantage because he's an independent, so he doesn't get the visibility in the televised debates the Dems and Republicans sponsor. Fortunately, Maxim's name is on everyone's lips, and he has invitations from all the morning shows, late-night shows, political shows—you name it, and they want Maxim. Our strategy is to flip the disadvantage to a plus because while their stages are crowded with ten to fifteen candidates competing for mic time and tearing each other down in advance of the nomination, Maxim has platforms to himself with plenty of opportunity to articulate his vison uncontested and usually in a less formal setting, which suits him best.

Once the meeting breaks, Kimba and I start packing up and preparing to leave for our apartment. It's almost been like college again, rooming together, but without the ramen noodles, frozen pizza, and sock on the door when Kimba gets lucky.

"Nix, could I have a minute?" Maxim asks, not looking up from his laptop.

Kimba and I share a cautious glance. He's been great about keeping his hands to himself and, other than the occasional *I love you thiiiis much* stare, discreet.

"Uh, sure." I wave Kimba on. "I'll see you in a little bit."

"Okay," she says, smiling knowingly. "See you at home."

I'm the last one in the office, and it feels strange to be completely alone with Maxim after a month or so of always making sure someone is around. We've shared a few stolen kisses, but we've been too busy for much more. Maxim still has a business to run, even though he's delegated as much as he can.

"Could you close the door?" he asks, his glance still glued to his screen.

"Uh, I'm not sure we should—"

"Close it." His voice is commanding, like I haven't heard in so long. My nipples respond immediately to the rough tone, beading up under my shirt as if he's licked them with his tongue instead of his sharp words.

I take a seat across the conference room table and wait. He clicks for a minute or so more and then closes the laptop. "Sorry. Jin Lei doesn't care about town halls or pop-ups. She wants me to get these Hong Kong investors off her back. She's on her way."

He stands abruptly, crosses over to the door I closed, and locks it.

"Doc," I say, a warning in my voice. "We've done so well, and this is definitely not the place."

"I hear you. We don't have to Tuesday, but we need to talk."

"Okay. What's going on?"

"Glenn." He slits his eyes. "He's a problem."

I release a relieved breath and a little laugh. "Gosh, you had me worried. How is Glenn a problem? He's a great speechwriter, which you'd know if you'd actually stick to any of his speeches."

"He's into you."

"You're reading things that aren't there. We're friends. We've known each other a long time. This is our fifth campaign together."

"He called you Nix."

Which is apparently the equivalent of first base in Maxim's calculus. "He doesn't know. How would he know not to call me Nix?"

"Somehow, magically, no one else does when they hear me call you that. Only him. Only Glenn."

"It's your imagination. We've worked together for years, and he's never tried anything."

Maxim reaches across the table and covers both of my hands with one of his. He pins me with the intensity of his stare. Even though it's over something silly, I bask in his undivided attention when there always seems to be something vying for it these days. Right now, I have him all to myself, completely focused on me, and I forgot how good it feels.

"If he touches you," Maxim says, his tone dangerous because it's so matter-of-fact, "he's fired. And do not try to keep it from me. I'll find out."

"How? From the security that I'm not supposed to know is there but I do know is there?"

"You agreed to the conditions. We can't let our guards down while Gregory's still on the loose."

With Maxim doing so well in the polls for an independent, it's easy to forget there's someone out there who wants to kill us. I hope Gregory isn't simply lulling us into a false sense of security and then striking when we least expect it.

"Any leads?" I ask.

"Grim thinks the CamTech rat is our best option."

"I hadn't thought of that."

"It's why he makes the big bucks," Maxim says, his grin coming and going before I have time to enjoy the warmth of it.

"That's the only person we know had some form of contact with Gregory when the vaccine information was leaked to him. We find the rat, and then we *break* the rat, which Grim is very good at, by the way."

"Oh, I don't doubt that, and is Wallace helping?"

He glances up, grimaces, rolls his eyes.

"Be nice," I say, chuckling.

"Yeah, Wallace and the CamTech team are cooperating."

Maxim stands and comes to sit on the edge of the conference-room table, pulling me up to stand between his legs.

"I don't want to talk about your ex-boyfriend," he says, ghosting his lips over mine. "Let's talk about your current one."

I don't hesitate, opening for him, as hungry as he is for any crumb, a kiss, a touch. Our love felt so vast in Wyoming, as wide and sprawling as the sky. Now it feels compact, reduced to the minutiae of a few crumb-kisses, stolen touches under tables, and long looks with our fantasies meeting across crowded rooms.

His fingers delve into my hair, tugging the elastic band free so the strands pour over his fingers. He tilts my head and whispers into our kiss, "Are you sure we need to keep doing this? I miss you so damn much, Nix."

I lick into his mouth, strain up, wrap my arms round his neck, and press into the erection at my belly, making us both groan.

"I miss you, too, but if it comes out, believe me, it will be such a distraction, and the people who are starting to take you seriously won't. They'll reduce us to a fly-by-night candidate screwing some young girl from his campaign."

"Young, huh?" He laughs. "Now you're trying to make me sound like some dirty old man."

"Hey, you *did* start lusting after me when I was only seventeen."

His smile fades, and his hands tighten at my waist. "You were so fantastic that day. I was in my dad's car, and I heard you before I saw you. The conviction in your voice, and then you were so... everything." He cups my cheek and rests his forehead against mine. "I never stood a chance."

"Neither did I," I whisper, curling my body in closer to his, loving how we fit together.

"I want our daughter to be just like you."

The word *daughter* jars me, and I drop my eyes. Being apart for the campaign is so hard, but doing the work of getting him elected, seeing how people already respond to him, makes it seem…possible. As adamant as I was about him running, I never stopped to think about what happens if he actually wins.

What happens to me.

Maxim's never proposed, but we want to spend our lives together. If he wins this election, marriage becomes a whole new world that would require sacrifices I never anticipated. Sacrifices I'm not sure I want to make.

"Did you hear me, Nix?" Maxim asks, tilting my chin up to lock our stares together. "I said I want our daughter to be just like you."

I'm still formulating my response when a key turns in the conference-room door. We hastily pull apart, my heart beating triple time. Maxim seems much more relaxed, sitting in the chair in front of his laptop as if that was his destination all along. Jin Lei opens the door. She's one of the few people who knows about us. She knows about everything in our lives, even Gregory.

"Oh," Jin Lei says, looking as startled as we are. "Sorry to interrupt. I forgot something. I didn't realize—"

"You didn't interrupt," I reassure her, avoiding Maxim's searching stare. "I was just leaving."

CHAPTER 42
LENNIX

"I'm not a monk or a priest," Maxim says from the small platform we set up in Philadelphia's Love Park, the iconic LOVE statue behind him with stacked red letters. "And, yes, at some point, I inhaled."

He pauses for the crowd's laughter. We finally convinced him to wear the campaign T-shirt. He felt weird wearing his own name across his chest. The man makes bras from recycled water bottles but has qualms about clothes that bear his name.

"But I'm not a liar," Maxim continues. "I'm not a coward, and I know how to build something from absolutely nothing. I look back enough to learn from our history but won't allow antiquated practices to keep us from the brightest future. Dig deep enough into my past, and you might find me saying something stupid or that I no longer even believe. Look closely enough, and you'll spot my flaws, but you'll also see someone with a vision and, I hope, the integrity to see through."

We kicked our policy pop-up tour off in New York, and our Cade bus has been tracking across states every day. Inherently, the viral, grassroots nature of the pop-up format means the crowds trend younger. I believe we'll have millennials on lock come November. They're the earliest adapting demographic, obviously. They're not as quick to mistrust Maxim's relative "youth," and the idea of doing something history-making—electing an independent president—appeals to them. Specifically, *Maxim* appeals to them. He's handsome and compelling, that leashed power and raw physicality drawing people to him, but it's the breadth of his intelligence and his unexpected humor keeping their attention.

"Ain't this some shit," Kimba mutters next to me on the periphery of the crowd.

"What?" I ask, forcing myself to drag my glance from Maxim.

"You can't take your eyes off him." Kimba nods to the stage. "And Glenn can't take his eyes off you."

"What?" I look around, and my glance collides with Glenn's. He stands a few feet away but averts his eyes quickly.

"Well, I'm sure that orange bra doesn't help," Kimba says wryly.

It's hot to be only May, and I decided to test-drive one of the "Make the Future" campaign tank tops. I didn't anticipate my orange bra strap sliding down my arm every five minutes.

"He's been staring at your tits all day." Kimba laughs. "You *do* know he's got a thing for you, right?"

"Who? Glenn?"

"You cannot be that oblivious, Lenn. How can a girl as sharp as you…" She huffs a sigh and rolls her eyes. "Lord, you are."

"Glenn and I have known each other for years. This is our fifth campaign together. We're *friends*."

"Uh, yeah. He heard you were working on the first three and made sure he was, too, and the last two campaigns, Owen's and Maxim's, you put him on. Dude's thirsty. He can write his little ass off, but his nose is wide open for you, honey."

Shock and chagrin take turns slapping me around. "Maxim said the same thing."

"Oh, my God. When Glenn called you Nix the other night, I thought Maxim would lose his mind. Glenn probably has a scar from that glare he cut him with."

"You noticed that?"

"I, unlike you, notice everything, see all the signs, and will interpret for a small fee."

We clap at a particularly stirring point in Maxim's speech along with the rest of the crowd.

"And when do you plan to put all this relationship observational skill to work for yourself?" I ask.

"Mama's got needs, and Mama gets 'em met, but I do *not* need a relationship."

"Did you see David at the funeral?"

"Girl, please," Kimba scoffs. "David was a youthful exploit. Seeing him again, even if it hadn't been at a funeral, there wouldn't have been any sparks."

"When are you gonna find a guy you'll give more than a night or two?"

A shadow crosses Kimba's face, and she fiddles with the gold ring she wears on her right hand. "Guys like Maxim don't grow on trees."

Before I can dig into that, Polly walks up. "Hey, ladies. I think Maxim has to do a little detour."

"Detour?" I ask. "What do you mean?"

"Jin Lei needs him in Connecticut," Polly says. "This afternoon and tonight. He needs to leave as soon as this is over. Apparently, it's kind of a last-minute thing."

"Tonight?" Kimba shakes her head. "He has dinner with local leaders tonight, and then we leave in the morning for Pittsburgh."

"Wait. Connecticut?" I ask. "Is it Millie?"

"Yeah. It's the twins' birthday, and Millie wants things to feel normal for them," Polly says. "They're doing a big party at her parents' place. The kids asked for Uncle Max to come."

"He has to." I nod, looking at Kimba. "We'll cover the dinner with the local leaders. As soon as they hear Maxim had a commitment associated with Owen, they'll forgive him missing tonight."

"Jin Lei says Maxim's dad has the company jet waiting for him at the airport," Polly says. "Must be nice, huh? You'd never know Maxim's *that* kind of loaded. I mean, except for his expensive clothes and that watch that costs more than some small countries."

I know his wealth is a huge part of who Maxim is. For him, it's an expression of his independence from his father, of his own innovative spirit. I get all of that, but there will always be a part of me that remembers our week in Amsterdam. Eating crusty bread and drinking wine in bed. Counting tulips in the field. Our bodies seeking and finding each other in a dark alley with rain-soaked kisses. God, things were simple. *We* were simple and at the genesis of not only our relationship but our adulthood. Figuring out who we were on our own, in blissful anonymity. Now the whole world watches his every move and he's running for president.

How is this our life?

"Anyway," Polly says, "Maxim can catch his daddy's jet, do the party and family commitment, and fly back tonight. We leave on the bus in the AM. Sound good?"

"Does he know yet?" I ask, returning my glance to him, now seated on a stool and taking questions from the crowd, which has tripled since word spread that Maxim Cade was in the park.

"Not yet," Polly says, "but Maxim's used to doing whatever Jin Lei says and going where he's told. A man like him gets used to trusting his schedule to other people. I'll tell him as soon as he's done."

I scan the perimeter of the crowd and the front of the stage, making sure the security is in place. Under his campaign T-shirt, Maxim wears a tightly fitted bullet-proof vest, courtesy of Grim. There's security at our SoHo apartment around the clock, which Kimba says makes her feel like a Kardashian, and Rick sits outside my hotel room in every city on this pop-up tour. I've gotten used to it. I know it's necessary, but I'll never like it.

Once he's done onstage, Maxim chats with people from the crowd, takes selfies, and generally wins over anyone within charming distance. The team huddles about the plan for the Philly leaders now that Maxim can't meet them. Kimba has the great idea of having him record a video we'll play at the beginning before we start addressing their concerns.

He's no longer in front of the stage, so I dash to the bus, hoping to catch him before he goes. Not only about the video, but because I miss him so bad I ache. I just want to smell him, to touch him, to remind myself the man it seems the whole world wants more pieces of is still mine.

I hop on the Cade bus, which is long and tricked out with every amenity possible. Nothing but the best for Maxim. If that man is on your bus, it'll be the best bus ride of your life.

Glenn is sitting in one of the booths, his laptop on the table.

"Hey, Glenn." I hope my voice sounds normal now that I know he's "into me," according to Kimba. And, well, I guess according to Maxim, too. "You seen Maxim?"

"Uh, yeah." He closes his laptop and looks up at me, his brown eyes intent. "He and I were going over some notes for Pittsburgh. I'll keep working on the speech while he's in Connecticut. He just left."

"Oh." I gulp down my disappointment. "I was gonna ask him to record a video for the leaders tonight."

The thing about pretending you're not dating on the campaign trail is it actually *is* hard to date on the trail. Some days Maxim and I barely see each other. Today is one of those days. My phone beeps with a text.

"Kimba says not to worry," I say, reading it. "She found out Jin Lei's riding with Maxim to the airport and getting him to record it now."

I slide the phone into the back pocket of my jeans. Glenn stares at the orange bra strap hanging down my arm, and I hastily pull it up again.

"Okay. Well, I better—"

"It looks like we've got some free time this afternoon," he interrupts.

"Um, not much actually. Kimba and I are taking the local leaders meeting tonight, so—"

"How about a late lunch?" he asks in a rush and reaches under the table, pulling out two of the boxed lunches organized by our local volunteers.

"Um, sure." I sit at the table across from him and open the box. "Roast beef. Yum."

"Don't let the candidate see you eating that roast beef." Glenn rolls his eyes. "He'll want to know if it's responsibly sourced or something."

I pause with the sandwich halfway to my mouth. It occurs to me that not only have I been slow to see how Glenn feels about me, but maybe I've missed his true feelings about Maxim.

"Climate change is a huge part of Maxim's platform," I remind him, studying my cold cuts. "Of course he's concerned about those things. Aren't we all? You not a believer, Glenn?"

"In who? Cade?" He snorts. "I mean, do I believe he's probably the next president? Yeah, I do, which is why I'm here, but let's just say he's not Owen."

I place my sandwich on the wax paper on the table, blinking at him owlishly. "He never claimed to be Owen. They believe so many of the same things, though, that it's easy for most people to support Maxim the way they did his brother."

I sip the bottled water included with lunch. "So you're only here for how it'll look on your résumé that you worked for the new president, *if* he wins?"

"That's not the only reason I'm here, Nix," he says, his eyes moving over my face, down my neck, tracing the satiny strap drooping down my arm again.

"Uh, could you not call me that, Glenn?"

"Sorry. I heard Maxim call you that and thought it was cute, so I..." He shakes his head like he's clearing it. "Never mind. Like I was saying. I'm not just here for the résumé boost. Over the years, working together so much, well, I've come to care about you a lot."

It's like a train wreck. The lights are coming at me so fast right now.

"I'd like to take you out some time. Dinner or a movie? Theater. I know you like plays. We could—"

"Glenn, I'm sorry. I think you know we have a pretty strict policy about dating people we work with on campaigns."

Unless you're my soulmate, of course.

"Oh, yeah." He pulls the ring on his Diet Coke can off, flipping it back and forth in his hands. "I get that. Maybe once the campaign is over—"

"Glenn, I don't..." I clear my throat and stare at the crust of my sandwich. "I think it's best if we just stay friends." I brave a look up at him. "Ya know?"

He blinks at me, a lot and fast.

Is he gonna cry? Oh, dear Jesus. "Glenn, I'm sorry. I never realized—"

"No, it's fine." He stands abruptly, scraping his trash into a bag with jerky movements.

"I am so sorry, Glenn. I hope this won't affect—"

"I'm a professional, *Lennix*," he says, emphasizing my full name. "You want to stay friends. I get it. It's fine."

He says *fine* in that way you know shit is for sure not *fine*.

I turn to watch Glenn leave the bus, walking down the aisle quickly like someone is chasing him. Two thoughts circle in my mind like a carousel.

One: I'm not sure I handled that well.

Two: I *really* don't want Maxim to know.

CHAPTER 43
MAXIM

I HAVE MY OWN PLANE.

It's a ridiculous thought, but walking toward the Cade Energy jet, I can't help but have it.

It's not even about *my plane is bigger than your plane, Dad*, or *look how rich I am*. I use my plane a lot less than most guys in my position anyway. It's the independence. The last time I was on a plane owned by my father, he basically told me I'd never make anything of myself without him. Every step I've taken away from him has proved him wrong. I was in my twenties then. Staring at forty, taking steps away from my family doesn't feel like the right thing to do, especially when we're all still reeling from Owen's death.

The demands of my business and the campaign distract me, but nothing can erase the pain of losing my brother. I try not to talk about it much because I know I won't be able to move forward if I do. I've been too busy for grief counseling, though I know I need it. The loss alone would be a lot to handle, but the guilt makes it worse—knowing Owen would still be here if I hadn't shot Gregory's brother, but I couldn't have done a damn thing differently. I couldn't have let him kill Lennix. I had to go get her, and when Gregory's brother held a gun to her head, I had to shoot him.

But if there was any one thing I *could* change to reorder the events that led to Owen's assassination, I would do it.

I settle into the leather seat and groan, scrubbing at my face, exhausted already. I don't know how I'll get through tonight, facing Millie and the twins.

"Mr. Cade."

The flight attendant stands there, uniformed and solicitous. "We were waiting for Ms. Pérez before we took off. I wanted to let you know her car has arrived and she'll be boarding soon."

"Salina's flying with us?"

"Yes, she is," Salina says from the curtained door, smiling at the attendant as she retreats. "I hope it's okay. Your father thought it would be."

I'm sure he did. He makes it so hard to be nice to him.

"Um, sure," I answer. "Plenty of room. I just didn't know."

"Millie wanted me to come." She takes the seat beside me and kicks off her stilettos. "Feet are killing me. I was in court all morning."

"You have an office in Philly?"

"No, I had a client here. Threat of deportation, but we got it sorted." She angles a wry look at me, her brown eyes laughing. "Maybe when you're president you can fix our immigration problem."

I chuckle, lean on the armrest, and place my chin in my hand. "I'll see what I can do."

"You really want to be president?" she asks, smiling.

"This isn't an elaborate ruse, so yeah."

"Your father's so proud of you."

Salina has her own connection to my dad, separate from Millie, since she served as counsel for one of his companies for a few years.

"Yeah?" I ask, twisting my lips into a grimace "We'll see."

"He thinks you'll win it all. He…um, does think you need a first lady, though, if you're serious about this."

I shrug. "It's not in the job description that I have one."

"But America's never *not* had one. You're breaking enough rules. Maybe you should be"—she reaches over and squeezes my hand, caressing my knuckles with her thumb—"conventional in that respect."

There was a time when I would have accepted the invitation so clearly engraved on the look Salina's giving me right now. I have it under excellent authority that there's a king-sized bed in the back of this plane. I know this because when I was in high school, I *may* have hijacked Daddy's plane to impress a girl or two. I may have made use of said bed in the back.

Some guys steal their fathers' cars. I stole Dad's plane.

"Salina, I think you're great, but—"

"How would you know?" she asks, her voice husky. "You haven't tried me yet. Though I've been practically throwing myself at you since Millie and Owen's wedding."

Has she? I hadn't noticed, but by then I'd met Lennix, and every other woman was a stand-in. It never really occurred to me that I wouldn't get Lennix back when the time was right for us both, so I stayed available. Did I have sex in the ten years we were apart? Of course I did.

Again. Not a monk.

But no one ever touched that place she staked out in my heart. The girl who chases stars landed on the moon and planted her flag, and I've been hers ever since.

"Sal, I'm in a relationship," I tell her. "It's complicated and can't really be public right now, but it's serious. I'm sorry."

Her long lashes flick down, and she bites into a bitter smile. The attendant comes back through.

"Welcome aboard, Ms. Pérez," she says brightly. "Could I get you something?"

"Vodka," Salina sighs, giving me a stiff smile. "And keep 'em coming."

The twins gather around a huge cake, sloppily cutting chunks for everyone with a plastic knife. Several kids their age laugh, spreading frosting everywhere, and you'd barely know anything was amiss if it wasn't for the strained, forced gaiety of their mother. Millie's trying so hard, but I know her. I see her pulling at the seams.

Within the hour, floodlights illuminate a line of large tents housing all the children from the party. I got a few minutes with each of the twins, and they seem to be doing well, considering. The young are most resilient. I haven't had any time alone with Millie, though, and I need to head back to Philly and get at least some sleep before we board that bus for Pittsburgh tomorrow. And three other cities that I can't recall right now.

"I remember when they were born," my mother says, tears in her eyes when we walk back into the house. "And now they're eight. Owen didn't get to see…"

I wrap my arm around her shoulder and squeeze her close. She's been on the verge of tears all day, holding it together for the sake of Darcy and Elijah, but she's fraying.

"I think he sees," Salina says, taking Mom's hand. "It's been a long day. Let me walk you to your room, Mrs. C."

Mom nods, her mouth working but releasing no sound. She looks at me, and the tears stream over her powdered cheeks. I stare back helplessly. Is she wishing Owen was standing here instead of me? Probably. Most days, so do I. He had the family, the following, someone to live for besides himself. I'd trade places with him in a heartbeat to spare Millie the torture lurking behind the blue eyes that used to be so lively.

Mom reaches up and touches my face. "I'm proud of you, Maxim. You were always such a good boy. You just never knew it." Her smile is shaky, her eyes bright with tears. "Owen knew, though. He always saw how good you were. Tried to tell your father. He'd be so happy that the two of you have made things right."

Have we? If Dad keeps meddling in my life with stunts like he pulled with Salina, things won't be right.

"Love you, Mom." I bend to kiss her cheek. "I'll call from the road."

She nods and walks off with Salina toward the stairs. I stand there alone in the large foyer for a few minutes, not sure what I should do. A door opens down the hall, and my father emerges, looking distracted. Probably business.

"Maxim," he says, surprise in his voice. "I didn't realize you were still here."

"Yeah. I want to see Millie before I get back on the road."

"Did your mother go upstairs?"

I nod. "Today's been difficult for her."

"Most days are. I don't think we come equipped with what it takes to handle the death of a child because it goes against the natural order of things, outliving your kid. It shouldn't happen. It hurts too much."

My father's always sure, but I know right now, he's lost in sorrow so deep he's drowning. As surely as my mother's hurting badly, so is he. He may not express it as freely as she does, but it's there—an unseen force, an undertow, pulling him down.

He closes the space separating us. "How's it going on the trail?"

"So far, so good. Just trying to stay relevant and be heard while the Dems and Republicans fight it out. My goal is to still be standing when Iowa rolls around in February."

"You'll be more than standing." He grips my shoulder, looking me in the eye. "You're gonna win this thing. Mark my words."

I hesitate. I should leave well enough alone. This is the best we've gotten along in years, but if we're going to rebuild our relationship, it has to be on a foundation of honesty. "If I do win, I'll choose my own first lady."

He stiffens but doesn't try to deny my subtle accusation. "Salina's a beautiful woman."

"She is. I'm sure she'll make someone very happy, but you already know who I want."

"Yes, the one girl who hates me," he says dryly.

"Oh, I'm sure there are lots of girls who hate you, Dad." We both chuckle at that, and it feels good to laugh with him even if for only a second, but when we sober, I drive the point home. "I told you before, if you can't accept Lennix in my life, we'll never be able to really repair things between us."

Neither of us breaks the stare or the silence following my words, and it's like looking in a mirror that reflects shared memories and moments from when we were closer. A torrent of emotions is unleashed in my chest—ever-present grief, sadness for how my mother's suffering, for how Millie's suffering, and a longing to share some of this burden with the man I used to admire more than anyone. I'm not sure how we'll find our way to anything close to that if he won't yield.

"Tell her there won't be any more Cade pipelines on protected land," he says softly, finally.

For the space of a few seconds, I'm too shocked by his words to even process them.

"What? Tell who—"

"Tell Lennix."

Not Ms. Hunter. Lennix.

My father and I were together the day I met Lennix. She was luminous and powerful and shone with her convictions. I still remember the way her voice broke when she said her mother's name—her indignation that day when she asked if we could see her. If we could hear her. Nightmares about her mother are built on the land my father stole from her people.

"Tell her yourself."

"What?" Dad asks, looking so much like me I wonder how Lennix stands it.

"*You* tell Lennix that you'll never put another Cade pipeline on protected land. She deserves that."

His throat bobs with the pride he's swallowing, and he nods. "I'll tell her myself, yes."

It's a huge concession. My father is too much of a strategist to give up something that crucial without an endgame in mind, something he gains.

"Why?" I ask.

"Because I've already lost one son." He glances up the stairs my mother took a few minutes before and sighs. "I can't afford to lose the other."

His words hit me in the solar plexus, and I'm short of breath like I was on that plane when I first got the news. Seeing both my parents suffer this way is more than I think I can take.

"I'll go check on your mother," he says. "Thank you for coming. It means a lot to her and Millie."

Before I can respond, he's heading up the stairs. I stand there, not even sure what to do or feel but knowing I need to get out of here.

Even though the grief is suffocating, I'm not cowardly enough to leave without seeing Millie, so I force myself to search for her. She's in the kitchen, loading the dishwasher. Unnecessary, because her parents have staff who would do that, but Millie needs to feel useful. She never intended to practice law for long. Her purpose was intricately laced with my brother's. With him gone, she seems adrift. She's young, beautiful, wealthy with no need to ever work again. I'll make it my business to protect her and the kids from predators.

It's the least I can do for Owen.

"You okay, Mill?" I ask from the kitchen door.

Her back is to me. The slim line of her shoulders tenses, and her hands go still in the sink.

"You know," she whispers, "you and O don't look anything alike."

She glances over her shoulder, showing me one red, tear-stained cheek. "But you sound so much like him."

I'm transfixed, my feet glued to the ground, and I can't even go over to comfort her. No one's ever told me that.

"Just now when you asked me that and my back was turned," she says, her voice growing more waterlogged, "for a second, it was like I had him again."

She turns to face me fully, leaning against the sink, her face collapsing in tears. I force my feet forward and stride across the kitchen, pulling her into a tight hug. Her whole body shakes with the force of her grief.

"I'm sorry we haven't talked much," she mumbles into my shirt, now soaked with her tears. "I want you to know I'm proud of you for running, and I know Owen would be, too. You have my full support. It's just...on the phone, it's too much. You sound like him, and I can't see your face, and it tricks my heart into thinking..."

She glances up, shadows painted under blue eyes dulled by pain. "I keep waiting for it to hurt less, but it never does. Every morning I wake up with this knife in my heart and no way to pull it out. I just bleed."

She doesn't say much else, and I hold her tight and promise to never let go. I can tell from the solace she seems to take from me being here that Millie doesn't blame me for Owen's death.

But I still blame myself. I probably always will.

CHAPTER 44
MAXIM

By the time I make it back to Philly, I'm completely wrung out. Physically, yes, but I'm used to an unreasonable pace. I've done it all my adult life. I've engineered my diet and workouts to get optimal use from this body, even though I don't sleep nearly enough.

No, I'm wrung out emotionally. I don't have a supplement or recovery shake for that. I'd take it if I did. No matter how stiffly I hold myself, I still feel Millie shaking, her sobs vibrating through every part of me.

In the hotel where the team is staying, a security guard trails me up to the top floor. I can't remember what time we leave in the morning for Pittsburgh, but it's early. Using the bus instead of flying everywhere takes longer, but Kimba and Lennix schedule all kinds of social media crap like live broadcasts on Facebook and Instagram while we're on the road to make good use of our time.

Lennix.

I need her.

Tonight, I need her so badly I'm tempted to go to her room and risk her anger and being discovered.

"Good night," I tell the guard, closing the door and leaving him to take the seat in the hall outside my suite.

The room is dark, only a small arc of light provided by one lamp. I stop in my tracks. Lennix is curled up asleep on the couch.

"Nix?" I sound hopeful, like she might not be real. Might disappear.

"Hey." She stretches, walking over to me, reaching up to wrap her arms around my neck. "Are you okay? I knew it would be so hard seeing everyone today."

"Yeah." I slide my hand into her hair. "I'll tell you about it tomorrow, but tonight…"

I trail kisses over her jaw and down her neck, back up to her ear. "I need it to be Tuesday, baby. Please."

She pulls back, searching my eyes, and then nods. I pull the tank top over her head, leaving her in that orange bra with the infuriating strap that kept sliding down her arm, tempting me while I was trying to concentrate on the pop-up questions today. I undo the front clasp of the bra, taking her breast into my mouth, groaning at the feel of her nipple hardening on my tongue. "Jesus, I missed them so much."

She chuckles huskily, unbuttoning and sliding out of her jeans. I yank the tiny underwear so hard one of the silk strips at her hip tears. She pulls the campaign T-shirt over my head, pausing when my bare chest comes into view.

"Where is your damn vest, Maxim?" Lennix snaps, her eyes furious. She's the one who got us into this campaign despite my fears for *her*, but she's as dogmatic about my safety as I am about hers.

"Calm down. I just took it off for the trip home." I pick her up, and she wraps her legs around my waist. I rush down the hall to the bedroom, already feeling morning much too close and my time with her going too fast.

In the bedroom, I strip off my pant, briefs, shoes, and socks. I'm naked so fast she blinks and then laughs.

"What do you want first?" she asks, her wide mouth soft, her eyes indulgent.

"What do you think?" I growl and slap her ass. "On the bed. Legs spread."

She scrambles onto the bed, laying back and spreading her legs, and it's so reminiscent of our rainy night in Amsterdam the first time we were together.

"You saved yourself for me," I say, grinning and crawling on the bed toward her.

She laughs, brushing a hand over my hair. "You mean when you deflowered me? Yes."

"I was so bummed when there was no flower down there."

"You didn't seem disappointed."

"Maybe there's one there now." I stand her on her knees and turn her around so she faces the headboard, her legs spread over my face. "Let's have a look."

I lift my face until the heat and scent of her pussy overtake everything. Her thighs are the walls of my city and her sweet, plump clit its crown jewel. She has me surrounded. I pull her down to sit on my face and devour her, pulling the lips open and eating like an animal long denied food. I've been caged, tied up, and now I'm let loose.

"Maxim, oh my God," she moans, riding my face and gripping the headboard.

She's the wettest, hottest thing I've ever tasted. I slide my finger back to her asshole, dragging it back and forth over the puckered entrance. I flick my eyes up to meet hers, silently asking. She looks down at me and nods, biting her lip. I ease in.

"Fuck, it's tight," I gasp. "The first time I fuck you in the ass…"

My dick stretches like a pipe at the thought of getting in there. I ease in an inch more, and her cheeks tighten around my finger.

"Touch yourself," I tell her.

She slides her hand between her legs, and I watch her slim fingers playing with my pretty pussy and almost come at the sight. She moans, rocking her hips.

"Fuck yourself," I say hoarsely. Obediently, her fingers slip inside, and then I match the rhythm of her fingers with mine in and out of her ass.

"Oh." Her eyes widen, and there's something so innocent about it—about a kind of pleasure she's never had. "Oh. Maxim."

"That's it, baby." I keep plunging my finger in and out while hers do the same. She grips the headboard so tightly with her other hand, the veins in her arm stand out. She's slack-jawed and her eyes roll back and her moans get louder and louder until she's sobbing and screaming, my name scrawled on the inside of her throat. Sexy as hell.

I sit up and pull her under me, spread her legs.

"I can't wait anymore, Nix." I pull her knees up and wide and plunge in.

"Dammit," I groan, planting one hand on the bed by her head and flicking her nipple with the other. "It's so good like this."

"Yes, so good." She rolls her hips to meet each thrust. "I missed your body."

Her breasts bounce with the frenetic, fucking motion of our bodies. "I missed yours, too."

I pull her legs down and lean in, needing to be closer to her, needing to feel her heart. I caress her arm and make my way over her wrist, the compass bracelet that signifies how we'll always find each other, until I can link our fingers. Our eyes lock, and the love there, the acceptance and devotion—it's too much. I close my eyes, sliding in and out but still seeing that love in her gaze.

Everything outside the door falls away, and my whole world is this room. This bed is our map, and we make love until it feels like we fall off the edge of the world. It's just us, the longitude of our bodies aligned and locked and loving. The latitude of our hearts, crossed, pressed together.

Later we're under the covers, the hotel comforter nowhere near as soft and fine as our bed in Wyoming, but I don't really care because she's with me.

"I needed this so much." I kiss her shoulder, pull her back into my chest, and cup her breast. "I needed *you* so much."

She nods, capturing my hand and linking it with hers. "I knew seeing Millie and the kids would be rough."

"It was so hard, but I think she'll be okay." I shrug. "We all will eventually. She misses him."

Matches are being struck inside my throat, a betraying burn. I swallow, trying to keep the scorching emotion at bay, but it won't be denied.

"Fuck," I mutter into her hair, tears streaming from my eyes. "Dammit."

She turns over, naked and beautiful, her eyes wet and concerned, searching mine in the lamp's anemic light.

"Oh, Doc," she whispers. "It's okay. Oh, baby, please let it out. Please let it go."

I grit my teeth, hoping to trap it, to cage it, but it roars out, wild and unwieldly.

"It's my fault," I mutter into her neck, squeezing her, needing something to hold on to when it seems the whole world is spinning. "God, Millie...she...the twins...it's my fault. O would still be here if..."

"Shh, baby." She rubs my back and kisses my jaw, my cheeks, my tears. "It's not your fault. It's his fault, and we can't bring Owen back, but we'll make Gregory pay, and we'll be there for Millie and the kids. We will. I promise, Maxim. I promise."

I don't know how long the tears fall, and I'm not ashamed or self-conscious. Not with her. She's an extension of me, and I'm an extension of her. She's a layer of my skin, a chamber of my heart. She's the tattoo on my chest.

Endurance.

I know what it meant when I got it, but Lennix brings new meaning to everything, even the word inked on my skin. *She* endures. This connection that started so many years ago, *it* endures. For the first time tonight, I think I can make it, as long as I have this. As long as I have *her.*

CHAPTER 45
LENNIX

"OH, HELL."

I jerk upright in Maxim's hotel bed, naked as the day I was born. There's light coming through the shades.

Light is bad. Very bad.

I throw the covers back and jump out of bed. We're supposed to leave for Pittsburgh at eight. I snatch my phone from the bedside table.

"Six thirty. Not great, but not the end of the world."

"Where are you going?" Maxim asks drowsily, grasping my wrist, his fingers catching in my bracelet. "Come back to bed. I'll make us breakfast later."

"Doc, we aren't in Wyoming." I pull away and search the floor for my clothes. "I have to go before someone sees. I'll meet you at the bus."

I speed out to the sitting room and locate my torn panties and jeans. Slipping the jeans on commando, I stuff the torn panties in my front pocket. I throw on the campaign tank top, not bothering with the bra but balling it into one hand and grabbing my shoes with the other. I have to make this the most discreet walk of shame in the history of hookups.

I open the door cautiously, almost overlooking the guard sitting in the corner of the small reception area. He quickly averts his eyes.

I'm not wearing a bra. Great.

Nippling in this tank top. Panties hanging out of my pocket. Barefoot. Well-fucked hair all over the place. This is some trashy shit right here and not my proudest moment.

I flash the guard an awkward smile while I wait for the elevator. The security staff know about Maxim and me. Most of them were with us in Wyoming. They probably think it's strange that we *don't* tell everyone. Fortunately, this is a private floor and you have to know the code to get up here. I should be safe.

The elevator doors open, and before I can step on, Glenn steps off. We both stand there, suspended in our mutual disbelief. I grip my bright orange bra so tightly, I'm sure I crush the wires in it. His gaze falls to my fist of orange satin, and his mouth drops open.

"Glenn, I can explain."

He grabs my wrist, flipping my hand over and forcing my fingers open. The bra, garish in the morning light, falls to the floor. He doesn't let my wrist go but squeezes.

"You little bitch," he says through gritted teeth. "Him? *Him,* Lennix? Miss I Never Fuck My Candidates. You hypocrite. What a cliché you turned out to be."

"Glenn, you're hurting me," I whisper because I don't want to alarm the guard, who will rush him if I show any sign of distress.

The door opens behind us, and I close my eyes, already knowing how ugly this will get and blaming myself.

"What's going on?" Maxim asks.

I look over my shoulder, and he takes in the whole scene at a glance, from my bare feet and the bra on the floor to Glenn's fingers manacling my wrist.

"Get your damn hands off her, Hill," he says, every word a knife aimed and hurled at Glenn's head. He strides over and pulls me out of Glenn's grip, glancing at my wrist, where Glenn's fingerprints have left livid red marks. I see the snap happen in his head and position myself in front of Glenn.

"Doc," I say, pressing my hand to his bare chest.

He looks past me to Glenn and then to the guard in the corner, who's on his feet but apparently unsure how to best intervene and awaiting instruction from Maxim.

"You just stood there? While he did this to her?" The guard opens his mouth, but Maxim puts up one silencing finger. "Don't. I'll deal with you later."

He turns a brimstone glare on Glenn. "You are fucking fired and lucky I don't shove my fist down your throat. If you ever touch her again, *mark* her again, I'll blackball your ass so hard you won't find a job sweeping floors. Am I being clear with you?"

"You fire me because I dared to touch your little whore?" Glenn snarls. Maxim lunges, but I push against his chest.

"Don't." I grab his chin and force him to meet my eyes. "Please let me handle this."

"Let *you* handle this?"

"I'm his boss, Maxim. I should deal with it."

"My boss?" Glenn scoffs, turning to press the button to call the elevator. "I'm glad you turned me down. There's no telling where that pussy's been."

Maxim steps around me and grabs Glenn by the collar, lifting until he's on his tiptoes. The guard pulls Maxim back by the elbow, forcing him to release his hold on Glenn.

"Sir, that's not wise," he says. "Mr. Hill, you should go. Now."

Glenn steps onto the elevator as soon as it comes and stabs the button until the doors close.

"What did he mean, you turned him down?" Maxim asks, his voice velvet-covered steel.

"Really? That's what you focus on?"

"When did he ask?"

"Yesterday after you left."

"You should have told me."

"Exactly when would I have had time to tell you, Maxim?" I ask, pitching my voice too low for the guard to hear. "You started growling and fucking as soon as you entered the room last night."

He closes his eyes and grips the back of his neck. "I *told* you he was into you."

"I missed it. I'm sorry." I stuff the torn panties deeper into my pockets. "I need to go catch him."

"Catch him?" He takes my elbow. "You don't go anywhere near him, Lennix."

"It's my job, Doc. I can handle myself."

"And that's how this happened?" He lifts my wrist between us, showing the marks Glenn left. He stares at the bruises forming, pulling my wrist to his lips. "Dammit, Nix."

"I'm okay." I need to get this situation under control. "I'll take Kimba with me, but I need to catch him before he leaves. I have to remind him he signed an NDA and is legally obligated to keep his damn mouth shut."

"You'll take him." Maxim nods to the guard. "Call someone else up here. You go with her."

I roll my eyes, call the elevator, and brace myself for the shitstorm ahead.

CHAPTER 46
LENNIX

"Maybe let me do most of the talking," Kimba says as we're standing outside Glenn's hotel room. "This needs to be handled diplomatically and firmly."

"And you don't trust me to be diplomatic and firm?"

"I *trusted* you to keep this from ever happening." There haven't been many times when Kimba has been truly irritated with me over the years, but her displeasure is sketched on her keen features now. "If you couldn't be celibate, I told you to be discreet. Leaving the candidate's room with your bra in your hand and your panties in your pocket is not exactly discreet."

I open my mouth to interject, but she holds up a hand, cutting me off.

"There's no defense, Lenn. We don't do this, and you know it. This Monica Lewinsky shit, not a good look."

"Monica Le—"

"I know it's not what it looks like. I know the truth about you and Maxim. I was in Amsterdam. I've seen it from the beginning."

"Not from the beginning, no," I tell her quietly. "You weren't there when I was seventeen and the most amazing man on the planet dropped into a desert and put himself in danger for me. That man needed me last night. He's hurting, Kimba. Doing this so soon after Owen… It's a lot."

"Yeah, well, doing *you* is not helping," she says with the first hint of a smile.

"I know." I blow out a quick breath. "I should have handled it differently, and I'll be more careful."

"Yeah, you will, or you'll be off this campaign."

That sobers me. We're equal partners, but I have no legs to stand on here. From the beginning, we agreed we'd never be sexually involved with our candidates. The fact that she's made the concessions she already has is a miracle. And she's right. It's bad optics. Bad business, but it doesn't feel fair. In hindsight, weathering the small storm a relationship between Owen's brother and his campaign manager would have caused is nothing compared to the scandal of a campaign manager and the candidate being "caught" with their pants down.

"Let's get this over with." Kimba sighs and knocks.

Glenn pulls the door open, his smile smug and his posture relaxed. "Ladies, come in. I've been expecting you."

We walk in, and he gestures to the sitting-room couch. "Please, sit. Let's hear it."

"Hear what?" Kimba lifts a neatly threaded brow. "Us reminding you about the NDA you signed along with your contract? You just heard it."

"Oh, surely there's more than that to sweeten this deal." He sneers and rakes disdainful eyes over me. "Miss High and Mighty got caught fucking not just any candidate but Maxim Cade, the press darling. That's a juicy story, and you know it."

"One you don't get to tell," I say, my voice even but knife-edge sharp. "Per the NDA we keep having to bring up."

"Oh, there are ways around an NDA," Glenn says, deliberately eyeing my breasts and dragging his stare over the length of my body. "Offer me something, *Nix.*"

"How's this for an offer?" Holding his stare, I lift my middle finger. "'Cause that's the closest you'll ever get to fucking me."

"Lenn, you know we have to give him more than that." Kimba

leans forward and raises her hands, both middle fingers up. "I'll double the offer."

Anger mottles his expression. "I'll talk," he spits.

"Do it." Kimba leans back and crosses one skinny-jean-clad leg over the other, flicking her silver Tory Birch ruffle sneakers. "And not only will I sue your ass, but I'll make sure everyone in town knows you were so inept, your writing so lackluster, we couldn't get the candidate to even use your speeches."

"That's not my fault," Glenn snaps. "The guy barely uses speeches. Half his stuff is off the cuff, and you know it."

"And Lennix is a damn good campaign manager who has earned her reputation working hard, not sleeping around," Kimba replies calmly. "And you know that, but it's all about perception, yeah?"

"Look, we can give you a letter of recommendation," I offer, my expression softening. "And an apology."

His eyes flick to mine at that, and he frowns. "An apology?"

"Glenn, I had no idea you had…feelings," I say softly. "We've worked together for years and been friends. I hate seeing it come to this. I want you to know it's not some affair. Maxim and I are in a serious relationship."

"Lennix," Kimba says, various warnings in the one syllable.

"I love him, Glenn," I continue, gambling that the guy I've worked with over the years to elect candidates we both believed in is still there somewhere. "This isn't some tawdry campaign fling."

"It isn't?" Glenn asks, a small frown denting his brows. "I didn't realize it was serious between you two."

"It…" I look down at my hands. "It is, yeah, and we'll share it when the time is right. Now is not the time, and we'll do it when we're ready. In the meantime, there's an NDA that says you won't talk about the things you saw here on the campaign, but that shouldn't even be the issue. You and I have been friends a long time. We should be fighting to save *that*, not fighting each other."

After a few moments of tense silence, Glenn nods. "You're right, and I understand."

"So..." Kimba glances between the two of us, cautious hope in the look. "We're straight?"

"Yeah, I could stay on with the campaign, if that's okay," he says. "Maxim's going all the way. I know that. Writing speeches for the future president will look good. I can get past this if you can."

Crap.

Kimba and I share a quick look because she knows as well as I do there's no way Maxim will go for this.

"I think, given the circumstances," Kimba says, "it's still best that we go our separate ways. We have friends working for the Dems who could use someone like you."

"Yeah, we'll be more than happy to give you a glowing letter of recommendation," I add. "I know we can have you placed in a day or so with another campaign."

Glenn's mouth tightens, and he rubs his palms over his knees. "That won't be necessary," he says stiffly. "I have a friend with another campaign who wanted me to go there initially, but I saw this as a great opportunity. I'm sure there's still a spot for me."

"Do you mind if we ask who?" Kimba frowns.

"I'd prefer not to say until it's definite," he replies, his look daring us to press.

I don't want to. This is as amicable as it will get.

"Well, if that's all," I say, standing, "the bus pulls out for Pittsburgh in a few minutes. We better get out there."

"Yeah," Kimba says, standing, too. "We can arrange transportation to anywhere you need to go."

"I'll get my own ride." Glenn stands, too, extending his hand. "Nice doing business with you."

Kimba accepts his handshake, and so do I. His grip on my fingers tightens, and I look up to find his face a serene mask. Even though there's no detectable malice in his eyes, I still feel like I just made some deal I don't understand with the devil.

CHAPTER 47
MAXIM

"Why didn't you tell us you were auditioning first ladies, Maxim?" Polly asks teasingly.

Everyone freezes, and then all eyes are on me.

Eight of us are spread across two booths on the bus, laptops, iPads, phones, and stacks of papers littering the surfaces.

"Excuse me?" I quirk a curious brow. "I'm not, as far as I know."

I sneak a look at Lennix, whose face reflects my confusion.

"According to *Page Six*," Polly says, showing us an article pulled up on her phone, "you may be just days away from the altar, and America might have its next first lady."

I roll my eyes. "Fake news."

Polly scrolls down the screen, and a few pictures pop up. All heads on that side of the table tilt in one accord to peer at the screen, including Lennix's. She and Kimba exchange a quick, unreadable look.

"Excuse me, guys," Lennix says. "I need to go read this policy paper."

She stands and walks to the back of the bus. Polly looks after her and shrugs, turning back to the *fascinating* piece on my potential forthcoming nuptials.

"Could I at least meet my bride?" I ask, holding my hand out for the phone. Polly laughs and hands it over.

Shit.

It was all innocent, but these photos of Salina and me make things look intimate and *arranged*. The two of us deboarding the Cade Energy plane. Photos some kind parent at the party innocently posted to Instagram from the birthday party. Salina and me smiling, standing side by side, our faces lit by the glow of birthday candles. Us sitting beside each other during dinner on the patio. I thought nothing of any of it at the time, but we present the perfect picture of a courting couple.

America's Next Camelot? the headline blares, and the sensational speculation that follows only gets worse.

Maxim Cade isn't the only candidate. Salina Pérez may be mounting a campaign of her own. Maxim for president. Salina for...first lady? Does she get your vote? A young, beautiful couple in the White House! First babies! We are here for it!

If my father leaked this...

Right on time, my phone buzzes with a notification.

Dad: I didn't do this. Just some reporter piecing shit together and speculating. Trying to take advantage of a slow news cycle.

Me: Why should I believe you?

Dad: If I did it, I would tell you. I'm not scared of you, boy.

Typical.

When I glance up from my phone, Kimba is staring a hole in my head. I lift my brows into the shape of *what?*

She tips her head toward the back of the bus.

Lennix has played it safe since the Glenn incident, barely looking at me the past few days.

"I need to ask Lennix something about this speech for Detroit," I tell the team at the table with a quick smile. "Be right back."

I set off down the long aisle. On the bright side, I get to be alone with my girl for the first time in days, even if it's in the back of a crowded bus. She's in the very last row, knees up against the seat in front of her.

"This seat taken?" I ask, nodding to the empty space beside her.

"Yeah." She scoots into the spot. "It is."

I move her slight weight over so I can sit.

"Could you not *touch* me in public?" she whispers. "We had a close call. We're lucky Glenn hasn't blabbered to the press."

"Is *blabber* a word adults actually use?"

Her mouth twitches, but she schools it into a straight line. I lean forward to catch her eyes with mine, glad the high back of the seat obscures us, provides a small measure of privacy.

"Look, I know you saw those photos of Salina and me at the twins' party. We just happened to be standing together and seated together. We were the only single people there. Everyone else had a kid and a spouse."

"Whatever." She shrugs but looks up to search my face. "You didn't mention the plane ride."

"It wasn't worth mentioning, and I didn't know about it until she got on the plane. My father—"

"Never mind. Enough said. I know he doesn't think I'm good enough for you, so I guess he has aggressively taken matters into his own hands to find a viable alternative."

"I told him to stop and that it's useless. There's no one else but you. He knows that. *You* should know that. Are you jealous?"

"Yes." She glares at me. "And you like it."

I chuckle because I kind of do. "I can laugh because it's ridiculous to even think I'd want someone else."

I lean my head out into the aisle to make sure no one can see us and interlock our fingers. Holding her hand is a privilege I'll never take for granted again.

She relents her first smile since Polly's little bomb. "It's probably a good red herring. Diverts attention away from us."

"You know the press will keep speculating and digging because America doesn't just elect a president," I say. "People have to feel good about the spouse, too. They want to know who that will be. We could end it," I whisper, bending until our heads touch and taking her hand, kissing her wrist. "If we just tell them I already have my first lady. An affair sounds bad, but an engagement sounds romantic. Getting married could solve all our problems."

A deep swallow disturbs the elegant line of her throat. Her shoulder tenses against mine. "Wow," she says with a stiff smile. "Did I miss the proposal?"

I lift her chin, locking our eyes and holding my breath. "Will you marry me, Lennix?"

Her eyes widen, and she snatches her hand away like I burned her. My palm feels cold as soon as she does it. She traps her bottom lip between her teeth and looks away, twisting her fingers into a knot in her lap. The silence following my question—*the first time I've ever asked that question*—is deafening. Slowly, the chatter and laughter of the team up front filter into my senses. Ironically, it's as the interstate flashes by through the bus window, the traffic and landscape blurring, that it becomes painfully clear.

"Are you…turning me down?" I force myself to ask. "Is this a no?"

She squeezes her eyes shut and presses her lips tightly together, looking like she wants to be anywhere but here with me right now. It's an ice pick slicing between my ribs. *How did I miss that Lennix does not actually want to marry me?*

"I love you," she finally says, her voice cracking. "But—"

"But you don't want to marry me?" I ask, forgetting to whisper.

"Shh." She stretches her eyes and tips her head toward the front of the bus. "I didn't say that. You know I want to marry you."

"Then what the hell? Why is this awkward? Why haven't you said yes? I asked you the most important question I've ever asked anyone in my life, and I get *this*."

"Let me finish. I want to marry you, but I'm not sure…" Her

glance slides away, and she closes her eyes again. "I'm not sure I want to be the first lady."

"What?" The word explodes from my mouth, and I don't give a damn who hears.

"Maxim," she hisses. "You have to lower your voice."

"What kind of trap is this?" I whisper hotly. "You practically forced me to run for president—"

"I did not. You want this, and you know it."

"Yes, I want it, but I wouldn't have risked your safety for it if you hadn't been so adamant, and I for damn sure wouldn't have done it if you'd told me you wouldn't *fucking* marry me if I won."

"I didn't..." She huffs a quick breath. "I didn't know. I didn't think in those terms."

"In the terms of I won't marry the man I supposedly love if he gets elected, so I think I'll get him elected?"

She reaches up, holds my face between her hands, and the contact feels so right, *so us*, that I lean into her palm, savor her touch, even in the middle of this fight.

"I know without a shadow of doubt that you're right for this country," she says, tears welling in her eyes. "But I'm not sure being first lady is right for me, Maxim."

Her hands drop from my face, and she swipes at a tear.

"I've worked my whole life for what I have, for who I *am*. I love campaigning. I love the fulfillment of putting leaders in power who will look out for the most vulnerable."

"You can still have impact as first lady. Of course you can."

"I didn't work this hard and this long," she says, some of her usual fierceness rearing, "to be the national plus one."

"The national plus one? Would you stop thinking about people's perceptions and expectations and just think about us? How does this play out? If I win you're the *first girlfriend* for four years?"

"Eight. You won't be a one-term president. Not on my watch."

"And kids? According to your plan, I'd be forty-eight when I left office. You'd be forty-one. You want to wait that long to start our family? Or maybe we won't wait for marriage and I'll be the first baby daddy in the Oval. I'm unconventional but not *that* unconventional."

I take her chin between my fingers gently until she meets my eyes. "I want a family with you. I want a life with you. Are you saying if I become president I won't have that?"

"I'm saying I'm not sure what's best for me, but I know you're best for America."

I drop her chin. "That's not an answer."

"Do I give up everything *I'm* supposed to do so that you can do what *you're* supposed to do? I know that sounds bad, but I'm trying to work through the implications of actual marriage if you win. Giving up my career, my causes to be first lady… It's just not what I signed up for, and I—"

"You signed up for *me*," I say, wanting to shout but keeping my voice low. "And I signed up for you, whatever that means, wherever that takes us."

"Easy to say when 'whatever' is you becoming the leader of the free world and me smiling and looking pretty for a 'say no to drugs' campaign or advocating for literacy. It's not what I want to *do*. That's not who I want to be. Don't ask me to know everything *today*. We had to move quickly. I just need some time to wrestle through this, Maxim."

I'll be damned if I'm losing my shit on a bus full of campaign staffers, and that's about to happen. I stand, but she catches my wrist.

"Let go, Nix. I have some things I need to *wrestle through* before I give this speech and convince Detroit to vote Cade."

I pull away and stride to the front, a small fire kindling under the collar of the golf shirt I'm wearing. I hate golf shirts. One of the pollsters suggested I try a golf shirt because some study showed they supposedly put people at ease. How does a damn golf shirt reassure someone they'll make rent? Or that their retirement plan will actually be worth something if this planet stays solvent long enough to use it? The world is on fire, and Lennix just turned down my proposal, and we're talking about golf shirts?

I rip the shirt over my head, and Kimba looks up from her phone, eyes pinging from my bare chest to my scowling face.

"I hate golf shirts," I snap. "Don't any of you ever ask me to wear a *fucking* golf shirt again. I don't care if millennials love them. I don't care if they make single mothers feel attractive or if the color blue makes men between the ages of thirty and forty-five trust me." I hold up the golf shirt for everyone to see, brandishing it like a weapon and then flinging it on the table. "No more golf shirts. *Ever.* Is that understood?"

"Seriously?" Lennix asks from behind me, walking up the aisle. "Don't be a jerk."

I swing around to face her. "Are you trying to get fired, Ms. Hunter? Last I checked, you work for me."

"Last I checked, *Mr. Cade*, you can go fuck yourself."

Absolute silence floods the bus, and we all seem frozen in some farce. Lennix gasps, covers her mouth, eyes widening, bouncing between me and the shocked staffers. "Oh, my God. I'm so sorry. We're all under a lot of pressure, and I..."

She falters, blinking at tears, running a shaking hand through her hair. My self-possessed girl is coming undone. It's not just the two of us being uncharacteristically undisciplined. I don't even think it's the fight we just had. It's *the wrestle*—the conflict of being in love with someone on a path you aren't sure you can take. As much as I want to resist her, to remain furious with her, I have no defense against this rare vulnerability. If all these people weren't gawking at us, I'd take her to the back of this bus and hold her, kiss her, assure her that we'll do whatever she wants to do. I'll *do* whatever she needs to do as long as we can be together.

And then I'd fuck her until she remembers it's just us. No matter what, always only us.

I glance at the shocked faces and the wide eyes of the team.

"I'm sorry, too," I tell them. "We're all under a lot of pressure, yeah, but I never want to take it out on you guys. You're amazing, and you deserve better than that."

I'm saved from more explanations or awkward apologies when the bus comes to a halt with a small lurch and sigh of brakes. I have to get off this thing and go regroup before I destroy everything I worked for, including my relationship with Lennix. I stride to the front of the bus. Quick footsteps follow me when the bus doors open.

"Doc," Lennix calls. "You forgot your shirt."

But I'm already outside, and as soon as my foot hits the pavement, a swarm of reporters gathers around me like bees, buzzing in front of our hotel, all stretching phones and mics toward me. Lennix steps off the bus, clutching my shirt, her eyes darting across the eager, curious faces.

"What the hell?" she mutters.

"Is it true?" one of them yells. "Is Lacy telling the truth?"

"Lacy?" Lennix asks, her mouth hanging open. "Oh, God."

"Who is Lacy?" I ask Lennix, but a reporter answers.

"Lacy Reardon alleges that you and your campaign manager are having an affair, Mr. Cade. Is it true?"

CHAPTER 48
LENNIX

"This is bad, right?" I ask.

Back at campaign headquarters in New York, Kimba and I stare at the iPad on the conference-room table. It's a charming photo of me standing beside a bare-chested Maxim, looking like we just rolled out of bed instead of stepped off a hybrid campaign bus.

*"Don't f*ck the candidate!"* the headline of the article proclaims. The piece goes on to say Lacy Reardon, former campaign employee fired by Lennix Hunter for sexual misconduct, accuses Ms. Hunter of hypocrisy since she is indeed conducting a long-term affair with her client, presidential hopeful Maxim Cade.

"That one's trending on Twitter," Kimba offers, her voice quite calm for the anger I suspect boils under the surface. "Don't fuck the candidate."

"Kimba."

"There's a GIF, too. You rolling your eyes with one hand on your hip. I'm actually secondhand embarrassed for you."

"I'm sorry."

"And a meme. Almost forgot about the meme and the surveillance camera footage was a *g-reat* touch."

Note to self: Never make an enemy of a tech genius who could mine the internet for footage of your lover coming in and out of your apartment.

And in. And out. And in. And out.

The *several* grainy surveillance photos of Maxim climbing into his SUV with security trailing him for sure made me seem like some little trollop he kept in a house and visited on a regular basis. Glenn confirmed my suspicions that he'd had something up his sleeve when he texted Kimba and me right after the story broke.

Glenn: Hey, ladies. Just wanted to let you know. That old buddy who had a spot for me on another campaign? It was Lacy. I'm writing speeches for Governor Dentley now. Glad we're all still FRIENDS. ;-)

Apparently Lacy and Glenn became pal-ish on that project they worked on together before, and he went straight to her bearing tales about Maxim and me. His text message was just enough to taunt us but not enough to prove he's Lacy's source. Certainly not enough to sue his ass for breaking the NDA. For all intents and purposes, Lacy talked. Glenn didn't.

"Oh, this might be the best headline yet." Kimba turns the iPad so I can see. "*Making it with the Kingmaker*. I think that's my fave."

"I know. I messed up."

"Messed up?" Kimba looks at me, disappointment and anger accumulating in her dark eyes. "Two of the candidates we had booked for midterm elections called this morning to say they've found consultants with 'less drama' and won't be needing our services."

I close my eyes and drop my head into my hands.

"Drama, Lennix. Do you know how long these people have been waiting for us to screw up? Two brown girls who think their shit doesn't stink getting taken down a peg or two. So *that's* how they made it so far, so fast. That's what they're saying. You *gave* them that."

"Kimba, come on," Maxim says from the conference-room door. "I think we both feel bad enough as it is."

"Oh, *you* feel bad?" Kimba laughs harshly. "That's not how it works, Maxim. These headlines aren't about you doing anything wrong or being suspect or not being great at what you do. Matter of fact, there are a lot of men patting you on the back for tapping that ass."

"Do you think I'm going to let you talk about her like that?" he asks, his eyes turning to slits.

"I don't have to talk about her." Kimba stands and points to the iPad. "Everyone else is. I *love* her. I've worked with her the last ten years building something we believe in. Now it and she are being laughed at, are being denigrated because of *you*. So don't come in here thinking you're gonna set *me* straight. I set *you* straight."

She walks to the door and stops in front of him. "Also, Ms. Hunter is no longer available for your campaign. She's being reassigned, but should you still want to retain the services of Hunter, Allen and Associates, meet me back here at eight o'clock sharp tomorrow morning so we can figure out how to salvage what's left of your campaign. Excuse me."

She pushes past him, through the door and out of the conference room. Her high heels echo down the hall to the reception area, followed by a definite slam of the front door.

In the quiet after her departure, I flip through the various articles and insulting headlines.

"My father called today," I say. "He wanted to make sure I was okay."

Maxim takes the seat across from me.

"He got into an argument with a colleague at work," I continue tonelessly. "The professor apparently had not-so-nice things to say about me, not realizing I was Dr. Hunter's daughter. He and Dad almost came to blows. He didn't tell me that part. Bethany did."

Maxim releases a sharp breath and reaches for my hand. "Nix, I'm so sorry."

"It's not your fault." I shake my head and push my hair back. "I knew this would happen."

"I'm not just apologizing for the fallout," he says. "I'm apologizing for what happened before all of this, on the bus."

I pause, flicking an uncertain glance up at him. It was almost easy to forget the volatile conversation we'd had before the press descended. I force a laugh. "Let me deal with one crisis at a time, okay?"

"Me asking you to marry me is a crisis?" He asks the question lightly, but I know him too well not to hear, not to *feel* the hurt behind it. I saw it in his eyes on the bus, too.

"When you asked," I start, meting out each word carefully, not wanting to do any more damage than I already have, "for just a second, it was scary how badly I wanted to be your wife. *Yes* was right there on the tip of my tongue. My heart wanted it immediately, but my head started asking, how would this work? How would I advocate so hard, so openly for Native issues when you'd have to be *everyone's* president? And what would we say when they call me biased? Or I take a stance that you don't agree with or that doesn't align with your policies? A first lady doesn't usually have *opinions*—at least, not that she voices. She has a *husband*, and her voice is swallowed by his."

He's quiet because he knows I'm right. His gaze is fixed on his thumb caressing the back of my hand.

"I've worked really hard to become myself, Maxim," I say softly. "To know what I believe, to live out my convictions, and to say what I think. I just want to make sure I wouldn't be losing all of that, losing *myself* in you and all that being the president requires."

A single hot tear slips over my cheek, and I brush at it with the hand he's not holding. "I saw the way Salina looked at you in those pictures."

He lifts his eyes to my face even though I don't meet them.

"She's a lawyer, like Millie. Attended Cornell and is a badass in her own right," I say, "but I bet she wouldn't think twice about giving it all up to be your first lady. I saw that in Millie for Owen, too. Hell, I see it in Mena for Jim. She loves being a senator's wife. It's enough for her. A part of me wishes I could be like that—so willing to see my dreams absorbed by yours."

He lifts my chin with his finger, forcing me to look at him. "Do you remember what you said in your speech that first day we met?"

I frown, sniff, and concentrate. "Um…which part?"

"You said, 'Do you see me? Do you hear me? I don't think you can,' but I *did* right away. I knew who you were, Lennix, before we even met. When I saw that dog headed for you, I didn't think about the fact that we didn't know each other. I didn't care what my father thought. There was no *time* to think. I couldn't have put words to it in that moment, but on some level, I knew who you were, and I knew you were mine."

I nod because I wasn't old enough to understand the connection between us that first day; maybe not even in Amsterdam did I fully grasp what it meant to meet the other half of your soul, but I know now.

"I'm sorry for not listening to you on the bus," he says. "I wasn't hearing you. I think I was afraid to hear what you needed to tell me."

He gestures to the iPad on the table between us. "Those headlines aren't real. The articles aren't real. *We* know what's real. I still very much want to marry you one day, and if this crazy plan of ours works, I'll be the president, but we can table marriage until you're ready."

I look at him, searching his face. That's all I want, time to make sure I'll be satisfied with the person that role will require me to be, but I know what it costs Maxim to give me that time. He's a generous man, but when he wants something, he takes. He wants me more than everything, so this is hard for him.

"Are you sure?" I ask.

"That day in my office with Chuck Garrett was one of the best moments of my life, hearing how you saw me. I want you to know that I see *you*, Lennix. You said run him as a rebel. If an independent finally manages to upend the two-party system and win the presidency, don't expect me to play by all the rules, including how my wife functions."

"Doc—"

"I believe we could blaze our own trail." The look on his face, in his eyes is passion and intensity and confidence and love. "I know you'd marry *me*. I'm giving you time to decide if you want to marry the president."

CHAPTER 49
MAXIM

"You sure about this?" Kimba asks for what feels like the hundredth time.

"Yeah." I check my tie in the greenroom mirror and stuff it into the vest of my three-piece suit. "Positive."

"Let the record show you are doing this against my expert advice."

"The record has been noted." I kiss her on the cheek. "I'm doing it."

"It may be disastrous for your campaign."

"Maybe." I shrug. "But it may help Nix. Which do you think means more to me?"

Lennix is already out on the campaign trail with the new gubernatorial candidate she's helping. She and I have spoken very little since yesterday, but she knows what I plan to do today. She, like Kimba, isn't sure it's the right move, but it's *my* move. My instincts tell me this is how we get past this, get back on message, and how I get to openly be with the woman I love.

And maybe still get to be president. There's a lot at risk, but I've gambled more than once with all my chips in.

"I'm sorry if I came across all hard yesterday," Kimba says.

"Hey, it's a tense time. We all say things we wish we could take back."

"Oh, I don't wish I could take any of it back," she says, shaking her head and chuckling. "I said what I meant, and I meant what I said. I'm just sorry it was kind of harsh."

"Oh. Well, as apologies go, I accept."

The door opens, and Alice, the producer, pops her head in. "We're ready for you, Mr. Cade."

I nod, give my reflection one last check, and follow her.

———————

"We're joined tonight on *Beltway* by the man everyone's talking about," Bryce Collins says. "Please welcome Maxim Cade."

When the polite applause dies down, I can almost feel the crowd's curiosity poking and probing at me.

"First, I'd like to offer my condolences for the loss of your brother, Senator Owen Cade," Bryce says soberly and, from what I can ascertain, sincerely. "Truly a fine man. I was honored to have met him."

"Thank you," I say, bracing myself for the flurry of questions I know will follow the sympathy.

"A few weeks ago, you announced your candidacy for president. How's that going?"

"Uh, up until a few days ago, swimmingly."

The audience laughs, and I offer a self-deprecating smile.

"Right," Bryce says, smiling, too. "Recent reports indicate there may have been some sexual misconduct between you and your campaign manager, Lennix Hunter. Is there any truth to that claim?"

"None whatsoever."

"Okay, you're not under oath here," Bryce says wryly. "So you can't perjure yourself or anything, but there is quite a bit of surveillance footage of you coming and going from Ms. Hunter's apartment. Would you care to address that?"

"You asked if there was truth to the accusation of sexual misconduct. I unequivocally deny that there was any misconduct."

"So Lennix Hunter is not your mistress?"

"My mistress?" I release a disbelieving laugh. "Is this Victorian England? Is Ms. Hunter being kept in a townhouse in Mayfair? That's a very backward way of discussing a consensual relationship between two adults. Maybe I'm her mister."

There are a few chuckles from the audience, and some women clap. I may have even detected one "amen."

"So you admit there is a romantic relationship between you and Lennix Hunter."

"Yes, there is."

A gasp travels through the crowd, and the silence that follows hints they're waiting for me to elaborate.

"Could you tell us how it started?" Bryce asks, his eyes gleaming with excitement for the illicit details. "Was it on the campaign trail?"

"No, long before that."

"You knew Ms. Hunter before?"

"I met Lennix when she was seventeen years old. I was twenty-four, but nothing happened, so please don't come at me about being a dirty old man."

Some of the nervous tension breaks, and most of the crowd laughs again.

"We met at a demonstration." I chuckle. "Ironically, she was protesting one of my father's projects. A Cade Energy pipeline that would go through ground her tribe considered sacred and that had been protected."

"At seventeen?"

"Yes. She was speaking, actually."

"And your first impression of her was what?"

"I heard her before I saw her. I'd never heard conviction like that from anyone so young. Not even at my age. I was twenty-four at the time, so seven years older, and, as noted, nothing romantic happened between us."

I pause and rub the back of my neck. "Well, that's not entirely true. I think that was the day I started falling in love with her."

"What happened at the protest?"

"We actually got arrested."

"You got arrested for protesting your own father's pipeline?" Bryce asks, delighted.

"He was not too happy about it," I reply dryly. "But that's where Lennix and I first met."

"There's a well-documented history of antagonism between your father and Lennix Hunter. Is it difficult managing that tension?"

"Sometimes, but listen. This nation has a painful, problematic past with its treatment of Native Americans. Someone like Lennix can't even hold a twenty-dollar bill without seeing Andrew Jackson. They buy their groceries with money celebrating the man who caused them arguably the most pain."

"I'd never thought of it like that."

"You and I don't have to. When people speak out about a past as painful as theirs, as long as they're not breaking the law, you don't get to tell them how to do it. So it's not awkward for me that Lennix objects to some of my father's business practices. So do I. That doesn't mean I don't love him or want a relationship with him. It means we don't agree. I won't tell Lennix not to voice her outrage on these matters. My role should be to listen."

"Are you concerned at all about the potential complications of running for president and dating someone like Ms. Hunter?"

"Excuse me?" A muscle in my jaw ticks. My teeth grind together. "You should define what you mean by 'someone like Ms. Hunter.'"

"Yes, well." He clears his throat. "Someone who has been so vocal protesting for a particular people group."

"Her people, you mean. Native Americans."

"Yes, but if you're president, it will be of the United States, all of them, all the people. Does it complicate things that in the interest of *her* people, Ms. Hunter has espoused views about our forefathers that some consider unpatriotic or un-American?"

"I think her views should be considered not un-American but

pre-American. They were here first. This was all theirs. We stole it. The implications of those wrongs are still being felt. And I think we get patriotism twisted a lot."

"You think we should redefine patriotism?"

"I think we should *remember* what patriotism actually is—that it's rooted in love of country and seeing a vision for life, liberty, and justice *for all* fully realized. Our forefathers wrote the truth but, in many cases, didn't live it out. Patriotism is loving this country enough to examine its problematic history so we *can* fulfill our forefathers' words."

"Some would argue that our forefathers did what all nation builders have done," Bryce says. "The strongest take over and make something good better, something that will last."

"Your version of colonization sounds like Darwinism, with the strongest surviving."

"It's not too far off," Bryce chuckles.

"I've lived all over the world, and America is my favorite place to be by far. I believe in it, or I wouldn't be running to lead it. Just because something ends up wonderful doesn't mean you don't expose the wrong in how it began. This country is amazing, but our origins are complicated and, in many cases, morally reprehensible. In the process of building something incredible, we stole, we destroyed, we took advantage of, we hurt a lot of people. We detract from our greatness when we not only refuse to acknowledge or examine our actions historically but don't seek ways to heal and make amends where we can. I believe that's the essence of what 'people like Ms. Hunter' are asking of us."

Bryce nods, his eyes narrowing. He turns over the card in his hand and picks up another.

"Thank you for articulating that," Bryce says. "Could we return to the romantic nature of your relationship with Ms. Hunter?"

"By all means."

"So you met her protesting your father's pipeline, and then what?"

"We reconnected briefly a few years later in Amsterdam when

she was on vacation and I was completing my doctorate. We didn't see each other again for another decade, when Ms. Hunter's firm started managing my brother's campaign."

"And you resumed your relationship?"

"God, no. She wouldn't give me the time of day. I literally moved to DC to be closer to her, but she wouldn't consider me for months."

"So when did it become romantic again?" Bryce chortles. "I guess mutually romantic, since Ms. Hunter had held out."

"Around five months ago."

"And why did you hide your relationship?"

"Because of what's happening right now. People making erroneous assumptions about her, about her work ethic, about how she became so successful. She's earned everything she has, including my love."

A sigh passes through the crowd at my confession.

"So you do love her?" Bryce roots around for clarity, which I'm more than happy to give.

"Yes, we're in a committed relationship."

"And marriage?" Bryce probes.

"Something we'll decide when the time is right for us."

"Americans like to know what we're getting," Bryce says. "It's a package deal. They want to know what their first lady would do, who she is."

"If they elect me, Americans can expect a man smart enough to ask for help when he doesn't know and bold enough to stand on his own when necessary. Someone who will fight for them in new, innovative ways, who will watch the bottom line ruthlessly and take risks that will propel us all forward. A man who will honor the past when we got it right and apologize for when we got it wrong and who is determined the future will be better than we can imagine."

I turn my attention to the audience and shrug, smile.

"Just consider the kind of woman that man would choose, and you've got Lennix Hunter."

CHAPTER 50
MAXIM

"I swear I'll try to make it," I tell Lennix, taking a sip of my coffee.

"I know how full your schedule is today," she says from the other end of the line. "You don't turn down *Good Morning America* for anything. This is a great chance for you to connect with voters."

"Yeah, Kimba sent me some policy notes last night to review. Basically *War and Peace* but slightly longer."

"She's thorough." Lennix laughs. "I'll give her that."

"We'll probably strangle each other before November. Being on the road without you as a buffer sucks. There's no one to protect me from her."

"Well, I'm on the road myself. The governor's race is heating up, and I think we've got a real shot of turning Virginia blue. I mean, it's a swing state, so it'll probably go red again in four years, but I gotta try, right?"

"Right." I rest in the easy silence for a few seconds, just enjoying the sound of her voice, the thought of her. "I miss you."

"Same, Doc. Same."

I smile even though it hurts to not be with her. "There are some guys in from Hong Kong. After *GMA*, I have to meet with them and try to save this deal, but I plan to catch a flight right after so I can be there in time."

"If you don't make it—"

"It's a big deal. I want to be there."

"Okay." I hear the smile in her voice. "Well, I have to go now. It's still really early here, but Mena will be up soon. I'm going for a run and then making *her* breakfast for a change."

"Tell her I said hi. I love you. It needs to be Tuesday really soon."

"We don't have to say that anymore," she says, laughing.

"I know, but I just like it."

"Bye, you."

"Bye, you."

I need to focus. Kimba really did send me a huge stack of policy notes. She wants me prepared for this interview. I already know they'll ask about Nix and me. There's no paper for that. Everyone does these days. Not in the "dirty little secret" way they used to. Now they want to know if we're engaged yet. Will she be my first lady if I win this thing?

Who the hell knows?

It's an act of faith, tabling our marriage discussion but moving forward on the trail. Maybe she'll warm to the idea of reshaping what the role of first lady could look like. I won't rush her. It *is* a huge sacrifice. Hell, if I win, I can't run my businesses while I'm in office. I built those from the ground up. The thought of someone else steering them, shaping them while I'm away, is galling. But I meant what I said. I'm running because I believe I can change things.

The door opens as I'm reviewing a few immigration laws that really do need to be struck from the books.

"Grim," I say. "Didn't your mama teach you to knock?"

"I think you'll be more interested in what I have for you than in my manners," he says dryly but with just enough excitement in the undercurrent of his voice to catch my attention.

"What've you got?"

"Him," Grim says simply.

My head snaps up, and I pin him with my stare. "Gregory? You got a lead on him?"

"Not just a lead. I know exactly where he is. I've got *eyes* on him, King."

"How?"

"We found the rat."

"How?"

"I'll let Wallace tell you," he says, dialing on his phone and coming around my desk so I can see. Wallace comes onscreen. He hasn't been around much since our confrontation at Lennix's apartment. Lennix and I have been on the road most of the time, first for Owen, then to Wyoming, and then for my campaign.

"Hey, Maxim," he says. It looks like he's home, based on the bedroom visible behind him.

"Wallace, how'd this happen?"

"Uh, yeah." He rubs his eyes. "There's this tech on my team, Chauncey. When I got back to work after Costa Rica, he was acting weird. Really weird. Missing work, checked out. Not at all like he was before my trip. Then he requested a transfer not long after I returned. CamTech never told anyone about the abduction, but he just kept watching me and gave me a sneaky vibe. So I gave Grim Chauncey's information."

"We cross-referenced him with what we knew about Keene to see if there were any intersections," Grim says, "and there were. They were at Stanford together. A search of Chauncey's home computer revealed some interesting payments that synced with several K&R incidents we suspect the Keene brothers may have been behind. Looks like he hacked into their systems for intel, but CamTech was the only company he infiltrated as an employee."

"Did you get a warrant to search his place?" I ask, frowning.

"No, he was the victim of an 'unfortunate home invasion,'" Grim says, tongue firmly in cheek. "While the burglars were at it, they tapped his phone."

"Nice." I fist-bump him.

"And then the day CamTech turned the vaccine files over to the CDC—"

"So they finally did it?" I cut in.

"They did, yeah." Wallace nods. "And our whole team knew because it essentially ends our research for now. We've been reassigned to a different project."

"So as soon as CamTech notified the team," Grim says, "we intercepted a text message between our rat and an untraceable number. The text didn't give any detail about Keene's whereabouts, but I had enough to question him." Grim's grin is evil. "Unofficially, of course. You know it doesn't take long to break these weak motherfuckers. Barely took any pressure, a few threats, and he gave up Keene's location. Sang like a bird."

"Where is he?" I ask, fists clenched and heart pounding with dark anticipation.

"Oklahoma City," Wallace answers, wearing a concerned frown and watching me carefully.

The world slows down, every second covered in tar. I can barely get my tongue to move. "Lennix is in Oklahoma."

"I know." A tortured scowl twists Wallace's even features. "If anything happens to her—"

"She's safe," Grim interjects. "Her security has her covered."

"You best be damn sure about that, brother," I say, my voice low and promising so much hell to pay if she's not.

"I told you, I have eyes on him and my guys are in position to move in as we speak."

"He's in the same damn city as Nix," I say. "That's not coincidence. Move the fuck in."

"There are a couple of ways to play this." Grim casts a careful glance to the screen where Wallace waits, watches, and listens. If I know Grim, he's about to tell me some off-the-record-illegal shit.

"Can we trust you, Murrow?" I ask.

"Of course," Wallace says, his voice tense. "Do whatever you have to. Just protect Lenny. I don't care if you break every law in the book. She's my best friend. I just want her safe."

It would typically irritate me to hear him call her his best friend, but I can't muster my usual possessiveness. I'm glad she has people in her life as loyal as Wallace—who care about her. Maybe he's not half bad.

"Tell us," I say, shifting my attention from Wallace onscreen to Grim by my side.

"We haven't alerted the authorities," Grim says.

"Don't." My voice is clipped. Curt. "Keene doesn't get a trial or handcuffs or a jury of his peers. They'll screw it up. He assassinated my brother, and he tried to kill my girl. No one I love is safe until we end this for good. I want to see his dead body."

Wallace sucks in a sharp breath. "Maxim, I—"

"If you think that asshole gets to see another day after what he's done to my family and what he's tried to do to Lennix," I say with complete calm, "then hang up the damn phone right now, Murrow. Forget what you've heard and don't ever ask me about this."

A tight pool of silence follows my words.

"Um, I was going to say," Wallace tells me from his screen, "that I agree. We need confirmation of death."

I nod, feeling a new respect for the man Lennix counts as one of her closest friends. "Glad we're on the same page."

"Except you also need plausible deniability," Grim says. "If there's ever any blowback from this, it can't come back around to the president of the United States."

"What makes you so sure I will be?"

Grim gives me the knowing look he's been working on for a decade. "You win everything eventually. Why would the presidency be any different?"

"An election is a little more complicated than a company

takeover." I pause, knowing both men will disagree with what I have to say. "I need to see it happen."

"I don't think that's a good idea," Wallace says.

"Should I define 'plausible deniability' for you?" Grim scowls. "It's too risky."

"You think I don't know that? But I have to see this all the way through. You're sure about these eyes you got on him, Grim?"

"Of course. I've got a feed to the very spot where he's hiding out. He moves, we see it."

"If he moves," I say, "kill him, but I'm still coming. I won't do it, but I need to *see* it, if I can." I clear my throat because the hot emotion there won't allow me to speak otherwise. "I owe my brother that."

Both men fall silent, and for a moment I think they'll disagree, but Grim nods, his narrowed eyes promising me the vengeance I crave but can't execute myself.

"Wallace, we need to go," Grim says, sighing and running a hand over the back of his neck. "I guess we have a flight to catch."

———

The man in the belly of the abandoned building doesn't strike you as a psychopath at first glance. He has a hot plate going, the aroma of bacon rising and filling the small space. He doesn't even flinch when a mouse scampers over his bare foot. His purple hair grows in a chaos of curls, but the roots are golden blond.

He seems simply eccentric until you notice the bomb in the corner. There are no flashing red lights or beeping sounds yet. No, he'll set those up when he goes to the Oklahoma State Capitol building up the street later today, according to Chauncey.

"Where's your mask?" I ask.

Gregory Keene whirls away from his bacon to face me. Immediately, a welcoming smile blossoms on his handsome face with its square jaw and blue eyes. "Maxim, you scared me."

"Sorry about that." I wave the gun I have trained on him in the direction of a stack of boxes a few feet away. "Have a seat."

"I actually have a very full day planned." Gregory nods toward the bomb in the corner. "As you can see."

"This won't take long. I promise."

"I've been meaning to call you," he says, settling on the boxes. "I've seen you on the campaign trail, and you might actually have a shot at winning this thing."

"Thank you for your expert assessment."

"I particularly like your take on health care. Innovative."

"Well, we both know how broken the system is. I really am sorry about what happened to your mother," I tell him. "No one should be abandoned and given up on that way."

The pleasant smile turns fox-sly, and the welcoming blue eyes go cold. "I guess as president, you'll fix it."

"If I make it that far, I'll try, but you won't be around to see it."

"I was really looking forward to seeing our girl today." He sighs, shrugging philosophically. "Killing her will have to wait since I suppose the cops are on their way."

My caustic laugh echoes in the dank little underground alcove. "Cops? You killed my brother, and you tried to kill *my* girl." I nod toward the bomb. "Three times now, if we count the car bomb."

"Oh, let's do count the car bomb. Killing your brother was some of my finest work."

Every muscle in my body screams in protest when I don't move, longing to lunge for him, to tear his throat out. Control is the friend urging caution.

"Peacefully in a jail cell after another fifty years is not how you die, Keene."

"So what?" Gregory folds his arms over his chest. "The future president of the United States is gonna kill me in cold blood? You can't."

"I deeply regret that you're right. I can't risk it." I turn my head to find the shape of Grim carved into the shadows. "But he can."

Gregory Keene never sees Grim pull the trigger. His head doesn't explode. The bullet leaves a large hole in what I've heard Grim call the T-box, dead center between the eyes. All the trauma is inside, a death shot that destroys the lower brain stem and all the processes necessary for life.

Gregory never had a chance.

The fatalism lands like lead on my shoulders, and I stare into the sightless eyes of the man whose life held so much promise. A genius. Stanford. Harvard. All thrown away because bitterness consumed him, eating its way through his morals and decency like parasites. He lost himself to grief.

Twice.

I know what that darkness feels like, how it crowds out all the light and makes you do things you would never consider before the loss. I wish things could have been different. I wish Gregory could have met Owen out on the campaign trail, aired his grievances, seen how O would change things.

Pain always carves out two paths. We all have pain. The difference is where it takes you. Gregory followed it down a path of vengeance that killed my brother and would have taken Lennix from me. I can feel no remorse for his death and still think what a shame, what a waste.

"King, go." Grim's words snap in the tomb-like quiet of the basement. "Rick's waiting in the back alley."

"Does he know?"

"No one knows but you and me. Didn't want to risk it. The rest of the team is standing down and awaiting orders upstairs."

"So the body—"

"I got it." He nods toward the shadows he occupied just minutes before. "Go through there and up to the main floor."

"And if they ask—"

"They won't. Go."

I follow the dark, narrow stairwell up to a door leading to an alley behind the building. Rick waits there, just like Grim said he would be. His inscrutable face reveals no more interest than usual.

"You ready, sir?"

"Uh, yeah." I pull out my phone to look at the screen saver. It's a girl and a guy kissing in a field of tulips, a freeze-frame of love in bloom. They look young and happy and unconcerned, no idea what the years ahead will bring, but it doesn't seem to matter. He's holding her like she's the whole world in his arms, and she looks glad to be there.

"Where are we going?" Rick asks.

I smile, glancing up to find the spire of the State Capitol pointing toward the sky.

"We're going to witness history."

CHAPTER 51
LENNIX

"This day has been a long time coming," Senator Jim Nighthorse says, spreading his pleased smile around the crowded room in the Oklahoma State Capitol building. "The number of missing and murdered indigenous women each year is staggering, an epidemic that has been overlooked, underreported, and unaddressed."

Mena and I stand behind him, holding hands, smiling, even as we both brush away our tears.

"I'm so proud of the bipartisan effort and commitment behind this groundbreaking legislation facilitating more efficient communication between tribal and local authorities. If we care, we'll keep searching, and we'll keep saying our sisters' names."

He glances over his shoulder, smiling into my teary eyes.

"This bill is the namesake of a national MMIW activist who lost her life in the field, in the fight. It is my honor to sign the Liana Reynolds Act into law today and to have her daughter, Lennix Hunter, here with us as a witness."

I step forward to sign along with several other witnesses and legislators, architects of the law. Looking out over those assembled, I find my father and Bethany in the crowd. He nods, approval and love and the same inevitable shadow of sorrow in his eyes I know he sees in mine. My hands are shaking so badly I can barely hold the ceremonial pen. Tears fill my eyes, and the words on the page blur.

"Lennix," Jim says. "Would you like to say a few words?"

I nod and open my mouth to start my prepared remarks when the door at the back of the room opens. Maxim walks in, accompanied by Rick. I honestly didn't expect him to be able to do *GMA* and his meeting and make it here on time. He smiles at me in that way that makes the rest of the world disappear for the space of at least one breath, and for a second, even with a roomful of people, it's just us. He blows me a kiss and leans against the wall, pride all over his face. I drag my eyes away from him and address the crowd.

"My mother was a fighter," I say. "Real fighters know you should never assume survival. She lived like every day was her last, being bold and loving loudly with no reserve, but she also lived like there were seven generations coming behind her. Always looking to the future and fighting to make it better. She lived for others. She fought for everyone who needed a champion."

My voice wavers, and tears escape the corners of my eyes as I see her again, glowing with pride after my Sunrise Dance. Taking pictures and dousing me with her love. I'm teetering inside, and I scan the room until I find Maxim again, righting myself through the sheer, steadying force of love in his eyes.

"She was the most vital, vivid person I've ever known," I choke out. "And for a long time, I had nightmares wondering how she died."

I shake my head, heedless of the tears or the way my voice cracks.

"I don't dream anymore about how Mama died. I celebrate how she lived. One of her favorite quotes was *'They buried us, but they didn't know we were seeds.'* My mother was a seed. She died when I was thirteen, but today, look at her *harvest* in this act that will search for, find, and save so many of our women in time. Look at her alive in *me*. Every morning I wake up and live with purpose, decide to make this world a better place, or decide not to just live for myself but to help those in greatest need, Mama lives on. *I* am her harvest.

"I used to despair that no one remembered her, that no one said her name or the names of the thousands of Native women who go missing and are never found. But today, I say her name. This act *bears* her name. Liana Reynolds."

The applause of the crowd, the smiling faces fade for a moment, and I'm back on that open plain for my dance. When I was a girl, I ran in the four directions, gathering the elements to myself—everything I would need to become a woman. According to tradition, that day unleashed my ability to heal myself, others, and my community, but being a woman is more than making the pain go away. It's living through it, learning from it, and putting it to good use, like we did today.

When Changing Woman heads east every morning, hoping to run into her younger self, I wonder what she would say if she ever did. Because now I know what I would say.

Nistan.

Run.

Keep running.

You don't stop running because it's hard. You don't stop running because it hurts. Don't you *dare* stop running because someone says you'll never finish the race or even that it's not your race to run.

Prove them all wrong.

Blaze your own trail.

Girl, woman, they'll *never* give you the world. You have to make your own.

And then I know. That thing I've been wrestling with, in this moment it's as clear as that girl running on a distant plain, cheered on by her community, by generations of ancestors.

Blaze your own trail.

Make your own world.

I won't let anyone define who I am, who I love, how I live. I'll do that. Will I have to make sacrifices? Of course. Compromises? Of course.

But will I have the chance to do something no one who looks like me has ever done before? And with a man I love more than everything else? A man who loves me the same way?

I signed on for you, whatever that means, wherever that takes us.

Maxim's words land on my heart, plant seeds, take root. All these years, I've been searching for the once-in-a-lifetime candidate, and I've found him. Maxim is my once-in-a-lifetime, and I'm his. Once in a lifetime and for the rest of our lives.

I excuse myself from the group of well-wishers and rush to the back of the room. Maxim leans against the wall, his smile spreading wider the closer I get, and the closer I get, the harder my heart pounds. Not caring if there are cameras or what people will say or what anyone will think, I reach up to take his face between my hands and kiss him long and possessively, claiming him. He shifts, his hands sliding down my back, tightening at my waist. He groans into the kiss, breaking away to bury his face in my neck.

"Nix," he breathes into my ear, chuckling. "Give a guy some warning. You want everybody to see the effect you have on me every time you walk into a room?"

I throw back my head and laugh, feeling freer than I have ever felt in my life. "Yeah, I think I do want them to see."

He cups my cheek, brushing my hair back from my face, the love in his eyes apparent.

"Let's change the world, okay?" My smile fades, and so does his. He searches my eyes, caresses my mouth with his thumb.

"Together?" he asks, his voice sobering.

I nod, pressing my hand to his heart. The compass charm on my bracelet catches the light, glimmers like the love that guided us from our first unlikely moment to this one.

"Yeah," I answer, practically *feeling* my face glow with the love in my heart, with the peace I've made. "Together."

EPILOGUE
MAXIM

"Love is such a dynamic force, isn't it?
It is the most inexplicable and yet the most beautiful force in life.
O, how joyous it is to be in it."
— *Love letter from Rev. Martin Luther*
King Jr. to Coretta Scott (July 1952)

"You're sure about this?" I fasten my cuff links, catching Lennix's eyes in the mirror.

"It's a little late to ask now, don't you think?" She smiles at my reflection. "With your parents waiting downstairs?"

I haven't spent Christmas in Dallas with my parents, *with my father*, in fifteen years. I was here for Owen's funeral, but this feels different. Then grief overrode every other emotion, but tonight, they all rise. Under the years of resentment and frustration lies anticipation.

I'm glad to be here. I just wasn't sure Lennix would be.

"If you've changed your mind," I say, turning to face her and leaning against the dresser, "Owen and I used to sneak out that window."

I tip my head toward my bedroom window overlooking the backyard.

"There's a huge oak tree out there." I cross over to her and splay my hands at her hips. "Me and O used to stretch to this sturdy branch and climb down, and Mom would be none the wiser."

At the mention of Owen's name, a familiar ache surrounds my heart. The ache of sorrow and, as much as I try to shake it, guilt.

"You okay?" Lennix peers up at me, her dark brows pulled into a frown. "I know this is rough for everyone, the first Christmas without Owen. I remember my first Christmas without Mama. I'm sure having you here will help your mom get through it."

"Thank you for setting aside your feelings for my dad to make sure we could be here for her."

"It's fine." She rubs my arm, looks me in the eyes so I know she means it.

"Well, let's get down there." I pull back to study her slim-fitting dress in scarlet, long sleeves that mold to her arms and the high heels that mean I won't have to dip as far to kiss her when we're under the mistletoe. "Merry Christmas Eve. You look beautiful."

"Merry Christmas Eve. So do you. You always do to me." Her gaze drops over my tieless dress shirt and dark slacks, inch by inspecting inch, lingering over my shoulders, chest, and legs. By the time she returns to my face, my body is responding to her blatant appreciation.

Hard. Ready.

I squeeze her waist and bend to whisper, deliberately brushing my lips over her earlobe. "We don't have time for how I feel when you look at me like that."

"When I look at you like what?" she asks with a smoky laugh, pulling back to peer at me through an upsweep of lashes.

"I think you know." I brush a thumb over her cheek. "But don't worry. I want it, too."

We grin, and I know we're both recalling a similar conversation on our first date at Vuurtoreneiland. A night of husky whispers and furtive touches that I'll never forget.

"Do you ever think how unlikely we are?" she asks. "You, being your father's son and all that represents, and me on the opposing side. And us meeting again in Amsterdam. Just all of it."

"We weren't unlikely, Nix," I say, no levity in the words. "We were inevitable."

Her smile dissolves, too, until we're staring at each other, and I'm feeling the weight of finding your person in a world full of somebodies. In a crowded galaxy, finding your star.

"Maxim!" My father's deep voice booms up the stairs and bangs on my bedroom door. "Dinner."

Lennix snickers when I roll my eyes. "Oh, my God. It's like you're thirteen."

"Except I'm not sneaking a girl up here. They actually know you're in my room." I take her hand and head for the door.

"Surely you weren't sneaking girls in *that* early, were you?"

"Huh?" I ask, pretending not to hear her. "You smell that? I'm starving."

She punches my arm, and we laugh together but freeze on the landing when we see my father standing at the bottom of the long staircase, his eyes fixed on us. Dad wasn't home when we arrived, so this is our first time seeing each other.

There's a subtle softening in his implacable features when he meets my eyes. The thread between my father and me has knotted over the years, tangled with resentment, anger, and pride, but there's no denying he loves me. I'm not sure he's ever known how to express it without the paternal possessiveness that made him pull the reins too hard—that made him push when he should have let me find my own stride. He made the mistake of trying to break me, like a wild horse he needed to tame. I was too much like him for that and had to leave, but I'm home now. My own man with my own woman.

He shifts his glance to Lennix, and the line of her body stiffens beside me, her fingers tightening on mine. I'm not sure if she's seeking or offering reassurance, but the contact reinforces our solidarity. My father pins his stare to our joined hands.

"Lennix," he says, his voice polite if not warm. "Welcome to our home."

"Thank you for having me," she replies, sliding her arm through the crook of my elbow. The claim she stakes on me is not subtle, but that's something she's never been. I've never needed her to be anything except who she was from the moment I met her—a bold, beautiful battle cry.

A wry grin of acknowledgment lifts one side of Dad's mouth.

"You still take for-damn-ever, son," he mutters, slides his hands into his pockets, and walks off toward the dining room. "Food's getting cold."

Lennix's eyes follow his broad shoulders in the expensively tailored sports jacket when he walks away. From behind, not seeing the lines on his face or the gray at his temples, he could be me.

The last name she used to see as a curse I hope she'll soon take. I haven't revisited the proposal. I may not win, and the implications of the presidency are a bridge we may never have to cross. We could wait and see, but there's something in me—*everything in me, if I'm honest*—that doesn't want to wait. I want to be the risk she takes. I want us to jump off this cliff overlooking the water together, certain that as long as we have each other, we won't drown.

"Ready?" she asks, a relaxed smile on her pretty red lips. I want to kiss her but don't want to ruin it, so I press my lips to her hair, and we walk down the stairs.

My mother doesn't do anything in half measures, especially not the holidays. The house is always fully decorated the day after Thanksgiving. On our way to the dining room, we pass one of several massive trees throughout the house, glittering with warm light. I pause, seeing not the empty living room but the floor littered with bright wrapping paper, two boys riding brand-new bikes into the hall, my father chasing us, my mother yelling for all the king's men to come eat breakfast on Christmas morning.

I grip Lennix's hand, struggling to master my emotions. She

leans into me, but she knows I'm leaning on her. If this is hard for me, how difficult is it for my parents?

"I'm right here," Lennix says, squeezing my hand back. "And I love you."

I glance down at her, my spot of sunshine in the lingering winter of grief, and manage a smile.

When we reach the dining room, my mother crosses over and hugs me right away and tightly. When she pulls back, tears swim in her blue eyes. "It's so good to have you home for Christmas, Maxim. Thank you for…" She bites her lip for a second before offering her warm smile. "Thank you for coming."

Shifting her glance to Lennix, she reaches for her hand, her smile warming even more. "Thank you for coming, too. For bringing him home."

"He wanted to be here," Lennix says softly. "Thank you for having me."

We make our way to the long table, and Lennix sits beside me. My father sits at one end of the table and my mother at the other. When my father picks up his fork, we all take that as our cue to do the same.

It's silent for a few moments, the only conversation the clang of silverware with fine china. I glance up to find my father's eyes fixed to the seat across from me, the empty one Owen always used to occupy. My fork freezes in midair, and the turkey turns to sawdust on my tongue. Dad swallows convulsively, obviously wrestling with demons dressed as memories. A single tear slides over one hard cheek, and his mouth goes tight and thin.

I'm at a loss. I've never seen my father cry. Not at the funeral or in the days that followed, even when I knew he was hurting. He's never shown any weakness, and maybe that was always our problem. Too much strength, not enough vulnerability. Too much power without compassion. When I was growing up, he was a deity. When I was older, he often felt like a villain. But now, in my maturity, I see him as he truly is.

Human.

Not perfect. Not evil. Not a god or a devil. Just my father, with whom I won't always agree but whom I'll love however he comes.

My mother rises from her seat, plate in hand, and walks the length of the table to sit beside him. They share a long look, and what passes between them is familiar because I know what love looks like, but it's foreign since they've rarely shown it this freely. He reaches for her hand and squeezes, and I know how that feels—to walk through life hand in hand with the woman you love, through good times and unimaginably hard ones. Their wedding rings glint in the glow of Christmas lights, and the longing to claim Lennix that way, to declare I'm hers that way, overwhelms me. I think we're all overwhelmed, but no one tries to fix it—to pretend it doesn't hurt or offer some stupid pat phrase that disavows the pain of the empty seat at our table.

We live in that silence, in that reality for a few moments, and then my father clears his throat, resumes eating. "So how's the campaign going?"

"Great," Lennix and I answer in unison. We share a glance and a laugh.

"It's going well," I say. "We're anxious to see how I do in Iowa come February."

"I think you'll win Iowa," Lennix says, slicing into roasted chicken.

"You could be a little biased." I reach under the table to touch her knee.

"I don't do bias," she says seriously. "The numbers bear it out, and so does my gut. Millennials will break hard for you, and you'll peel off some disillusioned Dems and moderate Republicans."

"So you're out on the trail with him?" Dad asks, a glass of wine halfway to his mouth.

"I'm, uh, helping a gubernatorial candidate right now," Lennix says, glancing at me and then down to her plate.

My father's eyes narrow at the small tell of her discomfort. "Why aren't you running Maxim's campaign?"

"As you know, there was a lot of gossip when our relationship came out," I say. "Lennix and her partner, Kimba, didn't want it to detract from the issues I want to focus on. I need to be taken seriously."

"Who the hell wouldn't take *you* seriously?" he nearly growls. "After all you've accomplished? This country is lucky you're thinking about running it."

"Speaking of bias," I murmur dryly, causing my mom to chuckle and Lennix to grin.

"Those are facts, and back to *you*," he says, leveling a stern look at Lennix. "You're gonna let some TMZ shit keep you from locking down Iowa? I thought you made kings, not governors."

You could hear dust settle the room goes so quiet. He and Lennix lock eyes down the length of the table, and the air hums with tension.

"Dad, Lennix—"

"Thought you said she was the best," Dad challenges, still staring Lennix down.

"I am," she asserts with quiet confidence.

"My son gets the best. You should be working on his campaign, not some governor in Virginia."

"How do you know it's Virginia?" she asks. "You're paying closer attention to my life than I would have thought."

"If you're going to be with Maxim," my father says, "you should get used to that. I keep track of mine."

Lennix glances down at the hands folded in her lap and caresses the compass charm on her bracelet. She meets my eyes and smiles. I shrug. I stopped being surprised long ago about my father knowing everything that goes on in my life and where I am at all times. Her bracelet is testament to the fact that I'm made the same way. I think she sees that now. I only hope she doesn't start wondering what else my father and I have in common. She might run for the hills.

Except Lennix already knows me, flaws and all, and she's still here.

"If he loses Iowa," my father says, steepling his hands, "he loses his shot. Am I right?"

After a hesitation, Lennix nods. "We have to win Iowa. It's psychological warfare. Whatever candidate millennials attach their ideals to, they'll ride to the end, even if they think that person will lose. Moderate Republicans, centrist Dems, older voters are more likely to use Iowa as a litmus test of Maxim's viability. If they see him lose Iowa, they won't waste their vote in the later primaries on someone they don't think has at least a chance."

"You mean they'll assume I'm like every other independent candidate who has ever run," I say, "and stop taking me seriously."

"Right," Lennix says with a brisk nod.

"Do you mean to tell me," Dad says, "that the girl I saw facing down dogs and rubber bullets when she was just seventeen years old grew up to be a woman afraid of a little gossip?"

"Dad, I don't think—"

"He's right," Lennix cuts in. "If you lose Iowa, I'll never know if my direct involvement could have made a difference."

"Then I suggest," my father says, spearing a clump of green beans, "you get back where you're supposed to be before you lose this thing worrying what people think. Cades don't care what people think."

"I'm not a Cade," she parries.

"Yet," I say. Our eyes lock, but there's no doubt in hers. It's only a matter of time. The *right* time.

"Goodness," my mother titters. "I'm surrounded by testosterone and..." She studies Lennix with a tilt of her head, like she's not sure how to classify her. "And whatever it is you have, Lennix."

We all laugh and dig back into our meal.

"I'll speak to Kimba," Lennix says, "about coming back to the campaign."

I pause my chewing. "Seriously?"

"That's right," my father says, raising his glass in a toast. "Fuck 'em."

Lennix watches him as if he's one of those pet boa constrictors who might turn feral without notice and squeeze the life from its owner during the night. Then she raises her glass, too. "Yeah. Fuck 'em."

The dining room becomes a war council, with my father, Lennix, and me strategizing for Iowa and beyond while my mother fakes looking mildly interested from time to time but surreptitiously plays Wordscapes on her phone.

"You thought about a potential running mate?" Dad asks, smiling at my mom when she slices the apple pie the staff brought in and sets a plate in front of him.

"Peggy Newcombe," I say.

"The congresswoman who was with you in Antarctica?" Dad asks.

"The same, but she's a senator now."

"She's a Democrat," Dad says.

"She is. That should help peel off a few more Democratic voters."

"Which we'll need," Lennix says. "Since Dentley's shaping up to be the Dem's front-runner."

It's galling that the candidate Lacy and Glenn work for will probably be on the ballot as the Democratic nominee come November.

"I have a few Republicans in mind for cabinet positions, too," I say. "To possibly garner some Republican support and because I think they'll do the job best."

"Whole-team-of-rivals approach?"

"Since I'm not party-affiliated, they're not necessarily my rivals. I'll have the advantage of choosing the people best qualified for the job, not based on which party they're from but on what they offer."

"And we'll get a few key endorsements lined up pretty quickly if Iowa pans out," Lennix says, forking the crust off her apple pie and tasting the filling.

"I know Millicent will want to endorse you," my mother says.

The three of us stare at her. That never occurred to me. I would never ask that of her.

Mom shrugs. "She told me she would, that she wanted to."

Millie and I haven't spoken much since I told her the truth about Gregory Keene's death. I could have let her believe the tale Grim wove that we leaked to the press. He planted a trail of crumbs for the authorities to follow leading to Gregory Keene's body and fingering him as Owen's assassin. My name was nowhere near that trail, and neither was Lennix's kidnapping. The picture that emerged was half-truth—a man with a promising future, driven to madness by his mother's demise as a result of our failed health-care system. Grim is as meticulous about covering up murders as he is about committing them, apparently.

Only Grim and I were in that basement. Only he and I know he pulled that trigger. Even though Lennix must suspect, she never asked me to confirm. She knows I'm as protective of Grim as he is of me, so that's a secret we'll both take to our graves.

The narrative provided much-needed closure for the public, but Millie deserved the truth. I went to Connecticut to tell her in person. Sobs didn't shake her body when I held her. There wasn't a tempo to her grief, but the unnatural stillness of resignation, like her body was just taking up space in the world until she can actually *be* here again. The twins keep her going through the motions of life. They necessitate she show up, but if she's anything like me, some days it feels like I'm watching myself smile, give speeches, interact with others—from this corner. Watching my body go through motions my soul isn't ready for yet. Those days are fewer and farther between for me now, but if I lost Lennix, I would probably conduct the rest of my life from that dark corner.

"Millie's in grief counseling," Mom continues, flicking a glance between Dad and me. "Something you'd both benefit from."

"I've been telling Maxim that," Lennix says, shrugging when I look at her like she's a sellout. "What? I have."

"Well, we're flying to Connecticut to see Millie and the twins tomorrow night," Mom says. "Where are David and Grim spending Christmas, Maxim?"

"David's with his family, though he's complaining about it, and Grim…" I shake my head. "I'm not sure. He just said he'd see us after Christmas."

"And the two of you are still flying to Arizona tomorrow?" Mom asks.

An edge filters into the air as soon as my mother says *Arizona*. That state, that *land*, was the genesis of our journey. Not just mine and Nix's but of her feud with my father.

"Yes," Lennix says. "My dad and stepmom are there."

"Yeah, well, we still have the morning." I stand, hoping to defuse the tension. "Christmas breakfast at nine, Mom?"

"Um, yes," she says, her voice pitching higher. She doesn't want a fight tonight either.

Lennix sucks in a breath, stands, and, with my hand at her back, turns toward the hallway.

"Lennix," Dad says, his voice commanding.

She goes still. So do I, tensed and ready to spring. She glances at him over her shoulder. "Yes?"

That single word hangs in the air, suspended in this fragile peace that one wrong move could shatter.

"I can't very well take up the ones we've laid," he says, his voice gruff and as close to apologetic as he's probably capable of. "But… there won't be any more Cade pipelines put on protected grounds."

She turns then, at first blinking rapidly, her mouth hanging open the slightest bit. As the shock of his statement wears off, skepticism pinches the corners of her eyes. "What's the catch?"

"You are. My son loves you. I love my son. I know I have a lot, but the older I get"—he touches Owen's empty chair, releases a heavy sigh—"the more I seem to lose. Priorities change."

"I can appreciate that. I'm *sorry* about that," Lennix says softly, fiercely, not looking away. "But you had no right. I know taking is in your nature, but just because you *can* take something doesn't mean you should. Doesn't make it yours."

Her outrage and indignation are arrows aimed for my father's heart, the same way they were the day we all met. I instinctively wanted to protect her that day from the dogs, the rubber bullets, *my father*—I want to stand between her and whatever retaliation he might offer now.

But he doesn't.

"I realize that. I'm sorry." He clears his throat and is nearly unrecognizable wearing remorse. "I know it's not enough, but—"

"It's a start," she interrupts, nods. "A good one. Thank you." She looks to my mother. "Dinner was delicious, Mrs. Cade. See you in the morning. Goodnight."

I start after her, but she puts a staying hand on my arm. "I'm tired, but you don't have to come right away. Spend a little time with your parents."

I search her face. We'll have to talk about this, but something in her expression, a pleading in her eyes, tells me she needs time alone more than I need time with my mom and dad.

"Okay." I kiss her hair and cup her cheek. "See you in a bit."

LENNIX

It's a night for ghosts.

At dinner, I felt Owen's presence so strongly, I almost expected to hear his jovial laughter if someone told a joke. And when Warren Cade told me about the pipelines, I could almost feel Mama squeeze my hand, could imagine seeing something in her eyes that I rarely witnessed: satisfaction. She always said injustice never rested and neither would she.

"Rest, Mama," I say, watching my reflection. "Tonight, you can rest."

Defying my valiant efforts to remain composed, tears track down my face no matter how much I swipe them. I rushed from the dining room because I felt something break inside me at Warren's words. A dam burst, and I knew once the water started, it wouldn't stop.

"This is a good thing," I remind the girl in the mirror with her puffy, red-rimmed eyes. "Stop crying."

I wash my face and put on a nightgown and a heavy silk robe. It's mine, but when I pull the collar to my nose, it smells like Maxim. I love that our scents, like our lives, have become so intertwined. There are traces of him at my apartment in DC and signs of me in his New York place, not too far from campaign headquarters.

A large bed, the centerpiece of the room, lures my tired body and racing mind. I sit cross-legged in the middle, resting my elbows on my knees. As soon as I'm still, the tears start again. I pass one embroidered sleeve across my cheek. A lot of people's rent costs less than this robe Maxim brought back from a recent business trip to Hong Kong. Those trips will be impossible as soon as the race heats up.

I finger the expensive silk, run my hand over the brocaded quilt covering the bed, still tasting the wine from dinner. By my calculations, a ten-thousand-dollar vintage.

I grew up on a reservation. Yes, my father was a professor, but for the first thirteen years of my life, I lived with my mother in a tiny house surrounded, in many cases, by great need. As a young girl, watching my mother fight, I dreamt of more and better for the people I loved. I didn't dream of Prince Charming and his castle, but seated in the middle of a bed that could easily sleep five, on a ranch that would swallow my entire childhood community, I realize I got both. Somehow I ended up eating with my enemy, sleeping in his home, and one day soon, I'm going to marry his son. And tonight, I *did* get more and better for the people I love.

Tonight, we won.

I think that's why there are tears. When Maxim's father said he would no longer put pipelines on protected grounds, it was a victory I didn't ever think I would taste. And in *this* fight, the victims often outnumber the victories. For centuries, our dreams had no borders, our lives, no limits because everything we could see, as *far* as we could see, belonged to us. Now ours is a displaced dignity, constantly fighting for our *place*—every acre, every plot, precious. And tonight, just the tiniest bit of that was restored. In a trail of broken promises, tonight one was guaranteed.

The door opens, and Maxim walks in. For just a second, my damp cheeks and red eyes make me self-conscious, but our glances connect, and the acceptance and devotion remind me I have nothing to hide or be ashamed of with this man. He closes the door, walks to the bed, and sits on its edge.

"Hey, you." He brushes the hair off my face, cups my cheek, and caresses my mouth with his thumb. "You okay?"

"Hey, you." I trace his dark eyebrows with my finger, follow the sculpted bevel of bone at his cheek, and touch his full lips. "I'm good."

"You sure? Did my father upset you? I know he can—"

"No, at no point tonight did he upset me. Not when he challenged me to resume my place with your campaign." I drop my eyes to the richness of the silk robe. "Certainly not when he told me about the pipelines. I'm… I think I'm overwhelmed. I never expected it."

"I don't think he ever expected to actually *do* it," Maxim says dryly. "It took a lot. He's been working up to it."

"You made him?"

"No. I told him if he didn't accept you in my life, there wouldn't be a place in mine for him. He said I could tell you there would be no more Cade pipelines." He pauses, takes my hand, kisses the center of my palm. "I told him to tell you himself."

It would have meant a lot coming from Maxim, but hearing it from Warren Cade, seeing him gulp down his pride, meant even more.

"Thank you," I tell him, leaning forward to kiss his cheek. He immediately turns his head, captures my lips with his, and runs his hands down my back to palm my butt. I pull back, affecting a shocked expression. "Why, Mr. Cade! Not in your childhood bedroom."

"My *childhood bedroom*? We're not sleeping in a bassinet."

I catch my bark of laughter in my hand. "Oh, my God. I don't want to disturb your parents."

"You won't. Their bedroom is basically in another zip code, and I'm sure the walls are soundproof. Thank God. I didn't need to hear that as a kid, and I certainly don't want to."

"Well, maybe I should give you your Christmas present now," I whisper, making my look and my voice seductive.

"Yes, please," Maxim replies, squeezing each cheek in one big hand. "I've been such a good boy this year."

"Close your eyes." I pull back and point my finger right in his face. He zeroes in on it, crossing his eyes comically.

"Don't make me laugh," I choke.

"You just laughed."

I wag my finger in his face again. "Stay right there and close your eyes."

He obeys, and I crawl across the mammoth mattress to the bedside table and pull out a gift box.

"Open your eyes." I present him with the box and bite my lip to keep from laughing.

He opens those peridot eyes, lifts his brows, and takes the small, rectangular box from me with a smile. "I thought we were opening gifts with my parents in the morning."

"I have another one. This is just something small."

"You spoil me." He pulls the ribbon and pops the top off the box. His shout of laughter draws an answering giggle from me. "Lube? You got me lube for Christmas?"

He leans over, pressing me until my back hits the mattress. His hand explores beneath the robe and under my gown. I laugh when he kisses my neck and palms my breast.

"Maxim, no! We can't *here*."

He lifts his head, looking both affronted and mystified. "You can't give a man lube and then deny him anal, Nix. That's just cruel."

"It's a gag gift."

"It is not a gag to me. It's basically a promissory note. This is you promising me anal."

"Yes," I hiss, laughing and pushing his shoulder, which doesn't budge. He keeps hovering over me. "But not here. Not in your parents' house. It was a joke, Doc. Ha, ha, funny."

"A gag gift is like…a whoopy cushion with holly on it, not dangling that pretty, tight little asshole at me and then telling me I can't have it tonight."

"You ruin everything." I chuckle, my laughter fading when I look up to find his eyes intensely fastened to my face. "But I love you."

"Same, Nix. Same."

A breathtaking tenderness filters into the dark center of his eyes and softens his expression. Inexplicably, tears sting my eyes again. Before I can even grasp what this is, he slaps my thigh playfully, shattering the mood. "I'm going to slip into something more comfortable and then come back for some run-of-the-mill missionary sex."

"Bastard." I swallow the unexpected emotion, forcing a laugh, and sit up to watch him undress.

He crosses over to the dresser and rifles through the drawer for a few moments, back turned to me. My heart might burst, I love him so much right at this very second.

"Dammit," he mutters, fumbling with his sleeve. "Babe, these stupid cufflinks. Can you help me?"

He walks back to the bed where I'm seated and proffers his wrist.

Removing the gold cufflink monogrammed with MKC, I glance up through my lashes to tease him. "What was so hard about that? Maybe you're losing some hand-eye coordination in your old age."

"Think that'll make people feel better about voting for a young whippersnapper like me?" He laughs, but that look, that breath-stealing intentness, lingers.

"Bet I could spin it." I smile and start on his left sleeve. When I flip over the cuff, my heartbeat screeches to a halt. My entire being, even my soul, breaks out in a sweat. My next breath queues up in my throat and just waits, suspended. A large cushion-cut diamond juts through the left sleeve's slit. I drop the sleeve like it's on fire, my hands flopping listlessly to my lap. Maxim watches me almost warily and drops down to his haunches in front of me. With his eyes never leaving my face, he pulls the ring out by its large diamond, revealing the delicate platinum band, which he takes between two fingers.

"I want the girl who chases stars," he says, his voice rough, that tenderness now full-blown and overwhelming in the way he looks at me—in the way he takes my left hand and just holds it. "Lennix Moon Hunter, will you marry me?"

My body slowly reacquaints itself with reality. My heart makes up for lost time, going from a screeching halt to a sprint in my chest. I'm aware of tears easing down my cheeks and into the corners of my mouth. I lick them, and I know with my rational mind that they must be salty, but somehow, they're sweet. Everything about this moment is sweet. The uncharacteristic uncertainty on Maxim's face. His lips pressed tightly together like he may explode if I don't answer him soon. I reach for him, sliding my right hand into his hair and leaning forward to hover over his lips.

"Maxim Kingsman Cade," I whisper, my voice breaking over his name, over the rightness of this moment. I offer my left hand, my fingers spread wide. "Yes."

Relief and joy stretch the smile on his face, and he slips the diamond, nearly blinding under the lights, onto my ring finger.

"You do know I could be president one day, right?" he asks with a hoarse chuckle. "I'm just making sure we're on the same page."

"Yes, I do realize that." I blink back more tears as I see how perfect the ring looks on my hand and caress the other jewelry he gave me—the compass charm. "I signed on for you."

He kisses me before I can finish the phrase that has helped me make peace with however our journey ends, but my heart recites the rest.

Whatever that means.

Wherever that takes us.

BONUS EPILOGUE
MAXIM

"This is our first dance."

Lennix's statement momentarily distracts me from the announcer addressing the crowd in the glittering ballroom.

"Obviously, it's our first dance." I gesture between my tuxedo and her glittering white formal dress. "That's kind of the point."

Lennix rolls her eyes and flashes an exasperated grin up at me. "No, I mean, I can't remember us ever dancing. I think it's our first time dancing *together*."

"Are you sure?" I frown, reviewing the nearly two decades since we met in that Arizona desert. "What about that Christmas party at the—"

"Nope."

"Did we not dance at that charity event in—"

"We didn't." She shakes her head and sighs. "Maybe we were too busy working every room we were in to dance in it, but I'm pretty sure this is our first time."

I take in the strategically placed diamonds contrasting against her dark, upswept hair, the shimmery white gown, nipped at the waist and flaring out over her hips and to the floor, and finally the large diamond sparkling on her finger. I lift her left hand to my lips and kiss the ring. I murmur, caressing the velvety sweep of her bare throat and collarbone.

"So our first time dancing together will be In front of hundreds…"
I peer just beyond the backstage curtain to see the sea of cameras
suspended from the ceiling and dotting the perimeter of the room.
"Correction, millions of people."

"Ladies and gentlemen," the announcer says. "The president of
the United States and first lady, Lennix Moon Hunter Cade."

The applause beyond the curtain where we've been waiting
backstage is deafening. When we step onto the stage, the lights
temporarily blind me, and I tighten my hand around Lennix's. This
moment feels fantastical, and it's the strong grip of her fingers that
grounds me in reality. This is actually happening. Long months,
countless speeches and campaign stops, millions of votes and
innumerable sacrifices have led to this historic night.

MISSING AND MURDERED INDIGENOUS WOMEN

As I interviewed Native American women for this story, an issue kept rising to the surface of our conversations: the epidemic of missing and murdered Indigenous women. Reportedly, in some tribal communities in the United States, Native women are ten times more likely to be murdered than the national average.

Ten times.

This is devastating and unbelievable. It's a complicated issue, and information here (uihi.org/wp-content/uploads/2018/11/Missing-and-Murdered-Indigenous-Women-and-Girls-Report.pdf) may help explain just how convoluted our systems make finding justice for these women.

As I approached Lennix's story, I knew many readers would see never finding her mother Liana or knowing what happened to her as a loose end.

It is intentional.

I wanted us as readers to have just the tiniest glimpse of how the hundreds of thousands of families feel who lose their mothers, sisters, friends this way. They, like Lennix, never know what happened. They only know she's gone.

Thank you for taking this journey with me.

ALL THE KING'S MEN
EXTRAS

Need to talk?

Enter the Throne Room,
The *All the King's Men* Duet Discussion:
bit.ly/ATKMSpoil

All the King's Men Playlist

bit.ly/ATKMPlay

All the King's Men Bonus Audio

kennedyryanwrites.com/product/allthekingsmenbonusaudio/

I'm always in my reader group:

facebook.com/groups/681604768593989/

Creative License

I must confess I took creative license with one aspect of the story. Bioluminescence in Tomales Bay is a real phenomenon! *But* tours and boat rides are usually conducted from May to November. Maxim takes Lennix much earlier in the year, which would probably not be the case in real life. ;-)

ACKNOWLEDGMENTS

In the author's note at the beginning, I thanked some of the women who guided me in writing this book, but it bears repeating. Sherrie, Makea, Andrea, Nina, and Kiona, thank you for sharing your tribes, your stories, your heritage with me. For teaching me, opening my eyes to so many things I had walked right past all my life. You are remarkable women, and I hope readers see some of your strength, courage, and wisdom in Lennix, the character your stories helped me create.

There are so many people who are always supportive, but there is a circle of friends who put up with me when I'm writing, creating covers, crafting blurbs. You poor, long-suffering souls know who you are! LOL! Thank you for being honest and patient and showing my projects the same loving attention you would your own. It means the world to me.

Jenn Watson—always and every time. Thank you for stroking my hair when I'm anxious and keeping a smile when I'm demanding and biting your tongue when I start trying to do your job and then fail and have to ask you to fix it. LOL! You and your butterfly hive are amazing, and I never take your thoughtfulness and professionalism for granted. Tia from Honey Mag, thank you for always being a voice of truth and for all your assistance. I'm so glad we found each other!

To my Kennedy Ryan Books group on Facebook, THANK YOU for being my virtual soft landing. You keep me encouraged and give me a safe place to celebrate every single day. I love you!

With every book, I'm reminded that this is all so great, but it feels pale and insufficient without someone to celebrate with. That's my #LifetimeLovah of twenty-two years and counting. Thank you to my husband who puts up with the mad rush to deadlines, the weeks of repetitive take-out food, the near-condemned state of our house when I'm trying to finish a book, with a wife who whispers dialogue under the sheets and talks to herself out loud all day long. I know it must feel like you live with a madwoman half the time, but you always make me feel loved and supported. You hold me when I cry, and you make laugh every day. I love you and "would do it all again."

ABOUT THE AUTHOR

A RITA and Audie Award winner and *USA Today* bestselling author, Kennedy Ryan writes for women from all walks of life, empowering them and placing them firmly at the center of each story and in charge of their own destinies. Her heroes respect, cherish, and lose their minds for the women who capture their hearts.

Kennedy and her writings have been featured in *Chicken Soup for the Soul, USA Today, Entertainment Weekly, Glamour, Cosmopolitan, TIME, O Magazine,* and many others. She is a wife to her lifetime lover and mother to an extraordinary son.

Connect with Kennedy!

Website: kennedyryanwrites.com
Facebook: @kennedyryanauthor
Instagram: @kennedyryan1
TikTok: @kennedyryanauthor
Twitter: @kennedyrwrites